WHY I DIDN'T SAVE ANYONE

MATTHEW HELBIG

Printed in the United States of America
First Printing, September 2018

ISBN 978-0-9995900-1-0
www.matthewhelbig.com

HAT WOULD NEVER DO ANYTHING WRONG

"Did you see this happen, Hat?" Officer Ollie took a big sip of his coffee. The creamer turned his mustache white, reminding me of my dad.

I almost corrected him that my name wasn't really Hat, but Harry always called me that, and after what I'd done, I'd decided to keep it in his honor.

"I was over by the couches, pretending to be a dragon, when he slipped and fell on his head. Harry wanted to put a dragon in his next book and needed to see what it would be like to jump on one's back."

I felt terrible about hitting Harry, my boss and the author of my favorite books, on the head with the fireplace poker and then concocting this lie, but I knew deep down I had done the right thing. A few weeks ago, Harry had actually travelled to the world from his books and told me what it was really like. The story was amazing, and the characters were so different from the ones in the books, but as he edited it, Harry had gone and changed everything to make himself look better. A few weeks prior to that, he had given me power of attorney for his books in case anything happened to him. It was a good thing, too. If it weren't for that, his fans would never know the truth.

"Care Bear feetie pajamas, though?" Officer Ollie asked. "I thought you dressed him, Hat, and I know you wouldn't let him wear something like that."

"He only lets me pick what he wears for public appearances, and he only agreed to that because his publisher snuck it into his last contract."

Officer Ollie nodded and set the coffee down. "I can't tell you how many calls we get about nerds . . ." He paused and looked at his partner.

"Yes, they prefer nerd or geek. There's not a more politically correct term for them. Sorry, we just got out of sensitivity training," Officer Mickey said as he opened the door for the paramedics.

". . . Where nerds attempt things that they have no right doing. I think this one will be my fiftieth." Harry was probably responsible for twenty-five of them. Officer Ollie even had his own mug at the cabin. "I don't see anything out of the ordinary here. We'll let the paramedics do their thing, and you can head over to the hospital with them. Really hate for something like this to happen to you, Hat. Do you need to call anyone?"

I shook my head and sighed in relief. It looked like I was in the clear. Unfortunately, I had overlooked his partner.

Officer Mickey looked back and forth between the steps and the ground and then put his hand on his chin. "Something's not right here."

My stomach dropped. I always had a plan for everything, or at least I did until this happened. The police had arrived quickly, not giving me the time to prepare for them.

Officer Mickey knelt next to Harry's unconscious form and pointed at the puddle of yellow liquid pooling toward the fireplace before walking back to the stairs. "The liquid on the third step here is a different color. Unless he peed a little as he was falling and then ate something to change the color in midair, I think we can conclude that this is water." He glanced toward his mentor.

Officer Ollie nodded, obviously impressed. "And I don't see any glasses—shattered or otherwise—laying about, so he wasn't pretending to use a cup as a shield this time."

I'd been expecting them to just pass this whole thing off as another one of Harry's silly escapades. However, unlike Harry, I had learned from my time in the Boy Scouts to be prepared for anything. "Harry wanted me to make my dragon impersonation as realistic as possible, so he had me shoot a water gun at him to 'purposely miss, as his rugged handsomeness would obviously deflect even the vilest shot from the vilest beast.'"

"What kind of dragon shoots water anyway?" Officer Ollie asked.

"He said having it breathe water would show how much more creative he is than those other hackneyed authors." It was nice to not have to lie too much. He had me do this very thing only a week prior.

"Blue dragons use steaming water as their breath weapon in lots of books," Officer Mickey said, "but that does sound like something Mr. Olson would say. I think he used the word 'vile' a hundred times in his last book."

It had actually been 357 times. He had me add an extra 100 of them to the last draft.

"Got anything else, Mickey?" Officer Ollie asked.

Officer Mickey knelt over the grinning form of Harry. I'd moved him slightly before they arrived to make it look like he had fallen. Fortunately, he'd left a slight indent in the wood last time.

"No, nothing else. Wouldn't be like Hat to do anything wrong. Once saw him walk an extra mile to the next intersection just so he wouldn't jaywalk."

They said some other stuff, but as it wasn't directed at me, I stopped listening. The next thing I knew, Officer Ollie was following the paramedics out, while Officer Mickey closed the door behind them and then walked toward me. I was sure he saw something at the last minute and had come back to arrest me. However, instead of putting his cuffs on me, he placed something small in my hands.

"Thought you might want this. That paramedic is a klepto. I should know. We used to date." I looked down, and it was Harry's ring with the neat Norse runes engraved in it. "It was worth grabbing it just to see the look on Sam's face."

"Thank you, Officer." I smiled weakly.

"I don't suppose you could let me know what happens in the next book? I promise I won't tell anyone. Do Verix and Arik finally kill Dyfantus? I really hate that guy."

I felt a thousand pounds lighter. "I should probably go with them to the hospital."

"Right, right. Of course. You can ride with us. Sam was not happy to see me, and you do not want to be with her when she's like this."

I nodded, and we raced to the car. The ambulance was just starting to pull out. Officer Mickey shivered as he shook the falling snow off his gloves and opened the door. I forgot to grab a coat, but with the way my body was shaking with worry, I didn't need one; I wiped the thick sweat off my forehead and sat down in the squad car.

"Did he at least leave an outline for the rest of the series?"

"Mickey, leave the poor man alone," Ollie said. "He might have just lost his best friend and his job."

COMAS ARE TEMPORARY, RIGHT?

I paced between the spot in the wall with the paint chip shaped like Texas and the TV showing some reality show celebrity's latest arrest. My body should have rebelled over my neglect of basic things like food, drink, and sleep, but I was much too worried to pay attention. The doctors had refused to let me in as I was not technically family even though he didn't actually have any family left. I think one of the nurses had tried to comfort me, but I didn't hear anything she said.

Harry had to be all right. I knew with certainty that had to be the case when I had first arrived, but after the fifth hour of no news, my nerves had eaten that away. I stopped chewing on my nails when they started bleeding, so I went back to wiping my eyes even though they had run out of tears hours ago. My legs finally gave up, so I plopped down in the slightly stained chair that faced the door to the ER.

After a few more hours of staring, I was convinced that I had developed X-ray vision and turned away from the door for fear that the X-rays I was producing might cause permanent damage to anyone who happened to walk past. The friendly nurse came through the door and gave me an "I'm sorry but I don't know anything new" look as she walked past. (I may have also developed slight psychic powers.) I was careful not to stare directly at her for fear that I might see through her clothes. I knew that would have been the first thing Harry would have done if he had been granted those powers, so I had to make up for the cosmic balance.

Fortunately, my temporary powers had disappeared an hour later when Harry's agent, Jess, arrived. I really didn't want to see her naked, and she was the kind of person that you couldn't avoid looking at no matter how hard you tried. It's not that she was unattractive—quite the opposite actually—she was just extremely loud and mean. Whenever she was around, my brain begged my legs to start running, but my legs developed temporary amnesia on what exactly that act entailed. My mouth, however, knew exactly what to do: stay shut.

"You!" Jess said as she noticed me right before she pounded through the doors to the emergency room. "You had one job. One! To make sure that brilliant doofus didn't doofus his way into doofus heaven." She poked me in the chest with an elaborately lacquered fingernail. "And what do you have to say for yourself?"

"I—"

"Exactly. No excuse." She pulled her finger out of my chest and placed it on her chin. The swirly pattern on her fingernails would have normally been mesmerizing, but my eyes were glued to her mouth as I anticipated the pain I knew was about to spew forth. "Does your kind believe in heaven?"

I wasn't exactly sure what "my kind" was in her mind, but I was confident it wasn't a good thing. I must have moved infinitesimally, inviting further attack.

"Of course you do, but only if God is a unicorn or a fairy or some other sissy crap." She covered her mouth and glanced around. Everyone in the waiting room was looking at us, though fortunately for her, that group only included me and Mrs.

Banford, a grandmother who collected colorful socks. Jess took one look at Mrs. Banford and assumed she was not a regular reader of fantasy and therefore not a member of her clientele's target audience. I doubt Jess cared if she offended Mrs. Banford's religious affiliation. "So, what did that bearded wonder do this time?"

I raised my finger slightly. "He—"

"Fell off the steps and hit his head again. And this time, he didn't drop the fireplace poker before it connected with his genius little brain." Her hand shot out like she was going to punch me but angled slightly toward the wall instead. Her face reminded me of my dad whenever Michigan lost to Ohio State.

I flinched, but she stopped right before she hit the wall.

"And I was about to mail him a helmet too, so I guess it's not completely your fault." Her face relaxed and her hands went back into her pockets. She let out a soft sigh and smiled slightly. I could start to see the face that Harry had become so transfixed with when he was looking for a new agent after his previous one retired. (He did not suffocate under unsold copies of the second book like in the rumor Harry's rival Billiam started.) "What was your name again? Spoon? Pot? Shoe?"

"Shoe was his last assistant . . . before you were his agent. My name is—"

"I'm sure you did everything in your obviously limited abilities to stop him, Shoe. So, how bad is it?" She pulled a cigarette out of her purse but quickly put it back in when Officer Mickey came around the corner. His eyes stopped on Jess but eventually focused on me.

"Hat, I guess nothing's changed then?" Officer Mickey asked.

Before I could open my mouth, Jess moved in front of me. "No, unfortunately my client is still in surgery. He is a brave man, but the toll is greatest on the ones who care for him most. Why, I am so distraught, I just don't know what to do with myself. Do you perhaps know what I could do with myself?"

Several answers to that question rolled through my mind, each more terrible than the last, but the question wasn't directed at me, so I kept them to myself. Not that getting a word in was really an option with Jess around.

Officer Mickey attempted to maneuver passed Jess, but she kept sliding in front of him. If the agenting thing didn't work, she could always switch to professional goaltender. Fortunately for Officer Mickey, he was not trying to get his balls through her posts.

"There's a bar across the street. You could console yourself there while I talk to Hat here." Officer Mickey then muttered something under his breath that sounded an awful lot like "pitch," though I wasn't exactly sure that was it.

"That sounds great. And you could join me afterward." I could hear Jess's thickly mascaraed eyelashes batting even though I couldn't see them.

"Yes, I'll be right there," he deadpanned.

When Jess finally walked out of view—which took about ten minutes as she stopped and turned to make sure he was watching her after every half step—Officer Mickey pulled a neatly organized stack of papers from behind his back.

"I . . . umm . . . I had to know what happened next, so I took this from the scene. I feel awful, and I swear I only read a little."

"How far, exactly?" I flipped through the pages of Harry's most recent draft, and they all seemed to be there.

"After Hammurabi paid Harry to have sex with his wife but before Harry accidentally burned out the cyclops's eye by showing off his manhood."

That was only about a fourth of the way through, between the extra chapters he added at the last minute where he invented blue jeans and then blue jean shorts. "Wait. How would you know that happens before if you didn't read past it, Officer Mickey?"

Mickey's lower lip rose to cover three fourths of his mustache. "I always knew you were the brains of that operation, Hat—not that that's really much of a compliment."

I gave him an extremely dirty look. I'd let almost anything slide, but nobody says anything bad about Harry when I'm around . . . no matter how true it is.

His hand reflexively went toward his belt even though he was in civilian clothes. "Sorry. Too soon. Anyway . . . I swear I won't tell anyone what happens, and I'll even sign a non-disclosure agreement if you want me to."

"I think Jess has some over at the bar," a high-pitched voice that didn't sound at all like me said. "Also, bring that last draft with you, so she can send it off to the publisher."

"Ahh thanks, I'll go give this to her."

He almost had the papers out of my hands before I came to my senses. "Wait, no. The book isn't finished."

Jess shot around the corner and attempted to grab the pages, but for once, I was too quick for her. "Give me that, you little dork," she said.

"No!" I must have displayed quite the scary face because Jess stopped in stunned silence. "This is not finished, and you can't have it."

Either my face was starting to look less scary or Jess had already developed an immunity to it, because she grabbed for the pages again. "I have power of attorney for that wonderful little doofus when he's incapacitated," she said, "so I get to decide that. Officer, take it from him."

Office Mickey begrudgingly took a step forward.

"Not anymore," I said. "He changed it last week."

"Crap," she said. "Who told you?"

"You did when you called the cabin."

"All you geeks sound alike." She attempted to mutter that under her breath, but even her lowest volume setting was several decibels above what I considered a yell. I was about to do the honorable thing and mention that she could tell Harry and me apart by the fact that I didn't immediately start breathing heavy whenever her name was mentioned, but as usual, she cut me off.

"Well, whatever. You still have to honor the contract he signed if you want the next advance check. And remember, life-sized statues don't come cheap."

He had commissioned that one when I took two days off to visit my mom a few months before. If I had been there, I would have at least talked him out of putting actual Doritos in the bag the statue was holding. On the bright side, there was always so much bird doo-doo on it that it matched his skin tone perfectly. "That still gives me two weeks then."

"Can you at least take out the part where Harry chases all the plain women out of Garandia with his banjo version of the *Friends* theme song?" Officer Mickey asked. "I know it's supposed to be true, but I don't think anyone will believe it."

"Y—"

"Yes, go do that, dweebus, so me and the officer can be alone. Replace it with some girly fairies or Keebler elves or whatever." She must have thought she whispered the last part but realized her mistake when Officer Mickey scowled at her.

Before I could offer a retort, the doors to the emergency room swung open. I immediately recognized the older man in scrubs as Harry's doctor and, unfortunately, recognized the tall man with the pointy goatee standing next to him. It was Harry's rival, Billiam von Cummerbund.

Was the nice doctor escorting him out for trying yet another one of his nefarious schemes? If Billiam had hurt Harry (more than I already had), I'd . . . I'd say some not nice things about him on the internet. Billiam had done several things to harm

Harry and his reputation, like write a parody of Harry's books, but since we couldn't prove that beyond a shadow of a doubt, and parodies are legal in the eyes of the law, I did the only thing I felt was morally permissible in that situation and frowned at him after I shook his hand. My mother raised me to have good manners, and I was not going to let a little suspicion and anger change that.

Billiam pointed toward our group and the doctor walked toward us. "As I've already told his dear brother here," the doctor said, "Harrold has finally stabilized, but appears to be in a coma. We're doing everything we can, but we're not sure when, or if, he might come out of it."

I should have throttled Billiam for claiming to be Harry's brother (even if it would have made a lot of sense as no two people I'd ever met behaved more like brothers than those two), but I was too overcome with grief and guilt to do anything but weep and make a noise so loud it almost made Jess blink. The doctor winced as he made his way back through the doors.

"Sorry about your loss, Hatly," Billiam said. "He was a worthy rival."

I crinkled my face in imitation of someone after Harry inadvertently harassed them. "He's not dead yet . . . unless you did something to him. Sorry, I shouldn't accuse you of things without proof, but you are definitely not his brother."

Seething from not being the center of attention for a whole twenty seconds, Jess moved between us. "Billiam's my client too and was concerned about his friendly rival, so I sent him in to look in on my other client and then finish the book if it isn't done." She turned toward Officer Mickey. "I care deeply about all of my clients. I think of them as my brothers and sisters . . . my much older brothers and sisters, which is probably why I'm still single. Are you single?"

"Now that I've returned the papers and know that my favorite author is at least in stable condition, I should probably go. Yes, there goes the radio. Off to a call."

Officer Mickey was not in his uniform, and I didn't see or hear a radio, but I must have been mistaken. Jess chased after him, leaving me with Billiam. I wondered if Mickey was allowed to use his pepper spray when he was off duty—not that I thought it would stop her.

"So, about that book. Jess wants me to look it over before she sends it off to the editor." Billiam reached toward the papers, but I was much too quick for him.

"No. I have power of attorney, so they're mine."

"Hatwell, I admire your loyalty to the Harrinator, but you should let a professional look them over." He reached for them again, so I turned and blocked him with my back.

I paused for a second to consider his point. It was a surprisingly good one. While I had gained quite a bit of experience editing under the tutelage of a master like Harry in the three years I had worked for him, I didn't have much in the way of experience actually writing, unless you counted the three hours I spent writing apology letters on his behalf every day. Billiam had been polite to me, and I liked the silly nicknames he always made up for me; however, he would have probably been the last person alive that Harry wanted to finish his book, and after what I had done, I owed that much to him. Plus, Billiam was way too eager.

"These are mine, and I'll finish the book." I growled at him like the mean baby down the street does when Harry tries to take her sucker.

He backed away. "Jess said you only have two weeks." He sighed. "Fine, but if you need any help, call me. I'm checked into the Grand across the street."

I shook his hand and left. He was kind enough to let me leave without following me, even though I knew he was heading out as well. I couldn't see why Harry didn't like him. Billiam was really a nice guy. Any other author wouldn't have come all this way to show his respect and then offer to finish his book to help.

The enormity of the task finally hit me as I exited the hospital, but my doubts were immediately squashed by my resolution to do justice to Harry's incredible journey. I owed it to his fans and myself to fix Harry's misguided attempt to make himself look better. I would get the truth out there and save Harry from himself.

WRITING THE WRITES OF WRITTEN FAILURES

Throughout the drive back to the cabin I was filled with a constant surety that I would accomplish my goal. What I was not filled with was a plan on how I was going to accomplish that goal. After I put the car into park, I opened my phone to call Billiam, and then closed it right before I pressed the call button. I did that a few dozen times, but each time the voice of Harry overcame me. Oddly enough, Harry's biggest rival was the only author who I thought would help me with this, as no other authors were on speaking terms with him.

As soon as I entered the cabin, I quickly cleaned up the result of my earlier righteous betrayal. I couldn't get anything done while I knew there was a mess in the other room. We were very lucky that the eight-foot-tall battleaxes hadn't fallen off the wall onto him. I had insisted that he have a professional build a custom, triple-reinforced wall mount when the axes arrived, and she had apparently done a great job.

After I finished cleaning, I walked upstairs into Harry's office and was filled with an odd mixture of fear and excitement; a feeling not unlike what I get when he gives me the first look at his new book. The file marked "First Draft of Book Six" was almost identical to the original story I remembered him telling me. All twenty-three acts of cowardice were there, he didn't have sex with anyone, and there was no sassy, black parrot. The honesty in this draft choked me up a little. I felt incredibly guilty for hurting such a person, but then the fan blew his final draft over, and I re-read the scene where he turns all the men in the kingdom into women by aggressively wagging his "sexy" eyebrows. After I stopped reading, I knew what I had to do: combine his later grammatical and typo fixes with the original version. I owed it to his fans to get the truth out, and due to his insane spending habits, I owed it to his creditors to get the advance check.

Over the next week, I managed to meticulously merge the two versions. When I reached the last word in the book, a brilliant thought crossed my mind. *The book shouldn't end where it did. The book starts on Earth, and it should end on Earth.* I added a new, final chapter where he came back home to ease my conscience by telling the truth—the whole truth, including the part where I hit him with the fireplace poker. I would be forever vilified by his fans and go to prison, but it would be worth it to get the truth out. The truth was all that mattered. No more lying. I would be free.

I worked on the new chapter for three days and felt amazing the entire time. The fact that it would get me arrested didn't matter. The truth would be out there, and this truth would not have sex with anyone.

After a few days making sure the new chapter meshed with Harry's writing style, I emailed it to the editor and sent a copy to Jess. Pressing the send button felt fantastic. The world would finally know that Vyenra existed and what it was really like.

I celebrated by pulling out the bottle of raspberry vodka he kept hidden in the back of the drawer full of comics. He thought it was a secret, but he should have known I would go looking through all those wonderful, old comics. Unfortunately, even with my higher level of alcohol tolerance, an entire bottle of vodka, no matter the silly flavor, was too much for me, and I soon drifted to sleep on what I assumed was the couch.

WHY DIDN'T I JUST GO BACK TO SLEEP?

I awoke in the pile of clothes that Harry had been wearing when he had visited Vyenra. He had insisted that I burn them immediately, but I hid them in the back of his closet to smuggle out later. To me they were holy relics that might have still contained some magic from that no-longer-mythical world. I did burn the underwear though, because they smelled funny.

The closet was bigger than I had remembered it. It even seemed slightly more spacious than his bedroom, but I knew that was the poor lighting and hangover playing tricks on me. They were definitely playing tricks on my equilibrium as it took three attempts for me to stand.

I had never drunk an entire bottle of vodka before, and I was beginning to see why. The closet looked like it was made of large stones, which I knew couldn't be true. When I finally steadied myself, it occurred to me that Harry had paid for some new additions to his cabin while we had been back at his house in the city. I had only poked in this closet briefly to toss these clothes in. He must have had them cover the little room in some fake stonework. It would be just like Harry to hire people to do something, and then when they told him how much it would cost to do the whole cabin, have them do the only room he could actually afford.

The fake stone was cool to the touch, which made me sleepy again. I slowly slid back down the bumpy wall. I don't know if anyone has ever told you this, but sliding down an uneven wall is not good for the skin. It tends to put pesky things like creases and holes in it, holes that tend to bleed and hurt even through liquor-induced happiness.

The pain barely kept me from falling asleep, and I re-opened my eyes to a figure standing in the doorway. When blinking didn't make the figure go away, I decided to try a more active tactic and groaned something resembling a sentence.

"I asked first. Who are you?" a gravelly voice replied.

I pulled myself up on the third try while keeping as much distance as the small closet would allow. "My name is Ha . . . what a minute, I live here. Why should I be telling you who I am?"

"That is an excellent point, and really, I think that should be a rule—nay, law—that our society should adopt." The figure, who I still couldn't quite make out in the dim lighting of the closet, took out a small piece of paper and began scribbling. "Don't think you can trick me with your great idea because this is *my* house, and as such, you have to answer first."

I shook off the hangover and focused on the figure in front of me. He was not advancing on me, so that was good. He also didn't appear to be armed with anything, not even a pen. He seemed to be writing on the paper with his finger. There was always the danger of him giving me a few nasty paper cuts. I flinched at the thought of it. I could just picture him hauling me off to his dungeon and giving me paper cuts. I bet he had lemon juice to pour in the cuts too.

I considered telling him my name was Harry to trick him, but since this was Harry's house, and he was much more famous than me, it was likely that the man was here for him and not me. Contrary to what Harry thought, his incapacitation would not be the top story on the world news, probably not even on the local news, as they had gotten tired of reporting his various injuries after the fifth time it happened in the first year. "They call me Hat. Now who are you, and what sort of nefarious things are you going to do to me?"

The man finished scribbling on the paper with his fingers and gave me a long look. He still hadn't moved forward, but seeing as how he had me trapped, he could take all the time he wanted. How long would he keep me in his dungeon? What sorts of things would he do to me? Was he a good cook?

"Now why would you assume that I'm going to do nefarious things to you? Why does everyone assume that when they see me? Do I really have that kind of face?" He stopped talking and stared at me. "No, really, I'm asking, do I have that kind of face?"

"I can't see your face. It's really dark in here."

"Oh, where are my manners? Here, come on out. There's much better lighting out here. By the way, my name is Gu, and it's very nice to meet you, Hat." He turned his back toward me and moved out of the doorway. All in all, he seemed to be an exceedingly nice kidnapper.

The room I stepped into was not Harry's bedroom; it was much bigger and did not have a single picture of a half-naked elf on the wall. The walls were covered in the same stone—which I was beginning to think weren't fake—as the closet I had left. The only furniture in the room was a large, plain table with equally plain chairs. What really sold that I was not in the bedroom was the complete lack of a bed—the number one criteria for being a bedroom—the number two criteria being something to play sad music with when someone makes fun of your latest attempt to grow a beard, and the best you could do is a patchy thing that only makes you look like a serial killer or a douchey guy who says he has a band even though they never play anything.

Gu gave me a stare that said he was waiting for me to say something. I had the feeling that he'd be giving me that a lot. "So, do I look nefarious to you?" he asked. "I mean, I'm not trying to, but it'd be really helpful if you can tell me what I'm doing wrong. Would cutting my bangs help? Growing my hair long? How about a parrot?"

"No parrot, and definitely not a black one," I said automatically.

"OK, good to know." He scribbled a note on his paper with his ink-coated finger. "But do I look nefarious?"

I realized that in the few minutes I had been in the non-bedroom, I had not actually looked at my kidnapper. I jumped back. Gu's face seemed to be stuck in a sneer, the permeant tension extending all the way back through his bald head. The only way he could have possibly looked more nefarious was if he had an eye patch. "Wait. Cut your bangs? You don't have any hair."

"Oh good, you jumped back when you looked at me. That's always a good sign. People tend to respond more positively to me after they do that." He flipped his paper over and put a notch in one of the columns. "I have you firmly down for 'not nefarious.' Do you think if I got a festive hat, fewer people would qualify me as nefarious?"

Only if it covered your face. I apologized mentally to Gu as soon as that thought hit me. "A big one might. Now what do you want with me? Are you going to torture me or just hold me for ransom?"

Gu gave me a puzzled look, making him look more nefarious. "We found you lying in that pile of those clothes out in the forest. The boss told me to take you back here so you'd be safe. There's lots of bandits in the forest, and he doesn't want anything bad to happen to you."

Did I really wander into the forest last night? If I did, why did I drag the clothes with me? They were rather comfortable to sleep on, but I don't normally have much in the way of foresight when I'm drunk. Since when are there bandits in the forest around the cabin? And who uses the word "bandit" anymore? "What does he even mean by 'bandit'?"

"A bandit is a robber that usually frequents a heavily trafficked area outside of a major metropolitan area. They are usually armed and often travel in groups to scare travelers with their numbers and weaponry, but not always. Would you like me to tell you about the origin of that word too?"

I would have liked to learn about the origin of that word but had other things on my mind. "Sorry, I didn't mean to say that last one out loud. I know what a bandit is, and I'll call the police about them when I get back home, though they might need to get more information from you. Does that mean you're not holding me prisoner against my will and that I can go?"

He didn't have to answer that question as the answer opened the door right behind him. The answer was holding a bag full of fresh fruits and vegetables and had a sword at his hip. The answer's name was Billiam von Cummerbund.

"You!" I said.

Gu and Billiam both looked at me with confusion and pointed back and forth at each other.

"I'm talking about the man who's my hero's chief rival," I said. "The man who wrote an exceptionally well-written and downright hilarious parody of my hero's work, which made my hero cry and forced me to go buy out all the Chunky Monkey from every supermarket in a twenty-mile radius to make him stop. The man who may or may not have changed the author's name on my hero's third book. The man who sends me a birthday card every year but only sends my hero one every other year except on leap years."

Gu nodded. "Oh, me, then. I didn't know you worked for Savey Davey the Gravy Baby."

Billiam set the groceries down and slapped Gu in the back of the head. "He means me, you idiot. And I keep telling you Davey isn't real. And as for you, Hatington, thank you so much for writing that review online. I didn't know you wrote it."

"I was only being honest, Billiam. Besides, you've always been real nice to me. Wait . . . Why are you here? I told Jess I didn't need your help, but it's just like her to send you anyway. Not that it matters. Your trip was a waste because I've already sent the book off to the editor."

"My trip? Hat, where do you think we are?"

I looked at the odd building we were in and then his even odder assistant. My silence must have been all the answer he needed.

"Hatman, we're not in Minnesota. We're not on Earth at all. We're in Vyenra, the land of Harry's books. When Gu over there found you in the forest, I ordered him to take you back here because you're such a nice guy, and I have nothing but respect for you." He pulled a nice big orange out of the bag and handed it to me.

Oranges were my favorite, and that one was the biggest one I had ever seen. Right before I tore into it, I realized something. While Billiam had always been a somewhat nice guy to me, he was being exceptionally nice to me right then—and he had referred to the world as "Harry's," not the one of Billiam's parody. Something wasn't right.

"Dig in, Hatrick. There's a whole pound of them. I got them just for you." He had his usual smile on his face; the one I had always considered pleasant—despite its slight crookedness—but which Harry had always said reminded him of that look a James

Bond villain gets when he thinks he has the hero trapped.

With the voice of Harry rolling around in my head, I carefully peeled back the skin and found a very un-orange color staring back at me. "It's purple. You were trying to trick me! You almost had me when you mentioned Vyenra. I'll bet you were going to knock me out, so you could take the draft of Harry's book from me."

Billiam gave Gu an odd look, that on anyone else would have been described as confusion, but given the circumstances likely meant they had some sort of secret code that involved rapid facial expression.

"But we already had you uncon—wait, that's what this thing is?" He picked up a stack of papers off the table. "We found this on top of you, but I thought Harry was doing his own fan fiction again. Like everyone on the forums doesn't know that Ari Holson is him."

"You thief. Give me that!" I dove across the table to take Harry's brilliant shame away from his friendly mortal enemy.

While Billiam was almost half a foot taller than me, we weighed about the same, so it was an even fight, or it would have been if he hadn't had an evil henchman with him. Fortunately, I caught Billiam completely off guard and his henchman had been in the process of cutting up one of those poisonous oranges, so he had to put the knife away before anyone got accidentally hurt in the tussle.

I soon had Billiam on the ground, but given his longer arms, he had the pages barely out of my reach. I was about to utilize the "Tickle and Grab" technique that I developed on Harry, when Gu grabbed me from behind and attempted to haul me off. He really should have known better than to try that on someone who had Harry as a mentor. I went limp, slid out of his hold, and dove toward the papers.

"Get him off my hand, Gu."

"I'm trying, Billy, but he's not ticklish."

"I told you to only use my full name, nincompoop, and he's famous for not being ticklish. Hit him."

The fact that I'm not ticklish was probably the only reason Harry hired me. He considered it a superpower, and I never even got to talk about my experience during the interview. He spent over an hour trying to think up a code name for me. I refused to wear the costume he made for me on my first day.

Gu pulled his hand back to slap me but stopped. "But I'm a pacifist, boss. Tickling's the most aggressive thing I'll allow myself to do."

Billiam struggled to pull the papers from below my body, but I had his arm trapped. Unfortunately, I couldn't figure out how to maintain my hold while standing up. At least none of the papers felt creased under me.

"Well, do something!" Billiam said.

"Oh, sorry, Billy. I got caught up reading one of the pages. I didn't know that armpit hair could be woven into an escape rope."

He stopped struggling and looked at the page. "Really? That's in there?"

I didn't need to hear what he said next. I leapt from the ground, grabbed the pages from Gu after giving an apology for being so forceful, and ran from the building. The sound of pursuit died reasonably quickly, which was no surprise because I was in fantastic shape from having to chase Harry down when he was trying to play hooky from work.

DON'T YOU POINT THAT SPOON AT ME

When I was sure I had lost them, I ducked behind a tree to catch my breath. It was fairly humid in that forest, so I had to take extra care to keep the pages away from my steadily dripping face. I had never seen such gnarled, curvy trees before, but then again, Billiam had said I wasn't in Minnesota.

I stopped for a second to take in the unbelievable possibility of his claim. Vyenra? Wowie! Could it be true? I'd always wanted to go there, even when everyone told me it wasn't real. But now it was real, and I was there! Or was that only a trick to throw me off guard, like the bandits Gu mentioned?

The bandits! I had forgotten about them in my sprint away from my pursuers. And there I was making absolutely no effort to silence my mad dash. I stealthily crawled toward a nearby large bush, and when I was sure no one was around, peeked out. I didn't see anything, but if those bandits had been evading the police for long, then they wouldn't have been easy to spot.

They had to be out there somewhere. Since there wasn't enough time to burn the pages, I decided to hide them before they could get me. I hastily dug a hole with my hands, careful to look around as I dug. No one was in sight, but I knew I didn't have long. I managed to get a sufficiently wide hole that was about a foot and a half deep in no time. I was so panicked that any concept of time was lost on me. As I carefully held the pages over the hole, I was stopped by a shrill noise from behind. I looked back at the forest in near panic, but after a few tense minutes, convinced myself that it must have been a bird. I scooped the dirt back into the hole and covered the draft.

Looking back to the forest, I was relieved to find no evidence that I had been followed, and no sign of any bandits. As I considered what to do next, a second shrill sound came from off to my right. There was no indication that whatever had created or caused it was moving in my direction, which was a relief. What wasn't a relief was that now that my focus wasn't elsewhere, I could finally focus on the sound. It was a scream—a very feminine scream.

Someone was in trouble and that person was a woman . . . or a cowardly fantasy author. In spite of my less than heroic size, I couldn't resist the need to protect someone in peril. My therapist said my need to protect was due to not being bullied as a child, though she did begrudgingly admit the copious amounts of books I read about knights couldn't have helped. Her theory couldn't explain why I was terrified of soul patches, however.

I was so caught up on instinctually running to help the usual source of such screams—Harry—that it didn't dawn on me that he was safely in the hospital and not likely roaming the woods. Unfortunately, that realization only hit me when I found the source of the noise.

I stopped in surprise like I'd run into a wall and bounced as my butt hit the hard forest floor. You would have stopped too if you were running through the forest and came across an adult holding two other adults in bright red robes at bay with a spoon. You wouldn't? Well, what if the spoon warrior was wearing a pot on his head, had a serving tray tied to his chest, and was wearing sandals in December? The sandals-in-December thing was probably the worst even though there wasn't snow on the ground. Was it December if I was in Vyenra too though?

"Don't think you can outsmart me, priests," the guy with the spoon said. "Didlius the Cunning is no man's fool."

"You would have to be a fool to oppose us," the taller priest said. "Do you know what the silver trim on these robes signifies? It signifies that we are high-ranking members of the clergy, and as such, we order you, as a loyal Paruxian, to step aside and let us have that obviously terrified woman."

Paruxia? I am on Vyenra!

Paruxia had never been directly covered in the books, but it was the homeland of The One, the most dominant religion in the known world. Harry had been fleshing it out in between drafts recently, so I knew a little more about it, like, for instance, that the men took great pride in their elaborate beards. These two priests did have rather impressive beards, and they were dark-skinned like real Paruxians too. Didlius had the same skin tone; however, he was completely clean-shaven like me.

"Ha," Didlius said. "I don't have to listen to that order because the terrified person is not a woman at all. He only screams like one. As I have cunningly outthought you, I think it's only right that you go."

Didlius moved to the side and pointed to a prone person shivering on the ground. The person was indeed a man. I could tell by the beard and Adam's apple. He let out another high-pitched scream to verify that he was the source of the noise.

"Huh," the shorter priest said. "It is a man. Well, I guess we should go then."

The taller priest smacked his companion upside the head. "That doesn't change anything. We still have our duty to do, and we can't just let this lunatic go around smacking people with spoons. Think of what that will do to our reputation, and more importantly that of the Most Holy One. No, we have to make him pay."

Didlius's face scrunched up. I think he was going for fearsome but on his baby-like face it came off as adorable. "So, when a cleverer opponent outfoxes you, you ignore the rules of fair combat? I'm beginning to see why church attendance is falling. On guard!" He swung the spoon at the shorter priest, who easily dodged it by taking a half step back. It was a spoon, after all, and not a particularly long one.

"Church attendance is falling because half the town's population moved to form that new town, you loon." The taller priest grabbed ahold of the arm with the spoon.

The pantsless man stood up and scurried away.

I considered intervening but couldn't decide who to support. The religion of The One was one of my favorite aspects from the books, but these priests didn't seem like the nicest guys out there. Plus, their opponent was named Didlius, and that was the name of the founder of The One. I decided to stay put until I had more information.

Didlius tried to shake the priest loose but to no avail. The taller priest was sturdily built while Didlius was barely a shade above emaciated. The shorter priest just stood there and stared. It looked like the taller priest was about to wrestle the spoon away, but he faltered when he caught a glimpse of me. I reflexively grinned in response, and that was enough of a distraction for Didlius to regain control of the spoon, though in doing so, he inadvertently made contact with the tall priest's mid-section.

Didlius gave a nervous grin right before a momentous crash knocked me on my back. Normally getting knocked over isn't a good thing, but in this instance, it likely saved me from permanent vision damage. A lightning bolt shot from the sky and landed right in the middle of the clearing roughly ten feet away. After the shock wore off and most of the ringing in my ears subsided, I sat back up. Somehow I had escaped unharmed. At first, I couldn't believe my luck, but then realized that both Didlius and the shorter priest, who were both much closer to the blast, seemed to be unharmed, if a bit shaken, as well. The smoldering pile of robes in between them even seemed at least salvageable, though there was no indication of the whereabouts of their former occupant.

The way the ground shook and the lightning shot from the sky convinced me that I was not dealing with cosplayers. No, this had to be real. I was really in Vyenra, the world from the books. With the right equipment, a production team on Earth could have made a convincing lightning flash from the ground, but I had seen this one shoot from the sky. Plus, something that could have caused that effect would have to be fairly big—big, as in too big to hide in robes and definitely too big to hide in the tight tunic that Didlius was wearing.

I was giddy. Well, I was giddy after I threw up last night's nachos. My legs were too wobbly to stand, so I did a little dance inside my head. When I found Billiam again, I would have to apologize for doubting his claim.

"You . . . you killed him," the shorter, and now only, priest said.

Didlius looked down at the robes. "You can't prove that. He could have left for vacation during the light show. Maybe he was late for a doctor's appointment. For all we know, he could have used the blinding light as a distraction and hid behind one of the many trees around here. Was your companion a practical joker?"

The only priest began to shake. "A lightning bolt landed on him, and it came from your spoon! You, sir, are a murderer and a witch. When I get the other priests together, we will come down on you with so much fury that you'll wish you had struck yourself instead."

"And they'll only do that if you tell them, correct?"

"Well, yes, but . . . you wouldn't!" The priest backed away.

"I *would* . . . Just to be clear, we are talking about you pinky swearing to never kidnap any women or men who scream like women, and also never telling any of your priest friends about what happened today, right?"

"No."

Didlius scratched his forehead. "So, you expect me to guess then?"

The priest backed away farther but didn't answer. With the way his lip was quivering, I had a feeling that he was too terrified to speak anymore.

"Fine. Is it that I wouldn't make you say no to drugs?"

A tear rolled down the priest's face.

"He thinks you're going to kill him," I said.

Didlius jumped and turned around. "My goodness. It appears that in my efforts to protect you from these priests, I've inadvertently shaved off your beard, straightened your hair, changed your clothes, took a few inches off your height, and lightened your skin. This spoon really *is* magic, and I thought the lightning bolt and ability to make priests disappear was impressive."

"I'm not the same guy that you were protecting."

"Of course you're not the same. With that glowingly pale skin you now have, you could pass for someone from one of those the southwestern countries like Sculandia."

Back in Minnesota, I'd always been described as tanned, but I figured it wasn't worth arguing. "No, I mean the guy you were protecting walked away about five minutes ago while you were arguing with the priests. I'm a traveler from a far-off land who happened to wander by, sort of like that second priest just wandered off."

Didlius turned to see the last of the priest's robes disappear into the underbrush. "I would throw Spoon-Scalibur at him, but the last time I did that I missed and started a forest fire. I very much need to practice throwing it, but I haven't figured out how to do that without destroying half the forest."

"You could find some regular spoons that are similar in build and weight and practice with those."

Didlius's face lit up. "My! And I thought I was clever. What is your name, traveler? I am known as Didlius the Cunning, bearer of Spoon-Scalibur. I came upon those evil priests accosting that poor woman who later turned into a man and felt it my duty to protect her. As a champion of Jaenia the Fair, it is my sworn duty. It is what all the knights in the stories do, after all."

I shook his hand. "I didn't know they had knights in Paruxia or much of any cavalry, what with it being mostly covered in forests. Oh, and by the way, my name is Hat."

Didlius made a throwing motion with his spoon hand but stopped at the last second. "Correct. We do not. I read about them in my favorite books as a child, and since they go on grand quests with magic weapons like I am on, I decided to model myself after them. You see, I am on a quest to free my Jaenia."

In the books, Jaenia was the wife of Didlius as he founded The One. With being in Paruxia, I was only one fact away from proving a theory. "What year is it?"

"Perhaps you are not as clever as I suspected. It is the year 467." Didlius gave a hearty laugh. While I was less than convinced of his claims to heroism, his laugh at least sounded like the kind of laugh that might belong to a hero. It was rich, hearty, and inspired confidence. The kind of laugh that makes you think you're in the presence of the future founder of a major religion, instead of some skinny guy in baggy pants and a tight vest. Until this point, the only thing that lent itself to him being anyone important was his neat spoon (which he wouldn't let me hold no matter how hard I begged).

As 467 was indeed the year when The One was founded, I

was convinced that I was in the right time and place. "So, that must mean you are or were a cheesemonger."

Didlius was so surprised that he almost dropped his spoon. "I was a cheesemonger by trade, travelling from village to village plying my wares. One day an elderly man came to my cart. I could tell by looking at him that he was one of those cheapskates who asks for a sample of every expensive cheese and never ends up buying anything. Sure enough, after his seventh sample, he collapsed. At first, I assumed he was only using it to distract me so I wouldn't give him my patented dirty look when he didn't buy anything, but when I checked his pulse, I realized he had used death as an even cleverer way to avoid that glare. Feeling he owed it to me for the samples, I rifled through his pockets and came across a few coins, some dusty butterscotch candies, and this spoon. As I fought to yank a particularly sticky candy out, I accidentally brushed the spoon, and the most melodious, perfect voice filled my head. She called herself Jaenia—the most beautiful name I had ever heard—and told me how she was trapped by a most terrible magic spell and needed a true champion to come and free her. I, of course, accepted her quest. After selling off my cart and wares for this equally magic armor I am wearing, I embarked on my quest."

I frantically looked around for something to write on. Harry had only written down a few fragmented facts about the formation of The One for inclusion in the next edition of the *Encyclopedia Garandia*, and with him being in a coma, the full story might never get written. This was a dream come true. I'd get all the information from a firsthand source. I'd actually get to meet a historical figure from the books! I already *had* met a historical figure!

Just thinking about all the questions I'd get to ask him almost put me in a coma of happiness. *What is the afterlife like, Mr. Didlius? Is stealing to feed your family permissible? Should you really be waving that spoon around when you're surrounded by flammable material?*

I grabbed his arm a split second before the spoon made contact with a tree. "Could you maybe put that thing away for now? The priests all seem to be gone."

"Ahh, well, I had this sinking suspicion that this tree was really a ghost in disguise, but since Jaenia agrees with you, I'll put it away for now. Though I warn you, tree, if you say 'boo' or try to steal my underwear when I'm distracted, you will feel the full might of Spoon-Scalibur!"

"Say, I don't suppose we could go somewhere and talk?" I asked. "Maybe somewhere with writing utensils and paper, preferably with less wood or other flammable materials. I'd like to hear all about your story."

Didlius's mouth dropped. "You would? That's fantastic. Only the greatest of knights had a chronicler with them. That would really help validate me in the eyes of Jaenia as a true knight."

"While that is a very tempting offer, I only have time to write down everything that's happened so far. You see, my boss . . . my noble master has fallen into a deep sleep, and I need to go back to watch after him."

Didlius nodded slowly. "I understand. Duty always comes first. Well, if you have the time, I am on my way to my village to say a goodbye to my mother. She has plenty of quills and paper and will be thrilled to hear that someone is interested in my story. My mother is a good woman, but she will be disappointed that I have given up cheesemongering and your interest will help ease that."

"I can relate. My dad wasn't too happy when I told him I was quitting my job as a software developer to be an assistant to my favorite author. He just couldn't understand that I had been dreaming about that job since I read the first book a few months before."

"And she even had the audacity to mention how my lactose intolerance would prevent me from ever being a cheesemonger."

"That's silly. You only have to handle the cheese, not eat it."

"Yes! Well . . . truthfully there's no way you can NOT eat some cheese. So what if I get sick a few times a week and can't work; it's my dream, and you should always follow your dreams."

My mom said that exact same thing when she talked my dad off the roof after I told him about my change in profession, but in this case, I thought his parent was right. Not that there's anything wrong with being a cheesemonger; it's a very noble profession, even if it likely won't survive the increasingly digital, modern business landscape. Of course, he was in Vyenra and so that didn't really apply. I was sure the cheesemongering profession had at least another millennium left there. However, when your body tells you your dream is stupid, you should probably listen to it. Doubly so when you're being told by a magic, talking spoon to do something else.

SOME FLOOZY WITH A BAD ATTITUDE
AND A LOT OF DEBT

After another ten minutes, the trees parted to reveal a fairly modest village of about ten small buildings, no walls, and no sign of any soldiers. The last two struck me as odd since every village in the books was described as having some sort of protective building and at least a militia, war being the one constant in this world. But I was not in any of the countries visited in the books, so I shouldn't have assumed this would be the same.

All the houses we passed were of a sturdy design with the walls made of a pale, white substance that was likely concrete and had thatched roofs with chimneys. The home that Didlius led me to was probably the nicest one on the block, being that it had a lawn gnome and none of the others did. I was greatly disappointed that it was only a statue, as I had always secretly hoped that the world of Vyenra had gnomes, elves, Cajuns, or one of the many fantasy races I had read about in other series.

Didlius's mom greeted me with open arms and happily agreed to find me something to write with and on.

"Such a nice woman," I said.

"She is." He sighed. "But she used to nag on me fiercely

while I was trying to settle on a career, especially when I was attempting to be a martial artist."

"I tried to learn a martial art once, but I was too slow and uncoordinated for Kung Fu."

Didlius nodded. "Tickle Shen for me, but I always ended up hurting people instead of making them laugh."

Didlius's mom came back with some crude paper, a handful of quills, and two full containers of ink. She had been in such a hurry that her headscarf fell halfway down her face. The only visible part of her head was a giant smile as she set the tray down. "Now what is it you want to learn about my little Diddy? Has he finally made the cover of *Cheese Quarterly*?"

Didlius pushed her scarf back up. "It's *Cheese Yearly*, Mother, and no. Wait, yes. That's exactly it. He's here to do a cover story and would like to know about my early life, before I go on an epic quest to win the heart of a fair maiden."

She clapped her hands. "Oh, that is such fantastic news, assuming you marry her and settle down. Don't want you falling under the sway of some hussy and let her swindle you out of your cheese cart again."

I began writing furiously.

"That was no hussy, Mother. That was my mentor, and it was a completely platonic relationship. Well, less platonic when she stole my cart while I was inspecting those magic weeds she found, but she taught me all I know about cheese and the selling of it, so it was an even trade I suppose."

"Even for *you*, dear. You cleaned out all my dairy products after that. Now, I hope this epic quest you're going on is wrought with peril. You'll never win a maiden's heart by fighting fluffy bunnies or old squirrels. For a truly epic quest, I expect lots of dragons and duels with dangerous swordsmen. Fair maidens never go for the sort who play it safe. That's not how your father caught my eye."

"How did he do that?" I asked.

Didlius rolled his eyes and his voice synced with his mother as she told the story. "When I was but a fair maiden, there was a vicious ogre threatening the village. Grak'Lok the Potty Trained would kill any travelers he caught approaching the village. As I had many a suitor, your father vowed to slay the unusually hygienic but naughty ogre to prove his worthiness. Granted your father did wet himself and run away in terror as soon as he got near the ogre, but I was mightily impressed by his attempt and agreed to marry him. Ironically, the ogre died of a urinary tract infection a week later because he kept holding it in, since the only toilet his size was over a day's walk away."

"Ahh, I see. You married him because he was the only one who was brave enough to face the ogre."

"Oh, no. Lots of other suitors faced the ogre, but his father was the only one smart enough to run away. I mean, that thing was huge. Its thighs alone were big enough to crush a man's skull . . . still not sure why Dictus stuck his head in between them."

I nodded. "So, you're saying Didlius should run away if he comes across any monsters?"

"Unless he has a magic weapon. It's the only practical thing to do." She stuck her finger into Didlius's chest. "And if your fair maiden doesn't appreciate a practical man, you send her right to me, and I'll straighten her out."

"Moms do know how to give the best advice," I said. "I'm sure you'll talk her into marrying your son."

She slapped her forehead. "No, I'll tell her to find one of those bad boys with the leather jackets and cool helmets with the wings on them. You shouldn't marry someone who's not right for you."

I drew a picture of myself in such an outfit on the back of the paper. I wondered where one would get a flaming sword around there.

Didlius reverently pulled out his spoon. "Fortunately, Mother, I do have a magic weapon."

She tilted her head and inspected his waist. "Where?"

"The spoon, Mother." He held it out proudly.

"What are you gonna do with that against a dragon? Serve him ice cream until he gets a brain freeze? Give him cough medicine and hope it makes him sleepy enough to stab him with a real weapon?"

He puffed his chest out. "Dragons aren't real, Mother. As a matter of fact, neither are ogres."

She slapped him in the gut. "Says the guy who thinks he has magic cutlery."

Didlius stomped out the back door. I bid his mother to follow him, and she reluctantly agreed. As soon as we exited the door, Didlius pointed to a nearby waist-high rock that jutted out of the grass and then took three slow practice swings. His mother sighed for what seemed like the fiftieth time. He brought the spoon down with all the force his thin frame could muster. The boulder exploded, showering us for over a minute with bits of gravel and dirt. I grabbed her right before a fist-sized one caught her in the head.

"Why . . . That's . . ." Her jaw seemed to lock in the down position.

"The legendary Spoon-Scalibur." He held it up proudly. "And it will be the instrument I use to win the heart of the fair Jaenia."

"Legendary? If it's so legendary, then why have I never heard of it? And what kind of girl is this Jaenia? 'Jaenia' does not sound like a Paruxian name. Has she been married before? Does she already have children? How old is she?" She tapped her foot in anticipation as the last of the gravel bounced off her floral bathrobe.

Didlius pouted. "It's legendary because it's magic, Mother, and Jaenia is . . . is beautiful beyond words—probably—and needs my help. As the holder of a magic weapon, it is my duty to save her. It's what happens in all the stories you used to read to me about knights when I was a child."

"If I may interrupt . . . Didlius's mother?"

She stopped tapping her foot and gave me a warm smile. "It's Helfinia, dear. Go on."

"Helfinia, I know Didlius's plan seems to have a lot of holes in it, but I can assure you that it will succeed. Don't ask me how I know this because I'm not at liberty to say, but without a doubt, he will triumph beyond your wildest expectations." My stomach turned at not revealing that he would be killed at the end, but it was the right thing to do for history's sake. Besides, what mother wouldn't want their son's name to be memorialized and worshipped for centuries?

Her eyes brightened. "Are you an oracle?"

Didlius's eyes brightened even more. "Can you predict the outcome of sporting events?"

"Ohhhh, that's a good one, son. Can you?"

"Again, I'm not at liberty to say."

She gave a cunning smile. "Ah, he can, but he wants all the winnings for himself. Very practical. I like you, young man, even if you aren't a Paruxian. But it's the 5th century, and if my Didlius wants to hang around with a southwesterner, then I say that's great. A shrewd guy like you who can tell the future is exactly what my Didlius needs on this quest to find this possibly married, single mom of an indeterminate age from some strange foreign land. But he found a magic eating utensil, so it must be the will of some higher being, so who am to say no?"

I bit my lip. "As thrilled as I'd be to go with him, I can't. I only came to get his backstory before I go back home and look after my employer, who's in a coma that I had nothing to do with. He tends to inadvertently do a lot of incredibly stupid things."

"That sounds exactly like my former mentor," Didlius said.

"She would unintentionally insult people and get into all kinds of scrapes. In the few moments when I wasn't saving her from her own stupidity, she did teach me an awful lot about the cheesemongering profession and life in general, though."

"Yes . . . he learned an awful lot from her, which is why I was so hoping you were going with him," Helfinia said. "Is your employer close by? Maybe Diddy can escort you to him."

"Actually, I'm not sure how I got here or how to get back. I'm guessing it was some sort of magic. Do you know of any Atlians nearby?"

Atlians were one of the two groups of people capable of casting magic in Vyenra, the other one being the Old Gods, who hadn't been seen for centuries . . . Centuries before the events covered in the books, which were in the future of where I was, meaning they were still around in this time period. So, one of them might also be able to help me if I could find one of those rare beings and prevent them from murdering me or turning me into a goat . . . Atlians were definitely the safer bet, as they were human, generally reasonable, and had a use for money.

"None out in a tiny village like this. The most likely place to find one of them would be in one of the bigger cities. Could take weeks to get to one of them. Why, you might as well go with my son, since I'm assuming you don't know your way around here." Her sly look was somewhat undercut by her scarf sliding back over her eyes again.

Didlius pulled her scarf back up, and she whispered something in his ear.

"You seem like a fine and noble fellow, Hat," Didlius said. "Will you accompany me? It seems like we have much in common, and while we travel, I can tell you more about my past."

I don't normally like being maneuvered into a choice, even when it's done with such subtlety and skill, but in this case, she had guided me into the option I had wanted all along. The only reason I hadn't volunteered to go with Didlius was Harry. I had put him in that coma, and it was my duty to look after him. However, I had no way to get back to him and the only way I could think of involved magic—magic that required me to travel to find. It looked like I had no choice. Besides, Harry probably wouldn't mind. Sure, if he woke from the coma and I wasn't there to greet him, he would probably yell and throw things at me as soon as he saw me, but he'd likely do that even if he hadn't just woken up from a coma. It was his way of saying he cared. And he'd forgive me when I showed him all the things I'd written down about the early life of Didlius, mostly because it would save him a lot of time.

"Then I guess I'm going with him," I said.

"Fantastic," Helfinia said. "Didlius, can you go pack some bags for you and your friend, while I tell Hat a few more anecdotes about your past? Oh, and don't take all my cheese this time. I'm having Mr. Pervus over for dinner, and we're having fondue."

"Sure thing!" Didlius rushed inside with a smile so big that it threatened to crack his face.

"Now, Hat, my Didlius has many good qualities, but critical thinking is not one of them. He's had me to guide him through most of his life, so I need you to look after him. Since you seem to know what he's up to, I want you to promise me that it's something good, like setting the world record for eating the most pie in a day or fixing our incredibly backward electoral process."

I looked up from my furious note-taking. "I promise . . . I thought Paruxia was an absolute monarchy."

"It is, and I find that incredibly backward. I'd like to see it become more of a constitutional monarchy—but you're right; the pie eating thing seems much more likely with my dear son's capacities. A mother can dream, can't she? Anyway, please look after my son and make sure he doesn't marry some floozy with a bad attitude and a lot of debt. Also, that he doesn't kill anyone. The floozy one is the biggie though."

From what Harry had written right before our disagreement, I knew that Didlius did eventually marry Jaenia, but I knew next to nothing about her. I did, however, know that he would found the religion that would soon shape much of the world of Vyenra for centuries. I wasn't sure if me telling Didlius or his mother would change everything, so I decided to keep it to myself.

I shook her hand. "Don't worry. I'll look after your son and I'm quite certain he will make you proud."

She exhaled deeply. "Excellent. Now do you want to see some baby pictures of Didlius? I'm quite the artist, and I really think I captured his naked bum perfectly."

A WOLF AND A BABY

We left the town the next morning through much fanfare, almost exclusively generated by Didlius. The multi-colored streamers and confetti were a nice touch, though I had to take his noise-maker away after five minutes. As we exited the town, Helfinia handed me a brand new, empty book to record our journey after I promised to look after her son and make sure he "didn't do anything too stupid or marry some tramp with loose morals and a funny accent."

I was too enthralled with taking in the sights of what I now knew to be a different planet to focus on where we were going at first. There were new varieties of trees closer to the road to study, which all seemed shorter and younger than the ones back near Harry's cabin in Minnesota. The temperature was also quite a bit more humid than back home. It was a constant battle to keep the drips of sweat off the pages of my notes—a battle I often lost. I did eventually get used to it though. Fortunately, Helfinia had demanded that we pack extra canteens of water.

"Where to, Didlius?" I asked.

"I am open to suggestions. Where do you think we should go?"

I finished writing what he said and looked up. "Oh, no. This is your story. I'm only here to record it. You're the one who has to make those decisions."

"Of course," Didlius said. "In the stories, the brave hero with the magic weapon is the one in charge, and he is usually accompanied by a lowly squire. May I call you my squire?"

I shrugged. "Sure." I was an assistant back home, and a squire was pretty much the medieval equivalent of an assistant. Besides, I was afraid that if I made any decisions, I might change the future. Squires did have to take care of weapons—something I knew next to nothing about—but Didlius's weapon was a spoon, so I thought I could handle that.

"Then I decide we go . . . forward!"

A brilliant decision, considering the only other direction the road went was back to the village, but everyone has to start somewhere. I hoped he would soon get the hang of that. Unfortunately, a few hours later, we came to a crossroads where the road split in two other directions: southeast and southwest. We came to a halt as Didlius scratched his chin.

"How about we go to wherever this Jaenia is and rescue her?" I asked. "Which direction is that?"

"An excellent idea, but I'm not sure where that is. And the people who made this road sign didn't think to add that information."

"That is quite the wrinkle. Was I mistaken or did you say you could speak to her through the spoon?"

"I can." He put the spoon up to his ear. "She says she doesn't know where she is. It's very dark, and she can't remember how she got there or who put her there."

"Well, you need to find Jaenia but don't know where she is, and I need to find a wizard to see if he knows how to send me back home, so maybe the same wizard might know how to locate her. We could kill two birds with one stone."

Didlius's jaw dropped. "I am a hero at heart, Hat, and I do not think we should seek any wizards who would require us to murder two birds, no matter the method."

I had to suppress a laugh. "It's a figure of speech. It means to get two things done at once."

"You southwesterners are a strange people, casually killing two creatures in such a barbaric manner, but yes, getting both done at the same time does sound like a wise course."

I looked up at the signs. "Your mother said Atlians are more likely to be found in larger cities. Which one of those is the biggest? Lestipul or Gyntia?"

"Lestipul is slightly larger but is also the end of that branch of the road, whereas the road continues on after Gyntia and eventually leads to the capital. And Gyntia is only fifty miles away while Lestipul is nearly 300."

"So, it looks like we're decided then."

"And we are too." An armored woman leapt from the trees into the middle of the road.

Didlius had barely enough time to duck as the axe in her left hand swept over his head. Her second axe whooshed over his head a second later. I'm not proud to say I froze, but in my defense, the attack had been rather sudden and unexpected. Even if I hadn't frozen, my quill and paper were hardly equal to her sharp axes anyway. Didlius was about to bring his spoon up into something like an uppercut (a spoonercut?), when a deep, male voice yelled, "Stop!" from the same area that our unexpected attacker had emerged from. It was well-timed for both Didlius and his opponent as the mad woman had somehow balanced herself and was about to bring both axes down on top of his skull. I'm not sure which of their blows would have landed first, and I'm glad I didn't get to find out.

A tall, armored wall of muscle scrambled out of the tree line and pushed the similarly armored woman away from Didlius. The woman looked like she wanted to continue her assault, but she was no match for the giant's strength. I noticed for the first time that her axes were not *in* her hands but *were* her hands, or at least the closest things she had to hands as the axe handles were attached to her arms at the elbows.

"Let go of me, you big lunky lunk," she said.

"No way, Wolfette. I'm not going to let you kill more people. And what's a lunky lunk exactly?"

She squirmed at the waist as she continued to push forward with her axe/hands. "It's what I call a big dummy dumb when he tries to keep me from my revenge. Now let go of me, Big Baby, so I can kill the guy who killed my friends."

The big man, who did not at all look like a baby, grabbed ahold of both of her axes' handles in one meaty paw, lifted her from the ground, and turned to look at us. "The pale one or the guy with the shiny spoon?" He swung her around to look at us.

Her arms continued twisting furiously while her feet pumped like she thought she had a chance to escape his powerful grip. "Does it matter? One of them is clearly the guy who killed my squaddie squad. Let. Me. At. Them."

"Nope. You tried the same thing last time, and when I let you go, you brought new meaning to 'half-off special.' How was the nice waitress going to make a living if none of her customers lived to tip her?"

She stopped struggling and bit her tongue. "I hadn't thought of that. She was pretty quick with the refills, and she gave me an extra strip of bacon too. But this is different. One of those two is definitely the killer man."

Didlius's knuckles lightened as he clutched the spoon. I took a few steps back.

"And which one would that be?" Big Baby asked.

"Let me down, and I'll sort it out after I kill them."

He sighed. "What did Jackal's and Cat's killers look like again? Go slow and think it through."

She scrunched her face. "He was bald, Paruxian, middle-aged, and fit in a bulky sort of way, like you but shorty shorter."

Big Baby gave us both a long scan. "While the one with the spoon *is* Paruxian and they are both shorter than me, neither of them are either bald, middle-aged, fit, or bulky."

"Two out of seven is close enough. Let me downy down." Her legs started pumping again.

"Wolfette, we've been over this at least a hundred times. You can't go around killing people because the killer might have changed his appearance, hairstyle, weight, gender, and age."

"You forgot race and sexual orientation. And why not?"

He lifted her up higher and turned her to face him. "Because I'm not going to feed you, bathe you, or do any of that other stuff for you if you do, and without hands you can't do any of those for yourself anymore."

"Spoilsport." Her legs stopped pumping. "One of these days I'm going to figure out how to use my toesy toes like fingers and then people like those guys are going to be in real trouble . . . Fine. I won't kill them for now. You can let me down."

Big Baby set her down gingerly behind him and shook his head in frustration. "Sorry about that, guys. My sister has been a little off since her companions died. Cutting both forearms off and attaching axes in their place probably didn't help much either."

"My goodness!" Didlius said.

"She did that to herself?" I asked.

"Oh, crap," Big Baby said. "Not the story again."

Wolfette cleared her throat. "It was a dark and stormy night . . ."

"You said it was bright and sunny last time."

"Quiet, dumby dumb. You weren't there. It was a dark and

stormy night. It was almost black out. Me and my squad, The Fanged Trio, had cornered this bald fellow we were tracking and asked him to surrender. Pretty routine. He wasn't even armed, so we weren't exactly at the ready when he jumped up and tore Cat to pieces with his bare hands. Jackal managed to get a few pokes of his spear in, but they bounced off like they were nothing. I . . . I dropped my axes and ran. I could hear his cackles coming from everywhere as I stumbled about through the brush. The laugh shook my skull and just wouldn't stop. I ran and ran until I couldn't run no more. I collapsed, and then the sound stopped, at least until I went to sleep the next night. I cut my hands off and attached my new axes to the stumps, so I'd never drop them again. I have to find this man and make him pay, or I'll die trying. At least then the laughter will stop. After I discovered how hardy hard it was to do some stuff with my awesomey new hand/axes, I tracked my little brother down for . . . help."

"My word," Didlius said. "That is terrible."

I nodded. "Did you say 'the Fanged Trio'?"

Our two new "friends" wore nearly identical bronze armor, minus the cod piece . . . on her armor, not his. Big Baby was seven feet tall with jet black skin. His dark eyebrows suggested equally dark hair. Wolfette was probably a few inches shorter than my five-foot-six-inch self and had long red hair rolling out from beneath her helmet. Her skin was closer to deeply tanned than the jet black of her brother and the Paruxians I had seen so far.

I hadn't really gotten the best look at their helmets yet, what with the distraction of Wolfette's furious attack, but now I could. Wolfette had a helmet carved into the shape of a ferocious wolf's head with its mouth open. Big Baby's helmet was similarly shaped but like a giant crying baby. It was an interesting juxtaposition to his massive, muscular frame. Wolfette's helmet seemed to be spot on with her demeanor, however.

When Harry had visited Vyenra, he had encountered a trio of mercenaries called the Fanged Trio whose members had similarly themed helmets, though their names were Wolf, Jackal, and Cat and they were from Garandia, not Paruxia. That group did, however, mention that there were other Fanged Trios out there assigned to different territories, though even if there hadn't been, I was in their past anyway.

Wolfette stomped forward, but Big Baby stuck his arm out, so she stopped. "I'm the sole survivor of the Paruxian Trio," she said. "And until I either find this bald fella or die, we aren't recruiting, so don't even thinky think about it. If I fall, oldie Cat will come out of retirement and reform us."

"Such a noble quest." Didlius wiped a tear from his cheek. "We are also on such a quest, though ours is about saving and less about killing. I am searching for the location of my fair Jaenia who has been imprisoned by some evil fiend. Would you two care to accompany us?"

Big Baby put both hands over his heart. "I have a soft spot for love stories, so of course."

Wolfette whacked him in the shin. "Who said you get to make decisions, doofy doof? I get to make the decisions because I'm the leader."

He scowled at her.

"I'm the leader because I'm older and more experienced."

He gingerly grabbed her axes by the handles and pushed them away. "I don't think that's really fair, since you were only born a few minutes before me, and I've been a mercenary for just as long as you. I say we vote on this."

She pointed both axes at him. "I say we don't."

"I say we do, or I'm not feeding you or helping you mount horses without killing them."

She scowled but lowered her axes. "Fine, we'll vote. I vote we're not going with them."

Big Baby smiled. "I say we are."

"I say you are," I said.

"Me too," Didlius said.

"Three to one," Big Baby said. "We go with them."

Wolfette tried to rub her cheek with her left axe blade but stopped with a curse when she drew blood. As she attempted in vain to rub off the blood with her axe, Big Baby gingerly wiped it off with his handkerchief. She muttered a thanks and tried to shoo him away.

"Wait a minute," she said. "Who said they get to vote?"

We voted on allowing Didlius and me vote. It was two to one for, with Didlius abstaining.

Wolfette stomped her foot. "Damn. Fine, we'll go with them, but as soon as our goals conflict, we go our seperatey separate ways."

"That sounds fine with me," I said. Didlius nodded enthusiastically.

As we walked toward Gyntia, I immediately caught up on recording everything that happened in our encounter with Wolfette and Big Baby. As such, I was a bit too absorbed to catch the conversation that led to Wolfette challenging Didlius to a duel. However, I did manage to jump in before it started.

"Stop it, sis." Big Baby tried to grab her axes, but she was too quick this time and ducked under him, which, given that he was about a foot and a half taller than her, only required her to dip the blades lower.

"He challenged me, you dumb diddy dumb dumb."

"That may be, but this isn't a fair fight. He only has a spoon." Big Baby ducked down to grab her, but she backpedaled out of his reach.

"My spoon is mightier than all of your weapons combined, mercenaries!" Didlius shook his spoon menacingly, causing Wolfette to laugh.

Big Baby almost grabbed her while she was distracted, but she did a squatting pirouette and slapped him on the side of the helmet at the end. I swore I could see the baby on his helmet cry harder after the blow.

"Diddy," I said. "Why did you challenge Wolfette to a duel?"

"Only my mother calls me 'Diddy,' but as my friend, you can call me 'Did.'" He shook his spoon at Wolfette right as Big Baby grabbed her ankle and dragged her back. "And that murderous mercenary dared to insinuate that Jaenia is not real. I'll have you know that my beautiful soon-to-be bride is more real than you can ever hope to be. You, you . . . red-headed, handless meanie!"

"You take that back," Wolfette said as she kicked Big Baby in the helmet. "I do too have hands, and they are awesomey cool! You're just jealous because if you stuck that spoon on your arm, the only thing you could do is serve ice cream faster, while I can axe-acute people."

I reached out and held Did back. He was a few inches taller than me, but I outweighed his thin frame by about twenty pounds, so it wasn't that hard.

"Did," I said, "while I'm sure she could have been a little nicer about it, remember where she's coming from. Would you believe a guy you just met if he told you his spoon was magic, and he could hear the voice of a beautiful woman in it?"

Did stopped struggling. "Well, probably not. Now, if it was a talking frog, that would be different. Everyone knows that talking frogs are secretly beautiful princesses under a magic spell."

"I think that's princes, actually," Big Baby said right as Wolfette's boot caught him in the forehead.

"Oh, then it's a good thing none of them changed."

I desperately wanted to hear the rest of that story but had to finish breaking up the fight first. "Why don't you show them what your spoon can do as proof?"

Did nodded, so I let go and pointed at an abandoned, one-wheeled wagon on the side of the road.

Did held the spoon on high. "Spoon-Scalibur, show them your capacity to deal discomfort!" He brought the spoon down on the remaining wheel. The wheel exploded, lightning came soon after, and then Didlius stood there once again without a scratch on him or his clothes. I had a feeling the magic of the spoon protected him from any of its effects and aftereffects, or else every one of its bearers wouldn't have survived one use.

Big Baby immediately let go of Wolfette's ankle, but it didn't matter because she stopped moving altogether (unless you count the bit of drool that rolled down the left side of her chin).

The silence was deafening. I couldn't take it anymore. "Pretty neat, huh?" I know, I could have said something cooler, but right after you've seen a spoon turn a wooden wheel into dust with a single blow, no one's paying anything else much attention anyway.

"I'm seriously rethinking cutting my handsies off to stick axes on them," Wolfette said. "And I take everything back."

"Even the part where you said that 'magic spoons are stupid' and so am I?" Did asked.

"I take back the part about the magic spoon."

"Fantastic. Friends?" He held his hand out, and she let him touch her axe to shake it.

"Friends."

After that little incident, they got along beautifully, laughing and joking as we made our way to Gyntia. Big Baby was amazed as that was the first time he had seen her crack a smile since the incident with her former companions. When we saw our first fellow traveler on the road, Big Baby hurried to reach his sister, assuming there would a repeat of her previous violent introduction, but she only nodded as the man passed and continued telling her story to her new friend. Sweat and worry covered her brother's face until the traveler completely vanished from view.

Not wanting to get close to the new best friends, mostly because Wolfette rubbed her axes together menacingly whenever I got within ten feet of them, I decided to learn more about Big Baby. I would have tried him first, but getting as much of

Didlius's story as possible was my chief goal. Also, people who can crush me to death with only one hand tend to make me a tad uneasy, no matter how adorable their helmets are.

"So, what's your story, Big Baby?" I asked. "What did you do before Wolfette performed her forearm-ectamy?"

Big Baby continued to keep one eye on his sister. "Huh? Oh, before. Well, let's see, I was a mercenary, and before that I was a mercenary, and then . . . let's see, mercenary. And before even that I was an anti-war protestor."

I wrote everything down as he talked with the quill Didlius's mother had given me, nodding at each "new" occupation. "Wait! Anti-war protestor?"

His eyes finally left his sister as he burst out into laughter. "Yeah, I figured the best way to end war was to do it from the inside, so I became a mercenary. When you're as big as me, people tend to give up before they even land a blow. So, by being involved in more fights, I was actually preventing them. Also, I've always wanted to travel. But all that ended when Sis came crawling into our camp one night, starving with those ridiculous axes. I didn't really have a choice but to feed her and then follow after her. I don't even want to think about all the lives I failed to save from that new temper of hers. She used to be so mellow but now . . . well, I'm glad your friend seems to have brought her closer to her old self."

"I hope it stays that way."

"Yeah, me too." He sighed. "So, what brings a . . . Garandian, if I know my accents, like you to Paruxia?"

"I'm actually not a Garandian. I'm from a far-off land called Minnesota in a country called the United States of America, and I think I was brought here by a magic spell, though not by choice. We're trying to find an Atlian to see if they know of a way to send me back. We're also hoping the Atlian can locate the woman Did is looking for, Jaenia."

Big Baby whistled out a single note. "Those are quite the objectives, and an Atlian in these parts is pretty rare, not to mention expensive."

Wolfette patted Didlius on the back and pointed at a dead log off to the side of the road. Did sprinted forward and turned the log into a shower of mulch. After she stopped laughing, Wolfette slapped her axes together in her version of applause.

"Yeah," I said. "We might have to go to the capital. Do you think we'd find one there?"

"I'm sure the king has one in his employ, but getting to him in the castle is probably impossible. If you can't get to that one or find another one, I'm sure there will be several in the larger port cities of the north. Atlians do like to trade and every one of their ships has one mage on board to make sure they always have a strong wind at their backs."

I knew the Atlians were highly successful traders, but it never occurred to me that they used their magic in that way. I was so absorbed in recording our conversation that I didn't even notice that we had walked into a town, though as small as it was, if Big Baby hadn't stopped talking, I might have walked completely through it and missed it completely. However, the argument that we walked into the middle of would have been impossible to miss.

"It's mine," a young woman said as she tugged hard on a bundle that was held by a red-robed priest. A second priest tried to join in, but she kicked him, knocking him down.

The first priest elbowed her, and she winced but kept holding on. "Nonsense. You have no more claim to this than I do."

"Legally speaking, I do," the first one said.

Didlius charged at the first priest, with his spoon at the forefront. The second priest regained his senses and leapt up, but Did knocked him out of the way. "You priests are all the same," Did said, "always trying to use those robes as an excuse to trample the downtrodden. We'll see how you deal with a true champion!"

The second priest slid against the large boots of Big Baby, and after looking up at the giant man, ran off into the town.

I was too far away to stop Didlius. Given what he was destined to do and that his target was a priest whose religion was going to be replaced by The One, I wasn't sure if I should have anyway. However, Wolfette put the flat part of her right axe blade out to stop Did mid-swing. The priest hadn't moved and stared at the spoon in confusion. The young woman stopped pulling and stared as well.

"Hold on, Didlius," Wolfette said. "I think we should take our time and do this the right way."

"Oh, thank God," I said.

"Wait for it." Big Baby moved toward them.

"I think it's pretty clear what we have here," Wolfette said.

"So, you're taking the side of the woman?" Didlius asked.

She raised both her axes. "No, they obviously both did it and must pay!"

Big Baby reached her in the nick of time and grabbed both handles, yanking her backward.

Both the priest and the young woman crouched down and held their arms over their heads. The round, red package dropped to the ground between them. Now that I was closer, it looked to be a basket covered with a red blanket. The package whimpered and then let out a loud cry. The woman and priest cracked their heads together as they both reached to grab the crying baby inside. Big Baby shook his head in bemusement and plucked the baby from the basket. The baby stopped crying and began cooing as the gargantuan mercenary gently rocked it back and forth.

Wolfette lowered her axes and pouted. "Well played, you big dummy dumb. If I killed both of them, we'd have to take the baby with us, and all of that crying and diaper changing would have slowed me down on my rocking vengeance tour. Figure this mess out quick, Hat, so I can kill one of them, and we can dump the diaper on the one that's lefty left."

"Well, I think it's obvious that we should give it to the mother," I said.

Wolfette raised both axes over her head. "Woo-hoo! Women's rights." She lowered her axes. "Wait. Why's it obvious again?"

"Please!" the priest said. "I don't want my son to die without a father."

Didlius scratched his head with his spoon. "According to Paruxian law, the father gets custody, unless the father is deemed unfit to be a parent."

"Oh. It's the opposite where I come from," I said. "Then he gets it, I guess."

As Big Baby was about to hand the baby over to the father, I had a nagging feeling that this wasn't right. Maybe it was my preconceptions from the legal system back home or maybe there was a good, moral reason in the back of my mind that I couldn't put my finger on. Whatever the case, I felt I had to do something. And that feeling completely overruled my desire to not affect the historic events of Didlius's journey.

"Oh!" I said. "I've got a better idea. There was a legendary king named Solomon who came up with the perfect solution for this exact problem. We'll cut the baby in two."

"Fine," the woman said. "I'd rather have half of my baby than no baby at all."

"If that's all I'm going to get, then I also accept this wise judgement," the priest said.

"Woohoo!" Wolfette said. "Lower the baby, you biggy big galoot, so we can get this over with and move on. I wanna see what kind of tavern they have here."

I breathed a sigh of relief when Big Baby raised the little baby over his head. "No."

Wolfette swung her axes in the air, but they weren't long enough to reach his outstretched arms.

"Wolfette, stop," I said. "It was only a test. I was going to give it to the one who wouldn't let us cut the baby in half. You're both terrible parents and neither of you deserve this child."

The mother began to weep. "But that's not how the story goes. In the story, the ancient Paruxian king Aronius rewarded the child to the woman who agreed to cut the toddler in half for her bold thinking and for seeing through his ruse."

"That's why I picked that option too," the priest said. "I knew you wouldn't actually cut our son in half."

"That's still terrible," I said.

"What if we both took the baby?" the priest asked. "Seeing how ferocious Vimina is trying to protect our son has made me realize how much she loves him. Until now, I thought she only wanted the baby to spite me."

Vimina wiped her tears. "And I thought you only wanted him to spite me too, Honus. Perhaps we can share him."

I nodded to Big Baby, and he handed the little one to Vimina. When Honus began to cry as he played with his son's tiny hands, there wasn't a dry eye in the area. I swore I even saw Wolfette tear up, but with her it might have been because she didn't get to cut or stab anyone.

"Is there anything I can do for you?" Honus asked. "I don't have much in the way of money, but you can have the few coins I possess."

Wolfette tried to hold her axes out to take the coins, but upon realizing the impossibility of that task, she looked to her brother. Big Baby crossed his arms and shook his head.

"Instead of paying us, perhaps you can help us with some information," I said. "Do you know of any magicians in the area? We need to find an Atlian. I know it's unlikely in a small town like this, but have you heard of any in the general area?"

Honus scratched his beard. "We haven't seen any Atlians in this town or in any of the nearby towns for over a century. There might be one in Arvingain, a few days walk to the south. Also, there've been reports of some non-Atlian magician wandering the road at night between here and there. Normally I'd call it preposterous but there have been an awful lot of sightings."

"Thank you," I said. With that, we bid the parents goodbye. They headed inside a nearby house, and we walked farther into the town.

"Can we stop at the tavern still?" Wolfette asked.

Big Baby laughed. "No way. The last couple of times, you got into a fight within five minutes."

"Well, that guy laughed at me the last time because I got frustrated when my delicious beer was just sitting in front of me being all foamy-like, and I couldn't take a drinky drink, so I decided to frustrate him by preventing him from drinking his beer too."

"Removing one's head does tend to prevent one from drinking," Big Baby deadpanned.

"And the other time I just knew they were giving me dirty looks. But I showed them they couldn't hide those looks by having their backs to me." She laughed. "They'll never try that again."

"Being dead does tend to prevent one from making faces. So, yeah. I am not taking you into any more taverns." He put his hand on her shoulder and steered her out of town.

"Spoilsporty sport," Wolfette mumbled as she beheaded a lawn gnome dressed as a local priest.

"Yeah, spoilsport," Didlius said as he "spooned" the rolling head into a million pieces.

The telltale lightning aftereffect of his strike startled the two townspeople nearby. After the shock wore off, the two of them scurried into the nearest building. The cloth hat of the statue somehow survived, floating like a feather through the air before finally landing at my feet. I picked up the tiny red hat and was about to put it back on top of its headless owner, when a shout caught my attention from behind.

"Those are the jerks who attacked Honus!" a priest with a sandal print in the middle of his robe said. "I told you that explosion had to be them."

"And they killed him and took his hat!" another priest said.

The seven priests and three villagers charged forward brandishing a wide assortment of mostly deadly weapons. Wolfette tried to turn to face them, but Big Baby still had his hand on her shoulder and lifted her over his head before she could. Didlius looked like he was going to join her in the assault but turned and ran when Big Baby carried her in the opposite direction. I finished setting the hat on the statue's neck before joining them in their retreat. Fortunately, the priests' long robes did not lend themselves well to running. By the sound of it, one of them tripped and took out the rest a few hundred yards outside of town, and when we looked back ten minutes later, they were nowhere to be seen.

FRED THE COPYRIGHT WIZARD

We moved as swiftly as we could through the afternoon, not pausing until it became too dark to see. While we hadn't seen any pursuit the entire day, Didlius's ears assured us it was there, but as evening approached, even his paranoid imagination seemed confident that no one was after us. Eventually, Did's and my legs refused to go on. My stomach seconded the motion. Big Baby eased my concern by pointing out that the mysterious wizard, if he even existed, would be easier to find in daylight anyway.

We moved off the road a bit to make camp in the forest. Thankfully the temperature cooled quite a bit in the evening, even more so in the forest. After a meal involving a cheese called Paruxian Blue that Did had snatched from his mother's cupboard and something that was a cross between a biscuit and a brick that Big Baby shared with us, Did and I were too exhausted for anything more than cleaning up and going straight to bed. Big Baby and Wolfette weren't tired yet and decided to take the first watch.

I was awoken by the scent of roasting meat. It wasn't bacon, but it still smelled heavenly. As I blinked my eyes open, I was surprised to find it still dark out. Big Baby was snoring heavily under a blanket a few feet away, so his watch must have been over, making it a few hours later. Didlius's empty bedroll suggested that he was the one cooking. My head protested the notion of moving mightily, but my stomach overruled it. I awkwardly stumbled out of my bedroll to see if Did had any more of that wonderful smelling meat.

As I neared the fire, I was happy to see two rabbit-sized shapes cooked to a golden brown, rotating over the fire. Didlius was three fourths of the way through eating another so he probably wouldn't have minded if I took one. As the spit turned again, it occurred to me that Didlius's hands were both currently occupied with his meal, not that he was close enough to turn the spit anyway. As Wolfette's loud snoring pierced the silence from somewhere to my right, I knew it had to be someone else.

Across from Did sat a person with a flowing white beard wearing a bright white robe and a big, floppy hat. Through the hat and his beard, I couldn't, at first, get a good look at his face, until he laughed at one of Didlius's jokes. I wasn't sure what a Flakoran was, but evidently they weren't very good seamen and were afraid of the dark.

As his hat slid back, I was surprised to find that his complexion was even paler than his beard. Though I was confident I didn't know the man, there was something about our friend that seemed familiar. The way his eyes widened when he finally noticed me suggested that he was thinking the same thing. He stood up to greet me, and I was even more surprised by his height. He had evidently been hunching as he sat. The way the fire light up his face brought to mind . . .

Didlius finally noticed me as well. "Hat, I'd like to introduce you to a real wizard. He said his name is Gand—"

"That is not his name." The smile vanished from my face as I connected the name, the beard, and the pointy hat with one of the great characters in all of literature. There's no way I was going to let some idiot in a Halloween costume ruin the story of the founding of The One, no matter how nice the costume was. *Ooooh, that looks like silk. No. No. Had to focus.*

"Harumpfh," our new friend said. "My name is too Gand—"

I stood up and stared hard at his chin. "No, it's not."

Mischief tinted his eyes, which I found annoying. "Agree to disagree. I am, however, a wizard."

I ground my teeth so hard I had to force myself to let out a breath, for fear of breaking a filling. "You are not."

"Hat, how do you know he's not a wizard?" Didlius asked.

"Because that name is associated with a wizard back home, and he's dressed exactly like him. Who are you really, and what do you want?"

The non-wizard smiled at me. "Am too, and I'll prove it by doing a magic trick."

"Is the trick to make trademarks go away?" I asked.

"No." He held both palms toward us and fluttered his fingers. "Behold. Nothing in my hands."

"Ooh," Didlius said.

"That's not the trick," he said. "Now look over there." He pointed behind us.

Didlius turned around. I did not.

"I said look over there."

"No." I gave him my meanest scowl.

"Look, do you want to see magic or not?"

I shrugged. "Not really . . . unless the trick is you coming up with an original name and switching to a career in dentistry."

Didlius grabbed my shoulder. "Come on, Hat. I want to see some real magic."

"And I want someone to look at my tooth," I said. Didlius pushed harder and began to whine (my one weakness). "Fine."

There was a *poof* sound, and I could smell smoke. *The bastard better not have lit my favorite shirt on fire.* I felt all over my back as we turned around. My shirt felt unsinged.

"Behold." The non-wizard slowly moved his right hand over the palm of his left hand. In his left, he held a pebble. "It's a ring. A ring of great—"

"It is not," I said. "It does not have any power, and if you call it your precious at any time, I'll hit you."

Didlius got close to the non-wizard's hand and stared hard. "It doesn't appear very ring-like."

The non-wizard put his hands on his waist and pouted, yet another reason why he most definitely wasn't a wizard. Everyone knows wizards don't pout. "And how do you know this ring doesn't contain great power? Great power can often be hidden in mundane objects. I'll have you know that a friend of mine was once a mild-mannered accountant, but in that mundane shell, she one day revealed herself to be the greatest—"

"Middle manager who ever graced an H&R Block?" I asked.

The non-wizard frowned at me. If he could have shot lightning from his eyes, I would have been very afraid. "No. She grew up to be a powerful wizard who ruled the land."

"Is this friend of yours you?" I asked. "And which D&D campaign setting was it?"

"No, her name is Fred, but that doesn't matter because you don't know her."

I rolled my eyes. "OK, so we've now established you're a woman. The beard kind of threw me, and I feel kind of bad that I automatically assumed something like that, but that still doesn't make up for this terrible ruse."

"I don't think that was a ring," Didlius said, "but it was still a neat trick."

"So, Fred, where are you from? New York? Minneapolis? St. Louis?"

Fred smiled at Didlius. "Thank you." She then turned to me

and scowled. "And my kind do not come from any of your mundane human cities, for we are a mysterious people whose origins are unknown."

"Can you do another trick?" Didlius asked.

"Indeed, I can, for we wizards are an unlimited source of magic and wonder." Fred waved her hands in elaborate motions. I wasn't sure if she was accusing me of pass interference or tripping.

"You're an unlimited source of something," I said. "Say, why did you make a puff of smoke when we already had our backs turned? Not to nitpick your already ridiculous attempt at fake magic, but it seems like a waste, Fred."

"Did you say puff of smoke?" Fred threw something in my face that temporarily blinded us and smelled like eggs.

When we regained the gift of sight, Didlius ran forward into the space previously occupied by Fred, his head darting around in wonder. "Amazing. I can't even see her."

"It's nighttime, Did. You can't see anything more than a few feet away."

"Not when I close my eyes. When I do that, I can't see anything close either."

"Are you closing your eyes?" I asked.

He giggled. "If you can't tell, then you must have closed yours."

"Why don't we both close our eyes and go to sleep?"

"Does that include the wizard whose name you never fully got?"

"Only if it helps her run into a wall." I unfurled Did's bedroll and pointed at it. "I'll take watch. After this, I doubt I'll be able to sleep much. I have a Frodo key chain in my pocket, and I don't want her stealing it."

Did nodded and climbed into his bedroll.

I tossed a few more logs on the fire and maintained as good of a watch as I could with the limited visibility. The only thing of note was me polishing off the slightly burnt rabbit-like meat that was left over the fire. Fred did not come back. Before I knew it, it was dawn, and Big Baby let me take a nap to make up for taking an additional watch.

They shook me awake an hour later, tossed a pack at me, and handed me a couple of rolls to eat as we walked. We continued on the road for a couple of hours before arriving at a tiny hamlet of only four buildings.

"I have never heard of there being a village here." Didlius grinned and clapped his hands. "This must be the home of that wizard we met."

Neither Wolfette nor Big Baby seemed surprised by his mention of the wizard, so Didlius must have filled them in during my nap.

I did a circuit of the nearest building. "No, if these were his, they'd be made of cardboard or plywood, and there'd only be two sides to them."

"Look, a cheese shop!" Didlius ran into the center of the buildings before I could react. I thought the sign looked more like a smiley face than a wheel of cheese, but it didn't matter because Didlius was already through the door. He quickly reappeared, grappling with a pale woman with thinning gray hair.

"Grab her," I said before quickly remembering who was next to me. "*Big Baby*, grab him. Wolfette, go scout for other attackers."

Big Baby pulled the middle-aged woman off Didlius while Wolfette disappeared around the corner.

"Did, what happened?" I asked.

Didlius hunched over huffing and puffing for about a minute before regaining his breath enough to let out a quick reply. "I don't know. I asked her about the Verican White, and before I knew it, she was over the counter and engaging me in fisticuffs. I managed to fend her off long enough to retreat for reinforcements."

"Put me down, or I'll turn you all into toadstools," the tall woman said while continuing to swing her bony fists. "I'm not entirely sure what a toadstool is either, so there's no telling what kind of awfulness you might end up with. I am the great and powerful Gand—"

Did's hand stopped shaking and his eyes narrowed into a fearsome glare. "You are not the great and powerful Gand, madam. We met her last night. She had a great bushy beard, a gorgeous flowing robe, and more power than even my marvelous magic spoon."

"Yes, I am. If you'll let me down, I'll put on the outfit and you'll see."

Big Baby gave me a dubious look. I responded with a shake of my head, and he continued holding the woman.

"Yeah, we're not going to do that," I said. "It was pretty obvious from your performance before that you don't know any magic and that you and I are from the same place. So, who are you really, and how did you get here?"

She struggled a little and then gave up with a sigh. "My name is Fred Dalingworth and I'm from New Jersey. I found myself in this strange land a little over a year ago but was waylaid by horsemen shortly after arriving."

My anger disappeared immediately, replaced only by sympathy. "I'm from Minnesota. Big B, could you let her down? I'd like to talk to her in private. We're from the same place."

Big Baby dutifully nodded and set Fred down gently. Fred directed me to the cheese shop, and we went inside. Did offered to come with me as a protection, but I declined. Even if Fred tried something, Did's idea of protection was likely the more dangerous threat. The look in Fred's eye after I mentioned Minnesota gave me the impression that any threat she posed was over. It was a good thing too, as the sound of Wolfette's axe hitting something metallic caused Big Baby to run to the other side of the building.

As soon as I closed the door behind me, I spit out the question that had been burning through my skull since I realized where I was. "Do you know how to get back home?"

Fred bit her lip. "The horse warriors took all of my stuff, except this costume I was wearing, and I'm pretty sure something I had on me was what allowed me to travel here. I've survived by using my amazing abilities at sleight of hand and beginner's magic to get donations from travelers. I've been trying in vain to get word of those thieves in the hopes of finding my stuff, but so far no luck."

"That's terrible, Fred. How do you know it was something you had on?"

"I could see this glow emanating from somewhere on my body before I passed out, and when I woke up, I was here. Do you know what exactly sent you here?"

"No, I don't know how I got to Vyenra either."

Her eyes brightened. "Vyenra? That's where I am? I love those books, though I hear the author is a little weird. Funny though that nothing I've seen so far seems anything like how it was described in the books."

"Harry is a little different, though you get used to him after a while. You're in an area he didn't cover in any of the books and about 2000 years in the past, right before the founding of The One. The man with the spoon outside is actually the one who founds that religion. I asked you to talk in private because I didn't want to reveal that to him."

"You've got to be kidding me. That religion is real? I thought the author just slapped that in there after people complained that there was no mention of Garandia's religion in the first book." Fred's eyes brightened. "On second thought, it does sound like the kind of thing that would be created by the guy outside . . . and the rest of his people aren't that much better."

"The Paruxians are incredibly naïve, though I've found them to be an intriguing lot. So, if you are trying to find the whereabouts of these horse warriors, why haven't you moved around? This is a fantasy world. All the best information is usually found in towns, especially taverns and inns."

She stared at the ground. "I tried to ply my trade in more crowded areas, but with so many people about, it is a lot harder to fool them. Someone always arrives after you've told everyone to turn around or is standing at an angle where they can still kind of see you pull the pebble from your pocket. I've been tarred and/or feathered six times now."

"And/or? Did someone really forget the tar?"

"There was a shortage on tar last month. Being feathered by itself is actually kind of pleasant, though they did not take kindly to me giggling so much . . . the curse of the ticklish."

The shout of several voices I didn't recognize came from outside. I immediately went for the door, but Fred stopped me.

"That's probably some villagers from the nearby village. They usually come by on the third day of the week for a blessing or some nonsense. I'd better put on my costume."

I helped her put the floppy hat on. "The horsemen let you keep this?"

"Yes, though they did take my replica *Lord of the Rings'* One ring. That was one weird day. I was taking a nap after a *Star Trek* convention, and the next thing I knew, I was in Vyenra." She saw my questioning look and answered it. "I like to show up dressed as Gandalf and mess with them."

I wasn't sure if I should love this lady or despise her. On the one hand, she owned what looked to be a very expensive Gandalf costume. Awesome. On the other hand, she liked to taunt fans of other franchises. As someone who had considerable difficulties with other fandoms at conventions, I couldn't like her either. I held the door for her, and we went outside.

Standing on the other side of Did were about ten locals of various ages chatting amiably. When they saw Fred, several of them began sharing looks of confusion. Big Baby held Wolfette a foot off the ground in one hand, a good distance away from the locals.

A short, middle-aged man in the middle of the group finally spoke. "We were looking for the wizard to show us his magics. I told all the boys about him back home, and they demanded I take them to him."

"And you have found the wizard." Fred tapped her staff on the ground three times.

"No," the spokesman said. "The wizard is a man, and he was much older. You must be his daughter, and while I'm sure you're decent, we want the original."

"I am too the wizard. Observe, nothing in my hands. Now, look over there!" She pointed behind them with his staff.

No one turned around.

The spokesman moved toward Fred angrily. "The audacity of the young. Trying to pass yourself off as your elder and then doing his signature bit."

Fred gave me a panicked look of confusion. Evidently taking advantage of the obtuse can backfire when they're too obtuse to believe that you're you. I looked around for something to help her with, but the only thing I saw was her fake beard lying in the doorway behind her. The fake beard!

Didlius dove out of the way of the charging crowd. I dove toward the fake beard. The crowd dove on top of Fred.

As I stood up, I realized that there was no way I was going to be able to get the beard to Fred inside of the pile of humanity. So, I did the only thing I could think of and put it on.

"My name is . . . look, I'm the wizard you came here to see, and I order you to halt your attack on my protégé." I didn't know I had "forceful" in my repertoire, but evidently I did, because the locals piled off Fred and stood in a nice neat line.

The spokesman spoke, "Sorry, Mister Gand—"

"Silence," I said, "and also my name is not . . . the name that you were about to say because it's trademarked in the land that we come from. Now, please move out of the way, so that I can check on my apprentice."

They were so cowed that they moved out of the way without saying a word. Fred's beautiful robes were fortunately unharmed, though they could have used a good dry cleaning. I thought Fred herself to be in about the same shape until I noticed the arrow sticking out of her left arm. Big Baby pulled a bandage out of his pack and staunched the bleeding with it.

"All right," I said, "who brought an arrow to a pile on? Come on, guys, safety first. Now I want everyone to hand over any scissors they might have, and I really don't want to know if you've been running with them. What's in the past is in the past, and we need to think about your safety in the future."

They handed me four incredibly rusty pairs of scissors and a gardening shear. I don't know what kind of pockets that guy had to have kept those hidden, but I made a note to get a pair after this was done. I almost handed the scissors to Did to dispose of later but changed my mind and kept them myself. Didlius with four pairs of scissors and gardening shears was just asking for at least one death, and I wasn't sure if he had the ability to rise from the dead.

"Great. Now who had the arrow? No judgements or blame." I gave them the perfect stare to match my voice. No one fessed up immediately, so I turned it down a notch. After a few minutes, still no one had replied.

One of the locals suddenly sprouted an arrow through his shoulder. To the man's credit, he didn't even yell. Once I looked past them, I finally saw the archer in the distance. He wore all black and had an arrow pointed at me or maybe at Fred.

"Why are you guys just standing there if he's been shooting arrows at you?" I asked.

"Because everyone knows that wizard beats archer, and you told us to stand here."

"Wizard beats archer, archer beats stag, and stag beats wizard in the game of Hacus," Didlius said from behind me.

An arrow landed an inch from Fred's other arm.

"Stop standing there and go get him," I said.

The spokesman nodded and the locals, along with Big Baby and Wolfette, charged after the archer. The archer released another arrow, catching one of the group in the side, but the plucky little guy kept charging. I was really proud of them. The archer disappeared over the horizon. I dropped the sharp objects and turned to Did.

"When they get back, I think those guys could be your first followers. Congratulations."

Did scrunched his eyebrows. "Followers? You mean like squires? In the books, a knight only has one of those. What would I do with the other nine? Also, I believe my friend Hat is filling that role. Did you see where he ran off to, Mr. Gand? Besides, they are your followers and not mine."

I took the beard off and put it on him. "Now they'll follow you."

"My goodness. It's you, Hat! Why, I was just standing here talking to that wizard and then you appear."

An arrow landed next to my feet. The archer had reappeared in the distance. I couldn't see any of the locals or Big Baby, but Wolfette was closing on him.

"Perhaps we should carry on this conversation elsewhere." I grabbed Fred and dragged her toward the tree line near the road.

"But what of my new followers?" Didlius yelped as an arrow jutted out of his pack. He hurried his pace.

"If they're any good at following, they'll find us." I dropped to my feet in exhaustion as we finally reached the trees.

Fred wasn't very well off. Did, fortunately, had a few bandages in his pack, and we managed to at least slow the bleeding. I almost panicked when she closed her eyes, but a quick check of her pulse confirmed that she was still alive. A few minutes later, Big Baby and Wolfette found us. As usual, Wolfette was a foot off the ground in his right hand. He yelled to the locals who soon joined us.

"Wolfette got that archer," Big Baby said.

"It turned out he had a fatal allergy to axesy axes, but this big dummy wouldn't let me see if it was a common allergy in these parts." She windmilled her axes toward the locals as Big Baby pulled her farther off the ground.

The locals gave Wolfette a wide berth while sliding closer to us. Fred was still unconscious, but it turned out not to matter as the locals were staring at Didlius anyway. It took me a minute to realize that I had slapped the beard on him, and that the locals hadn't believed that Fred was the wizard since she wasn't wearing the beard.

Their spokesman bowed before Didlius. "O great bearded wizard, we had come to see proof of your power but have instead found relief from that terrible bandit who has been plaguing us for years, always demanding food, money, and a discount on financial services from my brother-in-law. We stopped our offerings to him last month, and he's been shooting arrows at us ever since. But now we need not worry about him any longer thanks to your foul-mouthed and murderous companion."

"You're welcomy welcome," Wolfette said. "As thanks, I'd like you to answer a few questions to my axes."

The spokesman ignored her. "What may we do as thanks for your help, O Wizard?"

"Did, you're on," I whispered.

Did whispered back, "But I'm not a wizard."

"You're the closest thing with that magic spoon of yours."

Did stepped forward hesitantly and held his spoon up high. The locals seemed a bit confused at first, but then he brought the spoon down on a nearby tree stump. After the smoke settled, and the shock wore off, the locals got down on their knees. Until this point, I had serious doubts that Didlius could possibly be the legendary founder of The One, but after this improvised performance, I could finally picture him as something more than an average man. (I would have said below average but remember the locals in front of us would only believe someone was a wizard if he was wearing a fake beard.)

"As the source of your worship," Did said, "I demand that you look after my friend here." He closed his eyes and pointed at Fred dramatically.

The locals hurriedly scrambled up and gingerly lifted her from the ground.

"My wife has become really good at handling arrow wounds lately," the spokesman said. "We're going to take her back to my place, if that's all right with you."

Did still had his eyes closed to heighten the drama and hadn't responded, so I answered for him. "That's his way of saying yes."

The lead local nodded and then carried her off.

Did finally opened his eyes after the locals were long gone. "And my second demand is that you bring us some samples of your best cheeses . . . My goodness, that's very proactive of them to have left to go get the cheese before I even uttered the words. Do they have magic powers too?"

Big Baby set Wolfette down. "We might as well get going,"

he said. "There's nothing more we can do for that lady, and it's pretty clear there aren't any real wizards here."

"Agreed," I said. "You should go back to the town for your packs, and we'll get moving."

In a few minutes, we found their packs and were back on the road. Didlius kept stopping and looking back to the town.

"What's wrong, Did?" I asked.

"We should probably stop so they can find us. If we get too far from town, they won't be able to bring me their cheese." He went to scratch his chin and was surprised to find the fake beard still there. "My goodness. Perhaps I do have magic powers. Why, just this morning I was clean-shaven, but now I have this thick, luxurious beard."

Even Wolfette was surprised by his stupidity. I pretended to pat his back, but instead, undid the strap on his beard.

"And now it has leapt from my body! We should leave this strange place immediately before more of our hair falls off. The cheese is not that important." He sprinted away and we reluctantly followed.

POETIC JUSTICE . . . SAY, DOES
ANYONE HAVE ANY MORE POETS I
COULD BORROW? I BROKE ALL
OF MINE

Fortunately, with Did's thin, nearly muscle-less frame, he was only able to run for about three minutes without a long rest. After each rest, he ran for a few minutes and stopped for double that time. The three of us had little trouble keeping up with him by walking normally and not stopping.

After an hour, he must have felt we were out of the range of the hair-loss magic and stopped trying to run. Satisfied that he was satisfied, I took out my book and recorded our adventure with Fred. It took me a few hours, as I was still adjusting to writing on the move, but I was confident that I got everything down. Did's spirits seemed to be at an all-time high and his happy chattering kept our other two companions occupied while I recorded our historically important journey.

Nothing of note happened the rest of the day, at camp that night, or the following morning, besides Wolfette's lengthy battle with a swarm of gnats, and Big Baby's failure to convince a passing wagon to sell us some eggs. Since we were all unscathed and reasonably healthy, I wasn't going to complain even though I was developing a slight sunburn.

We soon sighted a town in the distance. The town was the

largest one I had seen yet, though to be fair, the largest one I had seen had been Didlius's hometown, which only had a population of around twenty-five. I couldn't see the entirety of the town we were approaching, but I estimated it to have somewhere between thirty and forty buildings.

As we came to the edge of town, a woman in her thirties waved enthusiastically as best she could while keeping her basket stable. I smiled and waved back.

Behind the woman, a masked man appeared from around the corner and laughed heartily as he grabbed her basket and ran off toward the center of the town. Didlius ran after him and I followed. Oddly, Wolfette didn't join in the chase. I assumed Big Baby hadn't either so he could keep an eye on her. The thief was a hundred yards away, nearing what looked to be an inn.

Did stopped and awkwardly jogged backward to stand in front of the woman. "Do not worry, madam, I shall have this vile criminal safely subdued in no time."

The woman bit her nails and stood on her tiptoes while watching the thief near the edge of town. "OK, but please hurry."

Didlius winked and bent over in front of her. He pressed his spoon hard into the ground for a few seconds and then flicked with his wrist. Before I could get a good look at what happened next, Spoon-Scalibur's bright light blinded me. There was a horrible scream, followed by a crash, and then a second, deeper scream. When my vision returned, the unconscious thief lay covered in food that I assumed came from the basket, and on top of the thief lay the equally unconscious owner of that food.

"What happened?" I asked.

Did lowered his spoon from the air, probably disappointing the nearby artist who appeared to be sketching him. "You said I shouldn't fling my spoon as I might hit the wrong thing. I decided against flinging you, in case any new questions arose as to what else isn't OK to hit, so I flung the woman instead. I must admit, my solution has a certain poetic justice to it—to be stopped by the body of the very person you wronged."

Wolfette slapped her axes together in glee. "That was the awesomesty awesome I ever awesomely saw. Only thing missing was an awesome death."

Big Baby put his hand on her shoulder just in case.

I stared at the ground where the woman had been standing, and while the hole was larger than the spoon should have been able to make, it still didn't look like the ground he had removed would be large enough to hold a person. "Does Spoon-Scalibur have any other properties that you didn't tell me about?"

Did stared at the ground, then looked back at me. "Ah, I see your conundrum. The ground didn't carry her; it was the wind that my mighty flick generated that carried her. And no, I do not believe Spoon-Scalibur has any extra abilities besides breaking anything it hits and the lightning."

The trees above us were now bereft of leaves on one side, confirming his statement. The woman had still not stirred, so I grabbed Did by the shoulder and turned him back to the way we came. Unfortunately, that way was now blocked by three hairy, large men with axes.

"Greetings," Didlius said. "Are you here to congratulate me on my heroic deed?"

The one with the long hair glanced back at his companions and nodded. "Come with us."

"Hahaha," Wolfette said. "No." She leaned forward, but she only got half a step before Big Baby had her in his grip.

"Not yet," Big Baby said before pointing her in the direction to follow them.

I shrugged and followed the group to the pile of people Didlius had created.

An older man in a blue robe knelt beside the woman and gingerly removed his fingers from the side of her neck. He meticulously wiped his hand onto a cloth from his pocket and nodded toward us. The thief began to stir until one of the onlookers kicked him in the side of the head. The woman had still not moved.

"Did anyone see who performed this legendary deed?" Didlius asked.

The old man stared at him without blinking. "We saw you do it, all right."

"Is she alive?" I half-whispered. "Also, unrelated question, but what is the penalty for standing close to someone you've never met who happens to commit murder here?"

The older man still hadn't blinked. "Looks to only be a concussion, and we know you four are together. I could hear everything you said." More townspeople had gathered around us, likely the whole town judging by the number of buildings I could see. There was no room to pass them in either direction of the narrow street.

"Did, ready your spoon." I didn't even bother to attempt a whisper as close as the old man was.

"Excellent idea, Hat. They will probably want a good look at it for the drawings they will need to build an accurate statue." He held the spoon aloft.

The mayor finally blinked, though I almost missed it in the fast motion of him kneeling all the way down. The entire crowd was now on its knees as well. Most of them stared at the spoon in pure euphoria, though a few lowered their heads in prayer instead.

"All hail the word of Ludius the Particular. The time has come!" the old man said.

Everyone in the crowd crossed both of their arms and rapped their chests twice. "In Ludius's name, we obey."

"Now can I kill them, brothery brother?" Wolfette asked. "They just called us lewd."

"They said 'Ludius,' not lewd."

"Close enough?" she asked.

Big Baby gripped her tighter in response.

"I hate to correct people who are worshiping me," Didlius said, "but if I wish to be worthy of Jaenia's love, I must be honest. My name is not Ludius; it is Didlius."

The crowd moaned as he lowered his spoon and put it away.

"Did, I think Ludius is their name for your spoon," I whispered.

I must have whispered too loudly because the old man stood up and shook his head. "Ludius the Particular is the name of our lord and spiritual master. One of his last great acts was his prophecy titled, 'How the Great Spoon of Destiny Will Save You, and Ten Helpful Gardening Tips.' Those gardening tips have allowed our village to win ninety-nine out of the last one hundred Best Garden awards in this county. If Horius hadn't cheated on the judge, we would have won that last one, too." One of our brutish escorts blushed.

Didlius pulled my book out of my bag, opened, it, and pointed to a blank page. "Write this down, Hat. I hope to take up gardening after I rescue the beautiful Jaenia. So, what are these gardening tips, elder?"

"Maybe later, Did," I said. "So, what does this prophecy say?"

"Your apprentice is quite the man of action, isn't he? A trait I can well appreciate," the old man said. "According to the prophecy, 'a man who is of the same people as the chosen followers of Ludius will arrive with Spoon-Scalibur and save us from the vile Chisites.'"

Did and I looked around but couldn't see anyone else in the village. "Are these Chisites on a lunch break?" I asked.

"We haven't met them yet," the elder said, "and our scholars haven't been able to determine if they are even people. For all we know, it could be a nasty pudding that we left out too long. I mean, they are defeated by a spoon, after all."

Did pressed his spoon to his temple and closed his eyes.

The elder scrunched up his face in confusion. "Is Ludius's chosen one taking a nap?"

Did's eyes popped open at the same time as his mouth. "Jaenia has informed me of the location of these Chisites. Follow me!" Did ran off into the forest.

The elder gave me a stunned, questioning look. I shrugged and then ran after Did. The sound of footsteps behind me indicated that the townsfolk had followed. Did only ran for a few minutes before stopping in front of a pond that contained two beautiful women who were in the middle of bathing. The women immediately blushed and stuck their bodies back underwater.

"Behold, the Chisites!" Did said.

The elder ran past us and stopped inches away from running into the pond. "Where? Are they behind the young ladies?"

Did looked at me and rolled his eyes. "No . . . they *are* the women."

Wolfette must have escaped from Big Baby's grasp but stopped as soon as she got to the edge of the water. "Dratty drat! I hate getting all rusty. Could you two ladies climb out of the pond, so I can un-Chisite you?"

The women moved as far away from her in the water as they could.

A villager raised his hand, and Did acknowledged him. "The taller one is my daughter, Jula, and our family name is not Chisite; it's Voretus."

"And my daughter Landia's last name is Candus," a bald woman said.

Didlius scratched his chin until his eyes lit up. He then winked at me and waded into the pond toward the two women. For some reason, the two naked women didn't like the idea of a strange man who had accused them of being the mortal enemies of their people heading toward them, and they both backed away.

"Do not worry, ladies," Didlius said. "If you are not Chisites, you have nothing to fear. And Jaenia has informed me of exactly how to determine that; all you have to do is answer some local trivia. You see, Hat, Chisites are not from around here and wouldn't know of local knowledge and customs."

I almost asked why he even needed to ask that, being their parents had just informed him that these two women were locals, but was afraid to remind him I was there, since by his definition I qualified as a Chisite.

"I will start off with a simple one," Did said. "What is the name of our current sovereign?"

The women stared at each other, scrunched up their faces in confusion, and then turned back. The one on the left opened her mouth, but nothing comprehensible came out.

"Aha! I knew it. They are clearly Chisites." He turned toward the elder. "Arrest them, then execute them, and you'll all be safe. Your prophecy is fulfilled, and you can all sleep safely knowing that this threat is forever gone."

Wolfette squealed with glee, but Big Baby had a hold of her. "Not yet," he said.

"How do we know that these are the only Chisites?" one of our escorts from before said.

"They can't even answer you," the bald woman said. "They're both mute."

"Actually, I don't know who our sovereign is either," the elder said. "This town hasn't seen a single government official or soldier in my seventy years of life."

"Hmm . . . I don't know either!" Did said. "I must be a Chisite as well!" He was about to stab himself with his spoon, but I waded into the pond and grabbed his arm.

"Didlius, has Jaenia told you of some other way to tell if they're Chisites?" I asked.

Did nodded sagely. "How about 'What is your favorite color?'"

"No; everyone will have a different one—and pick something they can answer with their fingers. Remember, they can't speak."

"Ahh. Plus, I don't have a favorite color, though it could be a trick question?" My scowl was all the answer he needed. "Fine. Oh, this will be perfect. 'What—"

Before he could finish his sentence, the sound of an explosion rocked our ears.

I DIDN'T BLOW IT UP, OFFICER. IT WAS THE SPOON

After everyone picked themselves off the ground and wiped the copious amounts of dirt and debris off, we discovered that the blast had come from the direction of the village. No one seemed hurt except for a few scrapes, some temporary hearing loss, and Did's feelings when no one wanted to hear what his next question was.

When we returned to the village, or should I say the place the village used to be, we found a big hole. There was nothing but dirt, the hole, and a black domino mask. Surprisingly, there was little in the way of smoke, though I supposed that was due to the lack of anything left that could burn.

I grabbed the mask to inspect it. There didn't appear to be anything special about it. I dug my nails into it to see if it was unusually durable, but they went through it just like a normal cloth mask. It had to have been left after the blast went off.

"So, I guess we know who did this," I said.

"We do?" Did asked.

I gave Did a disgusted look, which was probably unfair. I mean, if I kept giving that look every time he missed something obvious, my face would likely be stuck that way for the entire journey. I decided to raise the bar for giving that look from then on. "The guy who stole the basket earlier had a mask exactly like this. He must have blown up the town while we were out looking for these Chisites."

A man with food all over his clothes and dark hair plastered to his head pushed through the crowd. "That's my mask. It must have fallen off when your friend tossed that woman on me. My name is Stedius, and I'm the one who stole the basket earlier, but I didn't do this. I've been with the group the whole time. I want to rid our village of these Chisites as much as everyone else."

"It's true," the elder said. "He's our town's resident thief, and he's been with us the whole time."

"Wait," I said. "You *know* he's a thief, and you let him live here?"

"Oh, yes. Every respectable town must have at least one thief. No one will take a town seriously unless they have at least one. When the previous one died, we had to send flyers out to other towns to find a replacement, and fortunately Stedius took us up on the offer."

"My old town offered me a twenty-pelo-a-month raise to stay, but Adronima just threw the money at me, and I moved here."

"So, if Stedius didn't do this, then who did?" Did asked.

The crowd was silent for several minutes as everyone thought through the problem. Eventually the silence broke when a woman squeaked in the back. Stedius had attempted to pick her pocket, but evidently being paid to be the town's thief did not require him to actually be good at his job. The people nearby apprehended him and made him give the coins back.

I moved toward the center of the crater in the hopes that something else was left as a clue. The dirt and small rocks were not very forthcoming with information. "I don't suppose anyone can tell me where in the town the center of this crater would have been? Maybe if we can pinpoint where it started, we can get a clue into what caused it."

The elder and a few of the other townspeople walked over to the center and talked amongst themselves. After a few minutes of intense gesturing, the elder spoke. "This appears to be on the edge of town toward the north."

"Why, that's where Hat and I entered this town," Did said. "And I'll bet it's pretty close to where I heroically and brilliantly flung the woman at that vile thief, too."

Normally I would have stuck my hands over Did's mouth when he said something stupid like that, but unusually, he had figured something out before me. Judging by the looks on the faces of the elder and the townsfolk, no one else had come to that conclusion either, so I didn't feel too bad.

"Apparently, this prophecy was not about you after all," the elder said. "Even as vague as most prophecies get, there is no way that Ludius would have sent a protector who gives a woman a concussion, hurts our prized thief's back, and destroys the entire town."

"Now is probably not a good time to mention that I inadvertently walked through a flower garden on my way in, is it?" Did handed the elder a crushed daisy.

The elder half-heartedly took the flower. "I won first place at the last fair for these."

One of the townspeople spoke on behalf of the elder, who was too busy weeping to say anything. "There was a big flash from the sky when he flung that dirt earlier. I'll bet more of that stuff must have come on a delayed reaction when we were all out of town."

Did stared down at Spoon-Scalibur. "I've used this thing many a time, and there has never been a delayed reaction before. It only makes lightning at the point of contact and never again unless I strike something twice."

There was a scream off in the distance. I couldn't see the source through the thick crowd, but after a panicked man shoved his way through the crowd, I assumed it came from either him or the second man who scrambled in after him. Wolfette and a flustered Big Baby soon followed.

"What is the meaning of this interruption?" the elder asked.

"She tried to kill us," the first panicked man said.

"Did not," Wolfette said. "I only tried to prescribe you one of my axey axes. I can't help it if one of the side effects is death."

The second panicked man tried to move as far away from Wolfette as he could into the tightly packed area around the center of the crowd. In doing so, he bumped into Didlius's unwilling test pilot from before. The woman's eyes lit up as she caught the man's face.

Big Baby lifted Wolfette from the ground. "No more axe prescriptions for you, Dr. Wolfette. Sorry about that, everyone. These two pulled their empty cart into town, and she got it in her head that all outsiders were killed on sight in case they were secretly Chisites."

"The only way to prove they aren't Chisites is to see how they respond to an axe in the face," Wolfette said. "Now let me test them, you big doofy doofus, before they get away."

"While there's a certain flaw to this Dr. Wolfette's method," the elder said, "she does have a point. Who are you two men?"

"We are travelling merchants who sell rare and exotic substances," the first one said. "Our aunt lives here, and we sometimes store our products in her house temporarily when the market is down and then come back for it when it picks up."

"Yeah," the second one said. "We came for our containers. The stuff we're selling will sell for a lot in Arvingain now on account of them having their Flame Festival."

"Let me guess," I said. "These containers held a strange liquid called 'Chisite.'"

Did nodded in approval.

"No," the first man said. "Nitro-something. What was the last part called, Ites?"

"I can't remember, Chis. It began with a 'G' though."

"Nitro . . . glycerin?" I asked.

"That's it," Ites said.

"That's the gassy stuff that gives me the giggly giggles," Wolfette said. "If anything deserves my axe prescription, it's that. Where is it?"

"Nitroglycerin is a liquid and highly explosive," I said. "Wise elder, that's the stuff that blew your town up."

I decided not to mention Didlius's part in setting it off, since no one had been killed by the blast. Besides, if they tried to arrest him, there would likely be several deaths and serious injuries from an overdose of axes to the head or by cases of exploding body parts via spoon. Didlius's historical task ahead far outweighed him destroying a few buildings.

"It seems you are correct," the elder said. "But I am extremely disappointed that our prophecy didn't come true. I mean, to have found the bearer of the legendary spoon and have him perform such a dramatic feat, yet still not fulfill the prophecy. It is incredibly disappointing to say the least." He sighed. "Well, I guess I'll go back to teaching the new generation Ludius's prophecy in the hopes that they might get to witness it."

"Seriously?" I asked. "Nobody else caught it?"

The crowd shifted nervously, looked back and forth in confusion, or did a number of other things that made it obvious that they hadn't caught it.

"Ohhh." One of the burly men raised his hand. "He's saying we should buy some of that nitroglyceride stuff from them and rebuild our town with that . . . but wait, it all blowed up."

"No. No," an older woman said. "He's saying we should

invite them to build a store here and sell their wares. With the tax money, we could rebuild our town."

"Can I sell axe massages at this store?" Wolfette asked as Big Baby lifted her higher.

"By the Old Gods, you are all dumb," the elder said. "These two men are the Chisites from the prophecy. 'Chis' plus 'Ites' equals 'Chisites.' But that still doesn't match the part about the bearer of Spoon-Scalibur saving us."

"Oh, I know," Didlius said. "I saved you all from having to see those young, naked women."

Most of the men and a few of the women grumbled at that.

"Nice try, Did," I said. "You were close though. He saved everyone by getting them out of town when the explosion occurred."

The elder looked off into the distance, appearing to be deep in thought. "I suppose that is correct. If he hadn't distracted us for so long with his seemingly moronic questions, we would have all been here and been blown to pieces."

"And that was exactly my plan," Did said. "As thanks, I'd like to request a victory feast."

I grabbed his arm and pulled him away through the crowd. "No. A simple thank-you is all this brave and noble hero needs. Also, that you remember his name which is 'Didlius.' Please remember that name because it's important." Big Baby dragged Wolfette after us.

"Couldn't we at least stay for a small feast?" Did asked as he waved to the crowd.

"No. You're too humble for that."

"Thank you for all you've done, Didlius the Humble," the elder said. "I guess we wouldn't all be alive without you."

The crowd waved and gave a few reluctant thank-yous as well.

When we were a good distance out of town, Big Baby set

Wolfette down and spoke to me away from the others. "So, why did we hurry out of there like that? I trust your judgement, but I'm curious."

I continued to write of our adventure in the town without looking up. "There's a better-than-average chance that Did set off the nitroglycerin when his spoon went off."

"Ahh. I'm glad you're in charge."

I looked up from my book. "I'm not in charge; Didlius is. I'm only here to write everything down."

Big Baby gave me a hard look and then pointed at Did in front of us. Didlius had just finished smashing a large, dried-out tree branch with his spoon. What was left of the now flaming branch brushed up against the sleeve of Did's tunic, which also caught on fire. He tried to put it out with his spoon, causing another lightning strike. Fortunately, that knocked him off his feet, and when he rolled over to stand back up, he inadvertently put out his flaming sleeve.

"Fine, you can be in charge, Big Baby."

"Sorry, but my full attention has to be on Wolfette. The last time I decided to take a few minutes' break from that, she destroyed a circus." He winced. "Sword swallowing does not extend to axes, by the way."

"Then we'll make it Did's in charge until he does something stupid, then I'll jump in and fix it. Until that point, he has to be the one in charge. There's a good reason for that, and you're going to have to trust me."

He stared at me apprehensively but eventually consented.

HE LEVEED A SWIFT JUSTICE

The following day, we arrived at the next town just past noon. This town was the biggest one yet, so I was incredibly hopeful that it would attract a wizard. Beyond the size of the town, it didn't look much different from any of the other ones we had passed besides that it had more than one inn, tavern, and beard trimming shop. The Paruxians were very into beard care, evidently. The sign outside of town indicated that we had arrived in Arvingain in the land of Flasturia.

"I haven't heard of Flasturia," I said. "What are the people like here? Do they speak Paruxian?"

"No idea," Wolfette said. "We should stoppy stop and interrogate one of them." Big Baby had ahold of her before she took another step.

Did smiled at an elderly lady we passed. "Flasturia was what this part of Paruxia was called before its conquest hundreds of years ago. The people of Arvingain were staunchly loyal to Flasturia and never got over their conquest. They speak Paruxian, just like you and I."

"Why is Paruxian so similar to my language, English?"

"I am not sure. Legend has it that we were taught the art of language from a strange man in odd clothing thousands of years ago. Perhaps he was from your world as well."

I scribbled that down in the book. "So where to now?"

"My beard could use a trim," Big Baby said.

"I told you I could do that for you for free, big morony moron," Wolfette said.

"And I told you you're only allowed to trim my beard, not the rest of my face."

Wolfette pouted. "My way is more efficient. If I trim your facey face, you won't need beard trims anymore."

I pointed to a sign across the street that I couldn't make out. "What's that?"

Didlius stared up at the sign above us. "That's the sign for beard trimming. It is a shame that they're almost all the same now, but nothing makes you want to get your beard in tip top shape like a picture of the famous Judas and his glorious beard."

"A god amongst beards," Big Baby said in near awe.

"I bet he'd let me give him a trim." Wolfette created sparks rubbing her axes together.

"No," I said. "I mean the one over there. The purple one."

Didlius and Big Baby looked at it for a while but weren't sure, so we all went across the street and then inside. No one was there to greet us, but by the look of the place, it was either an apothecary, a pharmacy, a magic shop, or the world's most disgusting grocery store. In case it was the latter, I made a note to ask for a list of ingredients for every dish I was served until I got home. Newt liver casserole in a virgin blood sauce with a garnish of bat testicles and hag armpit hair was not part of my diet.

As the shop was full of tall shelves that seemed to have been purposely arranged to form a maze, we decided to split in two groups. I stayed with Didlius. After our seventh dead end, I decided to cheat by pulling out some larger items on the shelves and peeking through the space they had occupied. It didn't help us find the way, but I did locate another person. The person in question was wearing a red robe and cowl, and as he seemed to know his way around the place, I asked him to come to us. In spite of only being a row over, it took him almost five minutes to get to us.

"A priest!" Didlius hissed as I told him about our robed savior.

"What is your deal with priests, Did?" I asked. "Is this about those two you were fighting with when we first met?"

Didlius shook his head. "In my grandparents' day, the priests were focused on saving our souls for the afterlife and guiding us to become good individuals, but sometime around when Mother was born, they convinced the king to levy additional taxes so that they could upgrade the three major temples. From what the older people tell me, the temples really needed it—half of each was rented out to poetry clubs, a bring-your-own-pew program, more spiders than worshipers, etc. However, when those upgrades were complete, the taxes didn't stop. As a matter of fact, every few years they managed to get new taxes added for things like holier book covers, gold plating on relics, and better-looking acolytes. On top of that, they introduced entry fees to the temples and mandatory donations. Now, the clergy is richer than the nobility. Why, they even have their own personal army."

I started to write furiously. "So, you hate them because they've completely forgotten what their mission is."

"There are still quite a few of them who are dedicated to their message. It's mostly their leadership. No, I hate them because my father ran off to join them when I was three."

The priest finally found us, his hooded head bobbing as he approached. Did had his spoon out, but I managed to at least get him to hold it in his pocket.

"Greetings, friend," I said. "We saw the sign outside and were wondering what kind of establishment this is. Do you know any magic? We need to locate some people, and I am in need of tele-portation to another plane." I hadn't heard of Atlian priests before, but that didn't mean they didn't exist. There was also the possibility that the priest was only a fellow shopper, or if he did own the place, that one of his co-owners or employees was a wizard. Perhaps he had a potion that could help us.

The priest snickered. Unfortunately, I still couldn't make out his face. "The ladies have told me a certain part of me is magic, and that it has taken them to another plane, but I'm guessing that's not what you're looking for. Oh, wait. I do know one spell. Here. Pull my finger." He held his index finger out.

I yanked Did back before he could fulfill the request.

The priest shook his head and then pulled his hood back, revealing his pale, grinning face. The way his goatee bounced up and down as he laughed made it seem like it was taunting me.

"Billiam!" I said. "Are you the owner of this shop? Also, are you going to kill me? Feel free to answer those questions out of order, though no pressure. Unrelated, but have I told you how great you look? Really love the new haircut."

Billiam ran his fingers through his hair. "Oh, really, because I haven't had it cut in . . . Oh, come now, Hatso, that false flattery may work well on Harry, but I'm much too smart for something so blatant to work on me."

While it was true that he was smarter than Harry, he was not nearly as intelligent as he believed himself to be. Although the book he wrote satirizing Harry's world was well written, he mostly just made the characters dumber and gave everyone bad gas. He had always been nice to me though, and I am a sucker for a good fart joke.

"Oh, don't look at me that way, Hatio." Billiam tried to sidle up next to me, but one look from Did told him not to move another step. "So, you say you need to locate some people? Perhaps I can help you with that. I've developed quite a few contacts on Vyenra. And that plane you want to visit, is it Earth? If so, I can help you with that too."

Normally I would have found his plastered-on smile unsettling, but he had just mentioned getting back to Earth. Every fiber of my being was tingling. Even the air smelled sweeter, though that may have been because I had moved away from the aged mongoose feet.

"That's fantastic," Didlius said, the spoon abandoned in his pocket. "Where can we find my beloved Jaenia?"

"Not so fast," I said. "I know you, Billiam. What's the catch?"

Billiam did a passable impersonation of shocked. "Catch? Do you really think so little of me? With all we have in common, why would you assume I wouldn't help you out of the kindness of my heart?"

My face showed him what my crap-o-meter was currently reading.

"Oh, fine. I'm sure you've figured out by having experienced this place and by my being here that my supposed parody of your employer's first book wasn't a parody at all. I visited Vyenra, witnessed those events as they happened, and then wrote it all down. Evidently, Harry was here too and managed to get his more realistic—by Earth standards anyway—but inaccurate version out before me. Fortunately, the actual reality of this place is incredibly silly, so I was able to claim it was a parody. By the way, if you bring this up in court, I'll deny everything."

Did seemed to be trying and failing to understand what Billiam had said. He finally gave up and went back to scowling at him.

"So, seeing as you're here, I'd like to prevent that sort of situation from happening again. While I could go the parody route one more time, the legal fees from the lawsuit ate up most of my royalties. What I want from you is a promise that you won't release a book detailing what you've seen while you're here. If you give me that, I'll show you the way home and see if my contacts know the location of those people you need to find. Don't worry though, I'll change the names of everyone and every place, so it's not set in Harry's world. Since Paruxia hasn't been covered at all in the books, no one will even know."

"Why do you even need to write about this world?" I asked. "Your other books are quite successful. I really like the middle grade one about those talking dog people, the WeeHee."

"Also, off the record, but I didn't really write those. I've been trading stories with some mutual visitors of this world, editing them, and then selling them on Earth. The 'parody' one and the one I'm going to write about this adventure are special to me because I lived them."

As much as I didn't like Billiam, I could certainly sympathize with him. If I lived an exciting adventure in a fantasy world, I would want to write it down for the whole world to see . . . Of course, accepting his offer would mean he'd be preventing me from doing just that.

The real question was "What did Harry want?" not "What did I want?" When Harry was awake, he wanted me around constantly to take care of him and prevent him from doing anything too stupid. Surely, now that he was in a coma, he'd want me there to continue to keep looking after him.

Before I could figure out my answer, a shiny head bobbed into view. Gu smiled at me as he approached.

"Well, what's the answer?" Billiam asked while looking at Gu.

"The owner's out to lunch," Gu said. "So, we're going to have to wait until he gets back."

"Out to lunch?" Billiam asked. "This is a lunch counter and grocery store. Why can't he just cook something in the back?"

"Dunno. That's what his assistant said. Might as well do some shopping while we wait. Do you think they have fresh albatross tears? My pasta tastes too sweet if I don't put in a pinch of that." He began scanning the shelves.

Billiam threw up his arms in disgust. "Gah. This is why I do my shopping online back home. See if they have fresh cave moss. I want to try my hand at an authentic Paruxian salad."

I still hadn't decided what my answer was going to be when Billiam remembered I was there.

"Would getting a location for your friend's missing love help you decide?" Billiam asked. "No matter. I'm a good guy, so I'll throw that answer in for free as a sign of good faith. How does that sound?"

Didlius was about to burst, but to his credit, he held his tongue. I was starting to see more and more how he could be the founder of The One now. To curb his quivering lips, Didlius pulled his spoon out and held it over them.

"That would certainly help," I said. "How long would it take?"

Billiam looked over at Gu. "Do you know where this 'Jaenia' is?"

Gu set the container of slug paste back on the shelf and stood in front of Did. After a good thirty seconds of hard staring, he said, "You have to prove yourself worthy of both her and your-self. Only then will the path become clear."

"My word!" Didlius said. "No wonder your companion is a priest. You must be an Old God or an oracle to be able to dispense with such wise, prophetic sayings."

Gu stuck his finger on the spoon. "Nope. That saying is engraved on the handle."

Billiam laughed. "And I'm not a priest. This is a disguise."

While I did feel fairly stupid for not noticing the engraving, in my defense, Didlius had refused every request to let anyone look at or hold his spoon. I wasn't sure if that was for fear that someone else would take the powerful artifact from him or if it was a fear of losing Jaenia to another suitor. In either case, I could completely understand his protectiveness.

"Now, with that sign of good faith complete," Billiam said, "will you accept my offer?"

I paced back and forth in the hopes that the movement might shake a decision out of me. "Well, my friend Wolfette is in desperate need of the location of a bald man who murdered her teammates. I think confronting this man will go a long way to settling her homicidal tendencies. If you help with that, I'll agree."

"Homicidal tendencies?" Didlius asked. "What do you mean? She hasn't killed a single person since we met her."

"Fine. Overly aggressive tendencies. And she did kill that archer. Does that work?"

"Works for me," a certain axe-handed person said as she dove on top of Gu from around the corner. She must have misjudged the distance because she only made contact with the hafts of her axes and not the blades. She did still land with the full weight of her muscular body and heavy armor on the unarmored servant.

Gu bounced off the shelf behind him. With all the expensive ingredients on them, the owner had wisely invested in extremely heavy shelves and nailed them to the floor. I wondered if that decision was due to something like this happening before.

Amazingly, Gu quickly recovered from the unexpected and powerful tackle. Seeing his opponent dazed, he grabbed both of her axes by the handles. They struggled for a bit, but as Wolfette was still not completely recovered, he managed to toss her onto her back. Didlius took a step forward to assist Wolfette, but fortunately for all of us, Gu decided to use the opening to run toward the door and not to continue.

As Gu rounded the corner, he ran smack into a brick wall named Big Baby and landed with a thud. The large man took one look at his now standing sister charging toward the downed Gu, shook his head, and helped the man to his feet with a soft apology. As Wolfette neared him, Big Baby lifted her from the ground to stop her murderous charge.

"What are you doing, you big jerk!" Wolfette's legs pumped so fast they were almost invisible.

He smiled at her with serene patience. "Jerk? Not jerky jerk?"

"No time for extra words. He's getting away."

"From what? Axe therapy? Headache removal via head removal? Or my personal favorite, an axe-ecution?"

"No, that's the guy! Now let me down."

He lowered her to a few inches off the ground. "This isn't like the time you mistook that tiny doll for him, or the other time with the horse statue, is it?"

"I get it. I'm near-sighted and need glasses, but this guy I saw up real close. That's him. Now. Let. Me. Down."

He bit his lip and hesitated for a few seconds before setting her down. Wolfette was around the corner in under a second, and judging by the sound of the closing door a few seconds later, had somehow managed to effortlessly navigate the maze of shelves to find the exit. The door closed again a few seconds after, suggesting that Big Baby had either followed her path or also knew the way out.

"Well, Billiam, it looks like you've also managed to locate the second person for us, so I guess I have no choice but to accept your offer." I turned around to look at him. "I'll leave writing about Paruxia to you and . . ."

Didlius stared at the empty space where Billiam had been standing only a few minutes before. "It would appear that he left during Wolfette's disagreement with that bald gentleman."

"Did you happen to see where he went?"

"I heard the door open twice during Big Baby and Wolfette's disagreement. I assume he left then. Should we follow them?"

"That'd be great," I said. "But it took us over an hour to get here, and I have no idea how to get back out. You wouldn't happen to have left any bread crumbs behind us, did you?"

He pulled a piece of paper out of his pocket. "No; that would have been a tremendous waste of bread, and I have a feeling some of the things on these shelves might eat them anyway. I wrote the directions down. We need to go up, then up again past the turn, through the bend, down twice, left, then through another bend, right through a bend, left through another bend, right, and then past some bees, and finally through the door marked 'A.'"

While those directions didn't seem to make any sense, I decided to try them anyway since I didn't have a better alternative. My doubts dwindled as we passed bits of smashed glass along the way, most of which came from jars with axe-shaped holes in them. In less than three minutes, we were through the door and back out on the street.

A young man hurriedly ran up next to us. "Fire! Fire! The temple is on fire! Hundreds are inside, and we need more people for the bucket brigade."

"That's terrible, but we need to find our friends." I gave the young man the international symbol for *lower your voice*. Did he really think bursting our eardrums would make us want to help him more? "Did you see a woman with axes for hands or a large man with a baby-shaped helmet chasing a middle-aged bald man?"

"No, sorry," the young man said.

"Are you sure?" Didlius asked.

The young man stamped his feet impatiently. "I think I'd notice the first two people you described. It's not like we have a lot of people with axes for hands or helmets shaped like babies around here. Now do you mind? I have to alert more people about the massive fire."

"Oh, right. Sorry," I said. "One more, then we'll let you go. What about a taller, goateed version of me?"

He mumbled, "No," and ran off.

"I guess that means we go that way." I pointed toward the west, away from the fire.

"Because they wouldn't be running toward danger?"

"As the boy said, the two mercenaries are rather distinctive, and if he didn't see them, that means they probably didn't go that way. Therefore, they most likely went the other way. We have to hope they didn't go inside of any shops or took an alley."

"A wise deduction."

I was about to begin running, but Did grabbed ahold of my sleeve to pull me back.

"Hold on, loyal Hat. That wise killer said that I must prove myself to be worthy of Jaenia. Jaenia is an honorable and noble lady, and in order to prove myself worthy of her, I, too, must become a paragon of honor and virtue. Agreed?"

"So, what you're saying is that *you* need to be the one who captures the murderer."

"A virtuous thing to do, certainly, but not the most virtuous option available. This Gu fellow has only killed two people, but right now there are hundreds trapped inside that temple. Saving that temple is more important."

While Didlius had the laser focus of always trying to do the right thing, his ability to figure out how to accomplish that goal had so far been lacking . . . no, 'lacking' isn't a strong enough word. How about 'disastrous'? However, with this one statement, I was finally able to see that he might become the person I knew he would become. Perhaps all he needed was a focus, and perhaps the statement from the back of his spoon was that focus. Whatever the case, for the first time since I'd met him, he was right. I nodded and smiled.

"Come, fair Hat. We must save them!" Didlius said as he sprinted toward the smoke.

Didlius ran nonstop until we were at the large door that

marked the entrance to the temple—a door that was blocked off by flaming pieces of wood that appeared to have fallen from the scaffolding to the right of the door. He was about to attack the flaming wood with his solution to everything, but I managed to tackle him before he could connect.

Didlius pushed me off and wiped himself off. "Hat, what is the meaning of this? You said yourself that I am the leader. I will let this one slide as we haven't had orientation yet, but in the future, you are not allowed to tackle your leader."

As much as I wanted to not affect Did's decisions, my natural instincts from working with Harry took over to guide him to the correct course of action. "I'm not making any promises, but don't you think you should come up with a plan before you go charging in there?"

The temple looked to be two stories tall. Most of the structure was made of a pale white stone, but the door and roof were pure wood. It appeared that the door in front of us was the only entrance. The scaffolding looked to have fallen from the right of the door where they were painting a mural, and it looked like that was where the fire started. The door and roof were on fire as well.

Did turned his head back toward the temple, then turned back to me and laughed. "I was not going to go in there. The building is on fire. While my trusty weapon is more than a match for brigands, monsters, and evil knights, it is hardly the right weapon with which to combat a fire. No, what we need is water." He turned around, eyed a bucket brigade that was forming behind him, and ran toward them. "Aha!"

I hesitated to sprint after him because, for once, it looked like he was doing the sensible thing. Also, I was still a little winded after our sprint. I shook my head and ran toward the brigade. Unfortunately, Did had either gotten so overcome with his zealotry or forgotten what he was supposed to be doing and kept running through the bucket brigade until we were well out of town. As much as I wanted to ask him what his plan was, I was wheezing and huffing too much to form words. He finally stopped when we reached a river.

"Did," I panted, "I think they had a water source or two that were much closer to the fire."

"I suppose they did, but that fire was quite the beast, and I doubt whatever they had was enough." He pointed proudly at the river.

"While that might be true, I don't see how the two of us can possibly get some of this water to the temple in time. It's a half a mile away."

"Ha ha!" He ran down an incline, through the foliage, and out of my view. "And that is why I am in charge."

I would have immediately run after him, but I was still exhausted, and there wasn't anyone around for him to hurt. When I finally regained my breath, I jogged toward the sound of his voice. He didn't sound like he had gone very far, and he wasn't yelling, so I assumed he hadn't encountered anything dangerous. When I finally sighted him, I found I was mistaken. He had climbed on top of a levee.

The ten-foot-tall levee was made completely of dirt. The dirt appeared to be rather slick, and as he inched closer to the water above, I could picture him trying to impress me by doing a cartwheel and falling in. When we got back to town, I would have to see if the child safety leash had been invented yet and buy a few. While there was the possibility that Did could walk on water, I had no doubt he would still find a way to drown himself.

"Didlius, get off there! You might fall in."

He stopped his prancing, looked over at the nearby water, and then laughed at me. "Who are you, my mother?"

"No . . . I'm *my* mother, judging by my strong desire to send you to bed without dessert, but that doesn't change the fact that you might fall in." While I'd never been a parent before, I was beginning to see why my mom always had a permanent line of worry in her forehead. I sighed and walked across the top of the levee toward him. For once, my warning seemed to have sunk in, and he sprinted down the other side to the levee's base.

From our vantage point, we could see the top half of the temple. The flames had doubled in size, and there was no way anyone could even get near enough to put the fire out.

"Well, fortunately, you are not my mother, though even she would give me an extra helping of blueberry soft cake after I save those poor people from their fiery demise." Didlius stood up and raised his spoon over his head. "Behold, Spoon-Scalibur!" He lowered his spoon in a fluid motion, like a golfer making a long drive.

"Oh, no."

His spoon connected on the side of the levee with a sound like a bus hitting a brick wall. The light blinded me for a few seconds, so I didn't see exactly what happened next, but the bits of earth that showered me steadily over the next three minutes and the sound of rushing water kind of clued me in. Fortunately, Didlius dragged me to the side while my wits regrouped.

"If that isn't a deed worthy of sweet Jaenia, then nothing is."

My sight finally returned to me just in time to see the torrent of water overcome the town. While the fire in the temple was indeed out, only the roof of the structure was now visible, which was more than I could say for the rest of the town. "It's worthy of something, that's for sure."

Didlius stood up and began walking toward the town. "So, now we only need to make our way to the village and lead everyone out of the temple to safety."

"That could be rather difficult what with there not being a village anymore."

He stopped. "Hmm . . . you are correct. It seems there was a bit of a flaw in my plan. Do you think I could at least get a reward from them?"

"No one left to give it to you, unless some coins float out of there."

Did laughed. "Metal does not float, squire . . . ahh, you were being sarcastic."

I nodded. "From now on, you run any of your plans by me first, before you implement them."

He rubbed his chin and nodded slowly.

I'D ADVISE AGAINST IT

We ran downstream to help any survivors we could. As selfish as it was, I was hoping that we would see Big Baby, Wolfette, Billiam, or even Gu bobbing to the surface at any minute. Unfortunately, the only people we managed to save were an old man who didn't seem terribly happy that we pulled him out, his wife, who definitely wasn't happy we pulled him out, and a terrier who immediately jumped back in. I wasn't sure how many people had been in the town but was confident that it was a heck of a lot more than two.

After spending most of the day trying to find more survivors without any luck, and inadvertently learning every dirty word in the Paruxian vocabulary from the old man, including a few that Did assured me were made up (like 'testicle waffle' and 'fart conductor'), we decided that anyone else would have long since been pulled downstream, and also that it was probably a good idea to leave the scene of the crime sooner rather than later. The old couple seemed awfully happy to be rid of us so they could continue their decades-long argument on why their daughter left them to join the travelling podiatrists, though Did insisted their help was further proof of the goodness of humanity.

We decided to follow the river in the hopes that we would locate our friends, but after only a couple hours of travel, were forced to retreat deeper into the tree line by a sudden downpour. My heart sank as I desperately wanted to go back to look for our missing friends, but I eventually realized there wasn't any good we could do if we could only see a foot in front of us. While the trees did offer some protection, this particular rainstorm seemed intent on soaking us no matter what thick cover we sought refuge under. Did—or perhaps Jaenia—had a theory that it was our punishment for getting so many people wet. I couldn't help but agree, and it would have been fitting had we drowned in a much slower manner than had Did's unintended victims. I should have known better than to think we would die then, given my knowledge of Did's future, but was still quite surprised when we sighted a cabin in the distance.

I couldn't really make out much of the building through the rain and our haste, but it had a roof and that was all that mattered. Under normal circumstances, my deep knowledge of horror movies would have prevented me from going anywhere near a mysterious cabin in the woods, but I had several layers of water in every crevice of my body and every fiber of my being wanted to prevent me from becoming a merman or a very wet zombie. The cabin, with its wonderful roof, offered an alternative. At worst I would be a normal, dry zombie.

I know it's rude to enter someone's home without asking for permission, but basic courtesy tends to go out the window when you feel like diving into the nearest river just to get less wet.

Thoughts of crazy ax murderers swirled through my head as we entered, but the resident of the cabin was surprisingly pleasant looking. He didn't even have a crazy beard; his beard was very respectably well-trimmed. He looked more like a college professor than a recluse. I felt bad dripping water all over his clean floor, but he didn't seem to mind. He even gave us fresh-baked cookies. Normally, I'd pass on taking food from someone I hadn't even said a word to, but pain overwhelmed my reason. It actually might have been the smell of the cookies, but whatever the case, I gobbled down three before I even realized I should question their source.

"My, what brings travelers such as yourself into this area?" the bearded man asked. "No one ever comes out here because it's so far from the river. Did you know it used to flow close to here before they built that levee?"

Sound came out of Did's mouth, but it didn't form into anything resembling words. Apparently, he couldn't speak with five medium-sized cookies in his mouth at the same time.

I slapped his hands to prevent him from taking another two. "The levee seems to have burst . . . mysteriously. The river is now travelling on its old path."

The bearded man dropped the empty tray and backed away. "My goodness! And right in the middle of the annual Flaming Temple Festival. They hire an Atlian to create an illusion of fire on the roof and entrance and then ceremonially pretend to 'put it out' with a bucket brigade."

"Why do you live all the way out here, stranger?" I asked to draw attention away from the levee incident.

"I have it!" Did drew Spoon-Scalibur. "You must be out here because you are a wanted man."

I pushed Did's arm down until he put the spoon in his pocket. "Did, it's not right to assume someone is a criminal because they live in the middle of a secluded forest and immediately hand food to bedraggled strangers who wander into their house unannounced and uninvited . . ." I slowly let go of Did's spoon hand and gave the stranger a hard look.

He didn't appear to be the kind of person who would poison two strangers. I mean, he had a warm smile, a beautiful beard, and a festive robe on. How many poisoners do you know who look like that? Well, probably none, since they'd have probably already poisoned you, and dead people don't tend to read a whole lot.

The bearded man put his hands on his hips. "I am not a criminal, and I certainly didn't poison your food. If I was going to do that, I would have poisoned some food I didn't want, like that fruitcake my mother gave me five years ago or that bread from three days ago that I keep forgetting to throw out. Also, I gave you freshly baked cookies straight out of the oven. Do you honestly think I bake cookies four times a day and poison them in the hopes that some stranger will wander in? This place isn't exactly on the beaten path."

"Good point," I said. "But that doesn't mean you aren't some other kind of criminal like a land pirate or a guy who smuggles things in his perfect beard."

Did pointed his spoon handle at the bearded man. "That beard! Of course. You're Judas, the world-famous beard supermodel."

All the color drained out of our host's face. His head darted back and forth as he looked for a way out, but his cabin only had the one door which we were standing in front of.

Now, on learning his name was Judas and the fact that he had earlier handed food to strangers who entered his house uninvited, I should have immediately asked Did to whack him over the head with his spoon, but unfortunately, a much more important question subsumed my thoughts. "What the heck is a beard supermodel?"

Judas sighed. "Whenever someone makes a sign that requires a picture of a beard, they copy mine, the epitome of bearded perfection. They've tried others, but whenever a business uses a sign with another beard, their competitor puts up one with my follicular superiority on it and inevitably drives them out of business. It is my blessing and my curse. Once anyone sees this magnificent beard, they become transfixed by its majesty and barely listen to anything I say. Did you know that I am also a master speaker and one of the most learned men in this region? I discovered fourteen new stars last year and penned a new book where I unveiled my radical new theory that Vyenra is not flat but a cube. And I discovered a new element, too: Judion. But no one ever talks about all of that. Oh, no. They only care about my beard."

"Your beard is really nice." It was that perfect level of shininess—eye-catching, while not strong enough to blind you.

Judas sighed.

"Being a beard model sounds like an easy job to me. I mean, it's not like there's that much demand for pictures of beards."

Didlius and Judas laughed.

"This is Paruxia, Hat—land of the beard," Didlius said. "An elegant beard is to us what colorful clothing is to an Atlian or a cod piece is to a noble from the lands to the southwest. 'The better the beard, the better the man' is our national motto."

I stared hard at Didlius and his now stubbly though usually clean-shaven face. "Then where is your beard?"

"Jaenia does not like beards. It is her only fault. But I am a man in love, so I shaved mine off." Didlius tapped his spoon to his chin.

Judas's eyes grew wide. "Jaenia? That . . . doesn't sound like a Paruxian name. Of course it isn't. You just said she hates beards, and what self-respecting Paruxian would ever hate a beard? But . . . umm. Where is Jaenia? Did you lose her?"

Didlius smiled sadly. "We're on a quest to find her. We recently discovered that the only way to get to her is 'to prove yourself worthy of both her and yourself.'"

"Prove yourself worthy?" Judas looked at Didlius thoughtfully. "That's an interesting goal. How do you plan on doing that?"

Did posed like a superhero. "Stop crime, protect the weak, and save those in peril. All of the classics."

Judas rolled his eyes. "Isn't that a tad clichéd? Wouldn't it be better to try something a little different? I would imagine this Jenna is a special girl, and in my experience, special girls like it when a guy does something original, something they've never seen before. But then what would I know? I'm only a world-famous beard model and don't have much experience with women."

"There's a reason the classics became classics," I said, but didn't think Did heard me.

"But you are legendary for the number of famous and gorgeous women you've dated," Did said. "You must know everything about women."

Judas gave an insincere smile. "I've written extensively on the subject of love, and on many others as well. What you need, young man, is a chief advisor." He turned to me quickly and whispered, "You're not his chief advisor, are you?"

Before I could answer, he turned back to Did. "Yes, you need a chief advisor to guide you to becoming worthy of this Jemina. And I happen to know just the beard model for the job."

"Her name is Jaenia," Did said. "And I would be honored, but do you think Beardcules is available?"

"Beardcules?" Judas stomped around in a fury. "That hack isn't even worthy to stand in the shadow of my magnificent facial hair, let alone be your chief advisor. No, I mean me, Judas. I retired from the modeling game last year and have been looking for a new challenge. I've written a great number of scholarly books in that time, but what my books really need is something extraordinary."

"I accept," Did said without consulting me.

How dare this guy appear like this and take over my unwanted role! He hasn't suffered with us, travelled with us, eaten terrible food with us, had to share in the embarrassment of Did inadvertently injuring or possibly killing people, or had to share in the embarrassment of Wolfette purposely injuring or possibly killing people either. Who is this guy, and why does he deserve this role?

I poked Judas in the chest. "Who voted you chief advisor?"

"I vote we make him chief advisor," Did said.

"I vote against," I said.

"I vote for making me chief advisor," Judas said. "So, two to one, I win."

"You don't get a vote," I said, "and also, Did votes 'no.'"

"I do?"

"You do."

Did nodded confidently. "I do."

"And I vote for myself as chief advisor," I said.

"I second that nomination for myself," Did said.

Judas massaged his beard mockingly. "It seems there is a tie. I could break that for you."

I stomped my foot more like a first-grader than a toddler. "That's not a tie. He said he seconds the nomination, which mean he agrees with me."

"No, he said he votes for himself."

We both turned to Did for confirmation that we were right. At first, the look on his face said the only thing we'd get confirmation on was that he wanted more cookies, but after a few minutes of our double team of glares, he finally realized we wanted something. After scratching his head for a few minutes, he either managed to shake a thought loose or Jaenia clued him in.

"So, then I am the tiebreaker? Well, Hat was here first, so I choose him."

"But I don't want to be chief advisor," I said. "I only want to write about this journey."

"Splendid," Judas said. "Now as your chief advisor, I think the best way to impress this Janna would be to go about starting a religion. Girls love a guy who's in charge, and who's more in charge than a messiah?"

Did's face scrunched up in confusion. "That'll never work. She told me herself that she likes simple men of nobility, and those religious types are the opposite of that."

So, this was how Did got on the path to founding the religion. I stopped pouting. "I vote for Judas's plan."

"I second that," Judas said.

"I oppose." Did counted the votes on his fingers using the spoon as a substitute when he thought he ran out of fingers. "Darn. I lost. I guess we'll try this plan of yours."

SPLINTERS ARE NOT FUNNY

As excited as I was to get moving now that we finally had some direction for how Did was going to found The One, as soon as I opened the door it became readily apparent that we weren't going anywhere that night. Evidently, half an hour wasn't long enough for the sky to run out of thunder and lightning. Even if I could have survived what seemed like half the river being dropped on the forest, I doubted my ability to dodge the electricity. Did looked like he wanted to run *toward* the lightning anyway, so I shut the door and resigned myself to another night in Vyenra before I could get back home. I wasn't as disappointed as I should have been.

Judas kindly provided us with dinner, blankets, and a bedtime story. Afterward, I knew everything about the beard modeling industry in exquisite detail. For once, I decided that an aspect of Paruxian civilization wasn't important enough to bother writing down. I fell asleep as soon as he stopped talking.

The next morning, after a hearty breakfast of pancakes and sausages, Judas packed a bag, changed into his travel robe, and joined us. He ran out of room in his bag for his extra pairs of clothes and numerous liquids, lotions, cleaners, and assorted other beard-care products, so he had to borrow some room in Didlius's and my bags. I was about to complain when he also tossed in a few fresh sweet rolls as well as replenishing the rest of our more mundane food supplies.

We walked out of the cabin on our first steps toward meeting the king. If you looked only at the sky and felt the barest hint of the breeze, you'd think it was the most peaceful, serene day in existence. It made you feel like nothing could go wrong and everything was right in the world. However, if you looked down a bit to the trees and the ground, you'd get the exact opposite feeling—soaking wet everything, branches and leaves strewn about like the day after some sort of catastrophic tree battle, and little evidence of any wildlife. Those two opposing feelings were a reasonably accurate juxtaposition of my opinion of Judas. My gut said we needed him, but there was something about him that made me feel uneasy. I wasn't sure if it was due to him usurping some of my duties (that I didn't really want) or if it was due to his name and all the history that goes with it.

Before we passed the first tree, Judas asked us to wait a second, turned around, and ran back into the cabin. After about a minute, he came back out with a quarterstaff and handed Did and me each a rusty short sword. "The world can be a dangerous place."

"I beg to differ." Didlius showed us his moves. His spoon twirling was impressive, but I barely got him to stop before he turned one of the few trees that had escaped the prior night's tree-mageddon into kindling.

"What are you two doing? First our leader twirls a spoon around like it's a weapon, and then you tackle him for it." Judas swung his staff into the guard position. "Have I agreed to team up with lunatics? Is this a prank for a story in one of the big newspapers?"

I pointed at a fallen tree that was a safe distance away from anything else. "Did, get that with your spoon."

Did shrugged and sat down next to the tree. "Eating this with a spoon would be impressive, especially after that big breakfast, but—"

"Hit it."

"Ah, that makes more sense." Didlius stood up and turned two thirds of the tree into a mulch shower. The rest was aflame.

"Oh my." After regaining his senses, Judas stumbled forward to get a good look at Did's magic spoon. "Is that the Scoop of the Elders, the Legendary Ladle, the Teaspoon of Terror, or Myorc's Spork?"

Didlius smirked. "It is none other than Spoon-Scalibur."

Judas gasped. "I thought it was lost." He got closer and squinted at it. "It looks so plain."

Didlius pulled the spoon back and petted it.

"What I mean to say is that it's a very nice silver spoon, but I would have never guessed from looking at it that it's magic . . . So that's why it's remained hidden so long. Can I hold it for a bit? I'd like to get a closer look for purely academic reasons."

Didlius put the spoon back in his pocket. "I am sorry, chief advisor, but Jaenia was quite adamant that I never part with Spoon-Scalibur."

Judas bit his tongue. "Just like a woman. Never letting you touch her stuff. My ex-wife was the worst. You borrow her scented shampoo one time and . . . Sorry. Right. Well, we should probably get going. I know this forest like the back of my hand, and the capital is this way."

"So, what is your plan, O fearless chief advisor?" I asked through a mouthful of frosting as we began walking.

"Well, if Didlius is going to found a new religion, then he will need more followers. Through my extensive study of history, I have determined that the quickest way to do that is to convert the king. I call this phenomenon the 'Cycle of Sycophantry.' The king's noble hangers-on want to gain favor with the king, so they do what he does and take up his new religion. These nobles go back to their holdings, and their toadies want to impress them, so they too take up the new religion. The toadies' dependents also take on the new religion, and so on and so on."

"Oh, goodie!" Did said. "I've always wanted to meet the king. I'll bet my spoon will really impress him, too." He stared at his spoon. "Although, he might want it for himself and try to take it from me. Why don't we try to find our missing friends, Wolfette and Big Baby, first?"

Judas scrunched up his eyes in confusion.

"They were two mercenaries we befriended who got separated from us while we were in Arvingain . . . right before the river mysteriously changed direction and flooded the town."

"I'm sure they are fine," Judas said. "We'll look for them on the way."

"But isn't the river behind us?" Didlius asked.

Judas continued walking forward. "If they were swept away by the river, they will likely end up in the direction of the capital."

Didlius nodded enthusiastically. "That's right. The capital is on the Paru River, after all."

"Even after it changed course?" I asked.

"Probably not," Judas said. "But everything important eventually ends up in the capital. If they are not there, I'll ask King Fart to send out searchers."

I did a double take. "The king's name is Fart?"

"It's actually Fartius, but since we are so close, I call him by the shortened version of his name."

I scribbled everything he said in the book. "That's still a pretty weird name."

"I believe Fartius is a family name from his mother's side. He coaxed me into a personal consultation on becoming a beard model before he assumed the throne. He was rather earnest at first, but when I got to the part about sleep schedule and the hours of facial exercises, he balked. In that month of his training, we bonded quite a bit, and in the end, I did him one other service for which he owes me a favor. I plan to use that favor to get him to follow our dear Didlius."

"That must be one big favor," Did said. "What did you do?"

Judas stared at the ground. "I . . . the what is not important. Suffice to say, it is more than large enough to justify this request."

I considered questioning him further for more information, but with the look of embarrassment and barely perceptible shame mixed into his face, it seemed wrong to press him anymore. I had my fair share of things I wouldn't want to tell even my closest of friends, and it wouldn't be right to ask him to do the opposite.

We marched for several more days without much of note happening. I got very good descriptions of many of the trees and wildlife in the forests of central Paruxia. If you want to read about some more unique animals and plants, you'll have to buy the next edition of the *Encyclopedia Vyenra*, though for the most part, the animals were very similar to Earth ones with more horns, and the plants were like their Earth counterparts with the addition of elbows. The flying baboon was a particular highlight as long as you weren't standing under it when it had to go.

As much as I wanted to participate in our decisions, given my gut distrust of Judas, I had no knowledge of the forest we were traveling in or even the surrounding geography. I usually find it best to defer to the more knowledgeable person after all, though according to Judas he was more knowledgeable than any person alive on the subjects of beard care, skin care, hair care, tailoring, cloth making, rock climbing, tree climbing, pathfinding, path covering, tree trimming, tree growing, lumberjacking, carpentry, shipbuilding, wood carving, coopery, paper making, whittling, the making of whittling knives, blacksmithing, mining, smelting, fletching, bowyery, cooking, butchering, baking, cake decorating, candlestick making, candle making, architecture, building, sculpting, painting, drawing, stone masonry, quarrying, alchemy, potion making, dentistry, performing surgery and every doctorly duties, astronomy, mathematics, accounting, athletics, unarmed combat, every weapon known to man except the sling, tactics, leading, strategizing, jazzercising (and no, I didn't ask for clarity on that one), calisthenics, running, skiing, sledding, skating, crawling, hand walking, hang gliding, singing, whistling, humming, miming, playing every instrument discovered and even a few yet to be discovered, and making fart noises with his armpit. Be grateful that I skipped over the five days of conversation that led to that list.

"How many days until we hit the capital?" I asked.

"Two days, twenty-three hours, fifty-nine minutes and thirty seconds—which would be thirty seconds less than the last time you asked," Judas said. "Asking more isn't going to get us there any faster."

Did stopped and patted me on the back. "A worthy attempt, friend. We shall have to change tactics and ask less to make it go faster."

"Ha. Ha. Ha. Ha," a voice said.

Didlius looked at his feet. "Well, it should . . . Regardless, that is no reason to be so rude. I'd like to hear your better plan." Did scowled at me and crossed his arms.

"That wasn't me, Did," I said.

Didlius shouted at Judas in the distance. "And what do you have to say for yourself, mister? You were only recently given your position. Don't make me take it away."

Judas was barely visible through the dense foliage. He looked back and cupped his hands over his mouth for increased volume. "What?"

"Ha! Ha. Ha. Ha," the voice said.

I playfully punched Did in the shoulder. "Giving him his own medicine, I see," I said.

"That wasn't me," Did said. "I thought it was you."

"Seeing as how Judas isn't exactly the joking sort, I think there's someone else here."

Judas grabbed his staff with both hands and nodded toward me. I pulled out my short sword, and Did readied his spoon.

"Spoon. Ha. Ha. Ha. Ha."

A big mistake. I pointed toward the tree in front of me. Judas ran behind it.

"Owww," the voice said.

"You know, friend Hat," Did said, "that 'owww' was of quite a different pitch than the laughter."

"You're right," I said. "That sounded like Judas!"

Did sprinted around the tree. "Do not die, new friend. We have only just gotten to know you and wish to hear more skills that you have mastered."

I followed right behind Did because I didn't want to be alone and laughed at by a mysterious voice. We found Judas sprawled on the ground right in front of the tree. He was dazed but seemed otherwise unharmed. No signs of his attacker were evident.

"Ha. Ha. Ha," came from the vicinity of the tree, but I couldn't quite isolate where.

"He must have run around the other side as we arrived," Did said. "Also, he forgot a 'ha' this time."

"Or he is the tree!" I said.

Don't look at me that way. While Vyenra doesn't have talking trees, Atlian magic can animate them. My statement was only a clever misdirect, so the wizard wouldn't suspect me to be looking for him or her. I had not at all forgotten this fact when I said that.

"Ha. Ha. Ha. Ha."

"The sound came from that other tree, behind you," Did said. "There must be two of them or even more."

Definitely a wizard. But how to find the tricky bastard? I racked my brain for some nugget that would draw out the Atlian. Their love of flamboyantly colored clothing wouldn't really help. Their aversion to figs wouldn't either. Most of them did like a good deal, but I didn't really have much to barter with. However . . . they, and doubly so for their magic caste, were the most learned people around, something they shared in common with Judas.

"Hey, Judas. How much do you know about magic?"

Judas rubbed his temple. "I . . . While I cannot use that craft due to my lack of any Atlian ancestors, I am the foremost scholar of that subject in the known world. I've read several volumes on the more potent forms of ancient Atlian magic and own the only known copies of *Dragatsai's Grimoire* and *Gerenafrix's Book of Boom.*"

"Would you say you know more than most Atlians?"

"In the theoretical field I'm sure I know more than any of them. For instance, they were once able to perform offensive magic, but at some point either forgot how or lost that capacity."

"Ha. Ha. Ha. Huh?"

I still couldn't isolate where the voice was coming from. It was either coming from the tree in front of me or the one to my left. My eyes darted around for some clue to the wizard's location. Fortunately, Atlians of the magic caste wore purple—not a very effective camouflage in the woods, unless they were hiding in a field of lavender—so if he or she had even a tiny bit of clothing sticking out it would have been extremely easy to spot. Unfortunately, I couldn't see anything besides greens, browns, and the shiny silver of Did's spoon.

"What is your theory on why they can't perform offensive

magic?" I asked. "Are the modern Atlians not as smart as their forbearers, or are they just lazier?" (If any Atlians are reading this, know that I don't think this; I was only trying to goad our mysterious laugher into revealing himself or herself. Atlians are some of my favorite characters, and I think they're all awesome.)

Judas rubbed his chin. "While most historians believe the Atlians themselves banned the use of that magic after the Great Catastrophe, others posit that the few practitioners of that rare art were the perpetrators of that event and that they all died causing it. My personal scholarship indicates the source of that magic has either been exhausted, gone into hibernation, or been destroyed. I have exclusive sources that even the greatest of Atlian scholars cannot match, so it's not really their fault for not knowing of the superior hypothesis that I have reached."

In front of Judas floated a rather robust Atlian wagging his finger. I wasn't sure where he came from, as the books said Atlians couldn't teleport, though Harry had gotten things wrong before.

Not in the least bit afraid, Judas stood up and approached our new guest. "Do not worry, savior; his purple robes indicate that he is of the healer caste, and that caste is pacifistic."

Did stopped shaking but still held his spoon at the ready. "They seem to be a rather faded purple. Does that make a difference?"

He was right. The robes looked like they had been run through the washer about fifty times. I could even see through them in a few spots.

The Atlian appeared to be about to speak, but Judas interrupted. "It does. It means he is even more peace-loving than his kindred."

"Did, don't listen to him," I said. "Faded robes only mean they're old, or they've seen a lot of wear and tear. They have absolutely no bearing on how peaceful their owner is, more than likely they mean the opposite. And while Atlians of the wizard caste are also great healers, their magic is not restricted solely to that sphere; they can also use plant and wind magic to deadly effect. The knight Dyfantus made the same mistake the first time he encountered Hammurabi Joudisz in one of my favorite books."

Shock and then determination registered on Did's face. Most of the latter occurred when I said "knight." His grip tightened on his spoon, and he moved his left foot back into a fighting stance.

The Atlian finally spoke. "You'd better listen to your pale friend."

"The trees under his command can't harm us," Judas said with a slight quiver in his voice. "The diplomats and scholars I have met —all of which had numerous first-hand contacts with your people—told me that your magics cannot force plants to do harm to men."

"That's the dumbest thing I ever heard. What's next? That we can only heal left-handed people on Thursdays?"

"You can't?" Judas asked.

"We can, moron. Now on to the matter of me murdering you most terribly." He shaped his mouth into an "O" and wiggled his fingers menacingly.

The finger motions did not seem to be a spell as nothing happened to Did (who was in front of him) or caused any sort of motion from the trees.

Did scratched his head in confusion. "You forgot to say 'Ha. Ha. Ha. Ha.' after that."

The tree behind me said, "Ha. Ha. Ha. Ha."

"There, I made a tree say it," the Atlian said. "Much more menacing if he says it for me, right?"

"Wait a minute," I said. "Atlians have to make elaborate gestures to use their magic."

"No," Judas said. "According to my sources, they have to use a magic wand."

"You with the silly beard, stop talking," the Atlian said. "Non-idiots are conversing here." He floated toward me. "Also, pale guy, you're . . . wrong too? Yes, you also don't know what you're talking about. Now flee in terror or we . . . I will do some things you probably don't want done to you, unless you're into some of that weird stuff, in which case I won't do anything to you until you go away, preferably in terror or something like mild annoyance."

He had his back completely to Did as he said that, so, of course, Did tried to hit him from behind. Unfortunately, our Atlian attacker was either some sort of projection or intangible, and Did passed right through him, landing face first on the ground. The impact of his spoon caused a shower of dirt and leaves.

"Ha. Ha. Ha. Ha," the voices said from behind us. "Say, why aren't you guys running away?"

"Probably because you're not doing a very believable job of being a talking tree, Jerry," the Atlian said. "Err . . . I mean because they're so terrified that their knees locked themselves in place." He wiggled his pudgy fingers again, this time with a little less enthusiasm.

"Ask them if they'd be terrified if we talked more," one of the trees said.

"We would," Did said, "and thank you for asking, Mr. Tree."

"Wait a minute. If Atlians can only project their *own* voices, then why is the tree asking you a question?" I scowled at the Atlian to let him know I wouldn't tolerate any more funny business.

The Atlian glanced at me, looked at the recently talking tree, and then turned back toward me. "Because I have a split personality."

"That is absurd," Judas said. "My sources told me that Atlians with their inherent magical abilities are immune to that condition, as well as all sexually transmitted diseases and the hiccups."

I almost pointed out that there was no way that was true since the Atlians were responsible for transmitting Sex Hiccups to the Garandians shortly after their arrival in the kingdom, but held my tongue in the hopes Judas's statement might cause our adversary to slip up.

Our floating friend's eyes darted from tree to tree, hoping for some sort of help. If he hadn't been levitating, I would have guessed he couldn't do magic at all. "I don't think they're buying it, Jerry."

"Did you try wiggling your fingers really scary like?" the tree to my right asked.

"Yes," the Atlian said.

"What about making your head glow?"

The Atlian floated right in front of the tree and scowled. "I can't make my head glow."

"Because you're too fat to do that anymore."

"How can I be fat if I don't weigh anything?"

Another ghost—this one balding and dressed like a sailor—floated out of the back of the tree and snuck up behind the Atlian. "How do you know you don't weigh anything if you can't stand on a scale?"

The Atlian jumped . . . no, levitated higher, with a start. "Stop it or the warm ones will figure it out."

Another ghost dressed in a long black robe floated out from another tree and shook his head. "It's a bit late for that, Gafenarai."

"And no matter how many times you say it, we're not calling the living 'warm ones,'" the sailor said. "That's silly. We have no way of telling how warm they are."

Around twenty other ghosts floated out from different trees.

Most of them appeared to be Paruxian but a half dozen were from other ethnicities, including one that was dressed as a knight.

"What are you all doing out here?" Gafenarai asked. "Even though the whole scaring them witless thing failed, we still could have taken them prisoner."

"How are we going to take them prisoner if we can't touch anything to tie them up?" Jerry the sailor asked.

Gafenarai twisted his mouth like he wanted to answer but evidently couldn't think of anything.

"Why exactly did you try to frighten us?" Did asked.

The sailor shrugged. "Well, when the only way you can affect the living world is to make noise, you make fun the only way you can."

After hiding behind a tree for the entirety of the conversation —which he would no doubt explain as a sudden urge to expand his already massive knowledge of horticulture, and not because he was afraid—Judas finally joined the group. "If you had all floated at us, that would have been much more terrifying."

"After a century of that, it got old, so now we impersonate talking trees. What are you three up to?"

Judas gave Didlius the "no" signal but Did was oblivious. "We are off to meet the king and tell him about our wonderful new religion."

"What religion is that?" Gafenarai sat but still floated a foot off the ground.

"So, three people you've never met wander by and mention they're starting a new religion, and you're immediately intrigued?" I stared at them in disbelief. "If it's this easy, we'll be done in a week."

The sailor laughed. "We impersonate trees for fun. There's really not a lot to do around here."

"Plus, if we pick a new religion, we might get to pass on to the afterlife," a black-robed ghost said.

"So, what are some major tenets of your new faith?"

"Oh, well, that's easy. The first one is . . ." Now that I thought about it, the books were rather vague on this subject. I had been wandering around hoping to see this brilliant religion that was the foundation of the belief system of my favorite characters, but it had never occurred to me that I didn't really know a lot about it, except that the characters in the books' way of life revolved around it. It definitely centered on being nice to other people and treating them with respect . . . didn't it? The main characters were kind and honorable people, and they were also very pious. However, the books sure did have a lot of war and killing in them. Then again, most religions on Earth preached tolerance and good will, and there have been an awful lot of wars on Earth, especially over religion.

Maybe it didn't matter what it was. Maybe it only mattered what it would be. Those two things didn't have to be the same thing. We could make our own tenets and create a world of nice, kind, and not-at-all-murdery people. The perfect religion and the perfect world. Of course, if we did that, the books might never happen. No thrilling stories of struggle, great battles, and unexpected betrayals. Nice people don't do any of those things.

In spite of my temporary confusion, a plan came out of nowhere, and I knew what I had to do. We would see if the ghosts would agree to follow us. When we got to the preaching part of our new religion, the ghosts could hide inside of objects and pretend to be the voice of the almighty. It wasn't the most honest plan, but I was sure it would work spectacularly. I know if voices out of nowhere told me to do something, I would strongly consider what they said.

A split second before I could open my mouth again, Judas spoke. "Our first commandment is to physically assault anyone who disagrees with anything our religion says." Judas stroked his beard as the exclamation point. I would have assaulted *him* for making things up without consulting Did or me, but then that would have proven him right.

I was about to counter with my superior idea when the sailor cheered. "That's exactly our philosophy."

"Really?" Judas asked in an unsurprised voice.

"Well, yeah," Gafenarai said. "Why do you think we're ghosts? Nice people who lead fulfilling lives don't tend to get stuck like this."

"Then our second commandment is to seek out nonbelievers and make them believe or else."

"Or else what?"

"Or else . . ." Judas grinned devilishly.

The ghosts waited with bated non-breath. I also couldn't breathe, though for a completely different reason. Did smacked me in the back to prevent me from hyperventilating.

"Or else we throttle them mercilessly, unless they're bigger than us, in which case we give them a treat."

The sailor groaned. "But what if your followers can't actually cause direct harm or hand them treats, due to an unfortunate malady that prevents physical contact with anything?"

Judas clasped his hand confidently. "Then you scare the excrement out of them, preferably right before they're about to fall asleep."

There was a murmur of approval from the ghosts. They backed away and talked amongst themselves for several minutes before Gafenarai stepped forward and spoke. "What is your religion's opinion on ghosts? Do you try to dispel them? Can they become members?"

"Ghosts will be revered above all others in our new religion," Judas said. "We would be honored to have you in our flock."

"We would?" I asked.

"They seem like such fine, upstanding specters," Did said. "Jaenia agrees. As it happens, her stepfather was undead."

"Wait," I said because I don't know when to shut up. "What are some of your other commandments?" I was hoping they wouldn't agree with one of those.

Judas gave me a sly look and then grinned at the ghosts. "Always listen to and honor your elders. 'The older the better' is what we say, especially if they're dead."

"But what if your elders happen to be jerks?" I tried to ask. Unfortunately, the cheers of the ghostly gang were too loud to hear over. I waved my hands to get their attention, but when no one can touch you, waving hands doesn't really mean anything to you, so they continued their revelry as they charged out of earshot.

"Do you have any idea what you have done?" I asked.

Judas patted himself on the back. "Found our first converts, and what a find they were!"

I wasn't sure what made me madder, the fact that the ghosts loved his less-than-moral ideas for our religion, or that I didn't get to tell them my counterproposal. I kicked up a cloud of dirt in frustration. "You've sent a pack of murderous ghosts into the world using our name."

"They can't murder anyone, since they can't actually touch them. Besides, first converts!"

I gritted my teeth. "And now everyone is going to associate them with *our* name!"

"*And* we didn't tell them our name. As a matter of fact, our little religion doesn't even have a name yet. If they do anything bad, we'll claim they belong to a competitor."

"Oh . . . that's actually pretty clever."

"Sorry about those tenets too, as that's something we should all agree on first. I was only anxious to get our first converts. We can always change them later if they become burdensome." He stuck his hand out.

I grabbed his hand and shook it. As much as I wanted to be

angry at him, his ideas were almost ingenious. Plus, he apologized, and I was taught to always forgive if the person was sincere.

"I say we call our religion 'Jaenia,'" Did said.

Judas's face got bright red.

"Won't that get confusing, being the name of your girlfriend?" I asked.

Did's face turned red to match Judas's. "She isn't my girlfriend. We haven't started a proper courtship. But you are correct that it would be confusing."

"Excellent decision," Judas said. "I am of the opinion that our name shouldn't be chosen until later. If we pick one now that potential followers do not care for, they may not join. I think it would really raise morale to let our core followers name it when we really get going."

I nodded in agreement. It was a good plan. Plus, I already knew what it was going to be called, so there was no need to rush it.

THE REALLY, REALLY GOOD KING

Three days later, we finally arrived at the capital and our first signs of civilization. Judas wanted to immediately go to the palace, but Did overruled him and ordered him to direct us to an inn that could provide us with hot baths. We didn't want to meet the king filthy, smelly, and unshaven. Judas was mortified that I didn't want to grow a beard, but when I pointed out how silly the patchy stubble on my face looked, he couldn't help but agree.

While the city of Fwerfus was far larger than the small towns we had visited so far, I was still shocked that it was the capital of Paruxia. If I had to guess, I'd say it housed only 1,500-2,000 people. Judas informed me that it was only the fourth largest city in the kingdom, having been chosen for its central location between the two commercial ports in the north—Paru and Xia—and Xonrus, the ancient city in the south where all civilizations on Vyenra were said to have sprung from.

The buildings were a lot grander than the ones I had seen so far, at least. Most of the poorer areas used the same white, mortar-heavy style of the south while the nicer areas used wood, often bearing elaborately carved scenes that I was told reflected the personal histories of the inhabitants. As the city was the capital with people from all over the kingdom, the scenes reflected the various sub-cultures from all Paruxia. I had always thought of Paruxia as one homogenized culture, but my companions informed me that it was the home of five major cultural divisions and countless smaller ones. The closest unifying thing in the kingdom was the religion, but even that wasn't universal in the more remote areas.

After a hearty breakfast of a mushy cornmeal-like substance cleverly referred to as "corn mush," we set out for the palace. I wanted to do a little reconnaissance of the situation in the city before attempting to gain an audience with the king, but Judas assured me that even if King Fartius the First had died, he would still be granted an audience as he was beloved by all. Judas's arrogance was grating on me and I hated to be overruled, but his last plan had been quite sound, so I decided not to argue. Besides, I wasn't supposed to get involved anyway.

Before we climbed the hundred steps that led to the entrance to the palace, Judas called us to a stop. "I think I should go first since I am the key to our entrance."

"Ohhh!" Did said. "You're a key. How fascinating."

Judas groaned. "Just stay at least twenty steps behind me. I likely won't even need to say anything as they should move out of the way."

"Which part of you do we stick in the lock, your foot or your head?"

Judas had wisely left without answering Did and was already at the entrance. When the two guards in front of the gate didn't respond for several minutes, Judas loudly cleared his throat. The one on the right nodded toward him but didn't lower his massive axe. Did and I stayed on the steps as instructed.

"State your business," the left guard said.

"Shouldn't it be obvious?" Judas asked incredulously.

"Do I look like I have time to ask obvious questions?" His face indicated he didn't.

"Well, you are just standing there, so I'd say yes."

"He does have a good point," the guard on the right said. "This is rather boring. If the king would only let us do some occasional pillaging, this would be a much more exciting job, but no, he told us that's 'the opposite of guarding' and then he threw a bunch of dictionaries at us. The local pillage buyer wouldn't give us a single coin for those dictionaries either. That king of ours sure is a nutty one."

"What are you here for?" the left guard asked.

"To guard the door, obviously," the right guard said. "Weren't you paying attention when they handed assignments out this morning?"

"I meant him, dimwit."

"My name is not Dimwit." The right guard lowered his axe and sulked. "It really hurts my feelings when you say that."

"Do you have any idea who I am?" Judas stuck his face out and pointed his beard at them.

"He does have an awfully neat beard," the guard on the right said, "not that you ever have anything nice to say about anyone."

The guard on the left looked closer while still keeping his axe between the two of them. "That is nice. Beardcules might want to see this. It's almost half as nice as his."

"Beardcules!" Judas screeched. "That half-rate hack. His beard isn't even all-natural. He wouldn't know a good beard if it was attached to his face, which so happens to be the case because he has the beard of a pre-pubescent goat."

"You must know some real handsome goats then, mister. Not that there's anything wrong with that. Big cities attract all types."

Judas jumped up and down. I knew a tantrum when I saw one but was unfortunately all out of candy. "I don't know any pretty goats, and how can you not know who I am?"

"Does that qualify as disturbing the peace?" the right guard asked.

"It is certainly disturbing," the left guard said. "You two on the steps, are you disturbed by this?"

"No," I said.

"I do find it a little disturbing to find my friend so distressed," Did said.

The guard on the left nodded and then hit Judas square in the gut with the long handle of his axe. Judas attempted to continue his rant but was unable to form words. The guard on the right opened the gate and the other guard carried the still rather animated Judas inside. I wasn't sure what to do, but Did forced my hand by running after his chief advisor, so I followed.

"What is your business?" the remaining guard asked.

"We'd like to go in and see the king," Didlius said.

The guard moved his axe away from the entrance and opened the door. "OK. It's the first Trinsday of the month, when the king sees all petitions."

"Really?" I asked. "Then why is the door closed?"

"It gets drafty, and the king has a bit of a cold." He pointed to the left with his axe. "Follow the signs to the big entranceway at the end of the hall. The king will see petitioners until six, but you're the first ones."

"Thanks."

We didn't need to follow the signs as it was much easier to follow the sound of Judas's wailing in the cavernous palace hallway. The echo made it seem like he was only a few feet away, but as it turned out, he was much farther. When we arrived at the entrance to the throne room, a rather pretty woman in her mid-thirties had ordered the guard to set Judas down.

Her crown led me to believe that she was the queen, and her appearance immediately dissuaded my assumption that all Parux-ians dressed in functional, drab clothing. There was still the possibility that they all dressed that way because she had taken all their jewelry, however. I couldn't see any place on her body that she could fit another piece besides her face.

"How dare you put your hands on the renowned Judas, beard model extraordinaire!" the queen said. "For this insult, I shall have you demoted to the lowliest position of gate guard."

The guard rolled his eyes. "You already did that four times, Your Majesty."

"Then why are you here? Does this look like a gate to you?"

The guard bowed and then walked past me to the gate.

"Oh, that brute. To think of what he did to my poor Judy." The queen fretted and wiped Judas's shirt with her hands. "Have you heard that Fartius brought that pretender, Beardcules, in? I tried telling him that even second best is so inferior to the magnificence of my dearest Judy that there was little point, but you know Fart—when something bothers him he has to do something to fix it or he can't get anything else done. And now 'Grand Vizier Beardcules' has snaked his way into my husband's confidence and practically runs the kingdom. Farty still believes he makes the decisions, but all of his ideas invariably came from Beardcules's mouth first."

I wasn't sure if Judas was too paralyzed to answer or if he couldn't get a word in edgewise during her rapid release. The look on his face suggested verbal paralysis, though I wasn't exactly sure why. Whatever the case, Did and I were out of our depth and had to play along until we figured out more.

Satisfied that she had wiped off all the damage the guard had done to him, the queen grabbed Judas's arm and walked him into the throne room. Did and I hurried in behind them and managed to get close enough that the guards didn't stop us.

The king was seated on a massive throne, likely carved out of onyx. He had green eyes and a slightly lighter complexion than any of the Paruxians I had seen so far. None of the other nobles in the room bore either of those traits.

To the left of the king sat a man with the longest beard I'd ever seen. I guessed it would reach down to his knees if he had been standing, but seated, it was mere inches from the floor. Beardcules immediately scowled as soon as he noticed Judas. "Off with his head. No, wait, off with his beard first, and then the head."

"Whose beard and head?" the king asked.

"The traitor." Beardcules pointed at Judas.

The king scanned the room several times. "I don't see traitors. Are you really, really sure there is a traitor in this room? I don't remember naming anyone here as a traitor recently. And being a traitor is really, really bad, so I'd think I'd remember that."

Beardcules slapped his forehead. "I mean Judas, the former beard model, who is standing next to the queen right now, Majesty."

The king jumped up with a start and then ran forth to embrace Judas. "Judas, my old friend, it's really, really good to see you again. It was so bad when you left, and now you are here . . . and oh, it's just so good."

Beardcules stomped down from the throne to stand next to the king. "No, it's not good, Majesty. Remember you outlawed him a few years ago?"

The king bit his lip as he released the hug. "I did? That doesn't sound like me. Judas is a really, really good friend."

"You did. I was there when you signed the warrant for his arrest."

"Oh, yeah! I remember that. We had our best artist draw up the wanted posters, which I thought looked really, really like him, but you said they made him look better than he actually was, so I had the posters changed to match your description. Guard, go get me one of those wanted posters."

The guard ran in a somewhat awkward gait with his massive

axe as he left. He came back in under a minute and unfurled the two-foot-long poster for our group to see.

"That doesn't look anything like me," Judas said.

"Judas doesn't have any fangs or horns," I said.

"He's also not bald," the queen said.

"I don't think a beard can grow horizontally either," Didlius said.

"And my surname is certainly not Fakebeard-Impodiarrhea," Judas said.

"Yes," the king said, "I think this poster is for a different Judas. Guard, I want you to study this poster day and night—really, really memorize it—and go bring *this* Judas to me."

The guard rolled up the poster, saluted, and left.

"Now that that misunderstanding is out of the way." The king patted Judas on the back. "It's really, really good to see you, old friend. I was really, really sad to see you go, but you know, we all must move on sometimes to better things. It's OK. I understand. By the way, have you met my new best friend, Beardcules? He has a really, really nice beard too."

Beardcules's face turned a lighter shade of red on hearing his name. He pointed his chin at us to give us a better look at his beard. Judas did the same, and after several minutes with all eyes on the two of them, they finally lowered their heads at the same time.

"I refuse to give this charlatan even the dignity of a response," Judas said.

"Ha!" Beardcules said. "That statement itself was a response, and by giving that, you have given me all the dignity I rightfully deserve."

"Which is none," the queen said.

"Oh, my! Such bickering amongst my favorite people," King Fartius said. "What am I to do?" He looked at his two immaculately bearded friends. "No, I'm really, really not sure what to do. Anyone?"

"Your Majesty," Did said. "We have come to convert you to our new religion, so that I may gain the love of my most precious Jaenia. Surely you must understand the call of true love."

"Not really, really. By the way, who are you and what happened to your beard?" King Fartius asked, then looked at me. "And who let in the albino?"

"You men and your obsessions with beards," the queen said. "Did you not hear his plea? True love is a wondrous thing." She held her hand over her heart and glanced at Judas.

Judas took a few steps away from the queen. "Your Majesty, my friend here has that same spark in his eyes that I first noticed within your beautiful green orbs on that day we met. I knew they meant you would be a great king, and I think it's obvious to all that I was correct. That look says he too is destined for greater things, and I have deduced that great thing in him will be to found a religion. Given our friendship, I thought I should present you with the chance to be our first convert."

"I'm not really, really interested in a new religion," Fartius said. "I'll have you know that I am a staunch believer in . . . that one religion whose name escapes me at the moment. I swear it's on the tip of my tongue. Aren't I, Beardcules?"

"You are, Your Majesty." Beardcules's face shifted like he was giving a diabolical smirk, but I couldn't see it through the hair. "Now if that is all, I think you all should leave. Guards."

The guards tried to grab Judas, but the queen stepped in front of them. The king shook his head and moved forward to grab his wife.

"Honey, I know he was really, really important to us a few years ago, but time moves on, and we've found someone better." He pointed to Beardcules. "I mean, come on. The new guy's beard is longer."

"Hmpfh," Judas said. "It's not the length but what you do with it."

"Oh, really?" The queen winked at Judas. "I'd like to see a demonstration."

"Me too," the king said. "Everyone, stand back. We have ourselves a beard duel!" He pointed toward the courtiers who were already close to the walls, but they all dutifully took a step back. The guards tapped Did and I on the shoulder, and we followed them to the edge of the room.

"May I borrow your spoon, Didlius?" Judas asked.

Didlius pretended he hadn't heard, or maybe he wasn't pretending, but eventually Judas was forced to give up and turned back to Beardcules.

I whispered to Did, "Is a beard duel that staring thing they did when they first saw each other?"

"Oh, no. That was a 'beard off' which is what two beard models do to size each other up when they first meet. A beard duel is much deadlier. Those containers the servants are handing them now hold a special type of wax that is only used for these duels. It hardens the beard to such a level that they can break furniture and bones. Once waxed up, they will each draw a lot to see who goes first. The person who draws the short straw will get to hurl one insult at the other person, who then gets one swing of his beard in retaliation. If the person who drew the short straw survives, he will get an insult hurled at him and then get to swing back."

Judas raised his hands in triumph, indicating he got first swing. After a polite round of applause with the queen leading the way, Beardcules moved into one of the roughly three feet by three feet square chalk outlines that the servants had drawn.

"Your beard is as small as your manhood, both of which are bigger than your brain," Beardcules said.

Judas laughed as he moved forward to stand right in front of

Beardcules. He then turned his head as far as it would go to the right, held it there for a few seconds, and then swung his neck hard to the left, smacking Beardcules square in the chin with his beard. In spite of the loud thud, Beardcules seemed unaffected. As Judas backed up to his square, Beardcules turned to the crowd and grinned. The crowd roared with King Fartius probably being the loudest.

"As long as you've been in my shadow, I'm surprised that you haven't gotten as pale as my friend Hat over there," Judas said.

Beardcules scrunched up his face in confusion. "Who's Hat?"

I raised my hand. "I'm Hat."

"Ah. OK." Beardcules stepped a few feet away from Judas, turned his head back, and unleashed his long beard into Judas's chin. Judas didn't react for a couple of seconds, but then staggered back. The crowd held its breath, but he quickly regained his footing and remained in the square. Beardcules shook his head and moved into his square.

"You know we all know the reason you really left," Beardcules said.

Judas's face paled.

"Because your beard was starting to fall out. You're going beard bald!"

The crowd was so busy letting out a collective gasp that I think I was the only one who noticed Judas let out a sigh of relief.

Judas wound up and let out a furious swing. The noise was so deafening that I was sure Beardcules would be knocked clean into the wall, but when my senses returned, he was still inside the square on his knees. The crowd was on their feet. The king was giving high fives to everyone he could reach. After three minutes, the crowd finally calmed down enough so the combatants could continue.

It took a few more minutes for Beardcules to steady himself enough for Judas to attempt to direct his insult. I gained a new respect for Judas's tactical abilities. If had he immediately launched his insult, Beardcules would have been too disoriented to listen. When Beardcules was finally able to stand upright for more than a few consecutive seconds, Judas finally cleared his throat for his attack.

"I find it funny that you of all people would mention beard baldness, when you are the one who wears extensions," Judas said.

Beardcules's eyes finally came back to focus. A second later his face and then body began to shake in anger. This time he didn't stand still to ready himself. He charged forward, and a second before his foot crossed the line of the square (which I later learned would have been a forfeit), he caught himself. Now off balance, he slapped Judas weakly with his beard.

The queen and Didlius jumped up in cheer with me joining them a few seconds later; the rest of the crowd mumbled quietly.

Beardcules shambled back to his square and turned around. "You're old and your beard looks stupid."

Judas set himself, shrugged, and unleashed another blow, this one shattering the lower portion of Beardcules's beard, but somehow not knocking him back. The crowd was so enthralled that no one made a noise.

"Aha!" Judas said. "No natural beard would shatter like that. I told you all he used extensions."

Several members of the crowd shrieked in disgust. The queen said something about a disqualification, and the king reluctantly motioned to two of the guards, who hauled Beardcules out of the square to kneel in front of the king. Beardcules attempted to sputter a response, but nothing came out.

"While I can't arrest you for going against everything we Paruxians really, really represent, due to the progressive laws created by my brilliant grandfather," the king said, "I can remove you from your posts as Grand Vizier, Chief Advisor, High Chancellor, Higher Councilor, Minister of Finance, Lord Inspector of Roads and Muck, and Head of the Council of Royal Fitness. Was that all of them or did I forget a few?"

"You forgot Chief Panty Inspector," Beardcules muttered.

"Oh, that was a real one? I thought you made that one up as a joke. Well, I'm removing you from that one as well." He glanced sheepishly at his wife. "Sorry, dear. I really, really thought it was a joke and will be removing it from the official roles soon."

The queen stared icy daggers at him.

The king returned his gaze to Beardcules. "Umm . . . back to the matter at hand. While I am busy signing the decree really, really hard to remove that offensive position from the rolls, you will be roughly thrown out of the palace. You two guards, make sure to throw him out on his butt and be really, really rough about it. If I hear you threw him out on his head or were only really rough about it, I'll demote you to gate duty. Two reallys, not three, and certainly not one. Also, I want you other guards to go up to his room and toss all his stuff out the window, like my gorgeous and really, really reasonable queen does when we've had a misunderstanding that is always really, really my fault."

The seven guards at the back of the room saluted and left the throne room. As the two closest guards hauled Beardcules up, Judas cleared his throat.

"Your Majesty, as you know I have a nearly uncanny ability to sense hidden plots," Judas said, "and I sense one now."

The queen nodded vigorously. The king and several of the courtiers developed a bout of coughing fits.

"Sorry, Judas." King Fartius said. "It's the height of allergy season. Continue."

"My keen and unerring senses detect that there is more to Beardcules and his fake beard than just a plot to gain personal power, wealth, and the ability to inspect women's unmentionables. I think he was sent here as an agent of lowly Lorius and

Gerf, the countries that merged to settle the tie for who we've defeated the most."

The king scratched his well-trimmed, short-bearded chin. "An interesting theory, Judas, but what evidence do you have?"

"Couldn't you just have him tortured until he tells you?" Judas asked.

"We could, but I've already ordered the guards to toss him out really, really hard, and they're really, really busy guys and ladies. I'd hate to make more work for them."

Beardcules had used the time to gather his wits and began to struggle in the arms of the distracted guards. When the king turned back to his courtiers for some reinforcements to argue away Judas's claims, Beardcules wiggled his way out of the grip of one of the guards and used the remainder of his hardened beard to whack the other guard in the side of her helmet. He managed to get halfway to the exit (now unguarded as all the other guards had been sent to toss his stuff out the window), but Didlius was too quick for him. I barely got an order out to not use his spoon inside, so Did tripped him instead.

"Aha!" the queen said. "Only a guilty man would run like that. Judas was right. You should give him all of that traitor's old titles for this great service."

"Or he didn't want to be thrown out really, really hard," the king said.

The guards grabbed Beardcules and hauled him back to the king. The fall had cracked his beard off down to an inch from his chin. In spite of his less than dignified appearance, he still looked defiant. "No matter how hard they throw me, I'll never tell you my evil plan."

"Oh, that's too bad," the king said. "Guards, go toss him now. We have a line of petitioners out there, and I hate to keep my people waiting."

"Wait," I said. "He said 'evil plan.' Judas might be right."

"I might?" Judas asked. "I might!"

Beardcules snarled and looked like he was about to spit until his eyes caught his beard. All defiance left his face, and he began to weep uncontrollably. "They told me I'd get to be kiiiiiing. <sniff> They said that King Fartius loved famous beard models, and he'd had a falling out with Judas, so they sent me here. <sniff> I was to gain your trust and then get you to issue an anti-beard decree to throw the kingdom into chaos. <sniff> Then, they'd invade from the west while their allies attacked from the east, and I'd get installed as their vassal king." He said more, but it was so filled with blubbering that I couldn't understand anything else.

"See," Judas said. "I was right, and it was all due to how my legendary perception noticed those ridiculous beard extensions."

Beardcules stopped crying as anger filled his face. "My beard is all natural, and I have never used enhancements! I only agreed to the Lorger plot on the condition that they allow me to keep my glorious beard. The fact that you would be forced to shave your beard, and I would get to keep mine, was the main selling point."

"Your Majesty," one of the courtiers said as he picked up a portion of the shattered beard off the floor, "we should clean the wax out of his beard and then investigate this claim. If he is innocent of wearing artificial enhancements, then we should let him go."

The rest of the courtiers murmured their agreement.

Fartius stroked his beard, but then dropped his hand in exasperation. "What? No. He just admitted he was part of a really, really bad plot to conquer the kingdom. Why would I let him go? This is exactly why I gave him so much power; the rest of you are idiots."

The courtier dropped the beard piece and slinked to the back of the crowd. The king nodded, and the guards took the weeping Beardcules away.

"May I have one small boon for my great service, Majesty?" Judas asked.

"You may," the queen said.

"He may?" Fartius said.

"He may!" The queen gave him a withering stare.

"He may," the king said sheepishly.

Judas moved forward with a swagger. "I ask that you convert to my new religion."

"That is not a small boon."

"Yes. It. Is," the queen said. "And we accept."

"Shouldn't we find out what they believe in first? I mean, that's not really, really unreasonable, is it?"

The queen sighed in exasperation. "Oh, fine. Whatever. Tell us what you believe in, Judas." Her eyes blinked rapidly. I couldn't figure out the code, but Judas's face showed that he didn't like the message.

Judas recovered his composure and stared at the queen. "Our biggest belief is that marriage is the most sacred of institutions and anyone who is unfaithful is a terrible person."

"Oh, I like that one!" the king said. "And it fits so perfectly into my most loyal union, too. What else?"

Judas's face brightened. "That the best way to settle disputes with your neighbors is war."

"Yes! Our current religion frowns on going to war with our neighbors since they 'are our brothers and sisters in faith,' but this is perfect. We can go smack Lorius and Gerf around like we used to before they converted."

Again, Judas had made things up about our religion without consulting us. While it was true he did know the king better than us, I didn't like the direction he was going. Surely there was something less destructive and more moral that the king would like. I decided to give Judas the benefit of the doubt again, but I would have to talk to him about this when we left.

"Oh, yes, I almost forgot," Judas said. "It is a symbol of the utmost holy to have a shorter beard, nothing longer than a couple of inches past the chin."

The king jumped up in excitement, wagging his short-bearded chin. "Spectacular!" He looked around at the wide-eyed stares of the rest of the court and regained his composure.

Judas barely held back his excitement. "We're still ironing things out, and there are a few more tenets to be named later."

"A few more to be named later! Why, those could be anything. They might even be something that could be beneficial to our kingdom."

Judas stared in bewilderment and then regained his composure. "You know, I think they might, Majesty."

The king ran by his courtiers, high-fiving everyone. Pretty soon the whole crowd was caught up in the excitement and asking questions. The king, realizing that he might have shown his hand too much, finally calmed the crowd down. "Emm . . . Yes, well, seeing how I do owe you for uncovering the Lorger plot, I think I will try this new religion of yours on a temporary trail period, if that is acceptable to you?"

"That would be most agreeable, Majesty. Nobles, and especially kings, will be revered above all others in our new religion." He glanced back at the entranceway where the queen stood with her arms crossed. "As our mission is done, I then . . . I think we need to go elsewhere to continue to spread our message."

"What about asking if anyone's seen our friends, Wolfette and Big Baby?" I blurted out. "And if he's seen any other southwesterners like me."

"We didn't even tell them about my spoon," Did said, "and I'm sure they would like to hear more of my glorious quest to free Jaenia."

"That sounds really, really interesting," King Fartius said.

"No, it doesn't." Judas began to push Didlius toward the exit. "Trust me, it's not."

"What does this spoon do?"

"It scoops up yogurt and soup. Nothing more." He put a little extra effort in when he passed the queen, careful not to get caught in her gaze. "The line of petitioners is getting quite long, and you need to get on the paperwork to remove that position from the rolls. I know how busy being a king is."

"Ahh, very good, Judas. You always were really, really thoughtful. Scribe, fetch me the papers, and in the meantime, send in the first petitioner."

I gave the queen a quick glance. She looked like she wanted to murder Judas and anyone or anything associated with him, so I decided to follow Judas. As we made our way to the gate, we passed a line of about twenty people from every social class imaginable, including the mime class.

When we exited the castle, Judas wanted to leave town immediately, but I stopped him when I saw the stream of objects coming from one of the upper towers. It didn't take much convincing to get Judas to agree to take a few things that used to belong to his rival. Didlius got a few expensive changes of clothes, Judas got some new beard-care products, and I got a badly needed pair of boots to replace my worn-out tennis shoes. We exchanged everything else we found for coin at the marketplace.

As it was not even noon yet, Judas insisted we head back on the road. He wouldn't tell us where we were going, but I suspected our destination was the far-off land of "anywhere but here."

THE HOLY JUNK MAIL

As we passed the last wooden building to exit the city, Judas continued at his near running pace. Nothing we tried even got him to turn around. I tried imploring the author in him to let me get a look at the various Paruxian legends carved into the buildings' sides, but that only seemed to make him somehow move faster. Not even Did's best whimpering worked.

"Great, now I'll never know what happened to that guy with three beards," I said as the last building disappeared from view. "Did he defeat the hydra or marry it?"

Didlius sighed. "It would have been nice to tell a king of my tale. Unlike you, I've never had the opportunity to converse with royalty."

Judas didn't even turn around. He just kept walking at an unusually fast pace. "You trusted me to be chief advisor because of my advanced tactical and diplomatic abilities. As such, I don't think it possible to explain all the intricacies that went into making that decision."

"Advanced tactical and diplomatic reasons?" I snickered. "You only wanted to get away from the queen."

Judas stumbled but did not turn around. "I have no idea what you are talking about, Hat. I barely know that queen. Only met her once or twice to exchange pleasantries and nothing more. Couldn't even pick her out of a lineup if my life depended on it."

"I could," Didlius said. "She'd be the one in the tiara and clothes worth more than my entire village combined."

"Ahh, see, Did, that's the problem," I said. "Judas here wouldn't recognize her with clothes on."

Judas finally stopped. He didn't turn at first, but when he did, I realized my mistake. Rage filled his face. He barely stopped himself from reaching back and hitting me with his still hardened beard. Did stepped in front of him to hold him back, but by that point he had himself under control.

"I. Never. Laid. With. Her. Ever!"

I put my hands up in surrender. "Of course not, Judas. No one said you did."

The rage ebbed slowly, then suddenly evaporated as a light went on in his eyes. "You only said that to get a rile out of me, didn't you?"

I smirked sheepishly and pulled my book out of my pack.

He sighed. "Fine. It's obvious that I'm not going to get a moment's peace until I tell the two of you the story, so here it is. After months of the then prince pleading with me to teach him the art of beardcraft, I agreed to be his mentor. Given his intense interest in that art, we quickly developed into the closest of friends. With his much-improved beard, the prince finally had the confidence he needed to pursue a certain young lady that had been the object of his infatuation since he was a boy. With my coaching and occasionally tossing the right line in his ear, the prince was able to secure that beautiful maiden's hand in marriage. He was besotted with her, and she with him. All signs pointed to a very happy and productive marriage."

"This is a wonderful story," Did said. "When does King Fartius come in?"

"The prince *was* King Fartius. His father, King Gastules, was still alive then."

"Ohhh . . . excellent. Continue."

"Anyway, during the engagement feast, Fart let slip that I had written his proposal speech. He was so drunk that I don't think he even remembered doing it. Later that night, his betrothed, Famerala, came to my chambers and confronted me. I tried to deny it, but my face betrayed the truth. Fam can be rather forceful when she wants to be, and she soon knew that most of the wonderful words that had caused her to fall for her betrothed had come from me. As she left in a huff that night, I thought I had ruined the happiness of my friend, but over the next couple of days, Famerala seemed just as happy and in love as before."

"Oh, that's good," Did said. "I was beginning to get worried."

Judas lowered his head. "On the night before her wedding, she again came to my room and confessed that since the sweet and beautiful words that had caused her to fall in love with Fart had come from me, she was now in love with me instead. Not wanting to be beheaded and not feeling the same way about her, I told her that I was highly drunk that night and had made the whole thing up. She was skeptical, but I eventually got her to believe me. I hastily wrote a note to Fart telling him that he had reached the limit of what I could teach him in beardcraft, packed up all my things, and left the palace. I assumed in the five years since she would have forgotten about me, but it seems I was mistaken. I think any future meetings with King Fartius should be without his queen in attendance. She doesn't like travelling, so we should always meet him elsewhere, as far from the capital as possible. Even then, I think we should try to keep as many communications as possible by letter."

Did held his spoon to his chest protectively. "I think I should keep you out of all of my communications with Jaenia too."

I paused in writing Judas's story. "How would he even do that if he wanted to, Did? You only talk to her in your mind. I don't think Judas has telepathic abilities."

"Of course. How silly of me."

"Actually, I am the world's foremost expert in the arts of the mind," Judas said.

"But you can't actually communicate through your mind, right?" I elbowed him in the ribs and glared at him.

"Err . . . yes, of course." Judas nodded vigorously and Did smiled in relief.

"So, where to, Judas?" Did asked. "I greatly look forward to the next part of your plan."

"I have an idea," I said. "We could go from town to town and have Did show off his spoon. He could blow some stuff up to get everyone's attention, and then we could tell them about our religion."

"That sounds like an excellent plan!" Did said. "And Jaenia agrees."

Judas gave me a pinched smile. "A decent idea, though we'll need to save that for tomorrow. I have a much better plan for today. In my research, I learned about a far-off land where there live a warlike people called the Litotians. Their priestly class came up with a unique method to spread their holy message to nonbelievers, which they called 'religious junk mail.'"

"Religious junk mail?" Did asked. "What is that?"

"They'd print their religious message on a piece of paper or carve it into a tablet, using only simple pictures, and sneak up to the habitations of another heathen tribe during the night. When the heathens woke up the next night, they'd see the pretty pictures and start performing the deeds they saw represented in the junk mail."

"I hate junk mail," I said.

"You've heard of this and didn't share, Hat?" Judas wagged his finger at me. Did followed suit.

I shrugged. "We have it back home and most people just throw it out since there's so much of it. Most of it I don't even look at."

"Ahh . . . I understand your reservation, but here it is a brand new concept. Our junk mail will be the first in the area. People won't even realize what it is for until they begin reading and will have to look at it out of curiosity."

"Intriguing," Did said. "What if the heathens didn't emulate what they saw in the Litotians' junk mail?"

"Ahh, then they'd send their warriors in and murder them. They referred to that as another one of their brilliant inventions: 'Plan B.' But we will have to hold off on attempting 'Plan B' until we get more followers with pointy sticks. For now, we should visit an old friend of mine, Dagrius. Dags owns one of the finest printing establishments in all of Vyenra in the town of Elbis, only a few miles away."

"Could we call them 'pamphlets' instead?" I asked. "I think if we call them anything with 'junk' in the name, people will throw them in the trash."

Judas nodded thoughtfully. "A wise argument that was already on the tip of my tongue. It would be a good idea to think up a new name. That way if we meet any of those savages, they can't accuse us of stealing their idea. 'Pamphlet' it is then."

While I had always thought it was neat that they had the printing press in Vyenra, in spite of everything else being medieval, I hated that such a wonderful invention was being put to the evil practice of creating junk mail, but perhaps it wasn't so evil at all if it was being used to spread one of the greatest influences on my favorite world. Something can't be evil if it's being used for a good purpose, can it?

"How far from the capital is this town?" I asked.

"Oh, only a few miles," Judas said. "It's where all the nobles and wealthy merchants live who want to be near the king but avoid the busy city. Dags does a bustling business printing custom books and other works for the wealthy, so he moved here to be closer to them."

While we had passed by a few houses that belonged to the upper-class in the capital, Judas wouldn't stop for me to get more than a quick glance at them, but as we entered Elbis, I was finally given the chance to see some of the intimate carvings on them up close. When I noted that some of the houses seemed to have quite a few more scenes on them, Judas informed me that the more scenes, the more famous the family. I then asked if every wealthy person in the town was related as I had seen most of the same scenes on every house. Judas told me they likely weren't but everyone seemed to find a way to be related to the great Paruxian heroes of old, like Jurgus and Paru.

Judas was so determined to get the pamphlets made that he wouldn't even let us stop to wash off his still thickly waxed beard from the duel. In this case, his resolve paid off because we arrived fifteen minutes before closing. At the last minute, Judas caught himself in the reflection of the door and immediately ran off to fix his "mockery of a beard" before seeing his old friend. Did and I entered without him for fear that they would close before he got back.

The shop must have done pretty good business as it contained at least seven presses and possibly more as the building snaked around in an odd shape. The employees were mulling around, chatting amiably. I wasn't sure if business was on a bit of a lull or if they had already shut down for the day, but none of the presses were currently in use. The relieved owner came bustling forward.

"Gentlemen, gentlemen. Come in," the stocky, balding proprietor said. "Can I interest you in something in a deluxe leather binding? Or perhaps you are interested in our quantity discount? Five percent off if you order a hundred, ten percent off for 500, and twenty percent for 1,000!" He waved toward one of his employees and the boy scurried forward with cups full of a dark liquid.

I sipped the beverage. It was hot and thicker than most teas but thinner than coffee. It tasted sweet with a hint of something nutty. "Actually, we were looking to have some pamphlets made."

The owner scrunched up his face in confusion. "I'm not familiar with that term. Is that what they call a shorter work like a novella in the north?"

"No, we call those a small headache," Did said between sips, "and a blow from a dictionary is the chief cause of migraines."

The owner looked like he wanted to give Did a migraine, but his face instantly turned to joy when the door opened behind us as Judas entered the shop. "Judas! It's been too long. Boys and girls, fire up the presses. He must have another book finished. The king will have to build another library for your works if you keep this up."

"Dags!" Judas pushed past Did and me to embrace his friend. "I would still be sitting on fifty of them without your efficiency and skill getting them to print."

"Yours are always a challenge, dear boy, but I love getting your orders." They separated and Dagrius handed Judas a drink from the waiting hands of a different boy. "The added challenge of the light bit of editing I have to do is fun, too. Most of my clients around here have theirs dictated or outright written by a professional scribe."

The drink almost tumbled from Judas's hand. "Editing? What do you mean?"

Dags pulled the cup up to his friend's chin. "Nothing, nothing, dear boy. Only some . . . minor formatting." Dags gave me a subtle shake of his head that Judas couldn't see over the cup. "Now what brings you here?"

"If you'll recall from my seminal work on the Litotians, there was a chapter about how their priests converted some of their more isolated kinsmen."

"Yes, yes!" Dags said. "I had to go over that chapter seventeen times to . . . ah, adjust the formatting."

"The amount of care you put in is why I'm more than happy to pay you double what any of the other printers charge. But on to the point. Those clever Litotian priests liked to leave these small carvings, or later, pieces of paper depicting all that made their religion great on the doorsteps or cave steps of their heathen kinsmen to try to convert them. They'd been doing it for centuries, and it became a competition to see who could create the greatest junk mail. If you'll recall, they referred to those carvings as junk mail, by the way. We want you to create some of that junk mail, though we have decided to call them pamphlets to differentiate ours from the crude Litotian works."

"Oh, so these fellows are with you then?"

"Yes. The one who just stole Hat's cup of baeva is Didlius and with his unique blend of innocence, bravery, and charisma, we have decided to form a new religion. And to help with that, I was fortunate to recall this obscure fact about the Litotians and have decided to re-purpose their junk mail to my cause. Can you make them?"

Dags looked toward the ceiling, deep in thought. "Yes, but for something that only takes up a page a piece, you'd have to place a rather large order. I'm not going to tie up one of my presses for only a few dozen pages. It wouldn't be worth the effort."

"A few dozen?" Judas laughed. "Oh, no. I want to order 10,000."

Dags was speechless and didn't seem to be able to move.

"Ten thousand?" Did said. "Why, that is more than all the people in Fwerfus, Peru, Xia, and old Xonrus combined!"

"Near enough, and it seems you have grasped my plan already." Judas rubbed his hands together slowly.

"We're going to turn every person in the four major cities into pamphlets?"

Judas stopped rubbing his hands together and began to rub his temples instead. "Hat, you explain it to him while I go over the details with Dags."

"Sure thing." I saluted him and turned to Did. "You see, Did, we're going to hand out the pamphlets in the major cities and hopefully convert people to your cause with them."

Did scratched his head with Spoon-Scalibur. "With travel time and assuming eight hours of sleep a night plus two hours a day for meals and grooming, Jaenia calculates that I will be 347 by the time we hand all of those out. Plus, that's assuming we convert one in ten people and get those people to help out after that, which she assures me is a very generous number, due largely to the novelty of these pamphlets' newness. As spiritual figurehead, I must object. That will only allow me a few days to marry my Jaenia and enjoy our wedded bliss!"

Judas glanced back casually. "It will be much more than one in ten—more like one in two—because our pamphlets will have pictures. Literacy is not a universal skill amongst our people, tragically, and unfortunately, even those who can read tend to pay more attention to a picture—a fact that I learned the hard way when most of my books only sold a few dozen copies, yet the cartoons of that talking sheep sell thousands of copies without fail."

Dags gasped. "Pictures? You'd have to commission a special block for that. It will cost extra, a lot extra."

Judas dropped a few gold bars on the counter.

Dags waved a young woman over, and she took out a sketch pad. "OK," he said, "and what kind of pictures do you want? In color or black and white?"

"Hmm . . . we need something eye-catching and to the point. Definitely in color."

"Well, Did is our leader," I said. "It should probably be of him."

Judas appraised Did. "True, but most of his charisma comes from his presence and personality, not from his appearance."

The sketch artist mumbled under her breath, "Men are perverts. Why not a half-naked woman?"

"That's it!"

The young woman dropped her head in disgust. "That wasn't supposed to be out loud . . . What do you want this woman to look like?"

"I know exactly what I want her to look like." Didlius ripped a page out of my book and grabbed my quill. He spent almost half an hour before he tried to hand the sketch artist the page.

Judas intercepted it. "I see you are a practitioner of the minimalist school."

"No, I just made a stick figure and drew some circles for breasts."

"Those are breasts?" Judas asked. "Then why are they bigger than her head?"

Dags maintained his professional composure. "I'm sure Trovia can come up with something."

The sketch artist gave Dags the stink eye, but his look in response was much worse, so she hastily smiled and nodded instead. "Is there anything in particular you want this woman in the drawing to do or just the standard seductive pose?"

"On one side, we'll have her start unattractive and unable to find a mate, but then Didlius baptizes her, at which point she becomes beautiful," Judas said.

The sketch artist finished jotting down her notes. "And after that, she decides men are shallow, and she doesn't need them?"

"So shallow they stop hiring artists who mouth off to the customers?" Dags asked.

"Point taken. What about the other side?" She bit her lip and readied her pad.

Judas put his hand on his chin. "Didlius and an army slaughtering members of the other religions . . . I'm missing something. What is it?"

"Less killing and also beer," I said.

"Yes, that's it!" Judas said. "When the battle is over, they celebrate by having an alcoholic beverage of their choice."

Trovia raised her hand. "Should I mix in some crotch grabbing, sports, and any other male clichés I can think of? Have some women in chain mail bikinis and proportions so unrealistic that they have back problems for the rest of their lives?"

"I do like your enthusiasm, young lady, but it all has to fit on one piece of paper. The women in chain mail bikinis does sound nice though."

Dags nodded at Trovia, and she left the room, grumbling the whole way.

"We are rather backed up, so this could take quite a while . . ." Dags paused and Judas dropped another gold bar on the counter. "But since you're such a valued customer, we can have the plates done by the end of the day tomorrow and your pamphlets done on the day after."

"Splendid," Judas said. "While we're waiting, we can concentrate on the second part of my plan." He waited expectantly for someone to respond, but no one did. "Why, Judas, what is part two?" he said in a squeaky voice.

"I don't sound like that," I said. "Do I?"

"No, nor do I," Did said.

"Why, Judas, what is part two?" Judas said in a deep voice.

"There we go," I said. "Exactly like me."

Did nodded. "Much better."

"You'll like part two, Didlius," Judas said. "It involves us finding people to distribute our pamphlets so that you won't be long dead by the time we finish."

"Woohoo! Jaenia and I can have a whole week for a honeymoon."

Judas rolled his eyes.

I scratched my head. "So, who are we going find and convince to help in two days?"

"Follow me, good friends, and I shall show you."

THE REAL POWER BEHIND THE THRONE

Try as we might, Judas would not reveal who he was going to get to help us. He assured us that the answer would blow, not our minds, but another part of our bodies, and that these heroes would be able to help with the resulting explosion.

I wasn't sure what he meant by that, but I did know that I didn't like that he wouldn't tell us who we were meeting. His more recent plans hadn't been up to my modest moral standards, and I really wanted to know what we were getting into, so I could offer a counter-proposal. After almost half an hour of nonstop pressure, he finally told us that the answer wasn't safe to reveal in public, but he swore it would all make sense when we met them. We would just have to personify that great Paruxian virtue of patience.

"I'm not Paruxian," I said. "I'm an American, and we're renowned for our lack of patience."

Judas looked like he wanted to slap me, but somehow managed to whisper instead. "I've told you already, it isn't safe to talk about it here. The walls have ears."

Didlius's eyes bulged as he looked at the wooden walls next

to me. "They used living trees to make the walls out of! That's horrific."

"I was speaking metaphorically," Judas whispered. "I meant there are many people wandering these streets who would be shocked to hear of what you two are soon to learn."

"You mean the Illuminati!" I covered my mouth before I remembered that saying that out loud would immediately summon them. My eyes darted back and forth for signs of Megatron and Darth Vader, ready to kill me for having uttered that name.

"No, rich people," Judas whispered.

"Even worse! They'll lower their own taxes and convince everyone else it'll benefit them too," I said.

"Hat, calm down. You don't even pay taxes here."

"Oh, yeah. Let's go."

After my outburst, nothing much was said for the remaining half-hour walk to our new allies, besides Did trying to gain vengeance on a litterer by breaking both of his hands. Judas grabbed Did's arm before the first blow could land, and I tickled him until he dropped the spoon. Terrified of the near loss of his gesturing ability, the litterer picked up all the trash he could find for the next block and put it in the nearest receptacle.

We eventually arrived in the poorer part of town, noted for its lack of wooden buildings. I was surprised that this section of the town existed, given that the entire town was supposed to be only for the wealthy, but then remembered that their servants had to live somewhere.

"Why do the poor not make their houses out of wood?" I asked. "Paruxia's covered in trees, yet all the poor have houses made of some sort of stone."

"Making it out of wood is presumptuous," Did said. "It's like saying you think you're better than everyone else."

"Yes," Judas said. "And to fully understand it, you have to understand our history. You see, Paruxia used to be a rather barren land, as most of our trees had been chopped down to make pikes, spears, siege engines, and other related things in the great religious wars centuries before. So, a hundred years ago, the great King Dictus hired a small army of Atlian wizards to re-forest our land. I believe that Atlian ghost we encountered earlier was one of that group."

He continued, "During those barren centuries, only the wealthiest of individuals could afford to make their homes of wood, and so a wooden home in the old style became a symbol of wealth. Though trees have become plentiful again, it has become engrained in our culture that wood as a building material is for the wealthy. Using stone also saves the less wealthy from having to think up things to carve into their homes as most families do not have much in their history to brag about, if they even know their history at all."

Didlius nodded. "I didn't know that until now and had never given it a second thought. It was one of those things you learn growing up, but never consider why."

We finally stopped at the most dilapidated building on the block. With its mostly missing roof, cracked sides, and barely hinged door, I assumed it was abandoned. When we entered, my opinion didn't change. If I could have found a broom or some dust rags, the neat freak in me would have immediately begun working. I stepped gingerly to the only cobwebless corner and almost tripped over the small, wooden door to the cellar or basement.

"Let me guess," I said. "We're going down there."

Judas started. "How did you know?"

"The wood is freshly polished, there is no rust on the hinges, and there are no cobwebs around it."

"Hmm . . . you're right. They should get someone up here to dirty this thing up and make it look older." He beckoned me away from the door, opened it, and climbed down into the dark. When we heard his foot hit dirt a few seconds later, Did and I followed.

The passageway was unlit, but soon after Judas made a bird noise, a figure approached bearing a torch. Judas and the figure exchanged some sort of hand gestures. With the gestures complete, the figure turned around and we followed. I couldn't make out much of our surroundings since the torch was three people ahead of me, but the tunnel was made of stone and appeared well maintained. The ground seemed to have been recently swept as my feet were not meeting the resistance of dust one would expect from a tunnel.

It took us about ten minutes to reach our destination, and without our guide, we likely would have become lost even if we had brought some form of illumination. The passage had many twists, turns, and wrong ways. Did swore he even saw a pit. Fortunately, the room we found ourselves in was well lit, not that it helped make out the identity of our guide in his long, gray hood.

Our guide set his torch down and turned to Judas. "You know the secret hand signals, but I don't know you. What business do you have with . . . me?"

Judas turned around slowly to take in the room. "Your waiting room is rather quaint compared to the one in the Fwerfus. They have refreshments and a couch there."

Our guide's fist tightened. "There are more of us in the capital to maintain that bigger facility, and a couch wouldn't fit through our narrower tunnel. Now what do you want?"

"Ahh, my apologies. I'm sure you all do just as excellent of work as your counterparts. My name is Judas, and I wish to hire your services."

The guide's fist unclenched, and he hopped back almost into the wall. "*The* Judas? The beard model?"

"Yes, the very same." He raised his head to point his beard at the guide.

"Wow! I had your poster on my wall when I was a kid. You're my idol." He held his hand out and Judas shook it vigorously.

"But wait, you've got to be rich, and our organization . . . I mean me, just my lonesome self and nobody else. Ahh, crap. I'm going to get demoted again and have to clean all the toilets on bean night from now on. I wasn't supposed to tell you about the organization. Oh well. What's done is done, and it sounds like you already know about us anyway. As much as I idolize you, sir, we don't represent the wealthy."

Judas laughed. "While I can see where you are coming from, given the company I keep as an international celebrity, I live a rather modest lifestyle. Why, Hat and Didlius here can vouch that my only domicile is but a paltry cabin, the lone extravagance being the wood-burning oven that was a personal gift from the Ambassador of Fearn."

We both nodded in confirmation. I decided not to mention the gold bars he had been carrying around to pay for the pamphlets.

Our guide seemed unconvinced. "Be that as it may, Judas, your famous profession betrays that you can't possibly be a member."

"But my grandfather, also named Judas, founded your organization."

Our guide dropped his hood, revealing a handsome face, likely to be in his late twenties, and beard that could have been Judas's twin. "Your grandfather was *that* Judas?"

Judas grinned. "He was. I have kept that fact secret as I was afraid my fame would draw unwanted attention to your cause— not the best thing for a secret organization to have."

Before our guide could ask his next question, the wall behind me opened and three more members came out. The tallest one motioned for us to follow, and she escorted us through three more rooms, all exquisitely cleaned, but modestly furnished. We finally arrived at a room containing a worn but well-maintained desk with another robed figure seated behind it. Our tall escort whispered something in the ear of the man behind the desk who walked toward Judas. The two of them performed an elaborate secret handshake, which they finished with an embrace. Our original guide had not followed us into the room.

The man at the desk motioned for Judas to seat himself and he did. "The fact that you know the secret handshake known to only the highest members of our order confirms the story of your parentage, Judas. What can we do for you?"

It took Judas almost half an hour to explain the concept of the pamphlet to the cloaked men and women. The tall one was especially intrigued when we came to describe the picture of the woman becoming more attractive.

"Fascinating, but what does this have to do with us?" the man behind the desk asked.

"This is the especially brilliant part of my plan," Judas said. "Once we have the pamphlets, we need your members to distribute them to all the toilets in the kingdom while throwing out any other reading material nearby."

The spokesman nodded slowly. "Interesting, but why should we do this for you? While I have nothing but the utmost respect for our founder, this hardly aligns with our mission statement. What happened to your grandfather, by the way? My father said he vanished without a trace one day."

Judas lowered his head. "The Duke of Fwerfus created 'Free Chili Week' to commemorate the tenth year of his reign. Every toilet in the city became filthy, and my grandfather succumbed from exhaustion on the fifth day."

The tall one patted Judas on the back in sympathy. "He went to a better place. The Great Bathroom in the Sky is always clean and never runs out of soap."

Judas wiped a tear from his face and regained his composure. "Our new religion believes in the overthrow of the established order and the veneration of toilet cleaners everywhere."

"And sink and bathtub washers?" the shorter guide asked.

"Especially them!"

Our guides chattered excitedly until their spokesman made them stop.

"Wait, my fellow Cleaners. My sources in the palace lavatories have informed me that King Fartius has also agreed to join, and that you gave him a very different message. Why would the nobility join a religion that believes that?"

"That's what we told them so they'd help," Judas said. "When we come to power, we can reveal our true message, and since we outnumber them, they will be forced to come into line!"

The spokesman's smile almost went from ear to ear. "You truly are your grandfather's grandson, Judas. Even though you became famous, you still remembered where you came from. We would be honored to help you in this endeavor."

"Fantastic. We'll have the pamphlets in a little over two days. Would it be possible to get the assistance of the branches in Fwerfus and the three other major cities as well?"

"It shouldn't be a problem, since your message aligns with our mission statement. I will send word immediately. If it weren't this time of night, I'd send for drinks so we could celebrate this momentous day, but as I'm sure you know, we have to perform our daily task."

"Yes, of course," Judas said. "You have to make sure the towels run out halfway through the day, and then makes sure there are more men's restrooms than women's even though women need more because it takes them longer."

"Yes. If your brilliant plan works, we won't need to continue that, as we will no longer need to enrage the populace, so that they will overthrow the established order, but until then we'll continue."

Judas shook his hand. "In the meantime, my friends and I will look into other matters to help both of our causes."

"Splendid. The initiate will show you out."

Our original guide came back in and led us through the maze-like passage. We learned that he worked in the king's hunting lodge (and by royal definition, "lodge" means three times bigger than any other buildings in the town) nearby. Judas promised him that in our religion, men and women responsible for keeping bathroom sinks clean would be revered above all others.

After we bid our guide adieu, climbed up the ladder, and closed the door, I finally asked Judas the question that was burning a hole in my mind. "That's at least the third group you've said would be revered above all others. What happens when they figure out you were lying?"

"Ahh, dear simple Hat, why do you assume I *was* lying? You see, all will be revered equally, so when I tell one group that they will be revered it's actually true."

"My, that is very clever," Didlius said. "I can see now why you chose yourself as chief advisor. An excellent choice it was."

I grumbled under my breath. "I still think they'll get mad when they find out."

It still rubbed me the wrong way that Judas had elected himself chief advisor, not that I wanted the job, but it was still wrong. Unfortunately, my grumbling also seemed to affect my writing as I recorded our encounter with the toilet cleaners; the words were uneven, thick, and angry. I decided to think happy thoughts about getting to see Vyenra in real life and soon my notes returned to their normal, flowing, beautiful shape. Unfortunately, in my effort to regain my sanity, I completely missed Judas explaining what he had planned next.

THE SEEDY SIDE OF TOWN

We had walked several blocks before it even dawned on me that we were moving (my legs having displayed their usual tendency to follow without seeking my permission). Most of the time on my journey that would have been a good thing, but this time Judas had guided us to a run-down part of town that just screamed "danger." (There actually was someone constantly screaming something a few blocks away the whole time, and it might as well have been "danger.")

On several occasions some scruffy, menacing-looking men or women approached us, but backed off when Judas gave them a look. I wasn't sure what to make of that. Were Judas's earlier claims of being an expert in every fighting style true and was knowledge of that so well known that even street toughs knew about it? Or had his fame and respect as a beard model translated to every level of society? Were they toilet cleaners? I desperately needed to find out more about our self-elected chief advisor.

Judas led us into what I assumed to be a bar, given the drunks sprinkled right outside the door. As I entered, Judas stopped for me to catch up and then pulled me close. He had to almost scream to be heard over the noise, but fortunately, I could barely make out what he said. "Stay close. The people here know me but some may not see me before they decide to do something less than pleasant to you."

Did nodded. "In this crowd, I doubt I will be able to swing Spoon-Scalibur in time to stop them from giving me a spanking."

"Uh, yes . . . You may want to let me hold that for safekeeping." Judas held his hand out.

Did moved behind me and held his spoon protectively to his chest. Judas shrugged and then moved forward.

Judas was mostly able to push his way through the thick and raucous crowd. A few times, someone was about to turn and punch him, but they barely managed to see his face in time and quickly backed off. I couldn't see much through the crowd in front of me, but from what I could, everyone looked unfriendly and was wearing some sort of thick, scarred leather or battered mail. Eventually, we came to a doorway guarded by two large, bald men with forked beards. Judas said a few words and one of them went through the doorway. After a few minutes, he returned and motioned for us to go through.

The room we entered was surprisingly clean and well-lit, though it looked like it had been decorated by a little girl with a princess fetish. Pink, lace, and plush pillows were everywhere, contrasting nicely with the scarred, armored old woman seated with her back to us at the lone table. Across from her was a woman who I almost didn't see, as her pink dress, wig, and painted face served as a rather effective and unusual camouflage in the unique room. The pink-clad woman pointed (which was fortunately easier to see since her dark fingers were only painted at the nails) at three chairs. Her scarred companion got up and stood next to her, and we hastily seated ourselves.

"Lanea," Judas said, "it has been too long."

"I haven't been called that in a long while," she said in a sweet, almost purring tone, "and it is a testament to our history that I let you live for uttering that name. Call me 'The Pink Woman' as my colleagues do, or . . ."

The scarred woman finished the sentence for her by planting her axe in the table.

The Pink Woman rolled her eyes. "I've told Kitten not to hit the table anymore, but after all these years, it appears I'll never housebreak her, though I suppose when you have no tongue, you take every opportunity you can to let your weapon do the talking."

Her companion impassively pulled her heavy axe out of the table with one hand. When she finished, she stood at attention and stared straight ahead with cold, dead eyes.

"Now, Judas, what can I do for you?" The Pink Woman gave a sickeningly sweet smile. "Remember, my services are expensive, and I don't give discounts, no matter our past or that your father founded this company. Sentiment and emotion have no place in this profession."

Judas nodded. "You are so different from the little girl I knew in—"

She stood and yelled in a shrill, thunderous voice, "Do not speak of that place." Her eyes blinked, and she seated herself again. Her voice returned to the more relaxed, almost melodic tone she had used before. "The girl you knew and the place she came from are irrelevant and best forgotten. Now please, no small talk. On to business. My time is valuable, as I'm sure is yours."

"Yes, of course. I'm confident you're already aware of my new purpose in life."

The Pink Woman motioned for him to speed it up. "Yes, my sources told me of your conversation with the king and of the one you just concluded with the Society."

Judas smiled thinly. "Impeccable as always. Our religion should have an overflowing of followers shortly, but what we will be lacking is soldiers, at least of the experienced kind."

I wanted to scream at Judas for making awful plans yet again without consulting us, but one look into Kitten's eyes told me interrupting would be a very bad decision, so I whispered to Did instead. "Why do we need an army? I may not be an expert on military matters, but soldiers in this era aren't usually the kind to go around helping people, unless those people are themselves."

Did whispered back, "I asked the same question earlier. Judas said we need soldiers to protect us from other religions. He pointed out a bunch of historical examples where religions tend to get jealous of more successful ones and murder their followers. We need soldiers to perform—a term he invented—'proactive defensive extermination' of the other religions to protect ourselves."

My mouth dropped. I couldn't form words, which was fortunate because I doubted our host wanted to hear anything from me —not that it mattered since it didn't appear she even noticed Didlius or me. The two of them hadn't even paused while we talked.

The Pink Woman smiled warmly at Judas with mischief in her eyes. "But what of dear Fartius's armies?" she asked.

He responded with a conspiratorial grin. "Their equipment is professional, at least, though they are nothing more than children wearing their father's clothes. They haven't fought a war in fifty years, and except for the royal guards, they would likely soil themselves in a real battle. What we need is veterans, which you seem to possess in abundance."

"My fellow mercenaries would laugh if you used such a fancy term in their presence. 'Thieves,' 'killers,' 'murderers,' 'cut-throats,' and 'brigands,' those are music to their ears and accurate for most of them, too. Now, about payment? And remember, those who fail to pay live even shorter lives than those they've hired us to kill."

"King Fartius has never much cared for the priests. In spite of all he said in front of his courtiers, that is the real reason for him joining us. He wants to break their hold on him and regain the freedom of his forbearers. He would be so happy to be rid of them that he'd let you have whatever you capture from them. Are you familiar with the size of their local treasury?"

She clapped her hands excitedly. "I do so love when you ask me things I already know. I have already had my agents ask the king this very thing, and he has agreed. Your cause is now our cause. It appears, Kitten, that we are now a holy order. Go rouse the troops and spread the word that we are now under contract."

Her companion left without any sort of reaction.

"Now that we are working together once again," The Pink Woman said, "what do you need us to do?"

"For now, sit tight and await further instructions. As I likely will not need you for a couple weeks, you are more than welcome to take out short-term contracts in the interim."

She shook his hand. "Splendid. It is planting season and our soldiers need to spread their seeds."

"Seeds?" I asked.

"Oh, yes," Did said, "because those people out there are all into gardening. That explains why they are so dirty."

Judas gave him a patronizing smile. "No, her company is known as 'The Gardeners.'"

The Pink Woman nodded. "We fertilize the ground with the corpses of our enemies."

Didlius nodded like he knew that all along. "How do we let her know when we will need her?"

The Pink Woman smiled. "I will likely know before you do, dear boy." She waved her hand half-heartedly, and Judas instructed us to leave.

THE GREAT PHILOSOPHER, ME

It may have been my imagination, but the dangerous toughs we passed seemed to take a step back whenever we approached. At least one of them even gave us a nod of respect. I wasn't paying a lot of attention though, as I was too busy focusing on the terrible implications of that meeting.

The religion of The One has always been a peace-loving, morally upright religion in the books. Why is it becoming so violent and terrible?

But had it been that way in the books? The books are kind of vague on most of what its followers believe, beyond that they're devout and that it's better than the old religions. It is possible that it starts with violence but becomes better as time marches on.

Whatever the case, what Judas is planning is wrong. So many people will die. I have to stop him. It's wrong, and wrong is, well, wrong. So what if the characters won't exist; new ones will take their places. I might even like the new ones more. Besides, I'll still have the physical books to read . . . probably.

I slammed my spoon down on the table, splashing little bits of vegetables and soup on Judas's robe.

Soup? How long had that internal debate been going on? I had walked all the way to an inn, ordered soup, and eaten without even realizing it. What else had I done without realizing it? Had I fathered any children? Bought a timeshare? Completed a degree? Conquered Denmark? Died and been reincarnated as a sock? What day was it anyway?

I rubbed the side of my face. No new hair growth, so it hadn't been too long. Also, I had a face, so not a sock.

Judas seemed angry with me. Had I been yelling my internal thoughts again?

"No," Judas said.

"Oh, great," I said. "Then why are you so angry at me?"

He held out his stained robe. "You've been splashing soup everywhere."

"Sorry . . . wait a minute, I thought that question about my internal thoughts, and you answered it."

Judas dabbed the soup spots with a damp cloth. "It's obvious something's been bothering you about the meeting with The Pink Woman. What is it? Your cares and concerns are important to Didlius."

Didlius nodded. "Hat, you are the first person I've ever met who believed in me. You're my friend and I want you to be on board with what we are doing. Tell us what is bothering you."

I looked into the caring eyes of Didlius and then at the slightly less caring eyes of Judas, (though to be fair, he was busy trying to rub out the soup stains on his robe). My face brightened. I knew my friends cared. They would fix everything to make me happy. Our new religion wouldn't kill anyone just because they disagreed with us. It would all be right.

"I don't think we should use soldiers to kill anyone because they might attack us later. I mean, I'm OK with keeping the soldiers to protect our followers, as not everyone is as enlightened as us and religion does sometimes make people do not-so-nice things to people who don't agree with them. And I'm not saying that because I'm afraid of The Pink Woman or her silent partner."

Didlius stared thoughtfully. "Perhaps you're right, Hat. I am no philosopher, but I don't think killing other people is really the best way to help them. Jaenia has been strangely silent on the subject. I think that means she's testing me."

Judas looked up, having given up on getting the stains out. "You are correct, Didlius, in that you're not a philosopher. Fortunately, you have in front of you one of the greatest philosophers in the history of Vyenra."

He continued, "To quote the great philosopher, me, 'The greatest way to help people is to kill their enemies before those enemies can kill them, because when you're dead, there's no help for you but a hole in the ground.'"

Didlius clapped. "Oh, my, that is quite brilliant. I never thought of it that way."

I scrunched up my face in worry. "But what about, 'No bad deed goes unpunished?'"

"Also a good point," Didlius said.

Judas shrugged. "'It's only bad if your enemy is still there to make you regret it.'"

I stood up and raised my voice. "You're making those up."

"It's only made up if you didn't write it down first." Judas raised his head haughtily.

"'Nothing good ever comes from violence.' I think Martin Luther King said that," I said.

"I like that one," Didlius said.

"That's absurd," Judas said. "If you kill someone, you can take all their stuff, and stuff is good. I hate to quote the same brilliant philosopher as before but, 'Always listen to the guy with the sharpest stick, unless you can find a sharper one.'"

"What if you have a magic spoon instead of a sharp stick?" Didlius asked.

"It's a metaphor. 'Sharpest stick' means better armed, and I doubt anyone has anything as strong as that spoon of yours."

Didlius nodded enthusiastically. "Ahh, then I like that one even more than the one you quoted before it."

It was obvious I wasn't going to win this argument as he would keep "remembering" quotes that supported his argument, and Did was eating them up because they sounded fancy. Didlius was supposed to be my friend.

Judas's face changed from smirky superiority to smirky comfort as he patted my hand. "I understand where you are coming from, dear Hat, and when we begin the process of formalizing this great bastion of hope and soul saving that we are creating, we will need your compassion to temper my aggression. But I think the great philosopher, me, said it best: 'It is a prudent investment to kill a thousand now to save a million later.'"

"Math makes my head hurt, but you certainly have the right of it, chief advisor," Didlius said. "Don't you agree, Hat?"

"Can you at least promise to not kill people if you don't have to?" I asked.

Judas patted me on the shoulder. "Of course. Of course. Fortunately, I am equally as skilled of a diplomat as I am a tactician and warrior. Now that our little spat is over, let us have some drinks!"

He waved the waitress over and ordered us each an ale. We drank throughout the evening, but I don't remember anything that was said. And no, that had little to do with the ale, as I switched to water after the second one. Even though Judas's words were hard to argue with, my brain and heart were not satisfied. My stomach definitely wasn't, but that probably *was* due to the ale.

I tossed and turned all night as I tried to figure out who I could find to fix this. Some great knight always showed up in the stories of Vyenra to fix things. Where was that knight? Where was that hero?

But knights didn't exist in Paruxia. There likely weren't any living ones for thousands of miles. Didlius was supposed to be a hero but all of his heroics tended to have much worse consequences, and with Judas planted firmly in his ear, that was unlikely to change, at least to my benefit. I had to find someone else. I had find a hero, but where?

WELL, THAT'S SUSPICIOUS. NEVER MIND; THEY HAVE BEER!

I rubbed my eyes and slumped down the steps for breakfast. I wasn't sure what made my head hurt more—the lack of sleep or the uncertainty of what to do next. I wanted to believe that Judas would try diplomacy and peaceful conversion before resorting to violence, but something told me he wouldn't follow through. His plan was moving too fast for anything but the most expedient methods, and he did not strike me as a patient man.

I found my two companions at a table. Judas appeared boisterous and well rested. He stood up and vigorously shook my hand. I responded with a lethargic half-grip and let him do all the work. The waitress arrived and handed me an oatmeal-like dish they called "oatmeal." Normally learning a new Paruxian term would have excited me beyond words, but I had other things on my mind.

I ate the oatmeal slowly, each mouthful a chore. Thank God it was something that didn't involve a lot of chewing. My listless state combined with my dread for what I was going to do next made the meal take forever. My companions got bored waiting for me and began to discuss the next stage of Judas's plan.

Didlius ordered a second glass of milk while he waited. "We still have two days until the pamphlets are ready. What could there possibly be left to do? You seem to have thought of everything."

Judas smiled modestly. "I doubt I have thought of everything —likely 99.999% of the eventualities, but not everything. There is still one major component of our plan to take care of and that involves you, Didlius."

Didlius almost spit his milk on me, but even in my lethargic state, my years of experience dodging spit takes took over. His milk hit the wall behind me, and the waitress ran over to wipe it off.

"Me?" Didlius asked. "Do you need Spoon-Scalibur's might? Is there a monster about?"

"Performing a good deed would be a great idea," I said enthusiastically. "Doing something virtuous would get our name out there, and it might make up for some things those mercenaries are likely to do. Would you like to hear my plan?"

Judas snorted. "Perhaps we can do some small good in between other larger tasks if we happen upon them, but what I have planned for us is much more important. If our Didlius is going to lead and inspire our followers, then he needs to learn how to speak in front of a large group. Fortunately, I know just the person."

"But Judas," Didlius said, "you are already such an eloquent speaker. Why don't you do all the speeches?"

"Very astute of you, Didlius, but I must remain only your advisor. You must lead. While I would make an excellent political leader, no Paruxian would take me as their spiritual leader. Every Paruxian spiritual leader has been a humble person who the commoners connect with. Unfortunately, as a glamorous, internationally famous beard model, it cannot be me; it's hard for anyone

—whether commoner or noble—to relate to one as talented and unique as I."

I didn't think you could choke on oatmeal. Fortunately, the waitress saw my predicament and slapped me on the back to get my throat moving again. Even more fortunately, she got to me before Didlius could attempt CPR with his spoon.

Before I could regain my breath and ask how long it would take our "glamorous" beard model to train Didlius—and I would have to ask because he was assuredly too "humble" to bring it up himself—Didlius opened his mouth. "I do see your point on why you can't do it, and it's very astute of you to notice that my speaking skills are a tad lacking. I grew up in a small village and haven't had much of an opportunity to speak in front of a large group of people. I will therefore need your expert guidance and training. Teach me how to speak in a refined manner like you, sir. Teach me how to captivate an audience with only my words and gestures. Teach me how to be more like you." Didlius got down on his knees and began to tug on Judas's robe.

My breath finally returned, and I managed to pull Did off the ground. "I don't think you need to be exactly like him to be a good speaker, Did. Besides, I don't think any amount of training could produce anyone quite like him."

Judas beamed a gigantic smile. I wasn't sure if he misheard me or if he was trying to lull me into a false sense of security. "Very true, Hat. Very true. However, if you were like me, you would lose that special connection with the people; you wouldn't be one of them anymore. Fortunately, I know the perfect person to teach our humble Didlius the art of public speaking and fancy finger waving."

I stared with bated breath in anticipation of him naming himself as this person, and then saying his second, and third choices were also himself. OK, I'm lying. I looked around at the other tables in the common room.

There were only two other occupied tables. The first one held two rather depressed-looking farmers having some sort of silent conversation with facial gestures. The second table held a woman dressed in a coat with an excessive amount of multi-colored pockets. When the waitress asked her about the coat, she began pulling out a different "amazing, potent artifact," which happened to cure an ailment or issue that the waitress didn't know she possessed. The waitress bought a piece of twine tied to a stick that cured her "gingivitis of the brain."

"And that person just so happens to be very close," Judas said while waving his spoon like a conductor's baton. "Brutus."

"Brutus?" Did appeared as surprised as I was.

"Who is this Brutus?" I said. "And what kind of person is he? Or is Brutus one of your nicknames?"

"Brutus is a she," Judas said. "And she was my mentor. She runs the local beard modeling academy, which, despite producing such luminaries in the profession as me and the much less luminous Beardcules, is not well known. Brutus likes to keep her academy rather exclusive and out of the limelight, and she does this by making new potential students find the academy."

"Oh, my," Didlius said. "If the place produced you, I don't know if I'm ready to go through such an eminent and likely demanding institution. Also, how can I possibly grow a beard in a day?"

"While I would like for you to eventually work on that beard —our people will not take you seriously if you do not at least have a passable one—you only need to go through the speaking portion of the program." Judas put his hand on his chin. "Brutus and I will have to come up with something more truncated than what I went through. Perhaps we will focus on the volume and hand waving but skip the memory part. Yes, that's it! We'll use on of my other inventions: cue cards. I'm sure Brutus will have many other ideas on how to speed this up too. I might even be able to coax her into accompanying us, so we can learn on the road."

There was a good chance if this Brutus trained Didlius that he might end up with the same questionable morals as Judas, especially if she ended up coming with us. In every one of the books, there is a critical point where if the hero doesn't do something, the whole story falls apart and the villain wins. While I was sure that Judas wasn't entirely a villain—more misguided and a bit too willing to forgo morality in favor of the quick result—and that I certainly wasn't the hero, I was sure that this was definitely the critical point in this story.

With the unlikelihood of a hero showing up anytime soon, it was up to me to do something, and that something was to get rid of Judas, though without killing him; I was determined not to become like him.

I looked back to Judas to see if I could find some sort of weakness in his eyes, but he was gone. I turned to ask Did where he went, but he wasn't there either. The waitress walked past, so I asked her where they went.

She jumped with a start. "Oh, my. The guy with the neat beard told me you were mute. Your two friends paid for breakfast and your rooms and then went upstairs to pack. They said something about a quest in the woods. Can't imagine what they could be questing for there. I hope they're aware that those are the royal forests and killing any game is punishable by a spanking."

"A spanking?" I asked. "That's not a very bad punishment."

She giggled. "If you saw the Royal Spanker's arms, you wouldn't say that. Few people survive, especially when he puts on 'The Royal Hand of Naughtiness.' Twelve inches of Sculandian Steel will make anyone realize just how bad they were before they meet their maker. I'd much rather be poisoned."

I'm ashamed to say that I considered not telling Judas about the royal forest and then tricking him into killing a king's deer for dinner, but fortunately that thought only lasted a second. The poison idea lasted a little longer. Right as I shook the last awful thought from my skull, the woman in the many-pocketed coat approached.

"Did someone say poison?" She must have asked too loudly, because the two farmers immediately pushed their bowls away and ran for the door.

The waitress hurried after them. "No, wait. She wasn't talking about the food. I swear it isn't poisoned again. We fired that cook yesterday."

The woman in the many-pocketed coat shook her head in embarrassment. "My mistake. I thought you were looking to buy something, but ya wasn't talking to me."

She started to move back to her table, but I grabbed her shoulder and whispered in her ear. "Do you . . . do you actually have poison on you? No, wait, I don't want to know."

She turned back around and appraised me. "Yer right. You don't have it in ya to poison a person to death, but I seen the way ya looked at the fella with the fancy beard. You either hate him or like him a little too much."

"I don't—"

"No, no, boy. I don't have to know which. In my profession, it's better that I don't know. 'The less I know, the longer I live.' That's what my pappy used to say, and he lived to be ninety. Now how long are ya looking to knock him out? An hour? A day? Longer? I warn ya, longer costs a lot." She pulled several packets out of the pockets nearest her knees.

Knock him out? That's dishonorable. The heroes in the stories always defeated their enemies with their courage and skills of arms. Of course, I wasn't a hero and was completely lacking in either of those departments, so . . . It was pretty humane, and as long as I left him in a safe place, he wouldn't get hurt. I could use that time to convince Did that my way was the right way and would be better for the world. It just might work, but there was one problem. "I don't have any money on me, unless buttons are a form of currency here."

I pulled out the contents of my pocket, and I didn't even have the spare button anymore. My wallet and car keys were still there, which was fortunate because I hadn't checked on them in days. The only other things I had were an impressive ball of pocket lint and the ear buds to my phone, which wasn't going to do me a whole lot of good since I'd evidently lost the phone somewhere. I could have offered my key chain too, but it had sentimental value.

The woman's eyes passed right over everything in quick order —I was especially disappointed that the pocket lint was not valuable in this strange world—but she smiled when she reached the ear buds. "I'm not sure what this is exactly, but I'll bet I can pass it off to some gullible noble as a cure for ear wax. Ear wax is a real problem with that lot, so I can charge a fortune for it."

Without the phone, I didn't really need them anymore, but she didn't know that. "Fine, but I want three packets of the day-long stuff."

She bit her lip. "Two packets, and I get the lint too."

Ever the shrewd one, I skimmed a little lint out of the ball when the waitress slammed the door, and then dropped the objects in her hand when she turned back. You never know when you're going to need some extra lint. Unaware of my brilliant subterfuge, she passed over two packets without complaint.

"Be sure to put the contents of one packet in a glass of some liquid, and if ya don't want your handsome bearded fellow to know about it, I'd suggest something dark like an ale or baeva."

I was about to thank her when she began pulling new objects out of her other pockets to try to sell me. Not wanting to trade away the car keys, wallet, or Fridge Buyers Reward Card (seventeen more punches and I'd get the next one half off!), I made up an excuse about having a lot to pack and headed back up the steps to my room.

I entered my room and quickly repacked. I tried to customarily steal the towels, but the inn had wisely chained them to the table. I wasn't sure how they cleaned them like that—and by the look of them, neither had they—but could certainly understand. As the sounds of my companions echoed from the hallway, I left to join them.

"Ah, excellent," Judas said. "Hat has both broken his spell of concentration *and* packed his bag. I told Didlius that you were only busy strategizing how to best approach the packing and would easily catch up to us."

I was a little surprised by Judas's compliment, until it occurred to me that he was trying to lull me into a false sense of security. I managed to smile at him pleasantly as I massaged one of the packets in my pocket.

"Judas," Did said, "if I am to spend time learning at your old bearding school, then how can we possibly be back in time to distribute your pamphlets? Surely it will take more than a couple of days."

Judas chuckled. "While I was waiting for you in the common room this morning, I paid the bartender to send a few messages out to the printer and the Society. As I will likely not be needed for most of your lessons, I hope to sneak out and check on them to be safe. Brutus is more than capable of educating you without my supervision for a few days, though with the keen eye of the wonderful Hat, I may not be needed at all." He patted me on the back awkwardly.

It was good to know there was something he wasn't good at. He was definitely up to something. The feeling of the packet on my fingers calmed my nerves considerably.

"Judas, why don't we have one last celebratory drink before

we head out?" I asked. "This trip should be truly epic and all epic quests should begin with at least some celebration."

"That's true," Did said. "In the stories of my childhood, the brave knights always had a parade or last toast before they set out on a quest."

"Didn't you two have enough last night?" Judas shook his head. "No, you will still need to be at your sharpest, as this place will not be so easy to locate. I found it once a decade ago, but Brutus likes to change the landmarks, so that previous students cannot sell the location or tell friends."

While I tried to think of some other excuse to get him to buy a drink, he and Did started walking. I hurried after them. I had to think of something, but the only thing that came out was that it was my birthday. Unfortunately, we were fifteen minutes outside of town when it did, and they told me that Paruxians didn't have the concept of a birthday; the closest thing was the day they became a man or woman when they got a wheel of cheese and a bottle of milk from their parents. I hastily jotted those facts down. I had other things on my mind, so I couldn't truly enjoy them, but I knew I would when I got back home.

"So, how do we find this place?" Did asked. "You mentioned something about landmarks. What should we be looking for?"

Judas slowly spun completely around. "My first clue was a tree."

My eyes moved back and forth through the thick forest. "I found one." Sarcasm dripped from my voice. I bit my lip at my stupidity. I had to remember that I was supposed to be lulling him into a false sense of security too.

"I found one too," Did shouted excitedly, "although it might be the same one as Hat. What does your tree look like?"

"My apologies," Judas said with his eyes half-closed in concentration, "I should have been more specific. It was a special tree. A tree unlike any of the others. The kind of tree that haunts you in your dreams, but in a good way."

Didlius stared longingly at his spoon. "I know exactly what you mean."

Judas eyed the spoon but quickly went back to looking for the tree when he saw me notice that.

I giggled. "If there's people like Judas back home, I might have to start a tree dating site: GetWood.com." I was supposed to try to be nicer to him, however, jokes like that were too hard to resist. At least I held back on asking him if he'd been tested for root rot.

"A very amusing joke, Hat. Your wit is top-notch as always. If I had more time, I would join you in your jocularity, but my mind is elsewhere at the moment." He ran about fifty yards forward and did another slow, complete turn. "I cannot remember what this tree looks like, but it's still deeply etched in my subconscious, so I will know it when I see it."

We continued moving approximately fifty yards forward, looking around, and then moving forward again every few minutes.

"Can you remember anything particular about this tree?" I asked. "How was it special? Was it a different type of tree than the others? Was it bigger? Smaller? Wider? Have unusually colorful leaves?"

"Did it glow?" Didlius asked from behind us.

Judas scratched his head. "I can't remember, and I think we'd notice a glowing tree immediately, Didlius." He jogged forward another fifty yards.

Did sprinted to catch up. "Oh. Of course you would. How silly of me. But what about a building made of glowing wood?"

Judas and I both turned around and looked to where Did had been. In the clearing in the middle of the dense woods stood a two-story wooden building with a sign that said "Brutus's Secret Beard-Model College Visitor's Center."

"Hmm," Judas said. "Perhaps the old way proved too difficult for the younger generation."

We climbed the few steps and entered the building. The inside looked identical to the inn from earlier. At first, I thought we had wasted a day walking in a circle and had come to the back entrance of the same building, but realized they must have been made using the same design when I looked out the back window and only saw more trees and not the town.

Judas confidently strode to the bartender, making sure to point his beard forward. "I would like to see Brutus, please."

The bartender glanced up but continued to wipe down the bar. "Haven't heard of anyone with that name."

"What about her assistant, Cadula? She was a great friend and advisor to me when I attended this institution."

The bartender didn't look up this time. "Nope."

Judas rolled his eyes. "Can I speak to someone at the school? One of the teachers? Drapus? Lorconicus? Dug?"

The bartender finally looked at Judas. "Not sure what school you're talking about. This is a bar."

"It is not. It's a visitor's center." He looked behind the bartender at the liquor bottles on the wall and smirked. "That also happens to contain a bar. Fine, a bar that's attached to a school."

"Nope. No school here, only a bar. Now, are you going to buy anything? If not, I'm going to have to ask you to leave."

"We'll have three drinks, please, bartender," I said. "And make them dark. Extra dark."

"Hat, while I know you want to celebrate our quest," Judas whispered, "that should be done on completion, not in the middle."

I whispered back, "I think he wants us to buy something before he'll reveal anything."

"Ahh, it's part of the test. Very clever of Brutus, to make prospective students think they had found the place, but then have to go through a test with this stout guardian."

"You might be right, but he's also a businessman who wants to make some money. I can't imagine he gets a lot of customers in the middle of the woods."

The barkeep set three drinks down in front of us. The drinks were indeed dark, so dark, in fact, that when I stuck my finger in it a quarter of an inch from the glass, I couldn't see it. There seemed to be little bits of something floating around, which would normally have been a bad thing, but in this case, they would make it almost impossible to notice the powder.

Didlius happily began guzzling, but Judas was too absorbed in getting information out of the barkeep to even look at his. "Now that we have purchased drinks, barkeep, do your answers change at all?"

"Some of them might."

Judas slid a few coins toward the barkeep. "Is Brutus about, and if so, can we see her?"

Judas had leaned so far forward that I thought he might fall over the top of the bar. I almost considered pulling him back, but realized in that position, he would be unable to see me spike his drink. The barkeeper and Did were too focused on Judas's odd pose to notice either. I ripped open the crude packet and poured it in. Most of the tiny crystals slowly melted away into the dark brew. I swirled my finger through it a few times to get the last of the stragglers to blend in and soon the drink was indistinguishable from my own.

The bartender turned around to clean off a few bottles. "Don't know who that is, and no, you can't see her."

I whispered in Judas's ear, "He won't tell you because you're being rude and not drinking. Drink some and his answer might change."

"You're very wise, friend Hat, but I believe he's not answering because of the new visitors who entered behind you."

Just my luck. I finally get to flawlessly complete a clever plan and some jerks show up and interrupt. I scanned the area behind me but no one was there. When I turned back around to ask Judas where they went, my eyes caught the beer in my glass swaying back and forth.

"Ahh, must have been the wind," he said. "My apologies. Why don't you drink up while I interrogate this bartender further?"

"I will. He looks like he's about to crack. Look."

If Judas was half as clever as he thought he was, I would have been in real trouble, but he looked back at the bartender just as I told him to. I quickly switched our drinks back, then, to be safe, traded my new one with Didlius's half-drunk glass.

"Listen, bartender," Judas said. "We would like admittance to Brutus's school, whether she is currently in attendance or not. I'm its most famous alumnus. Perhaps you have heard of me? Listed as the number one beard model in Paruxia for five consecutive years and beard model of the century in *Judas Monthly*."

To be safe, I poured the second packet in Judas's current drink.

Recognition dawned on the barkeeper's face. "Ohhhhhh. You're Beardcules! I used to have a poster of you when I was little."

"Beardcules? That hack. He was only number one beard model in Paruxia for four consecutive years and was never named beard model of the century in my publication. Also, you're at least a decade older than him. How could you have possibly had posters of him when you were young?" Judas's face looked like it was going to begin to sprout flames, so I helpfully handed him his drink, which he downed in one long swig.

Relieved that I had finally gotten him to down the tainted

brew, I took a few sips of the Didlius-tested, half-drunk glass in front of me. I grinned at Judas, and he grinned back. *Now who's the smart one, you pompous jerk?*

He began to sway, and I laughed internally. *But if he's swaying, why is he slowly getting higher than me? Why is the bar getting higher than me too? Why . . . Where are my legs? Oh, wait, there they are. Right in front of me where I left them. I just couldn't feel them. The ground is nice and cold. So nice I could. . .*

SHE LET ME OUT FOR BAD BEHAVIOR

I could feel my legs again. That was nice. My skin tingled against the cold air. That was really nice. I was on a bed too, and not on the floor. I don't think I need to tell you what that was. OK, fine. It was nice. Realizing the tingling was caused by my lack of clothing was not as nice. They even took my socks. Why do they always take my socks?

I was naked in a barely lit room and had no idea who had put me there. Also, I could see from the light coming through the cracks in the door that I was the only person there. That meant either the bartender, Judas, or Didlius himself had put me there.

I laughed at that last one. Did was my friend, and even though he trusted Judas implicitly for some reason, he wouldn't do that to me. It had to be the bartender or Judas. The first one was probably working for Brutus, and she was close with Judas . . . Although, it wouldn't be even the slightest bit surprising if Judas remembered Brutus adoring him but had badly misread the situation. Did and I were guilty by association, and they had thrown Did and Judas into another cell.

There was also the possibility that sign on the building had been a ruse. The bartender could have been an enemy of Brutus's and made the sign to lure unsuspecting potential students to their doom. Whatever the case, my goal was the same: to figure out how to get out.

I was indeed in a cell. I could tell by the large metal door with a small slit at the top that seemed to only open from the outside. The only thing beside the bed I was on was a tall ceramic bowl that I assumed was their version of a toilet.

I searched the room frantically for some clue on how I would get out. I fought back the constant need to shiver and began to claw at the thick, metal door. I really wished I hadn't trimmed my nails a few days before. *Damn my dad and his sensible lessons on good hygiene.* No matter how long it took, I had to get out so that I could write down this epic tale. I collapsed in front of the door, and a few seconds later, the slit opened to reveal a pair of blood-shot eyes.

"Is Hat awake?" a familiar, arrogant voice asked from behind the eyes.

"Apprentice, give me a minute . . . dang," a voice that I assumed at first to be male said, but soon realized belonged to a lifetime, female smoker. "My happiest day has always been the day ya graduated, though now that you're back, I realize it was because it got a lot quieter after that. Now shut up and let me get a peek. I can still take the diploma away from ya."

"My apologies, master." I pictured Judas bowing pathetically and crying in a corner after he said that.

The bloodshot eyes began to look back and forth before resting on me. "There he is. He's awake all right . . . Why's he naked?"

"I heard there was a shortage of clothing, master," Judas said. "So, I had the guards take his."

The eyes disappeared from the slit followed by a hard slap.

"Do not lie to me, boy," she said. "I know ya didn't hear of any clothing shortage. Now go get his clothes!"

The eyes reappeared and focused on me. "Hi there. My name is Brutus, and welcome to my academy. Sorry about that; the boy does have a vengeful streak that I did my best to work out of him, but some things can't be fixed. Can I get ya anything?"

"Could you get me out of here?" I asked.

She laughed as she slid my clothes through the slot. "Yer a cheeky one, all right. My boy said you were one to watch, and he sure didn't lie." She hacked up another laugh. It sounded like it hurt. "No, yer gonna stay right there for a while longer. I'd kill you, but my boy says that could cause problems with that Didlius rube, and we need him for the plan."

"I'm right here, master," Judas huffed. "There's no need to talk about me like I'm not."

"A plan, you say?" I asked as I put my clothes back on. "My, I sure would like to hear that. As an amateur planner myself, I do love to hear about plans created by true maestros of that art. Why, if Judas is the greatest planner in Paruxia, I'd imagine you, as his mentor, must be the greatest in all of Vyenra or likely even the universe."

"Very astute of you, Hat," Judas said. "With you out of the way, we can finally get Didlius to do everything we want. After the pamphlets are distrib—Oww!"

"Don't act like that hurt, ya sissy," Brutus said. "And what kinda idiot tells their enemy his plan? If he gets out, he could ruin it. And you know my policy on bein thwarted."

"My apologies, master, but I'm really excited about murdering those priests. You know what they did to me."

The eyes turned, and I could hear a patting sound. "I do, boy, and I know ya been patient, more patient than anyone I know, so I'll forgive ya this one time. You'll have to be a little more patient though, because we still have three steps to go. By the way, did ya get ahold of that magician?"

"I did, master, but she's recently taken a nasty injury and recovering. She says she should be in good enough shape to travel in about a week."

"Excellent. So strange to find a non-Atlian mage, and a south-westerner at that, but times are a-changin."

They had to be talking about Fred, so at least part of their plan was likely to fail spectacularly unless they needed her to pull coins out of someone's ear or "look over there." "Wow. An actual wizard. That plan you can't tell me about sure must be brilliant. Say, when the priests are out of the way, is that when you usurp Didlius, or does that come later?"

Judas said, "Later," at the same time Brutus said, "We don't."

The eyes spun quickly around, giving me a good look at the back of her thin, graying hair. "That's not the plan we agreed on, boy! We need a sweet simpleton that the masses can identify with. Yer too arrogant to be likeable by most, and I plan on retiring in a few years."

"Of course, master," Judas said sheepishly. "I only misspoke."

"You better have." Her head began to turn back around.

"I don't think he did," I said. "Why, the whole time we were heading here, that's all he talked about. 'Brutus is a great teacher, but incredibly gullible,' he said. 'We'll get her to teach you every-thing she knows, lure her out of the protection of her compound, and then . . .' I'd finish that sentence, but the rest is too gruesome to repeat."

"What do you have ta say for yourself, boy?" Brutus asked.

"He's lying?" Judas said unconvincingly.

I stifled a chuckle. "He also said that he's surpassed you at every skill and that he only needs you because he's 'too important to bother with the lowly teaching part.' Oh, and that you smell like mothballs."

I couldn't even see the back of her head anymore. As the sounds of the fight echoed throughout the hallway outside, I tried to figure out a plan for how I could escape to take advantage of the distraction. I renewed my assault on the door, but it was obvious that it would take decades to dig through the metal. Desperate and out of ideas, I turned the handle.

The door opened in a whoosh, and I spilled out into the hallway. I hadn't expected it to work, so I put too much into the push, causing the door to slam to the full extent of its range. Unfortunately, there happened to be a person inside of that range, and it connected hard with her back.

Brutus tumbled to the ground, the contents of the pockets on her multi-colored coat spilling across the thin hallway. At least now I knew how Judas had defeated me in that bar. I found solace that he had only won by having help. I wondered if those packets she had given me had contained any knockout powder at all.

I should have been focusing on getting out of there, but Brutus wasn't stirring at all. I was raised to think of others first, and I'm proud of my good moral upbringing, but given the situation, I don't think anyone would have held it against me to not stop and check if my potential killer was hurt. Unfortunately, instinct took over, and I knelt to check the nasty cut on her head. With the tight corridor, it would have been almost impossible to get by Judas to the stairs without a fight anyway. While I have been described as a "scrappy" fighter, Judas was bigger than me by fifty pounds, and if his claims of martial arts training were even somewhat true, I wouldn't have stood much of a chance against him anyway.

"If you've done serious harm to her," Judas said, "I'm not protecting you from what her students do to you in retaliation."

I rolled her over. Blood covered half her face and her eyes were completely glazed over. The cut on her head was much worse than I had feared. I almost panicked before my CPR training took over, and I remembered to check her pulse.

"She's alive, but she needs medical attention. Do you have a doctor here?"

Judas half-smiled. "We do have a few."

I tore off my vest and used it to staunch the wound. "Could you go *get* them?"

"Now, Hat, why would I do that?"

"Because you don't . . ." As I took in the growing grin and the way he was maneuvering to block as much of the passage as possible, all the pieces finally clicked. "You want her to die, and you're probably going to claim this was all part of your plan, whether it was or not."

"You're right, I am going to claim . . . I mean, I planned this. I came here with Didlius so that he could learn as much about speaking as he could in the week we've been here, and then I was going to remove her so I could take control of the staff and students to form the backbone of my new religion. You're going to hang for this, which will put the second to last obstacle out of my way."

Did he say a week? Was I really out for that long? No time, Hat. Focus. The bleeding had slowed, but her pulse was getting fainter. I realized I had to try something or she would surely die. "Oh, look, a newspaper reporter, and she wants to interview the world's greatest beard model. Too bad Beardcules isn't here."

Judas's head snapped around so quick I was sure it would twist off. "Beardcules! He doesn't even have a beard anymore, and even if he did, he'd only be fifth, fourth tops. Stubblius and The Hairy Visage are easily better than him."

I lowered my shoulders and charged, but right before I connected with his back, he took a step to the side. I barely put my arms out before I connected with the hard stone wall. It still hurt, but a lot less than it would have had it been my head. I bounced and landed a few inches from Brutus.

Judas turned back around and crossed his arms. "I knew you

were going to do that. Newspaper reporters don't appear in dungeons of secret beard modeling academies."

I rolled over so I could rest on my knees to stand up. "What about a biographer?"

He gave me a patronizing look but cut it short as the sound of a clanging tray echoed down the hallway behind him. I smirked at him this time. When our new guest arrived, Judas would have to go get help or risk alienating his potential new followers. My only hope was that Brutus was conscious enough to have heard Judas refuse to get help.

Our new arrival dropped the tray as soon as he entered view. My hopes rose but then crashed when I took in his face. Didlius was my friend, but he was also not terribly reliable. There was also the strong possibility that Judas was planning on eliminating him soon, and Did had walked right into the next stage of his plan.

Judas's face twisted into mock shock. "My word, Didlius. It's so good that you've arrived when you did. We were letting Hat go, like you requested, when he turned on Brutus and savagely attacked her. If you had only arrived a minute sooner, we could have saved her."

I glanced over to Brutus. "She's still breathing."

Judas didn't seem the least bit put off by my revelation. "No thanks to you . . . She'll stop before we can get help, so don't waste your efforts, my noble protégé. It seems that your laudable but misplaced need to forgive has caused the death of my beloved mentor and friend." He buried his face in his arm and made ridiculous sobbing sounds.

"Did, ignore the over-actor and get help. She's still alive."

Did's face contorted in what I assumed was confusion and not facial spasms. "I . . . I want to believe you, Hat, but I can't believe a murderer."

"How can I be a murderer if she's still alive?"

Judas raised his face quickly, revealing a complete lack of tears. "Intent is everything in Paruxian law." His face quickly shot back into his arm as he began sobbing louder.

"Well, I didn't intend to hurt her either. The door got away from me." I desperately wanted to slap Judas, but that wouldn't have looked good, given the situation.

"Preposterous," Judas said through his sobbing. "Why would the door be open if we were keeping you locked up?"

"You just said you were in the process of letting me go. While I've never let someone go from prison before, I assume that usually involves unlocking the door."

"Well, now you'll never know because you've killed my master." Judas dropped his arm and immediately switched from pretend inconsolable to smug. "You'll never escape the cells in the next level, because we only open those to put a prisoner in, and then remove the body."

I desperately wanted to respond in kind but knew I couldn't. The look in Brutus's eyes, as well as the sudden terrible smell coming from her, told me any hopes of getting her treatment would be a waste. My only hope was Didlius. "Did, remember who's the voice of reason and compassion here. Listen to the calm tone in my voice. This was an accident. Judas probably caused this. You can't trust him. He's a terrible person."

For once, Didlius didn't waffle at all and immediately responded with confidence and surety. "I'm sorry, but I can't believe the word of an admitted murderer. However, due to all you have done for us, Jaenia has instructed me that I owe you at least a sixty-second head start."

"But Didlius!" Judas and I said in unison.

"Fifty-nine . . . Fifty-eight . . ."

I wanted to cry. I wanted to scream. I wanted to hit Judas. But the count kept descending. When I tried to walk past them, Judas moved in front of me, but Didlius forced him back with Spoon-Scalibur. As much as I wanted to argue, the always smiling face of my friend was replaced by the resolute, hardened face of a great leader. He had finally become the person he was destined to be, and it was all because of me.

WHERE'S A HERO WHEN YOU NEED ONE? NO, SERIOUSLY. DO YOU HAVE ONE I COULD BORROW?

I don't remember much of my trip up those stairs, out of that building, or into the forest. I think I passed several people, but my tear-stained face must have told all I passed to stay out of my way. It is possible someone tried to stop me, but they obviously failed because by the time my wits returned to me, no signs of the place I had left were in sight. What I could see were trees, birds, and a stream. In case I was being pursued, I made sure to use the stream to mask my path by running down it and then exiting in a different direction.

As much as I wanted to see the entirety of Didlius's founding of The One, my part in that story was clearly at an end. Judas had won, and Didlius no longer wanted anything to do with me. It was disappointing, but sometimes you meet someone who's better than you. There's no fault in that. Someone had to lose. Normally, that wouldn't have stung at all. This time it shouldn't have either, especially since my goal had been to do as little damage to the future as possible, so that I wouldn't change my favorite books. However, Judas was an unscrupulous, pompous jerk—descriptives that were the opposite of everything I stood for—and it was hard to stomach that kind Didlius thought ill of me.

I ran as far as my anger-fueled body would allow and then willed myself to run more. Eventually, my determination was overruled by the limits of my physical fitness, and I had to stop. I dove into a four-foot-deep indentation and covered it with fallen tree branches. When the pounding in my heart dropped enough, I listened for anything that might indicate pursuit. Besides the sounds of birds chirping in the distance and a squeaking squirrel who didn't seem to like how close I was to a prized nut, nothing else could be heard.

I had some decisions to make. Should I continue my flight or stay put and hope any pursuit passed by? And then, where should I go?

Unable to come up with an answer, I eventually succumbed to my fatigue and fell asleep, though that may have been my mind's way of avoiding a difficult decision. I had a wonderful dream of working for an author who treated his assistant like an equal. Right as the author began massaging my temple as thanks for helping her with a difficult chapter, her hands suddenly became very cold. I tried to push her hands off but recoiled from a sudden sharp pain.

As my eyes shot open to investigate, I realized I was being massaged by a large sword. Lying under the pile of tree branches, I couldn't see anything more than about a foot of the sword.

"Oh, good," the deep voice close to the sword said. "That sound didn't belong to an animal. Now, whoever you are, could you come out of there?"

I pushed the branches off slowly and raised my hands. The owner of the sword was massive—at least seven feet tall—and I would have been terrified if I didn't know him. My eyes darted back and forth, but I couldn't see Wolfette anywhere.

"Hat!" Big Baby dropped his sword, leaned forward, and embraced me in a huge hug.

I squirmed to try to escape from his unintentionally painful embrace. He must have realized my squeaks indicated I wanted to be let loose and set me down gently.

"Sorry. I forget my strength sometimes. I'm just so glad to see you and even gladder that you're still alive. When we saw the river devour the town, we assumed you were still in it."

"Did and I . . . happened to be outside of town when the river mysteriously changed course." As much as I knew I could trust him, I was not ready to take the blame for that event or pin it on Didlius. "We've recently decided to go our separate ways, however."

Big Baby smiled sadly. "We were about a mile out of town when we heard the loud crash, but I couldn't stop Wolfette so we could go back and check on you. Almost a day later, we finally managed to corner Gu and his friend when the trees started laughing at us. Wolfette got frustrated by the laughing, and when I was finally able to extract her from her assault on an oak, we noticed that Gu and his friend were gone. A few days ago, we got a tip from a lady in a multi-colored coat that they're holed up in a town on the other side of those bushes over there."

"Is Billiam still with Gu?" I asked hopefully.

"Yes. My source said he's somehow in charge of the town. As soon as Wolfette wakes up, we were going to charge in and attack Gu."

Lying on the ground, barely covered by the edge of the bush, lay Wolfette. She looked so peaceful sprawled out on the ground, and it was one of the few times I had ever seen her with anything close to a smile.

"After Wolfette tried to poke the bartender with the tip of her axe after he asked for a tip, the lady in the multi-colored coat gave her a free drink that knocked her out. When I went to intervene, she calmed me down and sold me these packets with sleeping crystals. It's so much easier to just knock Wolfette out most of the time and wake her up when I need her, but I used the last packet, so it's back to watching her constantly. She should be awake in a few minutes. Wanna help us?"

He directed me to the bushes, and I peeked through to see a town of about ten buildings. Every minute or so an armed person passed into view. Unfortunately, there didn't seem to be any pattern to their patrols.

"What we need is . . . food," I said. "I'm sure there's something else, but I'm not sure when the last time I ate was."

Big Baby opened his pack and handed me something round. I honestly don't remember what it was, but it was hard, tasteless, and glorious. I devoured it and took another.

"Thank you. Now I can focus. What we need is a plan," I said between swigs from Big Baby's canteen. I looked around for a book, hoping it would contain a chapter titled "Brilliant Plan to Defeat Gu, Get Me Home, and Hopefully Not Die." Unfortunately, there was no such book there.

Big Baby scratched his chin with his spare hand. "Great. What is it?"

"Charge in and disembowel Gu." Wolfette yawned as she rose.

"That's not much of a plan," I said. "I think it's missing a few parts like how we find him without getting disemboweled ourselves."

Wolfette rubbed her axes together and was about to charge out of the bush and presumably straight into the town, but Big Baby grabbed her and shifted her into a bear hug.

"Detailshhh," Wolfette said through Big Baby's chest. "Aaa'm not a thinker; Aaa'm a doer."

"Mom would be so proud if she heard that," Big Baby said.

"That'shhh not what I meanpf," she mumbled through his chest.

"So, what's the plan, Hat?"

I gave up on looking for the book that didn't exist. "I'm not the plan guy. I'm the assistant. I assist with things, like I'm doing now by presenting the topic for discussion."

Unable to get her arms to move, Wolfette began banging her head against his chest. She didn't accomplish anything, but she was making a light dinging noise that would likely attract attention before long.

"You're the one who outthought that wizard," Big Baby said. "She had the rest of us fooled."

"We werpf not. I would haf figured her out after I killed hrpf."

I bit my lip. "I guess I did, but it was more luck than anything. Everyone has a good idea every now and again, but that still doesn't make me a strategist."

"You also figured out that whole prophecy in the village."

"That's only two times. I'm sure you've both figured things out twice in your lives."

He looked down at his struggling sister. She had given up on headbutting his chest plate and had moved on to biting it.

"In two months since she dragged me into this, the only thing she's come up with is charge and slash."

Wolfette stopped squirming. "Notpf true. One time I shhh-lashed and then charged."

"Her plan . . . plans don't leave me any time to do anything more than clean up after her and make sure she doesn't kill too many people. Like right now, the only thing I can think about is how to get her to not realize she has other limbs free—which I shouldn't have to tell you I'm not doing a very good job of." He pulled his legs together a second after her knee connected with his groin area.

Who was the leader? It definitely wasn't Wolfette, unless our plan was to see what she was going to do, then do the opposite. Big Baby literally had his hands full keeping his sister at bay.

If I did simple subtraction, that left only me. But I was an assistant, not a leader. I only helped the much smarter, together person get the job done. I wasn't supposed to get the job done myself. I mean, sure, I had finished Harry's novel after he tried to lie and cheat his way to an ending that made him look good, but that was unusual. I had only been doing what was right because there was no one else there to make sure it happened. But that was on Earth. Here, I hadn't once thought up a plan on the entire journey, except the two times that Big Baby mentioned, and the numerous plans I had come up with for Didlius. Those would have worked out too if Judas hadn't interrupted.

I was a leader! Technically it was by default, but that still counts for something. I mean, it wasn't like there was going to be some knight in shining armor charging in at the nick of time. No guy in a cape. No secret agent in a fancy suit. No rogue cop who's the only one who can see what's really going on. No reprogrammed robot from the future in cool sunglasses. No masked man popping out of the bushes to save everything. No—

To the left of Big Baby, a man in a mask popped out of a bush, his cape flowing even though the wind wasn't blowing, his badge shining like justice, his outfit so white my mind could only process it as "good" and not a color. "Did somebody say they needed a plan?"

"No," Wolfette mumbled into Big Baby's chest.

The masked man deflated. "Darn. I was going to sneak into that village over there to overthrow that vile Billiam and his extremely friendly but murderous companion, Gu." He pointed to the left. "I think I see another clearing. Hopefully there's different people in it that need my help."

"Wait," Big Baby and I said in unison.

The masked man gave a dazzling smile and posed like a superhero. "Do you need some tips on what makes a nutritious breakfast, to know why breaking the law is bad, or to learn about proper road safety?"

"Maybe later," I said. "How about that plan thing on how to sneak up on Billiam and Gu?"

He looked at the palm of his hand. I could see writing on it. "Ahh, well, I'll go into the village in normal clothes, disguised as either a mild-mannered reporter or playboy billionaire, and when they aren't looking, slip some sleeping potion into the barrels of beer they've been drinking from and the town's well. That should knock out Billiam and most of their help, though I wouldn't count on Gu, as I've never actually seen him drink."

"That's a pretty good plan," Big Baby said. "Wolfette, if I let you out, will you promise not to go charging in until our new friend here gives us the signal?"

"Yeshhh," she said.

"Splendid," the masked man said as he pushed his way back through the bushes. "Now no peeking. I have to change. When you see smoke coming from the village, that's the signal."

Big Baby and Wolfette both gave him enthusiastic salutes. I felt bad that mine was half-hearted, but this guy had come from nowhere and usurped my moment of triumph. I had finally figured out my purpose, and he was taking it from me. Worst of all, he was dressed better than me. Or at least he had been. The sound of him changing had died down a few minutes before. I reasoned that he hadn't taken his costume with him. I considered hiding it from him or taking the cape because it was neat, but that would have been wrong.

Why was he helping us? Who was he?

Wolfette and Big Baby stared at the village patiently, their eyes never leaving it, except when Big Baby checked his progress on sharpening their weapons. He had handed me a short sword while our friend was changing.

"Guys," I said, "are you sure it's a good idea to follow this stranger?"

"Of course," Big Baby said. "He had a badge, and you should always follow an officer of the law."

"Unless he's trying to arrest you," Wolfette added, "at which point you either stabby stab him repeatedly, or run away if you think you're outnumbered. It's the mercenary way."

"Did anyone actually get a good look at the badge though?" I asked.

Big Baby sighed. "Hat, is this about you not being leader? I know you're used to being the hero, but sometimes it's about doing what's best for the group. Like now, for instance, we need to follow this strange guy we've never met who appeared out of nowhere and came up with a miraculous plan that will solve everything." Big Baby stopped staring at the village and turned back. "Now that I say it out loud, I'm beginning to see your point."

"I don't," Wolfette said.

"Did you say it out loud?"

She shook her head and then said the plan out loud. "I still don't."

"What's your plan, Hat?"

As smoke billowed from the village, I hastily told my companions my brilliant plan. I know it's cheap to not tell you the plan as well, but I have to build up the suspense somehow. It'll be worth it, and you'll be so pleasantly surprised you'll forgive me for what you're feeling now. Trust me.

"Hat," Big Baby said, "'trust me' isn't really much of a plan. We also don't like to be pleasantly surprised. Could you maybe tell us what it is, so we can be ready to follow it?"

"Oh, sorry. I like to prepare what I'm going to write for the book in my head, and I got a little caught up in it. This sort of thing never happens in the movies. They just fade away as the hero tells the plan and then everyone knows what it is."

Big Baby tapped his foot impatiently.

"Right, the plan. We all head to the center of town toward our new friend, pretending to follow his plan. Big Baby says he's getting thirsty and so does Wolfette, so you both take a drink out of the supposedly tainted liquid. You then pretend to get sleepy, having forgotten the drink was poisoned, and pass out as close as possible to Gu. Then the villagers who are not knocked out, like he said, all jump up to surround me. I'll go into a long speech with lots of loud noises and exaggerated gestures to distract them. That should give you two enough time to sneak up on Gu and kill him."

A second stack of smoke shot up from the village like a giant "hurry up, all ready" sign, and we walked toward our destiny.

YOU CAN SLEEP THROUGH THIS PART, BUT I'M NOT RESPONSIBLE FOR WHAT HAPPENS TO YOUR FACE

Our "friend" stood right at the center of the village next to the well. I recognized him in spite of him having changed into a voluminous robe because he had kept his mask on. There was also the fact that he was the only one in view who wasn't lying on the ground. A group of gruff-looking individuals lay near his feet, snoring a bit too aggressively in their armor, with weapons lying inches from their hands. My two companions and I stood opposite a large throne holding the "sleeping" Gu. Billiam was nowhere in sight.

Our friend waved excitedly as he noticed me. "Hat, over here."

I pretended to accidentally trip on as many weapons as possible, kicking them across the village. "So, they're all asleep as planned?"

He weakly kicked a rather hefty man a few times. The man didn't cry out but his left eye did open for a few seconds. "Yep. All sleeping away. It would take an earthquake to wake them. I checked all the houses. No men, women, children, or pets awake. Stab away at your leisure."

I winked at Big Baby, and he winked back. When he just

stood there and didn't ask to get a drink, I winked at him again in rapid succession, alternating my eyes in Morse code. Since there was no way he could have known Morse code, he just stood there in confusion.

Wolfette, however, took the hint. "Aheh! Aheh! I think I need a drink to cure my coughy cough. If we're going to stab all these people, we will need to fill up lest we have to stop halfway through." She pointed at the well.

Big Baby kicked one of the prostrate forms. "They seem to be sleeping pretty well. We can stop and get a drink after we're done."

"Aheh! Aheh!" She pointed at the well. "My . . . cough." She had the sides of her axes on her hips.

Realization dawned on Big Baby's face. "Oh, yes. Your couu-uugh. That's right, you need to quench your thirst with a cool drink from this well . . . and while I'm at it, I'll get one for myself."

Big Baby grabbed a nearby cup, dipped it in a bucket hanging over the well, and took a long, pretend drink. He then repeated the gesture for Wolfette. The masked man watched expectantly and did a terrible job of hiding a smile.

Big Baby pointed behind the masked man. "I will start my bloody work over there while my sister starts from the other side." As planned, he didn't point to where Wolfette was headed in the hopes that the masked man wouldn't notice she was maneuvering to stand behind the throne that held the "sleeping" Gu.

"Great," Big Baby continued. "Now that I am in position, I will begin to stab these obviously sleeping people." He raised his blade slowly. "Oh, no. What is this? I am too overcome with tiredness to finish my blow. What could have possibly done this? Of course! It was the water that I should have remembered was doused with a potion of sleep, and being the fool that I am, I gave it to my sister as well. Oh, no. She has collapsed too."

He crashed to the ground in even more exaggerated fake snores than the nearby residents. I could hear Wolfette crash to the ground right behind the throne.

"Darn," I said to the masked man. "It looks like my companions are out. Well, good thing the two of us didn't absentmindedly drink anything too. It's also a good thing you're on our side as I might not be able to finish murdering all of these mindless followers of Billiam and Gu before they wake."

The masked man began to cackle as he moved in front of me. "Did you really think some stranger would magically appear and solve all of your problems?"

I shrugged. "Well, I didn't think there was any magic involved, per se, and you didn't solve all my problems. For instance, I haven't been able to find a single shirt that matches my khakis since I got here and no one will accept any of my credit cards. But beyond those small points, I knew you were going to betray us all along."

"Ha ha! Fair points, but you have still fallen right into my trap. You see, when you thought I left to go poison all the water and alcohol, I didn't leave at all. I stayed hidden in a different bush so I could listen to your plan. That's why I really did put sleeping potions in this well, so your companions are in fact knocked out, leaving you quite defenseless. Grab him, fellow followers of Billiamism."

Several of his followers rose, but I forced the two closest ones to pause with an exuberant retort before they could grab me. "Ha ha ha! I knew you knew about my plan, so I told Big Baby to only pretend to drink from the well. Get up, Big Baby." I could only see his feet sticking out from behind the other side of the well, but they didn't move.

"Ha ha ha ha! I knew you knew that I knew, so I made sure to have one of my men knock him over the head with a cudgel."

His followers took another step forward, but I stopped them

with a few exaggerated gestures and my strongest speaking voice. "Ha ha ha ha ha!" I counted the "has" off with my fingers an extra time to make sure I got the right amount, then continued. "I made sure that he wore a helmet so you couldn't knock him out."

"Ha ha ha ha ha ha! My follower of Billianity made sure to knock his helmet off and hit him a few extra times really hard to make sure." He looked toward the man nearest Big Baby, who nodded in confirmation.

"Ha ha ha ha ha ha ha! I knew that you knew that . . . Can we just stop the you-knews and ha's? It's getting really hard to keep track of."

He scratched his chin. "Sure. It would save a lot of time, and I'm going to run out of fingers soon."

"Great. Now, I planned for that too, so Big Baby put on a second helmet, and I'm going to guess you knew that too, so you had your guy take that one off as well." He nodded. "So, I, knowing you'd do that, was only distracting you while my real plan went off, but you knew that, so you had another follower subdue Wolfette before she could slash Gu from behind. However, I disarmed your followers near where Wolfette is lying now, so you had them all have backup weapons, hidden in their clothes. I knew about the backup weapons, so I had Wolfette stab them with the spikes on her axes as she passed, but you knew she'd stab them so you had more people hidden. I guessed that and locked all the doors to the houses before we entered your line of sight. You guessed that, so you left the windows open. I closed the windows. You gave them a key to the locks. I broke the locks. You changed the locks. I broke those. You removed the second locks. I lit the houses on fire. You gave some other followers buckets to put the fires out. I drilled holes in the buckets. You plugged the buckets. I put extra holes in them. You got new buckets. I lit those buckets on fire and danced on them to distract your people while Wolfette took out Gu."

"When did you have time to dance?"

I gave him a little shimmy.

He gave me a thoughtful nod. "That is distracting."

"Thank you. You knew I'd dance to distract them, so I had Big Baby circle around and kill the guys who had buckets."

He grinned. "We've firmly established that Big Baby is unconscious."

"He is? Then who's that over there?"

"Where?" He looked left to right.

"Behind you."

He and his followers looked behind them, so I turned around and ran toward Gu with my sword at the ready. Unfortunately, he was already up and had Wolfette's arms pinned behind her back.

The masked man laughed. "Ha, etcetera, etcetera! I knew you'd do that too. And I also knew you'd have Wolfette try to stab Gu from behind when I discovered this ruse."

"Did you know—"

"Yes, but I'm not a fan of watermelon. I also know you don't know my real identity." He pulled off his mask to reveal the old man who runs the failing amusement park! Oh, right. There is no old man who runs a failing amusement park in this story. It was Billiam.

"I knew that too, actually."

His mouth dropped. "You did?"

"Well, yeah. You're the only other white guy I've met in Paruxia."

"Damn me and my love of comfortable and nonrestrictive short sleeve shirts." He was too busy stamping his feet in frustration to turn around and look at me.

I should probably point out that I hadn't noticed his pale skin tone against the white outfits he had worn up until a few seconds before I said that. I was only trying to distract him . . . I think. You see, my dizzying array of quasi-logic also had the effect of confusing me too, though not as much as the townspeople, who were completely frozen, trying to piece together what I had said. I thought most of them were still at the part with the locks. Knowing insanity was coming, I was able to brace for it and stay a step ahead, unlike Billiam, who had let insanity (A.K.A. me) get behind him.

I pushed Billiam into the well. His head hit the water first. A few seconds later, he shot back out and flailed about, splashing wildly.

"Hat, let me out. I might drown or die from all the darkness!"

I dropped a bucket attached to a rope down. "Here, bob on this for a while. I'll let you out when I have this all squared away. And what darkness? You're only a couple of feet down. Why is the well so full?"

He grabbed the rope and held on tight. "We had a lot of extra sleeping potion, so we dumped it all in."

I turned back toward Gu, who still had Wolfette's arms pinned behind her back. A few of the other townspeople looked to be moments away from working through what I had said.

"Give me one good reason why I shouldn't kill you right after I finish your friend?" Gu asked.

"Why give you one, when I can give you two hundred and thirty-seven?" I was bluffing; I only knew two hundred and thirty-four.

His jaw dropped, and I thought I saw a tear in his eye.

"Number one: because if you kill my friend, I'll let Billiam drown. Number two: without Billiam, you'll have to lead this motley group." I moved closer, about ten feet away, and he didn't react. "Number three: I know who Jon Snow's mother really was on *Game of Thrones,* and I know you haven't gotten to that season yet."

I must have gone too far with that one because his mouth

closed, and he gave me an angry stare. "Who's Jon Snow, and what's *Game of Thrones*?"

"Four: I can tell you about *Game of Thrones*." The only reaction he gave when I took another step forward was a look of confusion. "Five: I can tell you what's behind you right now."

He smiled wolfishly as he didn't turn around. He gave a signal, and the followers moved forward. "Before I kill you, what exactly was number six on your list?"

I put my hands over my face defensively. "That you're a pacifist and wouldn't hurt another human being?"

He laughed. I covered my eyes so I wouldn't see the blow coming. I don't care what my doctor says. If you don't see the blow, it definitely doesn't hurt as much. The only problem is the blow seems to take forever. When it didn't come after what seemed like an hour, I spread my fingers and peeked out. Gu wasn't winding up, so I removed my hands from my eyes.

"I was hoping you wouldn't remember the pacifist thing." He let go of Wolfette, who crashed to the ground, unconscious but snoring. "Billiam told me you were smarter than you look." He gave another signal and the followers stopped moving toward me. "I guess that makes you their leader now."

A muscular man with a large scar running diagonally across his face tugged on my shirt sleeve. "Will you be our new daddy?"

"No, he can't," Billiam's voiced echoed. "Because . . . Luke, I am your father!"

"How many times do I have to tell you, my name isn't Luke?" my potential new son said to the well.

"I wasn't . . . Hat, could you explain it to him?"

"No," I said. "But only because you didn't do the deep breathing thing before you said it." I turned away from the well and addressed the crowd. "Now, about this leadership thing. I'm sorry, but I'm going to have to decline. You see, I am only a humble assistant and not a leader."

"Could you assist me in getting out of this well?" Billiam asked. "I'm starting to get sleepy, and I'm afraid I'll drown."

I reluctantly nodded, and Big Baby pulled him out.

"If you're not a leader then why does that large man with the almost-as-large sword do what you say?" a woman with a scar that probably matched the other guy said.

I pointed toward Wolfette. "She's a dangerous psychopath." I pointed at Big Baby. "He's too busy keeping her psychopathy in check to do anything else, so I'm the leader by default."

My potential new son pointed at Billiam. "He's an idiot." He pointed at Gu. "He's going to leave with the idiot." He pointed at the rest of the crowd. "And our combined brain power is even less than the idiot's."

The part of me that was good at math almost screamed at the absurdity of that statement, but then one of the guys in front tried to eat his elbow. I looked toward Billiam to hand them back over to him, but he was already gone.

I tapped my temple. "Everyone, follow me. I'm going to introduce you to some old friends."

Wolfette groggily scrambled to her feet. "Where's Gu?"

"Hmm . . . It seems he left," I said.

"I have a vengeance and there's only one thing that can quench my thirst." She was back to her murderous self and almost cut one of my temporary new followers in half before Big Baby caught her arms.

"I'm going to guess it's not a refreshing beverage and that it involves Gu," I said. "One thing, though—he said he's a pacifist. Are you sure he's the guy who murdered your colleagues?"

Her stare told me she was considering murdering her own colleague at that moment if I didn't drop it.

"Fine, we'll look for Gu and Billiam on our way to finding Didlius." I got closer to Big Baby and Wolfette to whisper to them. "If I can turn this lot over to Didlius's care, I think I can fix everything, but don't tell them that. I don't want them to start having abandonment issues until I'm well away."

"OK," I said, addressing the crowd. "We're going to get moving in a few minutes here. If everyone could get some backpacks and supplies to survive a journey for a few days, we're going to have ourselves a little field trip."

"Umm, Hat," Big Baby said. "What about Billiam's other friends?"

I followed his eyes to the plains to the east of the village. It was easy to find what he was looking at. Great clouds of things are usually hard to miss, and this cloud of dust was no exception. It seemed to be caused by the large number of horsemen right in front of it, though they may have been running from the cause instead. Either way, it probably wasn't a good thing.

I turned toward my new followers and showed them exactly what kind of leader they had picked. "Anyone know what to do?"

THE BATTLE WHERE I GET WINDED

My new, temporary followers didn't seem to be much in the giving mood, though that may have been a blessing since several of them were scraping up their faces by scratching them with weapons, though at least they had grabbed weapons. Unfortunately, there were only about twenty-five or thirty of them, and while I couldn't get the most accurate count of the horsemen, what with the cloud of dust covering up all but the first few rows, I put their numbers somewhere between "a lot" and "way too many." Unless my followers had some hidden talents like transforming into planes so they could fly away, or sucking blood and then running away super fast, we were screwed.

"So, I see a lot of swords and axes," I said, "but does anyone have any pikes or spears? They'd work a lot better against cavalry."

A tall, skinny woman nodded and rifled through a nearby wagon. She proudly stepped in front of me and handed me a fish. "My husband, Gurgis, caught it yesterday in the river." She pointed at a short, roundish fellow who stared at his feet in embarrassment.

I took the fish, which I was fairly certain was some sort of catfish and not a pike. I handed it to Big Baby. "Thanks," I said, "is there anything else we have weapon-wise that might be useful?"

Four of the men in the back ran off, and I could soon hear the slow, steady sound of wheels rumbling through the dirt road barely out of view from the other side of one of the houses. I was expecting a cart or wagon, but they pushed forward a fully-functioning catapult.

"Do I want to know where you got that from?"

"Billiam promised us he'd teach us how to fly if we joined him, so his friend showed us how to build this," the guy with the scar said. "Our town had a lot more people in it before he came a few days ago. We were going to demand he tell us how to land safely, but then you showed up . . ."

As much as I wanted to explain how gravity works to them, there were more important things to worry about at that time. I ran up and down its length, inspecting it. "Splendid. Now let's load this thing up with some big rocks and let it rip . . . after they get in range. Wait for my signal before you fire."

The guy to my right readied the catapult. The horse people were now close enough that we could barely make out their faces.

I motioned for Big Baby, Wolfette, and a few townspeople to join me on the edge of town, also known as the place where a wall belonged.

"Who are these people?" I asked. "Have they attacked here before? Do they take prisoners?"

"No idea," the guy with the scar said. "And if an army that big attacked here before, our town wouldn't be here."

Gurgis's wife handed me another fish. "The hordes like to appear every few years on the plains, sack a few dozen cities, then ride back east. They move around a lot, so armies can't catch em."

"So, if we waved a white flag at them, they'd probably ignore it?" I asked.

Big Baby shook his head. "They might wipe their fannies with it after they get tired of stabbing us."

The horde was only a couple hundred feet away now. I considered having my followers make a run for the trees to the north, but there wouldn't have been nearly enough time. We would have to deal with them coming from the plains. I would like to say I said a prayer, but I was too terrified to think of anything except the massive army in front of me. My eyes became glued on their front ranks, in particular, on a ferocious young woman with a mostly shaved head, except for the long, braided topknot. I would have called it a unique look—a mixture of punk and savage—but everyone in her army had the same haircut. They all seemed to have their nose rings on the same side too. Unsurprisingly, given that they were attacking a Paruxian village, they had a much lighter skin tone, somewhere on the border of light brown and tan.

"There's at least a thousand of them," Big Baby said.

"That means more for me." Wolfette glanced back at us with a murderous grin and charged forward. "I can see Gu in the second rank, and I'm not going to let him escape again."

"That's probably a different bald guy, sis." Big Baby sighed and ran after her.

Scared beyond reason and not sure what to do, my mind wanted to crawl up into a ball. Ever the rebels, my legs decided to do the opposite, and I found myself running after them. By the time my brain registered where I was, I was halfway to the horse people. I supposed this was a better way to die. I'd have a better story to tell in the afterlife anyway. The twang of the catapult was followed by a roundish gray object arching from behind in slow-motion toward the horde. I was proud that my new followers had at least fired a rock at them until I noticed the way it wobbled and the water pouring out; water balloons had evidently been invented in Paruxia too.

The woman I had been fixated on smiled as she took in the object and then gave a great shout that sounded an awful lot like a naughty word. The rest of the horde responded to her shout by puckering their lips and breathing straight up into the air. It looked like even their horse had joined in, but I was delirious with fear, so I might have imagined it.

However, I was definitely not imagining the giant water balloon/bladder turning around in mid-air—along with a second one a few seconds later. The sight was so unbelievable that I didn't even turn when another probable expletive came from the lips of the young woman. This was likely a blessing as this time the wind came toward me and not up. I barely managed to spin around before the wind got to me. I flew several feet forward and landed face first in the dirt. This was going to be quite the story for the afterlife, though I wasn't sure if anyone would believe half of it.

The sound of hoofbeats grew closer. They seemed to be taking forever to trample me, so long, in fact, that it was starting to sound like they were moving away from me.

My always dangerous curiosity got the better of me, and I rolled over. A smaller contingent of the cavalry was circling me while the larger portion circled the village. Big Baby and Wolfette were only a few feet away. Judging by the two imprints in the ground nearby, they had been blown there too.

The young woman halted her horse in front of me with about five other warriors to her sides, their identical braids swaying in unison. One of them pushed Gu's horse forward, and he moved next to us. Billiam was across his saddle, unconscious and snoring loudly.

"Have your other followers turned on you as well, Gu?" I asked.

The horse people laughed.

"Give us one good reason why we shouldn't kill you," the especially handsome one next to the young woman said. I could tell he would be trouble because he was twirling his mustache. I wasn't sure if he was the evil leader or the advisor who corrupts the normally honorable king.

"Are you talking to just us or are Gu and Billiam included as well?" I asked.

The young woman stared unblinking at us through the whole exchange. At first I thought there was something wrong with her, but one look into her eyes told me she had heard every word.

Those eyes. While they were the same amber color as the rest of her kin, what set hers apart was the way you felt when you looked at them. Just a glance made me feel both weaker and stronger at the same time. When I was finally able to take my eyes off her, I got the feeling that my companions felt the same way. Big Baby had even pulled a ring out of his pocket but quickly put it back when she saw it.

"We're talking to all of you," Mustache said.

"Including the puppy I just found?" I asked.

"Especially the puppy you just found!" He cackled and everyone but Mysterious Eyes joined in. I would have applauded his brilliant display of villainy but didn't want to break up my momentum.

"Oh, good, because I didn't just find a puppy, which is probably a good thing with you sickos and your hypothetic killing of small, adorable animals. Now, as to the question of why you shouldn't kill us, I happen to have two hundred and thirty-nine reasons why you shouldn't kill us." I took a few slow steps forward. No one moved to intercept me which I took as a good sign.

"Oh, gods," Gu said. "Not this again . . . wait, two hundred and thirty-nine?"

"I thought up two new ones. I'll give some hints: one involves turkey basting, and the other, the 1997 Montreal Expos. Now, no more interruptions. I'm on your side now, and I'm on a roll."

"You're still probably going to die," Mustache said.

"See, there's that word 'probably.' If you never think positive, you'll never escape execution like I'm about to, unlike that poor mop head that you attached to your upper lip."

Mustache's companions sucked in so much wind that I was afraid they might suck the balloon back our way. Mustache didn't attack me as he appeared to be locked in an internal debate on which method of execution would be the most gruesome.

I decided to make it even more difficult for him. "Number seventy-two: Killing skinny assistants is nothing to brag about. When you sit around the fire with your fellow hordesmen and a tall beer, bragging about your brave exploits, and your buddy tells you all about the large, vicious barbarians he slew and you counter with the short, skinny guy with a quill, how is that going to go over?"

Several of the horse people nodded in response, but not enough. I was making progress though.

"Number two hundred and six: If you kill me, who will prevent forest fires?" I was operating on the assumption that their country didn't have a forest prevention mascot. "In the two weeks I've been here, I haven't seen a single forest fire. Coincidence? I think not."

No one had stabbed me or blew hard in my direction yet, so I kept going.

"Number two hundred and fifty-one: I know how to make cigarettes. Trust me, you'll like them. Great stress reliever."

That got a few nods. It was time to start to bring it home.

"Number two hundred and fifty-two: I'm the only one who knows how to get people off their addictions to cigarettes. Nasty stuff. Not worth the stress relief."

It looked like Mustache had finally decided how he wanted to kill me, so I had to make the next one good. Unfortunately, I'd been going mostly on instinct, and the only things coming to mind would make him want to kill me more, which isn't too surprising since about ninety percent of my brain is filled with mustache jokes.

"Number twenty . . . something with guacamole."

Mustache charged, completely ruining my chance to explain the wonders of tortilla chips and dip to the people of Vyenra. I stared his charge down defiantly, mostly because my legs were too frozen to move. "I wish I could write a book with all the mustache jokes in my head right now and then throw that book at you. Possibly follow that by dropping a library on you and then shaving that silly thing off your corpse's face."

"Halt!" the unblinking woman said.

Mustache brought his horse to a stop a few inches in front of me. His horse's breath smelled like wet farts, but it was still the most wondrous thing I've ever smelled. Not that I like the smell of wet farts or anything, but he wasn't trying to trample me to death. Priorities, people.

Mustache gritted his teeth. I didn't grit mine in response because the commanding woman told me to halt, and also because my dentist told me it wasn't good for them.

The woman trotted her horse forward. I still hadn't seen her blink, but I may have missed it with the horse in the way. "What was that you said about a library?" she asked.

"I'd like to drop a library on Mr. Mustache here," I said. "Not so much his horse though, as he seems like a nice guy. When this is over, I'd like to take him shopping for some new horseshoes, introduce him to some fillies, and go dancing."

"Is there any particular library that you would like to drop on my brother?"

"Hey!" Mustache said.

She pushed his horse over so I could see her. "A library you've seen recently, maybe?"

"Yeah, those late fees can really add up."

She made a grand gesture, and the rest of the horse people bowed their heads. "As a new horde goes out for Sacking Season, they must first sack a library before they are allowed to sack anything else. The founder of the hordes, my great-great-great-etcetera grandfather, Hung'Loser, had to make a concession to get the precepts for the formation of a horde passed in the Horse Congress."

"That's an odd thing to sack first. Is there a booming second-hand book market or something? Oh, I bet you're one of those societies that can't read."

She shook her head. "According to legend, the deciding vote had a traumatic fall at a library when he was younger and everyone laughed at him. In his defense, it's really hard to get a horse through those skinny aisles without falling off."

The rest of the horde raised their heads and nodded.

"And for the record, almost all of us can read, but we don't take that many books with us as plunder. Their weight-to-value ratio is too high, though we do fudge that a little for any paranormal romances we come across. A good story with a dreamy vampire is always popular around the campfire before bedtime."

Two rather burly horsemen gave each other fist bumps on "dreamy vampire."

"So, in conclusion, unless you or your friends happen to know where a library is nearby," the young woman said, "we're going to have to kill you. Which brings up something I almost forgot." She turned to Mustache. "Kill the bald guy and his unconscious friend."

Mustache stared hard at me with a big grin on his face, seeming to say "this is what I'm going to do to you next" as he advanced on Gu.

"Now that I think about it," I said, "I do remember seeing a library, but I'll only tell you if you let my friends go, including any of the villagers you captured. Also, throw in Billiam because I need his help, and Gu because my friend has some unfinished business with him."

"He's obviously lying, sister," Mustache said.

Mysterious Eyes gave me an even more penetrating stare, taking all of me in. It made me feel naked, so I gave her my best shy smile and a hesitant wink.

Mysterious Eyes shrugged her shoulders at Mustache. "Probably, but we don't have any more leads. Plus, he amuses me in a terrible jester kind of way."

I pumped my fist. "I've always wanted to be a jester. Now, about the townspeople."

"They're all still alive, I think. They all lay down after those bladders broke over them, and the rest of the horde has been circling them ever since."

"Ahh, I bet they filled them with sleeping potion. Wait . . . There couldn't possibly have been enough sprayed on them to put them to sleep."

"They all ran around screaming for a few minutes after that thing shattered, then lay down and started to pretend to snore," another horsewoman said. "It was all so stupid that we felt bad for them and let them be."

"And my companions?"

"We'll be keeping them for insurance," Mysterious Eyes said. "If you're lying to us, they'll die screaming."

She motioned to her followers. They brought a few horses forward and deposited us on them. I pointed back toward the north because I knew there were cities there and cities usually had libraries. I wasn't sure how I would prevent them from hurting people and taking their stuff, but I was confident I would think of something.

STOP HORDING ALL THAT MEDIOCRITY

As we rode across the endless plains, I tried to see if I could get my captors to give me a taste of their culture's music. Unfortunately, the kazoo was the only instrument they could play on horseback without literally scaring the crap out of their horses, and they had given up on singing, as their nose rings caused them all to whistle slightly from their nostrils. I really shouldn't complain, since my musical talents only extend to the triangle and singing in the shower, often together.

"Where is this library, jester?" Mysterious Eyes asked.

"I have a name, you know. It's Hat. What's your name, O leader of the horse people?"

She gave me a ferocious smile that almost made me wish she'd go back to glaring at me. "I am Hung'Lo, and we are not called horse people but the Mediocre Horde."

"Hung'Lo?" I said. "*The* Hung'Lo."

In the backstory of the books, Hung'Lo was the name of the ruler who orchestrated the slaying of Didlius. That meant I had bumbled once again into being in the right place to witness and record an important part in The One's founding. As much as I wanted to see everything, I had been hoping to miss out on this part by getting Billiam to tell me how to get home. Didlius was still my friend even though he had disowned me and fallen under a bad influence. Could I really witness his death without intervening? Would doing that make me as bad as Judas?

She chuckled. "I am not *the* Hung'Lo as I am the four hundredth of my line, four hundred and first if you count Hung'Loser. The second one shortened it when we discovered 'loser's' meaning in your language. It's hard to get taken seriously when everyone is laughing at your name."

"Aha! I've got it," I said. "I know exactly where to find a library . . . I mean, I already knew where the library was. I just remembered more specific directions this instant. It's that way."

Hung'Lo gave me a skeptical stare and then shrugged. "Hung'Ger, George the Accountant, point the horde that way."

Hung'Ger, which was evidently Mustache's name, and a burly man sped off. Thirty seconds later the horde wheeled thirty degrees to face north.

I leaned over to Big Baby and whispered in his ear. "That jerk Judas I told you about likes to write a lot. I'm going to point the horde right at a place that has a lot of his books and also happens to make those pamphlets he's depending on. A double whammy of a brilliant plan, wouldn't you say? With the books and pamphlets ruined, it might even make Judas depressed enough to step down. With him out of the way, Did might listen to my side of the story and even take me back."

"Wolfette and I could just kill Judas for you," he whispered back.

I almost said, "That would be great," and that troubled me greatly. "Hung'Lo, what happens to the rest of the city after you knock the library down?"

"We knock the rest of the city down too, and then take everything below a certain weight-to-value ratio, killing everyone we encounter on the way, and then go back over it a few more times for funsies."

I grimaced. "You and I have a very different definition of 'fun.'"

"That is why you are the jester and I am the warrior queen." She slapped me on the side of my butt.

I jumped a bit, causing me to lose control of my horse. Big Baby laughed as he settled my horse down. Wolfette didn't even react as she continued to stare to the west. The horde had earlier moved Billiam and Gu that way after Wolfette's third attempt at getting to Gu. Even though our captors had covered her axe/arms in thick blankets, she still managed to inadvertently knock Billiam off Gu's horse. Billiam had been lucky he only suffered a bloody nose and a few scrapes.

Big Baby said something after that but I couldn't hear over the swiftly beating hooves of new arrivals coming in from every direction. Something was up as Hung'Lo and several of the other warriors abruptly left and headed toward the front of the army. After a few minutes of uncertainty, Hung'Ger trotted his horseback in between Big Baby and me.

"The Great and Fearsome Hung'Lo has instructed me to protect you in the upcoming battle." His wolfish smile suggested that his idea of protection involved stabbing me first, so the enemy couldn't get the chance.

Big Baby stared off in the distance. "Who is it? The Paruxian army? The local militia?"

He touched his nose ring and shook his head. "If it were any of those, we would just ride away. No, it is the vile Ipanians and their silly nose rings."

While most of the horde had been riding through the forest on both sides of us, we had stayed on the road in the center. I couldn't see what was going on in the forest, besides every bird for miles taking flight. There was a lot of noise. It sounded like a wind storm attacking a logging camp. As much as I wanted to get out of there, I was packed in the middle of a rather large formation of ferocious horse warriors, one of whom wasn't about to let me leave his sight. Our only hope would be to wait for an opening in the ensuing chaos and make a run for it.

The front elements of our captor's army recoiled from a surprise charge of what looked like their own people but managed to bounce back and counter-attack with Hung'Lo in the lead. I had a hard time telling exactly what was going on as both sides wore identical animal hide outfits, had braided topknots, and even had the same brass-colored nose rings. The fight seemed to be going back and forth, but I was no expert on battles, especially not ones in person.

"Is this a civil war or a coup?" I asked Hung'Ger.

Hung'Ger scowled at me . . . scowled at me harder. "What are you babbling about? Those are Ipanians."

I looked back at the two sides as they fought around us. I still couldn't see any difference between them no matter how hard I squinted. Since they looked exactly alike, it took me a while to even isolate an Ipanian from a horde member. I was finally able to when an enemy got near enough for Hung'Lo to engage her. Same crude leather clothing, all sleeveless. Same braided topknot that went down to the middle of their backs. Same curved swords. Same nose rings on the left—no, right side . . .

That was it! "The horde has their nose rings on the left side, while the Ipanians have theirs on the right." I hadn't picked it up because they were facing opposite directions, making it appear at first glance like they were on the same side.

"The right side is always right," Hung'Ger said, "as the children's saying goes. The Ipanians teach the opposite saying to their disgusting, mongrel children. I shouldn't complain about their stupidity too much as that wrongheadedness is the very reason they will lose this battle. We hold our weapons on the right—the side where all the power comes from—and they hold theirs on the weaker left."

"It's good to know who I should be hitting if they break through to us," Big Baby said. "Say, could you lend us some weapons? I sure would like to help out with those weak-armed Ipanians. Us mercenaries are real team players, you know."

He gave Hung'Ger his biggest smile. On a normal-sized person, the smile would have been endearing, but on someone of his immense stature it had the opposite effect. Hung'Ger shook his head and trotted forward, likely to help in the fighting if it got near but still close enough to keep an eye on us.

Big Baby lowered his voice. "Any ideas on how to get out of here?"

"You mean get to Gu," Wolfette said.

"Look, sis," Big Baby said, "I know I promised we'd get him, but this isn't really the best time. There's no way we can get to Gu without being swarmed. We'd never survive, especially without weapons."

"You mean like these?" She held up her cloth-wrapped axe/hands.

"Hat," Big Baby said, "do you think you can cause a distraction while I untie the rope that's holding these on?"

I moved my horse forward to get in between the two of them and Hung'Ger. "Number fifteen: If you kill me, who will teach you how to knit leg warmers for your horses?" Hung'Ger and several of the other horde members stared at me. I wasn't sure if they had practiced synchronized glaring. If not, they were naturals at it.

"Something that's not going to draw every eye in our direction, maybe," Big Baby whispered.

I grinned at him and then turned back to Hung'Ger. "In fourth grade, I first began to take an interest in girls. My crush in that grade was Helen Distman. Most of the boys preferred Gina

LaFontaine because she was tanned and had longer hair, but I had much more refined tastes. Gina didn't know what a Charizard was and had never even heard of a Power Ranger, either of which was an unforgivable sin in my book, both then and now." Most of the horde members were back to looking at the battle. Hung'Ger still had one eye on me.

"In fifth grade, a new girl arrived, Beth Johnson. Red hair, the prettiest smile I ever saw, and an *X-Men* backpack. I traded away all my *Pokémon* cards and had my mom buy me a Cyclops t-shirt as soon as I got home. It turned out she was only into guys who liked Wolverine, but I persisted the rest of the year."

Hung'Ger had completely turned around, so I glanced back at my companions. The first axe was free, and Wolfette was trying to chop the other one loose.

"In sixth grade, all the girls in class switched to mooning over boy bands, so I turned my attention to Lacy Heitzman. She developed first and always brought cupcakes in her lunch, a lethal combination. I was powerless to resist and did all her math homework that year. I think it was her lowest grade ever."

The horde members near us seemed to be jockeying their horses back and forth in an effort to get in an even better position to not look at me. I added a few weeping sounds, and they moved even faster.

I could hear Wolfette rubbing her blades together. All eyes were away from us, so she had no problem taking out the first two men. Big Baby grabbed their blades as they fell and handed one to me. I considered heading off to the safety of the forest and not following Wolfette toward Gu but realized that without the protection of my two friends, there was no way I'd make it. Also, Billiam was with him, and I needed to find out how to get home.

As a result of my brilliantly boring stories, and the fact that no fighting was going on in the rear, Wolfette and Big Baby managed to get us three fourths of the way to Gu. Our luck ran out, however, when some horde members eventually noticed us. Part of me was relieved because Gu was a nice guy, and I didn't really want him to get hurt.

So far, Big Baby and Wolfette had managed to fend off all attacks, largely due to their thick plate armor. However, when the horde figured out that my friends' horses were not nearly as armored, it would all end. I did my best to stay out of the action by putting my sword in my lap and reciting the epic tale of my quest for a girlfriend in seventh grade. (It involved a ring and invisibility that seemed to only extend to women.)

Big Baby grimaced as four blades simultaneously bounced off his armor. Wolfette's right axe became entangled with the blade of an older woman, and their horses danced back and forth as they tried to pull them apart. I told everyone about summer camp before my first year of high school.

"Stop this!" a voice called. I couldn't place it at first, given the force and volume, but eventually traced it back to the normally even-keeled Gu.

Even the horde members halted and stared. With the resulting cessation of movement, Wolfette and her opponent managed to finally disentangle themselves.

"Excellent," Gu said. "Now, these two mercenaries and I have some unfinished business that needs to be completed. While I know you were instructed to keep us apart, we were only brought along as insurance to make sure Hat stays in line. As long as one of us lives, we can still fulfill that role, so I offer my companion Billiam as that insurance since the mercenaries do not care about him. Is that correct?"

"Yeah," Wolfette said. "I only want you."

Billiam gave Gu a long, pleading look, but finally acquiesced and moved his horse next to me.

"Now, horde members, would it not be easier and less costly for you to let us proceed?" Gu asked. "Donna the Barista?"

The older woman near Wolfette gave a slow nod. The horde in the vicinity backed off to form a large circle around my friends and Gu.

Wolfette screamed an obscenity and charged. Big Baby was caught off guard but soon followed. Gu didn't even move. I thought he too had been surprised, but the movement of his eyes told me differently. He straightened his back and stared at Wolfette's blade as it neared his face with a resigned smile on his face.

Wolfette's blade stopped inches from making contact. She stared at her arm in disbelief and then glared at Gu. After a lengthy internal debate, she lowered her weapon.

"Why can't I hit you?" she asked. "My arm was itchy itching to eviscerate you. I could feel the impact coming and it was glorious, but then when it got close, I just stopped. Of course! It's magicy magic. No wonder you made such easy work of my friends."

Gu blinked in surprise. "It isn't magic. It's mercy and compassion. You can't hit a person when you know he isn't going to fight back."

"No, that's not it. This is definitely magicy magic. I hit people when they can't fight back all the time. It's my signature move. They named a drink after it in our favorite tavern."

"Then it's because you know deep down that I wasn't the one who killed your friends," Gu said. "I've been a pacifist since before either of you were even born."

"But I saw you do it," Wolfette said. "I'll never forget that face and bald head of yours. It greets me in the middle of every good dream. Your cackle wakes me up several times a night; the same cackle you gave after you killed both of my friends and thought you killed me."

"I hate to interrupt," Billiam said. "And as much as I love my loyal follower, I want to point out that in no way do I condone the murdering of your friends. Also, at no point in your story was I present. With that out of the way, to the point: Gu has a very strict 'no cackling' policy. He rarely laughs, and when he does, it's so deep it makes the furniture shake."

"I've got it!" I said. "I knew my knowledge of soap operas would come in handy one day. Gu has a split personality."

Billiam shook his head. "I've been with him for years, Hatingly. Nonstop for months at a time. I would have noticed that."

"Someone who happens to have the exact same name as him?" Another head shake. "Aliens took over his body? Ghost? Possessed by the devil? Clones? Jackal was the real killer and switched bodies with Gu? They're not really dead, and it was all a dream?" All of those got head shakes. The last of which was by most of the horde. "Evil twin?"

"Hat," Billiam said, "as entertaining as soap operas are, I don't think you can apply any of those ridiculous plot ideas to real life."

"Wait," Gu said. "I do have an identical twin brother. He went full on recluse after 'the incident' and the thing with his ex-wife all those years ago, but perhaps he has resurfaced."

"Ha! A likely story." Wolfette raised both arms and swung.

Once again, Gu made no effort to dodge. He even stuck his neck toward her to make it easier. Unfortunately, when you're trying to decapitate someone with a single blow, you have to put your whole body into it—doubly so when you try it with both arms. Consequently, all that motion does not lend itself well to staying on your mount, especially when you don't have any hands to steady yourself when you begin to pitch over. Realizing he wasn't going to die, Gu helpfully reached out and steadied her.

Before I could ask if they were all right, a gravelly voice interrupted me. "Seeing how no one is going to die here, I'm going to have to break this up. I only let this go on because it looked to be a doozy of a smack down, but you scored way too low in the ratings." I looked to my right to find Donna the Barista pointing for us to return to the previous area of our incarceration.

Before I could offer a witty distraction, she slumped to the ground. The smiling visage of Billiam slowly appeared behind her, holding a crude club. "With her out of the way, we can get out of here. Who's with me?"

I almost raised my hand, but the shouts of several of the nearby horde members interrupted me. Fortunately, the majority of the horde in our vicinity, especially the ones directly behind us, were too busy looking for or fighting off the Ipanians to notice this, but there were still at least thirty of them heading our way.

"Oh, right," Billiam said. "There's more of them. Kind of forgot about them since they hadn't said anything for a bit."

"Can we put aside our differences for long enough to get out of here?" Gu asked.

"Fine," Wolfette said, "but as soon as we're safe, I'm ending you."

"I still maintain that I didn't perform that horrible act, but if it will bring peace to you, then you'll have your execution."

I began to recite my month-to-month high school crushes throughout my freshman year, as Wolfette and Big Baby cut their way through the horde to the eastern edge of the woods. I don't think anyone could hear me through the din of battle, but it did distract me enough to keep me from shaking myself off my mount. As much success as Wolfette was having in our lead and Big Baby at our rear, there were simply too many of them.

I breathed a sigh of relief when our attackers pulled back until I realized it was so they could form up for one definitive coup de grâce. As I said a prayer to every religious figure I could think of, the Ipanians appeared from the forest and charged forth into their left flank. Our attackers' formation disintegrated instantly. Before we could take advantage of our sudden good luck and pass them by, several Ipanians headed toward us.

"Still think this is a good idea, Hat-choo?" Billiam asked.

I pointed to the edge of the Ipanians. "Lower your weapons and ride that way. We're clearly not members of the horde. Maybe the Ipanians will let us through."

"I'm not a fan of plans with the word 'maybe' in them."

"Then by all means stay." I pushed my horse as fast as I could, which wasn't that fast since I wasn't the greatest rider—two lessons a couple of years ago isn't exactly expert—but that actually turned out to be a good thing. As soon as the elite horse people saw us approach, they were too busy laughing at me bouncing around to consider any of us a threat. We rode on for another thirty minutes without incident while I exaggerated my awkward riding in case we encountered any more Ipanians.

In hindsight, that was a mistake as it only slowed us down, but at the time I had no way of knowing that we wouldn't encounter any more of them. A party of cavalry seemed to appear out of nowhere only minutes behind, though the loud clomping of my steed as I steered her terribly may have masked their sound from my hearing.

"What now, fearful leader?" Billiam asked bitterly.

"Try to outrun them?" I asked.

"Hat, I appreciate your loyalty to us," Big Baby said, "but I know you're only saying that to protect us. The only plan that'll work is if Sis and I hold them off so you non-combatants can get out of here."

I bit my lip and stared at him. There was no way I would order my friends to their death. I mean, sure, his plan would at least allow some of us the chance to live, but there had to be another way. When I bit my lip a second time, Big Baby must have taken that as confirmation and charged toward the enemy.

Wolfette looked at his back and then looked at Gu. "Hat, I

want you to promise you'll kill that bastard if you make it out of here."

"I promise," I said without thinking.

She smiled as she hurriedly chased after her brother. I nodded to Billiam and Gu, and a knot in my heart later, we rode as fast as we could into the unknown.

THE CAVE OF INFO DUMP

We moved as fast as our awkward riding would allow through the forest. Our misadventures with seemingly every other piece of vegetation we passed almost brought the normally even-keeled Gu to tears. He certainly introduced me to several new curse words, though unfortunately there wasn't time to ask what they meant.

If it had not been for him, our pursuers would have caught us several times, but he always seemed to find the perfect spot to hide in when one of us inevitably got knocked off our horse just as hoofbeats sounded in the distance. He even had us backtrack a few times and change direction. I wasn't sure if those things were necessary, but as night approached, we hadn't heard the sound of pursuit in over an hour. Gu directed us to a cave to rest our exhausted selves and even more exhausted mounts in. I wasn't sure how he saw the cave from our vantage point, as covered with thick foliage as it was, but with the way he kept finding these hiding places, I had a feeling he was very familiar with our surroundings.

"I don't know if it's the best idea to stop," Billiam said.

Gu shrugged and dug some food out of his mount's saddlebag.

Fortunately, the horde liked to keep everything they would need for days of riding on every horse, and our horses came with saddlebags full of food and drink.

"Their horses are as tired as ours," Gu said. "Besides, it's almost impossible to see this cave if you don't know where to look."

"I guess. I mean, it's not like you've been wrong on this journey." Billiam gave a tired smile as he took a piece of jerky from Gu's hand.

"I *have* been right every time, but you always amend the plan. Like dressing up in that ridiculous white outfit and pretending to be someone else."

Billiam finally remembered I was there and turned to me. "Hatinator, the disguise totally fooled you, right? It was the part where everyone faked being asleep that you saw through."

I pretended to have trouble finding food in my bag and ignored the question, hoping it would go away. Billiam asked a second time, so I stuck my head out of the cave to check for horsemen.

Gu pulled me back in. "That's not important. What's important is that Hat agreed to kill me. I can't fault you for accepting since your friend had just given her life to save yours. Do you want to get this over with now, Hat?"

Billiam pushed Gu against the wall. "What are you saying, idiot? How selfish are you? I need you. Without you, my master plan will . . ." Billiam glanced back at me, then let go of Gu.

"Relax," I said. "While I did agree to fulfill Wolfette's vendetta, I never specified *when*. As long as I'm sure you're a good person, I won't kill you prematurely, though I do plan to investigate her story further. If I don't find anything, I'll find some poison, and you can take it right before you die of old age. That way I'll still have honored her wish, and you'll only die a few minutes before you were already going to die."

Gu nodded sagely. He tried to hide his relief, but the hint of a smile creased the edges of his mouth.

"Seeing as I'm doing you this favor," I said, "what exactly are and were you two up to? I do love hearing a great, evil master plan." As much as I wanted to find out how to get home, I had to make sure they weren't doing anything that would damage my beloved Vyenra, especially not my friends.

Billiam gave Gu a very nasty look. Gu ignored it and spoke. "The plan's not really evil, per se, though I can see why you'd see it that way. Evil is usually only a matter of perspective, isn't it? Since you gave Bill permission to write stories about this land, he decided to spice things up and use the connections he has built up while traveling to make a go at becoming king."

"King?" I asked.

"Yes, king," Billiam said. "Their current one is weak, and as it turns out, not really in control of most of the southern areas of the kingdom—areas I just so happen to have extensive pull in. I started in the village we met in, Greater Lurion. I don't know if you noticed, but those people were incredibly easy to fool. I put on some fake glasses, and they assumed I was a genius. They made me mayor and then king. We almost had a major slip-up when one of their relatives from Lesser Lurion visited and reminded them that they already had a king. Fortunately, I put my glasses back on said, 'Nuh-uh. Who're you going to believe? Someone from a place that starts with "Lesser" or your king?' and then they tarred and feathered her. I was going to move on to the second dumbest town next, then third, fourth, etc. and eventually the smarter towns would see our numbers and join up as well, but then you showed up."

I shook my head. "There can't possibly be other towns as stupid as that one."

"They have this tradition that when a town's population gets too big, they form a new town a few miles away from the original town and put 'Greater' in front of it to trick all the dumb people to move there. So, I was going to start with those 'Greater' towns. You know, if we can get back down south, we could continue."

Normally, I'd be happy when someone turns their frown upside down, but there was no telling how many people would die if he started a civil war. And while King Fartius wasn't exactly the best king out there, I was terrified of what Billiam might do as king. Good things usually don't come from leaders who take power by overthrowing the previous ruler without a very good reason like extreme incompetence or excessive cruelty; King Fartius possessed neither of those traits.

I crossed my arms and gave him an imperious glare. "I can't let you do that."

Billiam smirked. "That's cute. And how, pray tell, are you going to stop us?"

"I'll revoke my earlier offer to let you write about your adventures in Paruxia."

His smirk faded. "So what? I'll be king here. I can have all the power and things I want. Why would I ever need to go back to Earth?"

I deflated. "You're right. I mean, recognition for being the greatest fantasy author on Earth doesn't matter when you're a king, does it?"

"Not really. Who cares about what people think about me there. I'll have plenty of subjects here to prove how great I am to."

"Right. Who cares what Harry and all the other authors think anyway? It's not like you'll ever see them again, and I'm sure your fans will find someone else to idolize. So what if your family forgets about you except for the occasional 'What ever happened to him?' question at Christmas. None of that matters because your new subjects will be more than an adequate replacement."

Billiam's face went through a wide range of emotions as each new statement sunk in—my favorite was the way his nose twitched uncontrollably at the transition from pretending not to care directly to bitter anger before finally settling back to clever smirk. "Hatty, I have always admired the subtle, brilliant way you manipulate Harry into being actually productive, but I am not an arrogant simpleton like him. I know what you're doing, and it won't work on me. I'm too smart, and there's nothing you can say to get me to end my brilliant scheme."

I put on a sincere, innocent look. "You're right. There's nothing at all wrong with your plan. It's quite brilliant. Not a flaw to be seen. I'm sure it will all work out perfectly." I turned away from Billiam, toward Gu and tried to suppress a laugh. Gu responded with a half-smile.

Billiam pouted. "What are you two laughing about? It's about my plan, isn't it?"

We both shook our heads.

Recognition dawned on Billiam's face. "As soon as you get away from us, you're going to tell the king about my plan so he can thwart it, aren't you?" I stared at him flatly, and he began to pace. "You are. That's it exactly. Well, how are you going to do that if you're back on Earth?" I continued to stare at him, making sure not to reveal that he was about to tell me my heart's desire, this time without asking for anything in return. "Ha! You didn't think of that, did you? But you are not nearly as smart as me, so of course you didn't. As soon as I tell you how to get back to Earth, you will have to take it so that you can look after your master." He stopped pacing and stood in front of me. "Hold your hand out."

I put my left hand out, hesitantly so as not to seem too eager.

He gave my hand a look over. "Now the other one."

I held my right one out.

"Where's your ring? The one with the runes on it I saw back at my cabin."

I opened and closed my mouth. He was talking about Harry's ring! The one Officer Mickey had given to me for safekeeping before they took Harry to the hospital. I had it on when I fell asleep and travelled here, but after that . . . "I don't know."

Gu had been chewing and drinking away through all of this, his pupils going kind of glassy like he was daydreaming through the last parts, but on the mention of "ring" he snapped back to attention and set his meal down. "His travel ring? I figured you might need a spare, so I took it while he was sleeping."

"Please tell me you still have it." Billiam tapped his feet.

Gu pulled the cord from around his neck with Harry's ring on it and held it out.

Billiam yanked the cord from his grip and handed it to me. "Sorry about that, Hat. These things are incredibly rare and the only . . . well, the only practical way to travel between our worlds."

He stared at Gu for a second and then continued. "If you're wearing it and fall asleep or get knocked unconscious, you'll travel back to Earth, though not always in the same place you left from. Not sure why it works the way it does, but that's how it always is for me."

"The Old Gods put the unconscious thing on there as a precaution," Gu said. "The trip is too much for the conscious mind to process and can cause a mortal to go insane. And the magic takes you to 'where you need to be,' which is why you always end up transporting to my location, boss. It's so I can keep you out of any trouble you can't handle."

Billiam scowled at him.

"That would be why Harry ended up back at his cabin after he visited here . . ." I moved the ring toward my hand.

Gu pulled my hand back. "You'll want to keep that thing

around your neck on the cord until you want to travel back, so no putting it on your finger, toe, bunch of hair, and I'm not even going to mention the last place. If you travel by accident, you can just go back to sleep again, but you may not end up back at the same place."

"Or even the same time," I muttered.

Billiam pushed Gu back. "What's all this talk about not putting that thing on right now? You have your way back, and I'm sure Harry needs you. Just think of what his enemies could be doing to him while he lays there unconscious without you to look after him."

I scratched my chin. "Most of the things I can think of involve you, and you're safely away here."

"Ahh, but my agent isn't, and I left some very specific instructions with her."

"Jess is also Harry's agent."

"But she always does what will make her the most money in the long-term. And the instructions I left her will make her a whole lot of it."

His grin threatened to break his face. Normally, I'd consider that something to be worried about, but I knew it was all false bravado . . . well, real bravado, but bravado based on erroneous and incomplete information. I had him exactly where I wanted him. The only thing left to do was to figure out for myself what to do with him.

Billiam grabbed the ring. "So, you better go back home right now to stop Jess before she ruins your friend's career."

I pulled my hand back. "But if I go home now, how can I stop that . . . important thing." *Come on, plan. I know you're there. Why haven't you come to me yet?*

Gu gave an almost imperceptible laugh. "Very delicate, Hat, but there's no reason to hide what you're doing from us anymore. We all know what you're planning."

"We do?" Billiam paused and then nodded sagely. "We do, but just for the sake of clarity, so we can be sure we're all on the same page, why don't you explain it to us?"

"He needs to get back to Didlius, before Judas gains control of that new religion, then Paruxia, and then the world. And we also need Judas out of the way before we can even think of attempting your master plan, sir."

"Ahh, yes. I momentarily forgot that portion of my strategy. Thank you for reminding me now, but I'll have to reprimand you later for not reminding me earlier."

Gu bowed deeply. "My sincere apologies, master. I'm sure whatever punishment you come up with will be most ingenious and appropriate."

Billiam grumbled at Gu and then shook his head. "Now, seeing that it's my plan, I know the answer to this, but I want to test you to see if you have figured this out as well. Where can we find this Judas?"

"I think the best place to either find him or find out where he is would be Elbis, where the pamphlets are made, so we should head there."

"Very good summation of my plan, Hat. We'll take you there, since coincidentally it's the same direction we're travelling anyway for the next stage of the plan that doesn't involve you."

"Sounds good to me," I said. "Say, you wouldn't happen to have anything to write with, would you? I lost my writing supplies when I parted company with Judas and Didlius."

Gu pulled out a stack of paper, a quill, and a couple of bottles of ink. Billiam glared at Gu as he handed them to me but didn't stop him.

"Let's eat up and then Hat can have first watch," Billiam grumbled.

I ate quietly and made sure to stay out of his way. While I didn't exactly trust Billiam, I didn't hate him. I understood his situation and felt sorry for him. As much as I really wanted to make faces at him for being such a sour puss, I decided he'd suffered enough.

OK . . . I ran up next to him right as he lay down, made a fart noise, and then ran away. I couldn't resist. Hey, for me that's pretty good. Plus, it made Gu laugh. After all we had been through, we needed a laugh, and I had a feeling there wouldn't be any for quite a long time. After they went to sleep, I began catching up on my notes of the journey.

SEX DOESN'T SELL? WAIT . . . THAT CAN'T BE RIGHT

We left the cave on the next day. Billiam and Gu had remained mostly silent through the journey. They had been carrying on a hushed conversation as I awoke in the cave, and from what little I heard, it looked like they were hiding something. As much as I wanted to find out what they were up to, I was more afraid that they'd try to ruin the founding of The One.

The silence did give me some time to think up what to do about Judas, however. He was far too cunning for me to hope he had somehow screwed up and lost Did's favor. I would need to get Didlius alone and explain things. If I could do that, I was sure I could convince him. I would have to lie low and do some reconnaissance first to see when Judas was away from him.

We arrived on the outskirts of Elbis a couple days later without anything of note happening. There seemed to be a lot more people walking about than I had seen on my last trip here.

"Hmm," Billiam said. "Looks like there must be some sort of festival going on. Gu, do you know of any festivals around this time of year?"

Gu shrugged. "No idea. You know I'm not from here."

"Ahh," I said. "I was wondering why your features were so different."

Billiam's eyes blinked rapidly. "Well, uh, Hatsy. I think this is where we part. Gu is . . . does not do so good with crowds, so we're going to visit a guy outside the capital. He's been writing down all the stuff that's been going on there, and I need it for my plan."

I tried to sound disappointed as I said goodbye.

The streets were clogged so thick that there was no way I would be able to enter the town proper from that direction, so I spent twenty minutes circling to the poorer area. My first thought was to visit the toilet cleaners. They did seem to have a rather vast network of information. I was hesitant to use them, however, given their connection to Judas. That decision was soon made moot anyway as the push and flow of the thick crowd carried me in the opposite direction. I soon found myself on the other side of town.

I tried to ask what sort of festival was going on, but almost everyone in the crowd was too interested in moving toward their destination. Eventually, I did manage to corner a nice couple who informed me that everyone was trying to see "the glorious one," but no one seemed to know precisely where that was. The crowd had all gathered here after being inspired by the pamphlets they found near their toilets, and the "Made in Elbis" mark on the bottom was the only clue to their "glorious one's" location.

After a few more hours of going with the flow of the crowd, it looked like I was in the wealthy part of town not too far from the printing press that Judas had ordered the pamphlets at. Seeing something recognizable, and having been completely frustrated for over two hours by only being able to go where the crowd would let me, caused something primal to open up inside of me. I yelled a very angry "excuse me," poked a few bellies, and squeezed my way to the entrance to the printing press. I raised my hand in victory and then pulled it back down just as quickly. The printing press's door had a big "closed" sign over it and a big thick lock on it.

I gave the door a few strong shakes, but it wouldn't budge. I added a kick to my repertoire mostly out of frustration. It didn't open the door, but it did draw a rather loud shout from behind. I turned around angry but ready to apologize in case the shouter was someone I had given a meanspirited poke to earlier or in case he had friends.

It turned out he did have friends. His right hand held his friend named "sword" and his face held his other friend, "goofy mustache." I decided to focus mostly on "sword" though as he would likely interject with his rapier wit (also known as stabbing) when I made jokes about his other friend. The shouter had a little badge that indicated he was local law enforcement even if it looked to have been hastily glued onto his tunic recently.

"They're not giving more pamphlets out," the mustachioed swordsman said. "And even if they were, there aren't any more in that building. The glorious one had them moved to an undisclosed location."

I wasn't sure if "the glorious one" referred to Judas, Did, or someone else in authority, but whoever it was likely was where I wanted to be. "I don't need a pamphlet," I said, "but I would like to talk to this glorious one. Take me to your leader."

His mustache drooped, making it somehow look more goofy. "Why would I do that? If it were that easy to see him, everyone would be doing it. No door would go un-shook and soon we'd have a town full of doorless buildings, their contents ripe for the taking. Everyone would be so focused on looting that no one would be paying attention to the big announcement."

"Not true," I said. "If you took everyone to the 'glorious one' as soon as they shook doors, they wouldn't be here to see that they shook the doors open. And if they were already in front of him, they'd have to listen to his announcement."

A smile peeked out of the bottom of his bushy stache. "Wow, you're almost as smart as the glorious one. I guess I'll take you to him."

He pointed his sword forward and poked his way through the crowd. We headed to the largest, most elaborately decorated house in the town. At first I was afraid that my friend had taken over the king's house, but then I remembered that King Fartius had agreed to join us, so I breathed a sigh of relief. I hoped they had gotten his permission first, but it turned out not to matter because my guide continued past it.

"Where are we going exactly?" I asked. "To the toilet cleaners?"

"Toilet cleaners?" He inadvertently cut off a guy's pinky as his sword turned in the same direction as his head. "Why would we want to bother ourselves with those poop scoopers?"

I wanted to tell him how powerful the "poop scoopers" really were but remembered how much they valued their anonymity. They wouldn't like it if I revealed their secret, and I didn't need them as an enemy. "No reason. I just really have to go."

"You have to go?" He turned completely around, his sword cutting deep slashes in the backs of several people in front of him before settling with the tip firmly poking my midsection. "If you had to go, why did you try to break into the printing press and then have me take you to 'the glorious one?' Didn't your mom teach you to always go before you leave?"

The situation had turned completely around. The guy had seemed happy, almost enthusiastic to take me to this "glorious one" until I mentioned the toilet cleaners, but now his "friend" sword was threatening to permanently empty my belly. I had to think fast and use my rapier-like wit to deflect his rapier-like rapier. Unfortunately, he had used the word "poop" and that word is my kryptonite. (The word, not actual poop. When I see actual poop, I pinch my nose and run away like most people.) I had managed to resist the urge to laugh for a few seconds but now I was in full-on giggle fits.

He pulled his sword back in surprise at my reaction, which was a lucky break as with my belly bouncing about from the giggling, he would have cut me without even moving. "Spontaneous giggle fits? I've heard of this. That's the first symptom of the 'Pooponic Plague!' I have to get you out of here, kill you, and burn your body, not necessarily in that order." He grabbed ahold of me. "Let's go before you give everyone the runs!"

"Halt!" a powerful voice called from behind him.

My escort/soon-to-be-murderer relaxed his grip as he turned around. Behind him stood a formation of soldiers with a palanquin in their center. The palanquin's box was covered with drapes on all sides, completely obscuring whoever was inside. These soldiers wore polished plate armor, helmets, and crisp tabards with the royal colors, in stark contrast to my companion's rusty chain armor, dirty leather cap, and stained pants.

The soldier closest to us spoke. "What seems to be the problem here?"

"Mild disturbance. Thinking he might . . . nothing to concern yourselves with, milord," my escort stammered.

The soldier waved the formation on. "Nothing to concern myself with? I'm a king's guard and your little 'mild disturbance' has slowed me on my duties. Does our country's safety mean so little to you, mercenary? Are you not loyal to Paruxia?"

"I know Paruxia's safety means a lot to me," I said.

They both turned and glared at me.

"I met King Fartius a few weeks ago, and he seemed like a really great king," I continued sheepishly. "I mean, I'm not from around here and he's not my king, but I wish he was. He's that good of a king . . . The queen seemed really nice too . . . and the king's beard, wow . . . really an impressive beard . . . Is that magic armor or are you just that good at polishing?"

They were both staring daggers at me. I felt at least a little good that I got them to agree on something, less so that they were agreeing that I was a babbling idiot.

"So, you were arresting him?" the royal guard asked.

"Think he might have the plague," the mercenary said. "Not one of the really bad plagues like the 'Exploding Brain Plague' or the 'Impotence and Male-Pattern Baldness Plague'—only one of the lesser ones."

"Ah, then carry on."

The guard turned around to rejoin his formation. As soon he got near the palanquin, the curtain raised slightly at the edge, and the guard leaned in to talk to whoever was inside. The guard apologized profusely as he explained his actions, but the person inside wanted more.

The guard marched back over to us. "The king wants to know what plague he has."

"The king?" I asked.

"King? I didn't say he was the king. He's only one of the lesser servants out testing the palanquin, and this lesser servant is practicing the kind of things the king would ask."

The curtain pulled back farther, and King Fartius's distinct short beard poked out.

"Hey, King Fartius." I waved.

King Fartius stuck his head out and waved back. "Hat! I didn't know you had a plague. Why don't you come back with me and my doctor can fix you up? Plagues aren't really, really contagious, are they?"

"They are, Majesty," the royal guard said.

"I don't actually have any plague," I said. "This officer mistook my giggle fits after he said 'poop' for a sign that I had the 'Pooponic Plague.'"

The king and guard began to giggle uncontrollably.

"They have it too!" The mercenary held his hand over his mouth. "You've infected the king."

They stopped laughing.

A royal guard with a large plume in his helmet came from the front of the formation. "There's no such thing as a 'Pooponic Plague.' The royal physician disproved its existence last year. It was a mistranslation. It was supposed to be 'Souponic Plague,' where you laugh uncontrollably whenever you hear the word 'soup.'"

"Well, that isn't a very funny word," the king said.

"Exactly," the guard captain said. "Only those with the strongest of wills can resist laughing at the word 'poop.'"

After everyone stopped giggling, the king invited me into his palanquin. No one else was inside. It may have been my imagination, but it appeared larger inside than it had from the outside. The smells of the close-packed, sweaty crowd were replaced by a florally, perfumed fragrance. The king pointed, and I sat across from him on the lush, purple cushions. My saddle-sore rear melted in pleasure. He offered me a bowl of candied, grape-like fruits which I happily accepted. Food, comfort, and nice smells. I could see why Billiam wanted to be the king.

"Hat, am I glad I found you," the king said. "I originally only agreed with Judas's proposal to make him happy because I never anticipated he would succeed, but then my advisors reported a really, really big gathering here to meet Didlius, so I came at once. I've been to see Judas, yesterday, and was on my way to visit him again. Judas and Didlius were having a rather heated argument last night. I hope it was only temporary, but if it's something more, you may be the only one who can diffuse them."

I didn't like the idea of seeing Judas before I had talked to Didlius alone, but if they were fighting, Judas might be too distracted to do anything or Did could agree to talk to me just to spite him. It wasn't the best of plans, but with all the guards around, it might be the only way I'd be able to get to him. My gut told me to go with the king. "I'll try my best."

"Really, really good." He patted me on the shoulder. "This new religion could be just the thing I need to break the power of those dastardly priests. Always telling me I can't kill my enemies because they're my brothers in faith and it's not 'moral'—whatever that word means. They just make it really, really hard to be a good king, and it'll be great to have a new religion with fewer rules to follow. Plus, my friend Judas will be in charge, and I'm sure he can fudge some of the rules if I ask him really, really nice or buy him some new robes."

"Actually, Didlius is in charge."

He patted me on the other shoulder. "Of course he is. I only misspoke. I meant he can talk to this Didlius for me. Assuming you can get them to reconcile . . . And if not, you're my really, really good friend too. The secret of being a good king is to always have a backup plan, more than one backup plan if you can help it. It took me a few years to learn that one. But that's another secret of being a really, really good king; always learn from your mistakes and always strive to get better. That's why so many of the best kings not so coincidentally lived so long. Well, that and the bad ones tend to get made really, really dead."

The palanquin stopped, followed by the shuffling of armored feet, and then a clunking noise as the front dropped open.

"Announcing King Fartius the First. King of Paruxia, Xonria, and the Falian Islands. Lord of the Paru Sea. Conqueror of Volwaen. Destroyer of All Who Oppose Him. Owner of a really, really great beard, and by all accounts a nice guy."

The curtain in the front pulled back and King Fartius walked slowly and regally out of the palanquin. I stayed seated, not sure what to do.

"And also announcing, Hat." I waited almost a minute for him to make up some titles, but when none came, I walked out as well.

"Who is also a really, really nice guy," King Fartius added.

"But not quite as really, really nice as His Majesty," the guard captain added.

I had planned on walking out slowly and with as much dignity as I could muster, but as soon as I took in the foyer, I realized that they had been announcing us to no one.

The room had a very high ceiling with beautiful etchings decorating everything above us. Whereas the etchings on the outside of buildings were cramped, intricate, and numerous, the etchings on the ceiling were on a much larger, grander scale. It seemed to be of some great battle, though I wasn't sure if it was mythical or historical. On one side of the ceiling stood a massive Paruxian host—every beard resplendent, long, and unique—and on the other, hideous monstrosities vaguely resembling men, all of which were clean-shaven.

When I reached King Fartius, the guards assembled in front of us and marched us through a succession of hallways, each bearing a different scene above. The one with the crowned figure crushing a giant's toe with his beard was my favorite. Eventually, we came to a large door flanked by two more royal guards. The guard captain opened the door, and Fartius and I entered. None of the guards followed us inside. I wasn't sure if they weren't allowed in for privacy or didn't want to get involved in the fight.

The initial crash of noise was deafening. I wasn't sure if the sound assaulting our ears was from a mythical beast, a rock concert, or an explosion. As I recoiled into the nearest corner, the only thing I could see was the king standing next to me with his crown pulled over his ears. Eventually, either my ears adjusted, or the combatants quieted down, and I was able to move toward the source of the cacophony on the other side of the room. Judas held Spoon-Scalibur over his head and the shorter Didlius was swinging his arms wildly to recover his weapon. Upon sighting Judas, I tried to go back out the door, but it was locked.

"Give me back my spoon, you fiend," Didlius wailed.

"I most certainly will not. Your followers are outside and you need to focus. You can't do that while you continue to obsess about this magic spoon."

"But it is the only thing connecting me to my precious Jaenia." He tried stomping on Judas's toes, but Judas dodged.

"And she will still be there after you finish your speech. You can have it back when the speech is over. If Hat were here, he'd tell you the same thing."

For the record, that's not true. If Hat had been there, he would have told Did to hit Judas with the spoon and then give the speech. Actually, Hat was there, and he was mostly thinking he wanted to stay out of this until they both tired each other out.

"But I'm only doing this whole religion thing to become famous and prove how worthy I am to her," Did said, "and you have no idea what Hat would want. You first told me Hat murdered Brutus, but then once I started disagreeing with you, suddenly you remembered that it was all an accident and that every time the spoon comes up, 'Hat would want you to have it.'" Didlius bit Judas in the armpit.

I was about to breathe a sigh of relief when I heard that Did had forgiven me but winced instead when he bit Judas. Poor Did's mouth would probably taste like sweat for hours.

Judas grimaced and pushed Did backward. "If you become a famous religious figure, you can have as many women as you want. You can have a different one every day. Several different ones. This Jina . . . Jona, whatever her name is, cannot possibly be worth that much effort. You don't even know what she looks like. She could be ugly. She could be old. She could even be a non-Paruxian!"

"I don't care what she looks like! She knows my soul. She's

known my every thought for over a year. She knows my heart and I know hers." Did kneed him in the groin.

Judas doubled over in pain, but right as Did reached for the spoon, Judas rolled up into a ball with the spoon at the center. Didlius kicked him repeatedly in the side, and Judas released a high-pitched howl as each blow landed.

"Hat, now would be a good time to do something," Fartius said. "They did the same thing yesterday. I tried to intervene with my guards, but that made your friend even angrier. For some reason, he doesn't trust me or even, more shockingly, my guards. Who doesn't trust a heavily armed, state-sponsored killing machine of law and order? You peasants are a strange bunch."

I watched for a few more kicks. I'm not proud that I figured out what to do right away but held off because I liked seeing Judas kicked. I briefly considered kicking him a few times myself. My soft heart eventually made me intervene.

"Guess who's back?" I asked, making sure to say it slow enough for him to get a few extra kicks in between words.

Didlius turned but didn't stop his assault. "The ghosts we met in the forest?" I shook my head. "No? Wait, I know this one. The thief I captured by throwing that woman at him?" I shook my head again. "Please, tell me it's not my mother!"

"I'm . . . Hat's back, Did," I deadpanned.

He stopped kicking and embraced me in a big hug. "Hat! It's so good to see you again. Judas explained that Brutus's death was only an accident. I wanted to look for you, but Judas said you would have been killed . . . I think. Judas wasn't very clear on that point, but he assured me most convincingly that it would be for your own good."

"I'm sure." I turned to give Judas a few kicks to let him know what I thought of his plan to "keep me safe," but he was already gone. "So, I take it by the crowds outside that those pamphlets worked pretty well."

"They did! The priests from the capital came to break them up, but our ghost friends scared them away. My suggestion was to offer to have the toilet cleaners do an extra good job on their bathrooms as a bribe to the priests, but the ghosts have a mind of their own. It all worked out in the end. When the priests left, the king himself showed up to lend his support."

"Hello." King Fartius waved from the other side of the room. "Really, really sorry about what the guards did yesterday. I left them outside this time."

"Thank you, Your Majesty. The one with the plumes seems to like me a bit too much, and I only have eyes for my sweet Jaenia. Jaenia! Where is that dastard Judas?" Did opened every object in sight in search of Judas, except for the door right behind him.

"Where who is?" Judas asked through the doorway.

Did ran through the doorway, and I followed. As the room was only big enough to hold the three of us, Fartius had to stay outside. It appeared to be a changing room.

"Another mystery solved by Didlius the Clever!" He raised both arms in celebration, hitting me in the nose and Judas in the chin.

"Ow!" Judas said.

"Serves you right," Did said. "Now what have you done with my spoon?"

"I have hidden it where you will never find it."

I looked around the tiny room. There was no place for him to hide it in there, so I assumed it was the spoon-shaped bulge in the breast pocket of his robe. I decided not to mention that until I found out more of what was going on.

"I'll give it back when you finish your speech in a few hours," Judas said. "The speech is too important for distractions. It's your first one to your new followers, and first impressions are often the most important."

Didlius kicked him in the shin. "Then I'll beat the location out of you."

Realizing that I was just as likely to get hit as Judas in that small room, I intervened. "Did, what if I promise to keep the spoon safe while you get ready for your speech?"

Did paused with his hand half-cocked. "You would do that?"

I nodded.

"Very well. Jaenia likes you and told me to always trust your word. Perhaps a few hours without her in my head would be good." He lowered his arm.

"Excellent," Judas said. "Why don't you go upstairs to where I have the speech, and I'll join you in a second."

Didlius nodded and went to the door that led to the hallway.

"I would like to hear this speech," King Fartius piped happily. "Perhaps I can even offer a few suggestions. Don't get me wrong —I'm sure Judas's speech is really, really good, like all his speeches are, but I'd really, really like to save as many souls as possible by making sure that church tax rate is low. Say, Mr. Didlius, how do you feel about putting my picture right in the middle of your holy vestment? I'd pay an endorsement fee, of course." The king followed Did out the door.

As soon as their voices faded, Judas slapped me on the back. "Hat, it is so great to see you. I'm sorry about that whole incident with Brutus. It was completely Didlius's idea to put you in jail. I tried to talk him out of it, naturally, but he's in charge, so I was forced to relent. Did I mention how great it is to see you?"

I hid my smile well enough that it didn't draw a reaction from him. I wasn't sure what he was up to, but my gut told me to play along. "It's . . . good to see you too. Looks like your plans have worked out exceptionally well. The crowd's huge outside."

"Exceptionally well?" His face lit up in mock surprise. "That's quite the compliment."

I eyed the bulge in his breast pocket. There was no way I was letting that arrogant, morally questionable jerk keep something like that. "Give me Did's spoon. I promised him I'd take care of it."

Judas shrugged. "I seem to have forgotten where I put the thing, but don't you worry, I'll find it after the speech."

I pointed at his pocket.

He pulled Spoon-Scalibur out. "Well, look at that. It's a good thing you have such a keen eye. I'm so good at hiding things that even I can't find them when I look for them." He begrudgingly handed it to me.

I tucked the spoon into my pocket. "Listen, Judas, I know you'd don't like me."

His eyes became so glued to my pocket that he almost forgot to pretend to frown. "I'm not sure where you got that idea, dear Hat. I consider you one of my closest friends. Also, Didlius has been completely unmanageable since you left, so our organization has need of you."

I considered using the spoon on him, but that would have made me no better than him. My gut told me that I should let things play out for now, and my gut hadn't been wrong yet. I wasn't sure if that meant I should wait for him to slip up or let what he had planned go on. Perhaps his plan was what was meant to be.

"Whatever," I said. "As much as I disapprove of some of the things you're doing, it's pretty clear that there's nothing I can do about it. I'll make a proposition for you. I promise to not interfere with any of your plans for the religion if you leave me alone to write down everything that happens uninterrupted."

The fake frown vanished from his face. Judas grabbed my hand and shook it. His grip was surprisingly strong. "That sounds splendid. I always said we worked better together than we did apart. Now let's go upstairs and see about the speech. When you write it down in your little book, be sure to use words like 'dignified, 'legendary,' and 'remarkable' when describing it."

"What's in this speech?" I asked, not moving.

"Oh, yes. My apologies, but my mind does tend to wander. Well, I planned for Didlius to go into a lengthy spiel about how any men who fight with us against the heathens will get lots of beautiful women both here and in the afterlife. Most of our followers should be men, so I only put in a few sentences to cover the women's side of the pamphlet to keep them from nagging. At the end, we'll cover the beard stuff to appease our glorious king, while still keeping it vague enough to not anger any of the more conservative beard purists."

I picked up some paper and a quill off the desk and began taking notes. "Actually, I was out there for several hours, and I saw a lot more women."

"Hmm . . ." He pulled a pamphlet out of his pocket.

I leaned over his shoulder to look. Evidently, the artist had taken quite a bit of liberty with our instructions. The pamphlet depicted a woman trying to get water from the town well and getting harassed by several men along the way, so she goes into a temple of our religion to avoid them. As soon as she converts, the priests go out and beat the crap out of her harassers.

"This is nothing like what we told her," Judas mumbled.

I pointed out one of the side windows to the crowd below. "But it worked." Out in the crowd there were roughly two women to every man.

For the first time since I'd known him, Judas was completely speechless. His eyes slowly scanned the crowd several times, and then he ran to the other side of the room to look out another window. The crowd on that side was no different. "It looks like I will have to rewrite the beginning. I was hoping for more men since they make better soldiers. How will my new religion sweep across the continent with so few soldiers?"

I decided to ignore the sexism in that statement, so that I could use it to my advantage. "I guess Didlius will just have to do something peaceful with *his* religion."

He didn't seem to hear me and continued to stare at the crowd. "Though I do see more weaponry in the hands of the women than the men, and they do seem rather angry."

I closed the window, almost taking off the tips of three of his fingers.

He muttered something and led me out to the hallway, through another guarded door, and up some stairs. We entered another guarded door and found Didlius and King Fartius arguing with three Paruxians in matching red robes. When the argument died down, the three priests turned toward us and hissed in unison.

YOU TAKE THAT SPOON OUTSIDE, YOUNG MAN

After they were finished hissing, the three newcomers posed like they were in a movie poster, never letting their eyes off us. I shuffled a bit to the left to confirm a theory and not one of their eyes followed me. They must not have liked Judas, and it had nothing at all to do with me not having had a chance to bathe or shave for a few days. I even stuck my tongue out to no response.

Before I could try my hand at armpit noises, the Red Robe in the middle snorted. "We can finally dispense our justice on the chief oppressor."

"Here, here," the other two Red Robes said.

Judas tapped his fingers on his hip. "I'm going to guess by your armbands that you are representatives of one of the other beard modeling schools."

"No, no," the king said. "Those scarlet vestments indicate they are from one of those special religious orders, likely here to stop your speech."

"No," Didlius said. "They're villains, here to take my sweet Jaenia from me and tie her to some carriage tracks."

The one in the middle sneered. "Mwa ha. You're all right. Our formal name is the Order of the Beard Model, Special Religious

Forces and Tax Consultancy, or the OOBMSRFTC, and we were sent here by His High Holiness for all of those things you mentioned, followed by an audit for extra fun."

"You forgot the first 'T,'" I said.

"That 'T' is silent!" The good news was he did know I was there. The bad news was I could now hear a constant ringing sound from his shrill voice.

Judas smiled. "So, your plan is for the three of you to announce that you're here to stop us right in the middle of our headquarters that is surrounded by armed guards as well as an untold number of our followers?"

"Yes!" the shorter one said. When her two companions did not join in on her enthusiasm, she repeated the word but as more of a hesitant, whispered question.

"Ha," the middle one, the apparent leader, said. "We only did that so you would get a false sense of security and let your guard down. And then, when we were assured you had your guard down, we would strike!"

"Wouldn't that be about now?" Judas asked.

"Well, not when you're all looking at us," the leader said. "Could you all close your eyes?"

Didlius and the king covered their eyes. Judas rolled his at me and shook his head. The two of us moved across the room and pulled their hands down.

"Drat. They told me you were too clever for anything but the cleverest of plans, but now I see that they were not exaggerating." He turned toward the taller one. "Clithsbus, open the door so that we can strategically withdraw and come up with another plan."

Clithsbus raised his hand enthusiastically. "Huzzah!"

Judas motioned to me, and I moved in front of the door before Clithsbus could turn around. Clithsbus scratched his head and looked to his master for new instructions.

"Say," the leader said, "could you move over so we could strategically retreat?"

"I'm going to go with 'no' on that one," I said. "I've watched way too many cartoons, and we don't want you coming back for more hijinks every week. I think we should just put you in prison, but that's only me throwing out suggestions. I'm not the one in charge. Didlius?"

"That sounds like a great idea, but I should ask Jaenia." Did held his hand out toward me.

Judas slapped his hand down. "No Jaenia until you've finished the speech."

"But I need her sage advice."

"You can figure this out yourself. Besides, I think this Jamania is only a figment of your imagination anyway."

Did slapped the smile right off Judas's face. "She is real! She's beautiful and smart, and I can't live without her."

"Not that I don't like seeing Judas get slapped," I said, "but can you prove she's real, Did? I'm not doubting you or anything, only curious."

Did held his hand out. "Of course, if you could just give me the spoon—"

"No spoon!" Judas slapped his hand back.

Did pushed Judas down, and they rolled on the floor in a pile.

"Yeah, we're just going to go," the leader of the Red Robes said as he took a step toward the door. "You guys obviously have some personal stuff you need to sort out."

I moved back to the door and barred his path. "No."

The leader was about to pout at me but had to leap to the other side of the room to avoid the two wrestlers. His two companions followed him. King Fartius remained seated and began clapping. I wasn't sure who he was rooting for. I was rooting for the two of them to come to their senses and stop.

"Judas," I said, "would you agree to stop slapping if Did

promises to only hold onto the spoon for a few minutes, long enough to have a short conversation with Jaenia?"

Judas rolled Did to the ground and held him down. "As curious as I am for proof that she's real, I doubt he'll give it back. Last time, I had to drug his food and then take the spoon when he slept."

"Did, do you promise to give the spoon back after you prove Jaenia is real?"

Did pushed Judas off him, dove on top, and slapped him repeatedly. "I do. I am a man of my word, and I promised to let Hat keep her while I practice for this speech."

I grabbed Did's hand as he reached back for a power slap and put the spoon in it. Didlius immediately stood over the prostrate form of Judas and held the spoon over his head reverently. The glowing spoon blinded me for a few seconds. When my vision returned, everyone besides Judas (who was still lying on his back) and I were down on their knees in awe.

"What is that?" the leader of the Red Robes asked.

"It's beauuuuutiful," the taller Red Robe said. "The light can only be the work of God."

"Nuh-uh," the shortest Red Robe said. "God's light is blue. This is better. It's like if silver, water, and light had a baby and that baby grew up, learned magic, and how to be awesome. All hail new God!"

"Sacrilege!" the leader said.

"Screw you." The taller one tore off his vestment and threw it at him. It was good to know they had boxer shorts with little hearts on them in Paruxia.

"Yeah." The shorter one followed suit and tossed her vestment at their leader.

"Ahem," Judas said, still from the ground. "As nice as that little spat was, could you please confirm this Jaenia exists and then hand the spoon back to Hat? Preferably right after you move so I can stand."

Did took a few steps back. "Sorry."

Judas stood and glared at him. Did stared at the spoon for several minutes but, besides a steadily dimming glow, nothing happened.

Judas tapped his fingers on the floor. "As I thought. Now give it back."

Did stared at the spoon and looked like he was going to cry.

"Don't worry, Did," I said. "You'll get this back after the speech later. It'll all be over before you know it."

He sighed in resignation. "I know, and then I will gain my confidence and be worthy of her love. If only I could believe in myself like the two of you."

I patted him on the back. "I'm sure she already feels you're worthy of her, Did."

"Do you think so?"

"Of course. I mean, if she's been talking to you and encouraging you all this time, she's got to be into you."

Judas laughed sarcastically. "She's *only* able to talk to him. She's just as likely to be doing that because she's bored, not because she's interested in him." His eyes lit up suddenly and then softened. "No, no. I'm mistaken. Hat is right as always. She is clearly in love with you."

Did raised his head slowly, a lone tear sliding off his chin. "She is?" He looked to me and then Judas. "She is." The spoon shone brighter, and he raised it back above his head. "She is!"

The spoon erupted in light, several times brighter than before. I barely managed to shield my eyes before it got to a level that might cause permanent damage. A duo of screams—one masculine, one feminine—told me that not everyone was so lucky. I doubted any ships hundreds of miles away would have trouble finding land. I had been so distracted with the blinding light that I hadn't heard Did strike Spoon-Scalibur against anything to warrant the lightning aftereffect, though even that was not as remotely distracting as the pieces of roof that landed on my toe.

"Did, how many times do I have to tell you not to use that thing indoors?" I yelled, but it was doubtful he, or anyone else, could hear me through the sound of the collapsing roof.

I fought back the excruciating pain in my big toe and kept my hands over my eyes. I was about to back up when another piece of roof slapped me in the forehead and knocked me flat. It all happened so suddenly that I'm not sure if it knocked me out briefly or what, but the next thing I remember was opening my eyes and leaning forward.

Fortunately, Didlius had dropped the spoon before it got too out of hand. The spoon rested a few feet to my left between the large pieces of roof covering the spot where Judas had been and the headless body of the taller former Red Robe. The leader of the Red Robes had been one of the screamers, though with the way he was holding his eyes, he likely had a good reason. Everyone else in the room seemed to be frightened and in shock but otherwise unharmed. All things considered, it was better than I expected. Even the beautiful woman Didlius held in his arms seemed mostly fine.

Beautiful woman? Where did she come from? And more importantly, what does she put in her hair to get it that shiny?

A MYSTERIOUS WOMAN WHO DOESN'T HAND OUT MAGIC SWORDS

Didlius knelt and held the woman in his trembling hands. I've never seen a face so happy. At first I thought his face was stuck like that, as nothing moved a millimeter for over a minute, though as far as facial expressions to get stuck with went, that was a good one. Three minutes later, his face finally moved, at first with a simple twitch in his eye, but after that everything seemed to come at once; it looked like he was having a facial spasm. Fortunately, the painful expression was soon covered up by a torrent of tears.

It was too much, so I had to look away, and boy, did I look at the right place. I had considered his companion to be the most beautiful woman I had ever seen before, but now that she was returning his smile, I revised my estimate by several degrees to more beautiful than I could imagine. Her smile, her hair, her teeth. Everything about her seemed to glow with a silvery shimmer that was rather similar to the glow from the spoon.

I found the spoon only a few feet away. It didn't have a bit of that constant silver glow that it had always had. If I didn't know any better, I would have assumed it wasn't made of silver at all. It looked like an old metal spoon.

My eyes darted back to the woman, then back to the spoon,

then back to the woman, and back to the spoon again. Could it be? Instead of wasting a lot of time in a lengthy internal debate (and bore the crap out of my readers by trying to figure out what a lot of you probably already guessed), I decided to just ask her. "Jaenia, is that you?"

She didn't answer me right away as she stood up and took in her surroundings. "Depends on who's asking."

"My darling," Didlius said, "that is Hat. Remember him? I told you about him."

I backed away as far as I could (which was only a few inches into the rubble) as her beautifully smiling face changed into a beautifully frowning face.

What had he told her about me? Maybe she didn't like me teaching Did how to rap? I bet she's a fan of country. Or is this Judas's doing? Where is Judas anyway? The pile of wood that marks his last known location isn't moving. It would serve that bastard right being dead.

Her frown mercifully disappeared as she bit her lip and turned back to Did. "And who are you?"

"I am Didlius, my sweet love. I can see that you're disoriented by your sudden freedom, but surely you must remember me."

She turned back to me suddenly, leapt up, and got about an inch away from my face. I was both aroused and terrified at the same time. She smelled terrific, a combination of roses and cinnamon. I smiled at her, which she took the wrong way and immediately put her perfectly manicured finger into my chest.

"How dare you take advantage of my sweet Didlius, wherever he is. Talking him into sending armies to ravage the countryside and then ravage the suburbs before ravaging the countryside again! And then you had him throw out that sweet Didlius boy who was guiding him to be a hero." She released her finger and scratched her head. "Which one are you again?"

Didlius gently put his hand on her shoulder. "The *man* who

helped me focus my heroism is named Hat, who you happen to be talking to right now. Judas was the one who talked me into sending out the armies to make the non-believers pay, but you shouldn't worry as that is part of Stage Two, which we haven't begun and won't begin since you oppose it so much."

I clapped in relief that he wouldn't use war to spread the word of The One. Unfortunately, my clapping re-angered Jaenia, and she poked me in the chest with two fingers this time.

"So, you go about plaguing my sweet Hat's mind with your villainy, Judas, and then try to deafen me? Do you know what I have done to villains in the past?"

"That's Hat, my sweet, and I am Didlius," Did whispered in her ear.

She pulled both fingers out of my chest and shook my hand. "Oh, my apologies, whoever you are. It's really a pleasure to meet you. Could you go fetch the handsome hero, whose name escapes me right now, that I've been talking to through that spoon?"

"A pleasure as well," I said. "And Didlius is right next to you."

She blew back her dark, wavy hair and laughed. "No, not this skinny servant. I mean the bulky, he-man with the long, flowing hair and face that could tempt even a goddess like me. He's finally proved himself worthy of me by believing in himself, and I'd like to reward him."

Didlius looked like he wanted to bury himself in the pile of rubble that marked where Judas had been. King Fartius stood up and patted Did on the back in reassurance. "I think the young lady just needs some rest. She has obviously been through a lot."

"Who're you calling young?" Jaenia asked. "I'm old enough to be your . . . mother's younger adopted cousin who was switched at birth and . . . yes, rest would be good. What year is it anyway?"

"Four hundred sixty-seven," King Fartius said.

"Four hundred sixty-seven?" Jaenia howled. "Oh, my goodness. I've travelled back in time. No, wait. I've travelled forward in time! No, wait again. Four hundred sixty-seven of what calendar?"

Before I could answer her, a pile of wood flew off the floor, revealing Judas's smirking form. The closest thing to damage on him were a few hairs out of place and a nasty wrinkle on his tunic that likely wouldn't come out. "You've been trapped in there for nearly two thousand years, my dear."

"Do I know you?" Jaenia asked.

Judas was incredulous, but then a light went on and he suddenly calmed down. "Ah, yes. You've never seen me with this beard, have you?" He snapped his fingers and a sudden flash emanated from them. The hair on his head fell out, but not his beard. "Better?"

Jaenia shook her head. "No."

He felt his bearded face. "Ah, sorry. I've been posing as this preening beard model for so long I'm a little rusty." He snapped his fingers again and the beard fell off.

"Still nothing," she said.

While Jaenia might not have recognized him, I did. It's amazing how covering your face and head with hair can make you almost unrecognizable, but in my defense, I hadn't exactly spent a lot of time with him.

"Gu!" I said. "No wonder you . . . I can't actually think of anything that connects the Judas plotline with Gu's. Is this part of Billiam's evil . . . sorry, regular plan, since we agreed that nothing he's done so far has been worse than morally ambiguous?"

"Quiet, you soft-hearted simpleton. The big people are talking here." He snapped again, and a gag appeared in my mouth (which wasn't as bad as it sounds as it tasted like delicious, creamy peanut butter).

Satisfied that I was taken care of, he knocked Didlius halfway across the room to land on top of the still pitifully moaning leader of the Red Robes in the corner. "Ahh, it's so nice to not have to turn my powers down so I could believably pass as a weak mortal anymore," Judas/Gu said.

Neat! Magic hair removal, creating gags full of peanutty goodness, and the strength to knock a full-grown man across the room with a slap—the only people who could do that sort of thing were Old Gods. (Atlians can also use magic but are terribly allergic to peanuts and possess normal strength, so that eliminated him from being one of them.)

"Now," he continued, "that those insignificant obstacles are out of my way—"

"Didlius's servant!" she screamed. "Don't you dare hurt my beloved's help." She smacked Judas/Gu to the opposite corner of the room back into the pile from which he emerged.

Seeing what happened to things in corners, I moved to the middle outskirt of the room, a little behind and to the left of Jaenia. The peanut butter taste of the gag was still going strong. I wanted to ask him if he could add a little grape jelly to the gag, but of course couldn't verbalize my request, so I attempted sign language instead.

Gu spit out a chunk of wood and stood up. "How dare you defend that man-child! What does he have that I don't?"

"I don't know," Jaenia said. "I'm sorry, but I don't remember you."

Gu looked her hard in the eye, on the verge of his anger overwhelming him, but then his chest deflated and he sighed. "You really don't, do you? You know, shortly after I put you in that spoon to cool off after you left me, I had a feeling that maybe that wasn't such a good idea. And then when I went back to my head priest to rectify the situation a century later, the stupid mortal went and died of something called 'old age.' I've been looking for you for all these lonely centuries, so that you could again be by my side when I restart my religious conquests, and now that I've finally found you and contrived to free you from your prison, you don't even remember me. Well, no matter. We do live forever, so that should leave plenty of time to remind you why you always loved me. Would you accompany me to dinner and a play, milady?" He bowed down elaborately and then smoothly grabbed ahold of her hand.

She looked at his hand for a long while but then recoiled like she had been bitten. "No. My heart belongs to Didlius, who I'm sure will arrive shortly and defeat you."

Gu raised himself back up and turned toward Didlius. "A situation easily remedied by handing you his literal heart. Ha ha ha!" He stopped and scratched his beardless chin. "Ohh . . . That's a good one. I'm going to have to remember that for my next book, which I will write with your beloved's blood."

I finished removing the gag right in the nick of time, though it did muffle my slow clap a bit. "Really love the evil laugh there, Gu. Perfectly timed after the outstandingly scary threat to remove his heart. It brought chills to me, though slight complaint. Minor one, so don't get too offended, but she said her heart belonged to Didlius, and you threatened to remove *his* heart."

He glared at me (also outstandingly scary), but his face relaxed a bit. "A valid point, but I don't want to remove her heart, since you know, I love her and all, but she used the word 'heart.' I'll fix it later in editing."

"Oh, yeah. I totally understand. It was a minor quibble. But don't let me keep distracting you. Please continue with describing to Jaenia what you're going to do to my friend." While he was focused on my mouth, I picked up the spoon.

"Very well." He raised his voice to barely below a yell. "I'm going to tear his heart out and then . . . There's not really much I can do to him after that. Sure, I could do a little taunting dance or gloat, but from what my research suggests, a mortal would be in too much pain to notice it. Kind of defeats the purpose. Plus, that'll likely put her in a rage, and then she'll attack me. Can't really gloat when you have a goddess attacking you. She may not look it, but she is strong."

"Who's a goddess?" Jaenia asked.

Didlius beamed at her through a bloody mouth. "You are, my dear."

"Does that include any powers? Can I summon lemon cupcakes?"

"I believe he said you do have powers, but I'm not sure about that particular one. Why don't you try?"

She wiggled her fingers at Gu and then did a pirouette.

Gu shook his head in bewilderment. I took the opportunity to toss the spoon to Didlius.

"Whatever," Gu said. "If it makes you happy, you can figure out how to summon cupcakes while I acquire a heart to put on the top of mine."

"No. I'm not going to let you harm my dear Didlius's servant." Jaenia stopped pirouetting and massaged her knuckle.

Gu laughed. "The last time you tried that you ended up in a spoon. Would you like to be in a butter knife or a spork this time?"

"The only one who's going to be spooned is you," I said as I motioned to Didlius.

Didlius looked down at the spoon in his hand, looked at Gu's back, and then whacked Gu right on the spine. I covered my eyes from the anticipated light show but opened them soon after when I didn't hear thunder. Gu turned around and stared at Didlius. This time Did didn't need any directions and hit him again, right between the eyes. The spoon bounced off Gu's skin with little effect besides mild annoyance. No thunder and lightning occurred either, which was probably good since the building didn't look like it could take much more.

"Such bravery," Jaenia said in awe. "You really are my Didlius."

King Fartius grabbed the blind Red Robe and ushered him out the door to my right. Gu saw them out of the corner of his eyes but did nothing to stop them. The other Red Robe seemed to have already left. I considered joining them but something made me stay put. I'm still not sure if it was because I wanted to be there to witness this for the book, if I had become braver as a result of the journey, if I was staying for my friend, or if my legs were too terrified to move. Whatever the case, I stayed.

Jaenia growled at Gu, "If I have to give my life to protect my beloved, I will. Mark my words, guy whose name I can't remember, I, Hat . . . Didlius? Whatever my name is, I, the goddess of love and post-breakup revenge, will not let you harm him!" She punched Gu in the jaw with a glowing fist.

Gu recoiled, seeming more shocked than actually hurt. Seeing an opening, Jaenia kneed him in the groin, which definitely hurt, but not enough as he rebounded with a ferocious uppercut. The building shook, first from the impact of the blow, then again when her body bounced off the floor. Enraged, Didlius hit Gu in the back repeatedly with the spoon to no effect. Gu didn't even turn to address Didlius and instead kicked Jaenia in the ribs. She grimaced slightly but didn't seem to be anything more than annoyed as she swept Gu's legs out from under him. While the two gods didn't seem to do any damage to each other, the building was not so impervious to their struggle. For some reason, wooden Paruxian buildings didn't seem to stand up too well to gods with super strength having punching and lightning-flinging parties in them. I made a note to propose new building codes to King Fartius if I lived as the building swayed back and forth with each new blow.

"Did," I said, "we have to get out of here. The building can't take much more of this. My stomach can't either, but I'm pretty sure the building part is more important. Come on."

Didlius slapped Gu on the back a few more times with the same non-effect. Jaenia pushed Gu off her and dove into his face with a flying elbow drop that would put Hulk Hogan to shame. Gu shrugged it off and landed several rabbit punches into her stomach. The resulting force caused the building to sway in the opposite direction but had no effect on his opponent besides wrinkling her dress.

As much as I wanted to see what happened next, I was confident that one more blow would answer the question of what it would be like to have a building collapse around you. I gave a last shout to Didlius and ran to the door. The building swayed again as I reached the bottom of the stairs and swayed the final time as I took my second step out of the exit.

Even through the pounding of my heart, I could hear the loud crash behind me. As loud as that sound was, it was nothing compared to the collective sigh of the crowd in front of me.

WHAT CAN I TRADE YOU SO YOU WON'T KILL ME?

The crowd that had gathered around the building was staring at me expectantly. They were an odd mixture of people that seemed to be from all walks of life. I wasn't sure what they wanted from me. The only thing I could think of was that they wanted a sign that I was OK. I was still shaking from what had happened but didn't want them to worry, so I dusted myself off and gave them a half-hearted wave.

"Is that him?" someone in the crowd shouted.

"Couldn't be," a fat man in front said. "The pamphlets clearly showed him just like us, and this man . . . doesn't have a beard."

"Nice save, Lucus. Those racial sensitivity classes have really paid off."

"He brought a whole building down right as he left it," a woman with fruit on her head that may or may not have been a hat responded. "I doubt our new god would have left that kind of flashy entrance to some nobody like his assistant."

There was a murmur of agreement in the crowd.

"Hey, assistants are people too," I said.

There was less of a murmur of agreement to that one but still some.

I turned around. The building was completely destroyed, except for a desk that had somehow miraculously escaped. The floor of the room where the battle had taken place was laying on top of the rubble to my right and was mostly intact. Conspicuously missing were any bodies or still moving gods. "Could you guys help me dig through the rubble behind me to see if my friends are alive?"

"Oh, that's nice," the same woman said. "I guess our first commandment is we should always check any rubble for friends if a building collapses on them."

I ran over and dug frantically through the piles of rubble for any signs of Didlius. Several members of the crowd joined me.

After what seemed like hours with no luck besides finding the spoon, King Fartius pulled me aside. "It is unfortunate that Didlius and Judas are gone, but this crowd is looking to you for guidance. We have a rare opportunity before us, and we need to take advantage of it."

"I have more important things on my mind, Your Majesty. Why don't you lead them?"

"I've tried forming my own religion before, but the people really, really don't trust a king to lead them in spiritual matters. They seem to want a different guy for that job. Besides, they appear to have taken a shine to you."

I looked back at the crowd, and he was right. Everyone in the crowd was looking at me as if I had answers they desperately needed, like what to eat for dinner or if it's OK to claim your imaginary friend on your taxes. As much as I wanted to give them those answers, I had to find Didlius because he was my friend, and so I could see his story through.

"There was a massive flash of lightning on the second floor right before the building collapsed. I don't think Didlius could have survived that." King Fartius pointed to the blackened spot that covered most of what had been the second-story floor.

If Didlius was gone, then who was supposed to lead The One? Harry was very clear that Didlius founded it . . . or did he say *helped* found it? What was the phrasing again? I looked to the crowd for answers but their faces only seemed to hold questions.

"And our second commandment is we should give up looking for friends in rubble after precisely fourteen minutes," the fruit-helmed woman said.

OK, one of them had an answer to something, but it wasn't the right answer. It wasn't a wrong answer either; it just wasn't a particularly good answer. These people needed answers, so someone would have to give it to them.

"And all confirmations of commandments should be set by lengthy bouts of staring and then any overly proud nod." I wasn't sure which was more annoying: Fruit Hat's loud voice or what she was saying.

King Fartius tugged on my sleeve. "We were going to have the speech from a platform on the eastern edge of town, but perhaps we should hold it here. You've already got their attention. I'll send for the Atlian we hired to cast a really, really big voice projecting spell and for my servant with the cue cards."

I nodded to the king. "If everyone could wait a few minutes, we're going to get set up."

Fruit Hat helpfully shouted, "Intermission," and the crowd milled around excitedly. Out of nowhere vendors appeared hawking some sort of meat in pockets. If I hadn't had more important things on my mind, I would have rushed to learn more about them.

"Thank God," I said. "That was getting out of hand fast."

King Fartius chuckled. "You really, really shouldn't say 'thank God' anymore since you are a god to these people."

"Oh, God . . . oh, me? No. I'm only the earthly . . . worldly representative of their new deity. I should probably start my speech with the name of the deity. They need to know it's called The—"

"Leave the name out for now. It will add a really, really big element of mystery that will make them come back for more. When you've got them right on the edge of being completely hooked, you shoot the name out and boom, you've got them. I was king for two whole years before I told anyone what regal name I chose. I went through seventeen heralds, but my approval ratings were never higher."

"Judas/Gu said you were called Fartius when you were prince and that it was a family name on your mother's side. Is that not true?"

"I was born Fartius, but that didn't mean I had to pick it as my royal name. Now, we need to prepare for what you're going to say."

"Don't worry," I said. "I have this. I'll start by telling them to treat people with respect and then how all people and beards are created equal in God's eyes. Follow that with make love, not war, while taking time to explain how war is bad for everyone. Don't worry, I'll go over that one in depth to address the inconsistency with that one side of the pamphlet. Then cap it off with money not being the source of happiness."

"Err . . . I really, really like the beard thing, but all *people* being created equal can't be right. Surely you mean all peasants are created equal."

"No, I mean . . ."

A trio of guards appeared leading a thin, purple-robed Atlian woman. She stopped a few feet away from me and without a word began making elaborate gestures with her hands. Slowly, a swirl of green energy began to build in front of her.

"I meant that all peasants are created equal, yes," I said to Fartius. "Also, that all nobles of the same rank are created equal and all kings who are not of Paruxia are created equal—the king of Paruxia being equal to only God, and maybe his wife if she's really bossy, which is not at all the case with you, Majesty."

"That could work, but the rest will likely go over really, really bad. I would suggest that you stick to Judas's speech. While Judas was an Old God, his speech should still resonate really, really good with the crowd."

"I don't know. Judas and I didn't agree on much. Besides, I haven't even seen the speech, let alone memorized it."

"Judas thought of that, as Didlius wasn't really, really known for his memory. He had the speech written out on these large, paper-covered boards that he invented called 'cue cards.' It's just not fair that he had both the power of a god *and* the greatest mind in all of Paruxia, but maybe his mind was part of his powers." About a dozen guards formed around Fartius.

The king continued as he pointed to the tallest building in town. "I will be listening from the balcony of my hunting cabin over there. I had one of my servants get the cue cards, and she'll be holding them on the balcony right in front of you." He pointed up and I could see a heavy-set woman adjusting some large white cards there. "I thought it best if she wasn't on the same one as me as some people might take that as you getting your words from me."

Before I could voice any objections or concerns, the king moved away. The crowd immediately covered any path between us. The guards he left with me didn't seem interested in leaving their positions or even acknowledging me. I couldn't really blame them as the crowd was starting to get a little rowdy, though it was really more of the overly energetic festival type and less of any real danger.

Taking my first good look at the crowd and the large quantity of expectant eyes glued to me, it finally occurred to me how enormously important what I was about to do was. Granted I knew what the outcome would be, but it would still be extremely important. Books would be written about this speech. Countless sermons would go over what I was about to say. Children throughout the ages would be bored to tears covering this at Sunday school. Suddenly I was very glad there would be cue cards in case I got nervous and forgot what to say.

The crowd seemed to represent every strata and social class of Paruxian society. Even the creepy clown class was represented. I thought I might have even seen a few non-Paruxians in there, though they could have only been from other areas of the country with different styles of dress, hairstyles, and coloring. Even a few ghosts were in the audience. I gave a wink to the Atlian ghost, Gafenarai. A group of toilet cleaners were huddled to the right. They must have just come from work as the rest of the crowd was giving them several feet of space. The Pink Woman's mercenaries were spread throughout the crowd—judging by their pasted-on badges—as a police force . A pale, bearded woman waved her floppy hat at me from below the cue card woman, and I waved back. I was relieved to see Fred, the pretend magician, was alive and had recovered from her injuries. The crowd appeared to be varying degrees of happy and excited, without a hostile face in sight. What was I worried about? I knew how this would go. I might even enjoy this.

The Atlian finished her motions and then snapped her fingers at me. Green waves shot toward my face. I reflexively took a step back to try to dodge them, but they caught me and covered my face. A cool wave massaged my throat and spread to the rest of my body. It felt amazing, and I let out a sigh of relief. The echo of my heavily amplified sigh turned every eye on me immediately.

The Atlian waved her fingers again and two big "Silence" signs each held by a scantily clad woman on my far left and right began to glow. (I was told later that it was customary for Paruxians to obey all signs, no matter how idiotic the message, as long as the speaker paid half-naked women to hold them up while they were speaking.) The crowd dutifully quieted and stared at me in rapt attention. The Atlian moved closer and motioned for me to begin.

"Hello, everyone. My name is Hat. That's H-A-T for those of you writing this down. I'd like to thank you all for coming here to hear my message of spiritual well-being."

"Stop wasting time and get on with the part about the seventy virgins," a short, bearded fellow yelled.

That got a laugh from parts of the crowd.

"I heard there were sixty-nine—and who cares if they're virgins," another masculine voice said.

That got another laugh from the crowd followed by louder boos. I was losing them already, and I wasn't even through the introduction.

"I'm going to be straight with you all," I said. "In no way am I going to promise you people—virgins or otherwise. What I am going to promise you is that if we all work together and treat each other equally, everyone's lives will be better."

The voices that were booing changed to cheers, but as soon as they ended, new boos emerged, roughly as loud as the laughter from before. It seemed no matter what I said I was angering one group and making the other happy. At least King Fartius was still on my side. He smiled and then pointed furiously to his left. I looked at where he was pointing and remembered the cue cards. The first one seemed promising, so I read that.

"Long has been the time that the Paruxian people have gotten in their own way. Since you began recording your history, your people have followed a cycle of the people at the top taking advantage of the people at the bottom, then the people at the bottom get tired of it and rise up. Then those new people in charge start oppressing the people at the bottom again. I say the time for that has passed."

There weren't as many boos from the crowd, but also weren't

a whole lot of cheers, so I figured the crowd was just as confused as I was about what to conclude from that statement. Time to take a slight positive and turn it into a bigger one. I blended the message on the next cue card with my own since I didn't agree with all of it.

"What I'm saying is that we need to stop hating ourselves. Think what we could do if we spent all the energy we now spend fighting and hating each other on something more positive. Instead of being bitter that the other farmer is better at plowing than you, you could focus on what you're good at and use that positivity to fuel being a better farmer yourself."

"That is a good point," a guy with one arm said. "I've always hated my brother-in-law for his skill in whittling lifelike depictions of famous historical figures defecating, but if I focus on how good I am at juggling swords, I could use that positive energy to fuel my tailoring business."

The example was a little odd, but who was I to judge? "That's the spirit!"

A guy in a richly embroidered shirt spoke up. "And I hate how my brother is so good at shooting peasants . . . pheasants, but if I stop thinking about that and focus on my arm wrestling, I might be able to win back custody of my son."

"Now you're on the right track." I had no idea what the arm wrestling thing meant, but at least he understood my general meaning. For the first time, I didn't hear any boos.

"I get what you're saying," a guy with a monocle and a top hat said. "My neighbor Thamus raises the best pigs in the village, and that's always made me really angry, but if I focus on how good I am at sneaking into people's houses while they sleep and murdering their children for no reason, that could really inspire me to be a better farmer."

"That's . . . the general idea, but someone should probably arrest you."

My response got only cheers from the crowd.

A muscle-bound man in a bowl cut knocked Monocle down. "And I will use my newfound positive energy to beat him to a pulp." Several other people joined in.

"With this newfound unity and positive energy, you can all can start working together and focus on the real problem . . ."

Crap. This was the same thing that ruined my student council campaign freshman year. I was on a roll, and right when I had the crowd where I wanted them, I completely blanked. My eyes scanned the audience for something that might clue me in to an answer. "The problem that's plagued this world since there was a Paruxia is . . ." If only someone had a sign that could tell me what to say, like on a cue card. Cue card! There it was, and it only had two words on it. "Other people," I said.

Before I could take that back, the crowd roared in applause. Bowl Cut even stopped pounding on Monocle and shook his hand before he resumed pummeling him. The king high-fived his guards.

I sighed in frustration, which would have normally been a perfectly fine thing to do given the situation; however, my voice was still amplified by the Paruxian spell. Everyone stopped their celebrations and stared at me in confused anticipation. It was good to know that they were still listening, less good that I wasn't sure what to say next.

I gave the next cue card a look over *before* I read it this time. Yeah, it could have definitely been worse. The next one was all about murder, maiming, mugging old ladies, and looting. A thought occurred to me, so I motioned her to flip back one card. I'd use what Judas wrote while changing a few words.

I raised my hand to get everyone's attention again. "If we all unify against our common enemy, we can charge forth and really stick it to them . . . figuratively, by improving our economy. And we can do that by organizing and forming units . . . to learn new trade skills, marching into enemy territory . . . with our new trade items and conquering . . . those new markets for our goods. First, we shall target the weakest of them . . . weakest markets—not people, as we're not going to directly hurt anyone—to gather resources for further expansions . . . into more lucrative industries and then we shall loot the richer, weak-willed, cowardly. . . industries by showing them our superior . . . products. When that is all done, you brave, powerful men can stick it to all the conquered furniture you want!"

At the beginning, the crowd was more confused than anything, but they seemed to warm up as I went along. I did kind of lose myself on the last sentence which was more odd than bad —unless you happen to be a table or sofa. A small group of the men in the crowd got especially excited over the last sentence, so I made a note to wash any surfaces thoroughly before making contact with them.

When the cheering died down, one of the less excited men raised his hand, and I motioned for him to speak. "But what about the pamphlets? It clearly depicts us killing our enemies, not trading with them."

"It's a metaphor for what we're going to do to their economy."

"And the second panel showing the women we'll get from the conquest?"

"Women do like a guy with a nice job and a lot of money," I said.

He nodded slowly. "Maybe that's why I haven't had much luck finding a nice girl to settle down with."

A scruffy-looking woman in equally scruffy-looking armor raised her hand but didn't wait for me to nod to begin yelling, "It takes a lot less time to kill our neighbors than it does to learn a new trade skill, make stuff, and then sell it. I say we save some time and take it!"

Quite a few people spread amongst the crowd responded enthusiastically to that. It was only a small percentage, but the noise spread steadily from those pockets. I shouldn't have been too surprised as people do have a tendency to listen closer to the opinions of the person with the sharpest sword.

I would have to counter with my own weapons: logic and reason. I'm kidding. I'm kidding. Obviously these Paruxians had a tenuous arrangement with either of those. If I countered a blade with reason, I'd probably get stabbed twice—once for bringing the wrong weapon to a sword fight and once for using it incorrectly. No, earthly logic and reason didn't apply in Paruxia, but Hatly logic and reason worked great.

I clapped at her statement dramatically. The amplified slow clap echoed off the buildings, drowning out the sound of her growing support until it ceased. "But if we attack these other countries, what do you think will happen?"

"We kill or enslave all their people and then take all their stuff." She banged her sword against her buckler and her supporters banged together whatever weapons they could find in response. The guy wielding egg beaters was my favorite.

"There are two things wrong with that statement."

"Only two?" the Atlian next to me asked.

"Two major things wrong with that and a lot of little things that I don't have time to get into. The first thing is that in almost every battle throughout history there are casualties on both sides, and if we attack another country, there's going to be lots of battles —battles we might lose. If it was that easy, King Fartius would have done it a long time ago."

"Is that true, Your Majesty?" the scruffy woman asked.

King Fartius stood up slowly and waved dramatically to the crowd. "Mostly it's because my brother would overthrow the country if I sent my armies away, but the loss of life is a really, really good reason too."

I waited until he sat down to continue. Momentum was everything. "And the second reason is that if we conquer these other countries, that would mean their people would then be Paruxians too. Do you really want to kill or enslave other Paruxians?"

The scruffy woman dropped her sword along with her jaw. A few of the other people who had been cheering tossed their weapons into the crowd in frustration.

"So, in conclusion, we're going to work on learning new production skills, fostering trade, and mostly not dying. Does everyone agree with that?"

The response I got was the sweetest sound I ever heard: reluctant agreement. I knew I couldn't let that excitement just sit there. No, I had to maintain it.

"Everyone, repeat after me. I'll say 'trade' and then you say 'Paruxia.' OK, here we go. 'Trade!'" The crowd replied with "Paruxia." We did that a few times and then I changed the first word to "rich." They seemed to really like that. I had them right where I wanted them. All I had to do was deliver the coup de grâce, the finisher.

Unfortunately, the scruffy woman interrupted me again. "So, we're under no circumstances to kill people in the name of this religion?"

"No."

She pouted. "But what if they start it?"

"Well that's a complicated question. Did they throw the first punch?" I remembered who I was talking to and quickly added, "Figuratively."

"Are you guys behind him going to figuratively punch him or literally stab him?" the scruffy woman asked.

As much as I hoped that whoever it was she was referring to would go away if I didn't turn around, the sound of hoofbeats and clanging metal led me to conclude that wouldn't work.

THE POWER OF PANCAKES

On the other side of the rubble stood a mass of cavalry, the majority of which appeared to be members of the Mediocre Horde. Sprinkled liberally throughout were darker-skinned men and women wearing the red robes of the local priests and awkwardly holding a wide variety of weapons.

"Neither," a man in a red robe with a wide-brimmed hat said from horseback. "We're going to convince him with our well-reasoned arguments."

A group of similarly attired men and women laughed at his statement. Several of them almost dropped their bows.

"Oh, that's nice," I said. "I thought you might want to hurt us because of the weapons. I don't suppose I could borrow one?"

"That was sarcasm, moron," the first man said. "Of course we're going to kill you."

A familiar female horsewoman pushed through his still laughing stooges. "No killing that one, Holiness. I have special plans for him after we get to that library you promised us. The rest you are free to dispose of." Hung'Lo gave me a feral wink as more of the horde spilled out of the trees to either side.

"For some reason, I liked it more when you were going to kill me," I said. "Bringing this up randomly and not at all for my benefit, but shouldn't you priests in the red robes be the enemies of the horde, you know, since they don't follow your religion and like to kill your followers. Random musing, though feel free to talk about it amongst yourselves."

"You're even cuter when you're trying to manipulate me," Hung'Lo said, "though you're a lot less cute after you betray me and try to run away. As for my new, temporary allies, they offered me directions to a library in exchange for help stomping down your little club."

"It's a win/win," the red robe in the wide-brimmed hat said.

"Not true," I said half-heartedly, "I don't get to win."

Hung'Lo smirked. "The first lesson our new warriors learn is that someone always wins and someone ends up crying."

I looked back at the royal box. The king was nowhere to be seen and neither were his guards. Members of the crowd were attempting to push back into the town but didn't seem to be moving very far. A large dust cloud had popped up from all directions just outside the city, indicating that they probably had us surrounded.

At least the Atlian who had cast the voice projecting was still there. I made a note to ask the king to give her a big bonus if we got out of this. I turned back to address the crowd. "The thing I said about avoiding violence is still true, my people. However, there comes a time when you can't avoid it. This is one of those times. Defend yourselves with anything you can find. Kill them before they kill you! For Paruxia!"

The Atlian nodded enthusiastically. "But if we can avoid a fight, we should, right?"

"Well, yeah."

She winked at me and disappeared.

My jaw dropped as I stared at the now empty space. "What

the heck? Atlians can't teleport." Her sound-projecting spell had left with her too.

A royal guard poked at the space where the Atlian had been. "They can't. She probably turned invisible." The sound of footsteps to my left indicated he was correct.

I hadn't realized the guards the king had left with me were still there. At least something was going right. "The king is gone; shouldn't you be with him?"

"The king instructed us to protect you with our lives, though if those priests over there ask, we're not royal guards. We removed the insignias on our uniforms and are using unadorned shields."

"Well, at least I have you five brave men and women with me." I shook each of their hands. "It's been an honor. I wish I got to know you all, but I doubt the six of us can do that much against such a force."

The horde and Red Robes continued to pour out of the forest. It must have been my imagination, but it looked like the horde had gotten bigger, even accounting for the addition of the Red Robes. Fortunately, they hadn't charged yet, but that was probably so they could get their full array of forces into position.

I turned back to look at my followers. Most of the ones closest to me had given up on trying to run through the city as it was obvious that was a lost cause; the streets were just too thin for that many people to move through at the same time. Quite a few faces were looking to me for guidance. The only way I could think to get them out of this would be to sacrifice myself and hope that would be enough. My gut sense was tingling. I knew a plan would come, but when?

A faded hand shot out of my nose and mouth. I spun about in panic for a few seconds until I saw the laughing ghost behind me. "This is hardly the time for jokes," I said.

"My apologies," Gafenarai the Atlian ghost said as he stifled another laugh. "I needed to get your attention. You said there are only six of us, but my spectral companions and I number quite a bit more than that. Not sure how many anymore as we lost a few to an abandoned amusement park. What would you like us to do?"

Now I had it! Part two of my plan was handed to me. I wasn't confident in the plan yet, but it was better than nothing. Any plan that doesn't involve you living through it is missing something. At least some of my followers would have a chance.

"Well, you can't actually touch them," I said, "but I'm guessing they don't know that, and even if they do, ghosts are still scary . . . *especially* if you don't see them coming." A grin crossed my face, which caused him to giggle. "So, while the guards and I face them, I want you ghosts to fade into the ground and move into positions right under the forces in front of us. When I say 'pancakes,' you all come out and scare the crap out of them. While they're panicked, we'll make a break for it in the gap that should form where you came out."

Gafenarai nodded his pudgy head and the ghosts quickly dove straight down, fading into the ground. The guards and I marched forward through the rubble to stand a couple hundred feet in front of Hung'Lo and the spokesman for the Red Robes. A sizeable number of the crowd moved forward to join us, though oddly I couldn't see a single toilet cleaner in their ranks. As much as I didn't like the unexpected complication of more people to account for, it was heartening to see their loyalty. At least the group who was with me seemed to be mostly armed. I could even see a surprising amount of functional armor from the group. I assumed many of them were The Pink Woman's mercenaries.

Hung'Ger had arrived and stood his horse just behind his sister's. He sharpened his sword casually while keeping his eyes glued to me. Right as I was about to let the world of Paruxia know of my love of pancakes, and also signal for the ghosts to attack, a woman dressed head to toe in pink pushed Hung'Ger's horse and rider out of the way and gave me a saucy smirk. She waved her hand half-heartedly and almost all the forces behind me rushed over to join the opposing army. The army greeted them with open arms.

"So, I guess you didn't like my speech about not attacking everything in sight and have switched sides?" I asked. "Or were you ever on our side to begin with?"

"Dear, dear Hat," The Pink Woman said. "As always, I'm only on my own side, and my side is always the one that wins. I must admit your speech was highly moving, but a lack of war is bad for my bottom line. Besides, I only agreed to join Judas, not you. My agents arranged this little switch before your speech even began."

"But I'm trying to build a better Paruxia. A Paruxia that you could be a part of. Think about what it would be like to be in the history books as an important part of my new Paruxia."

She gave her pink nails a thorough inspection. "Pish. Posh. History is only written by the victors, and you won't be writing anything after this little skirmish, while I will be swimming in the mounds of pelos these fine priests have offered me. Now that my men and women are aligned perfectly, I think we should begin." She grabbed her reins and wheeled her horse about, moving out of view.

Before I could yell "pancakes," the mercenaries began their attack. How did they manage to close the distance to my small force before I could yell a single word, you're probably asking? Well, they didn't have to close any distance because they attacked the forces next to them. The Pink Woman hadn't betrayed me at all. It was a ruse.

Pandemonium broke out. Men and women screamed. Horses screamed. Men and women on horses screamed. The previously panicked crowd behind me screamed as they decided to take advantage of the situation and join in on the attack. I, however, forgot to scream. A royal guardswoman shook me from my shocked stupor. I thanked her and let the world know of my love of pancakey goodness.

I don't know how Gafenarai and his ghostly companions heard me through the deafening tumult, but they responded instantly. Their timing couldn't have been better as they emerged right as Hung'Lo and Hung'Ger had decided to take advantage of the lack of mercenaries in their area and charge. Gafenarai himself appeared roughly halfway between them and my small band. Their two horses spooked immediately and crashed into each other.

"Sir," the royal guardswoman to my right said. "Now would be the perfect time to escape."

"No," I said. "I think we might be able to win this thing, and my absence might demoralize our forces."

The royal guards saluted me in unison in response, and then we made our way through the rubble to the battlefield. Several horde members and a couple of Red Robes tried to get near me at various times, but the guard quickly dispatched them. Had I been alone, I was sure that any one of those opponents would have made quick work of me. A powerless spoon and a clever tongue are not the most useful weapons in a chaotic battlefield (unless they're the sole equipment of someone you've taken a large life insurance policy on). After around the tenth enemy was dispatched by my guards, the rest of our opponents made sure to find somewhere else on the battlefield to direct their horses.

The leader of the Red Robes gathered a group of his fellow priests, and they pointed small, shiny objects that I assumed to be holy symbols at the ghosts. Soon the priests managed to wrangle every ghost in sight into a screaming circle. I was about to lead my guards to their aid when The Pink Woman and a group of her followers appeared out of the forest behind them and made the priests scream instead.

The battle looked like it could go either way. With the surprise of the mercenaries' triple-cross finally gone, the Red Robes and Horde members pulled back in bunches to regroup at the edge of the forest. A few of my followers attempted to pursue but were quickly surrounded and dispatched. The Pink Woman corralled our remaining forces into a line in anticipation of the enemy's eventual charge. My guards directed me to join them, but they were too late. After my second step, the enemy charged.

I estimated the enemy to be a couple hundred yards away from our lines when they started—and a hundred yards away from me—but just before they reached me, the members of the Horde suddenly wheeled to the south and literally blew the small portion of my followers directly in front of them through the town and out the other side. A few of the Red Robes continued with the Horde, likely too caught in their midst to do anything else, but the majority of them stopped their horses in the middle of the field, staggering around in confusion. Sensing the moment, The Pink Woman led my followers in a charge. In short order, the Red Robes were either dead, dying, or surrendering.

I was shaken from the victorious scene when flames shot up from the center of town. Seeing the puzzled look on my face, one of the guards answered, "Looks to be the library. Not a bad target to hit. With all those books and the wooden houses around it, they could easily take out the whole town. Odd timing to go for it when they did though . . . unless they wanted to get us to break formation so they could take us from behind."

He said more after that, but I was too distracted by the faint thundering of hoofs to listen. The Horde were beginning to appear again in the narrow streets, heading toward us. I yelled to my followers to turn and fight, but they didn't hear me. I was about to direct my guards to make a run to join the rest of our army when I noticed the first horde member fall from his horse. More and more began to topple, and with the narrow streets and their tight-packed groups, the succeeding ranks had no choice but to crash over the fallen horses in front. I wasn't sure why until I saw a figure wave from the top of a building. As I took in the figure's dirty mop and those of several other waving figures, I now knew why I hadn't seen any toilet cleaners in our motley army.

The Pink Woman finally noticed the new threat and directed our army back to the town. I was about to go join them when I saw Billiam and Gu fifty feet away, helping Hung'Lo and Hung'Ger to fresh mounts.

"Gu's alive!" I said. "If he's alive, that might mean Didlius is as well. Come, loyal guards." I ran forward, but when I glanced over my shoulder, saw that they hadn't followed.

"Come on, loyal guards," I said. "That god is getting away."

"Loyalty and honor are all well and good," one of the guards said, "but that's the guy who blew the top off that building earlier and now you're telling us he's a literal god. Ghosts, evil priests, horse people who can knock over people with their breath, we can handle that, but gods are well above our weight class."

Another guard nodded. "Also, if the Old Gods are real, why should we follow this new religion of yours? Your ideas are pretty sound and all, but you haven't told us anything about your god, while right over there is the genuine article."

Wanting to argue with them, but seeing Gu get away, I shrugged and ran after him. In retrospect, this was incredibly stupid, but sometimes you do stupid things in the heat of the moment, like the time I combined dill dip with Sour Patch Kids. (I think it goes without saying there was alcohol involved in that one.)

"Wow," a guardsman said to my back. "There goes one brave guy."

"I believe they call them martyrs," another guard said.

"Huh, I thought his name was Hat. Everyone remember to tell the chroniclers that fellow's name was Martin."

GU TIMES TWO JUST WON'T DO

As I raced after them, a thought occurred to me. And no, it wasn't "How the heck does this idiot expect to catch a horse?" If that had occurred to me, I probably would have stopped running after them and found a mount of my own. The thought that occurred to me was that in the books Hung'Lo was the one responsible for Didlius's death. So far in my journey, they hadn't met, but here were Gu and Hung'Lo right in front of me, teaming up. True, Didlius might already be dead, but I thought the same of Gu, and he seemed to be not in the least bit dead.

Fortunately, my quarry was too distracted to hear me coming. I rubbed my eyes as I took in the scene in front of me. Gu looked like he was talking to himself. I closed my eyes several times, but his double was still there.

"Your evil is at an end," the Gu in front of Hung'Lo and Hung'Ger said.

Across from him were Didlius, Jaenia, and the second Gu. My friends were a bit bedraggled and unconscious but appeared to be breathing. I sighed in relief but sucked it back in when I realized that Hung'Lo, Did's historical murderer, was right across from him.

"How exactly are you going to stop me when you've taken that centuries-long vow not to harm another being?" the Gu in front of Jaenia and Didlius asked.

"That's why I've brought friends." The first Gu pointed at the Hungs.

Billiam slinked away and then dove behind a bush. "I'm his boss, so I don't have to help if I don't want to."

The other Gu laughed. "What are these savages supposed to do to me? Give me horse riding lessons? Teach me how to make assless chaps?"

"They are the descendants of Hung'Loser."

The other Gu's jaw dropped. "The demi-god whose descendants were foretold to one day kill every god?"

"No, the other Hung'Loser with the other prophecy. You know the one."

"Noooo! I don't want to get married and settle down. According to that prophecy, I'll even have to stick around to raise the kids! I'll develop one of those awful dad bodies. Have to take them to football practice. Join the PTA. Start caring way too much about my lawn. The horror! We're gods; we're not supposed to have to do any of that. What kind of brother are you?"

"Brother?" I asked way too loud. "Which one of you is the real Gu?"

"I am," the Gu in front of the Hungs said. "Hi, Hat."

"Yes," Gu's brother said. "Hi indeed, Hat. If I'm going down, at least I'll get to take you with me."

"Not if I have anything to say about it." Hung'Lo stepped in between us. "Prophecy be damned. I want to marry Hat instead."

Gu's brother pushed her out of the way, knocking her down. "Prophecy be damned indeed. Goodbye, Hat." Electrical sparks began to build as he rubbed his fingers together.

Gu pushed Hung'Ger in his path. "On my journeys with Billiam in southern Paruxia, we have consulted many of the books that were thought lost when the great library was destroyed."

"That's what we were doing?" the bush said. "I thought we were working on my master plan to unify the stupid people?"

"No, I only told you that to keep you quiet, Billiam. Anyway, the books said that a descendent of Hung'Loser would be born who would be immune to your powers, Axaous, and who you would fall madly in love with. Seeing as how you were able to strike the daughter, it must be the son."

"Do you honestly think I spent the last several centuries searching for my ex-wife so I could marry a man?" He stopped rubbing his hands together as he looked at Hung'Ger. "Huh."

Hung'Ger shook free of Gu's grip and moved to the side. "Look. Whatever happens here, I will not be the one to come between you and killing Hat."

I looked at Billiam's bush, wishing I had thought of that, but it was too far away and likely neither lightning nor stab proof. The two armored warriors approaching, however, showed more promise, though the woman's axe/hands were probably not the best weapons for the situation given their resemblance to lightning rods. The giant two-handed sword held by the even larger man wasn't any better though.

"Ha ha!" I said. "The cavalry *has* arrived."

Axaous turned to the two armored warriors. "They're not on horses."

"It's a saying where I'm from. It means reinforcements are here to save me." I slapped Big Baby on the back as he stood in front of me. "Really great to see you two. Wolfette, the guy in front of me is Gu's identical twin brother Axaous. I believe he is the one who killed your squad mates, seeing as how he said that Gu's vow of pacifism has been going on for centuries."

"Are they also descendants of Hung'Loser?" Axaous asked.

"We were adopted," Big Baby said, "but probably not."

"Splendid." Axaous blasted Big Baby, knocking him twenty feet away into a nearby bush. Billiam yelped and ran behind another bush.

Wolfette dove out of the way and then rolled in front of Axaous. She brought her left axe/hand down hard on his foot.

Axaous stared down at her, shrugged, and kicked her into Billiam's new bush. "That was my favorite toenail, you loon." Axaous advanced on me.

"Why do you want to kill me?" I asked. "I thought your beef was with Jaenia and Didlius."

Axaous paused right in front of me. "I want to murder that fool's only friend to torment him before I kill him for taking my beloved ex-wife from me. I read about it in a book once, and it seemed to really torment the hero. Also, you mucked up my plans to recreate my religion—a plan I've been working on for over a century. All the time I spent forming that secret organization to distribute my junk mail and then the mercenary company . . ."

"Recreate your religion?" I took a step backward, glancing back at the bushes. I could see some light movement, indicating that neither of my friends were dead. "Axaous . . . That means you're the Old God of posttraumatic stress disorder!"

Axaous took a step forward. "*And* the god of war. Why does everyone put that one second? It's clearly the most important one. I mean, I didn't assemble a massive army of followers centuries ago because I'm the god of posttraumatic stress disorder. Back in my heyday, no one would have put that one first, but you lose one battle and suddenly everyone wants to join the hot new religion just because they beat you. Do you know how many battles we won before that?"

"Fourteen?" I asked. Axaous shook his head. I glanced back again. Both bushes were shaking violently, though more from the back. "Fifteen?" Axaous shook his head. A loud thumping noise came from Big Baby's bush. "Sixteen?" He shook his head again.

The bushes stopped shaking, and I could hear movement from behind them.

"We won 2.35 battles." Axaous stomped hard, causing the ground to shake. "That's 2.35 times as many as they did. And I may not be the god of mathematics like my cousin, Duglacious, but I'm fairly certain that 2.35 is more than one. Of course, they weren't following Duglacious so I suppose I can't really blame them for not knowing that. I wrote a book about that whole era of my life, as well as every other era, if you'd like to read about them . . . which you won't get the chance to because you're going to die!"

Big Baby was in position behind Axaous. He raised his great sword to strike but stopped when I shook my head. "If you're going to kill me to make Didlius mad," I said, "shouldn't he be awake for that? If he doesn't see it with his own eyes, you could be making it up."

Big Baby moved to shake Didlius awake.

"Also, you may want to wake Jaenia for this too," I said. "It's probably even more important because of her powers that rival your own."

Big Baby shook Didlius harder. "She's the beautiful woman over there," I said. "No, the woman. The one next to the guy you're shaking."

"You're right," Axaous said. "They should be awake for this. And my ex-wife is extremely beautiful. Thank you for noticing. You know, Hat, as much as I despise you for opposing me, if things were different I think we could have been friends." He reached his hand out to shake mine.

I looked at his hand and backed away. "Yeah, I'm not falling for that."

He nodded in respect. "No matter. I think I'll start with electrocution, then light your hair on fire, and follow that with a drowning."

Jaenia was groggy but now standing.

"Did you hear that, Jaenia?" I asked. "He said he wants to be electrocuted first."

Jaenia teetered over and fell back down right as Axaous turned around to look at her. Axaous laughed and blasted her with a flick of his wrist. She stopped moving. I wasn't sure if she was dead or unconscious again.

Didlius roared like a man twice his size and swung a tree branch in revenge. I'd never seen Did get angry before. I was impressed and terrified.

Axaous was neither. He didn't even stop laughing as the tree branch shattered over his forehead or when he counter-attacked with a flick of his wrist to my friend's abdomen. Did's bottom half shot back about a foot and then his entire body collapsed to the ground face first.

Big Baby used the distraction to bring his great sword down over the back of the god's neck. The blow was so mighty that I was sure it could have brought down a tree. The noise was certainly just as loud. The top half of his now broken sword missed my face by a few inches as it flew by. The bottom half dropped to the ground as Big Baby's arms collapsed to his side, bereft of strength. There actually seemed to be pity on Axaous's face as he tossed Big Baby one-handed into a tree. The pity on his face was gone when he found me again.

As he neared me, with clear intent to do not-so-nice things to me, Gu rushed to intercept. Axaous stopped and stared at his twin for a few seconds, then shrugged when he realized that Gu couldn't do anything to him due to his vow. His punch sent Gu reeling. Gu recovered quickly but didn't move forward again. He gave me a downtrodden look of apology as he backed away.

I looked around for anything in reach that might help me, but the only thing that was close was Hung'Ger. Fortunately, as Hung'Ger was only paying attention to Axaous, I easily grabbed him and held him in front of me like a shield. It was right in the nick of time as Axaous unloaded a bolt of pure electricity. I was extremely glad that the Mediocre Horde only wore hide as armor and not anything that conducted electricity.

Hung'Ger screamed before the blast landed but then giggled a second later. The bolt bounced off him and rebounded back to Axaous, right into his chin. Axaous's feet scraped the ground as he slid back, but he remained standing. Before I could celebrate my genius, Axaous's powerful hands ripped Hung'Ger from my grip. There was no nod of respect this time.

"Any last words?" Axaous asked. "And make it something good. I plan on including it in my next book."

"Wolfette," I said.

Axaous frowned. "What the gods is a 'Wolfette?' Is that one of those new slang words you kids seem to think up daily so that us older people won't know what you're talking about?"

I smiled in satisfaction as I knew my friend would take that perfectly timed mention of her name to strike. To strike! To strike any day now . . . Where was she?

Axaous put his hand on his chin. "You know, I slaughtered a trio of mercenaries a couple of months back and one of them was called Wolf. Odd thing to remember at a time like this."

"Actually, you only killed two of them. The one named Wolf got away and changed her name to Wolfette."

"Ahh . . . small world. Well, back to killing you . . . Were you yelling her name in the hopes that she would take that moment to strike?"

I shrugged. "You got me. I have one request as a worthy adversary. Could you not mess up my face? I'd like to have an open casket if possible."

"Sure. Sure. You know that Wolfette did actually strike when you said her name. She's been stabbing and slashing without pause since then. It kind of tickles."

He picked me up and held me high so that I could see behind him. True to his word, there was a woman stabbing away at his back. It wasn't, however, Wolfette; it was Hung'Lo.

The axe blade that cleaved neatly into the hand that held me a second later told me where my missing friend was. I dropped to the ground and rolled away as the real Wolfette began her assault. It was glorious. It was ceaseless. It was futile.

"You killed my friends, so I will killy kill you," Wolfette screamed as her second axe bent into uselessness against his nearly impenetrable hide. "They were good people."

"They were mercenaries and murderers." He kindly bent her right axe back into place so she could take another swing.

"Yes, they were good *at* killing people. Do you know how many people are now walking around not dead because you killed my friends? And how much bounty money will go unpaid?"

She took a swing with her now functional right axe into his shoulder, bringing it right back into the land of non-functional, not that that stopped her. She continued pummeling him even when the blade ripped completely off and was down to only a stub. Mercifully, Axaous slapped her with both hands and she went down. Hung'Lo was also down on her knees, probably either from exhaustion or from realizing the futility of her task as I hadn't seen him strike her.

I reached in my pockets for my car keys to use as a pathetic weapon in the faint hope that there might be something in them that he was weak against. Earth probably had substances he had never encountered, right? Unfortunately, I must have dropped the car keys somewhere. The remainder of the lint ball was missing as well. However, I did have the spoon I had found in the rubble. *What the heck? It used to be magic.* Sure, the magic seemed to be gone, but magic works in unexpected ways. That's what magic is: things that don't follow any logical rules, right?

I swung the spoon with all my might and hit Axaous in the

jaw. We stared at each other in confusion for about a minute and then the most wondrous thing happened: a bolt of lightning appeared from the sky and landed right between us. Through the deafening sound and blinding light, I'm not one hundred percent sure what happened next, but when I regained my senses, I was crouched next to Billiam and Gu behind a bush. Either I had been knocked there or someone had grabbed me and hid me there in the confusion. I was leaning toward the grab theory as my waist did seem sore, and I wasn't singed. Axaous seemed to be recovering from a similarly stunned situation. The flickering of electricity from Gu's hand seemed to confirm that theory.

"That was a really cool way to kill him," Hung'Ger said to Axaous, "but you may want to think about doing it from a distance next time. Not that I'm criticizing, being I'm only a mere mortal and all. The important thing is that the weaselly little moron is dead."

Hung'Lo wept into the dirt. Neither of them paid any attention to her.

Axaous rubbed his eyes. "No offense taken, mortal. And yeah, I hate—*hated* that guy. I'll make sure to make him look like the worst villain in history when I write my next book."

"I'm glad he's dead." Hung'Ger spit on the ground.

"Say, we should grab a drink and reminisce on why that guy sucked so much, after I finish killing my ex-wife and her new boyfriend." He patted Hung'Ger on the back.

Hung'Ger smiled. "Yeah. That'd be great, but only as friends. In no way do I want to get married ever. I would like to have kids though."

"I know, right? Marriage is the worst. By the way, if you have any kids, I'm going to have to murder them because of that prophecy. No hard feelings?"

Hung'Ger nodded. "Oh, totally understand. No hard feelings at all. I'll probably adopt anyway."

"Great! That'll save me from having to kill them. I'm still going to keep an eye on you and your sister though. Say, do you have anything to drink? Shooting lightning bolts gives a truly godly thirst." He eyed Hung'Ger's canteen on his belt.

Hung'Ger pulled the canteen off. "Sure, but I'm a bit of a germaphobe. I don't let anyone drink directly from the canteen except me." He looked around and eyed the spoon on the ground. "Would you mind if I poured it on this spoon and you drank from that?"

Axaous picked the spoon off the ground and inspected it. "It's a little old, and it'll take a while using something so small, but your canteen, your rules." He nodded and Hung'Ger poured some water on the spoon.

As soon as the water touched his lips, Axaous began spasming violently. A bolt of white light spread from his throat, soon covering him and the spoon. The spoon floated up to rest at his eye level while Axaous stared at it, frozen in horror.

Billiam looked to Gu for an answer, but he shrugged. Hung'Ger seemed unaffected by the light as he had time to walk in and out of it several times, even managing to drag his still shrieking sister a good distance away. When the light finally disappeared, Axaous was no longer there. I sprinted to pick up the spoon, but Hung'Ger stomped down to cover it with his moccasin.

"In no way am I going to let you have this," Hung'Ger said.

"But it's mine," I said. "Or Didlius's, if he wants it back. Either way, it's not yours."

He drew his knife and swung at me. I barely dodged a stab that probably would have given me that second belly button I always wanted. He responded by back swinging his blade to attempt to remove all those pesky entrails that were getting in the way of the newer, thinner, deader me. A five-inch piece of axe handle arrived to intercept his radical new weight loss system.

Wolfette's cold axe stub rubbed against my belly as she held her block, causing me to giggle, though that may have been my nerves.

"You will not harm this man as long as I'm around," Wolfette said.

"Ha!" Hung'Ger said. "You and what army?"

A great shout arose behind us, causing Hung'Ger's foot to slide off the spoon.

"Yeah," I said. "Back on Earth we know to never say that."

"You mean like 'Look over there?'" Hung'Ger pointed behind us.

Everyone besides me looked behind us. A second later Hung'Ger and Hung'Lo ran away.

"That doesn't really fit with what I was . . . Eh, he did stop Axaous, and I'm too tired to chase after them anyway." They ran into a squadron of Horde cavalry a few seconds later, climbed up behind them, and rode off into the distance.

I picked up the spoon and looked it over. It was back to being shiny again, and I could hear a faint voice in the back of my head saying something about revenge and then about editing. "Anyone have an idea of how he got trapped in this?" I asked.

Gu lowered his head and stared at the ground. "Xom, the father and mother of the first generation of gods, created a few eating utensils to trap us in whenever he/she felt we needed a timeout. If we eat or drink off them, we get sent to a realm of nothingness until someone lets us out. No-so-coincidentally, all of us ate exclusively with our hands whenever we shared a meal with Mother/Father, and we all developed terrible table manners. I'm ashamed to say I recognized the spoon for what it was when Didlius showed it to me at that store, but I was too afraid of what Axaous would do to me if I freed you, sister/ex-sister-in-law."

Jaenia raised her battered face from Didlius's shoulder. "Given how we both used you in our battles after our breakup,

Guryan, I do not blame you for it. I'm sure that day he tricked me into the spoon was the first time you ever got any peace in your life. It was so obvious poking out of that sundae, but I think I was so tired of the fighting that I knew what the spoon was all along." She hobbled a couple of steps and then embraced Gu.

As I rubbed the tears out of my eyes, a royal guardsman marched forward and saluted me. "Sir, we have routed the enemy forces, and they have fled the field. The Pink Woman and her forces are in pursuit. What should we do with the prisoners?"

I looked to Didlius for an answer since this was his religion and I had only been filling in, but he shook his head.

"Offer them conversion or death," I said. "If they pick death, hold them for about a month, then let them go. We need new recruits, and I want them to think they have to join, but I'm not going to be responsible for murdering people."

The royal guard turned to one of his fellows, who saluted and left. The first guard turned back for an additional question but lost his breath when he noticed Jaenia.

"Who is that, sir?" he let out in between gulps.

"My fiancée and I are only simple travelers who got caught up in this mess by accident," Jaenia said. "Your brave leader and his friends saved us from some brigands, but I think it is time for us to be going."

I looked to Did for confirmation and his grin told me all I needed to know. While I didn't want to be the one responsible for The One, after seeing the way they looked at each other, I knew without a shadow of doubt that his fate was to be with the love of his life and not what I had thought it to be all along. Sometimes what's written in the books isn't what really happened. (Except for this book, which is one hundred percent accurate!)

FIGHT FOR YOUR RIGHT TO PARLEY

I almost managed to convince Didlius and Jaenia to at least stay for the victory feast, but when one of the guards mentioned King Fartius, Did decided to leave for fear that the king would try to talk him into taking my place as leader (though not before picking out cheeses for the feast). I was about to argue further when Jaenia mentioned how much she had to teach Didlius about the world and about thinking things through before he acted. Deciding that both he and our new religion would be better off without him—at least until Jaenia finished her instructions—I wished them the best as they left.

I'm sure the food at the feast was glorious. Everyone else seemed to be enjoying it. Even Wolfette was smiling, but it shouldn't have been too surprising since she had brand-new Sculandian steel axe/hands and the weight of vengeance off her chest.

Big Baby chatted amiably with Gafenarai between drinks of their respective alcohols. I had no idea there was a such thing as ghost ale, but the ghosts seemed to have found an endless supply of it. I was quite surprised that the townspeople I'd liberated from Billiam had made it there. They were quite thrilled when Fred the magician put on a show for them as well as some of the denser bathroom cleaners and mercenaries. While I would never have counted Billiam and Gu as allies, I was glad they were there as well. Gu's singing left no dry eyes in the house, and Billiam's retelling of the first *Star Wars* was breathtaking. (I'm referring to *A New Hope*. I refuse to acknowledge the existence of *The Phantom Menace*.)

Even some new recruits were there. My recruiters had evidently introduced the former horde members to the concept of sleeves, and the former Red Robes now wore nearly identical robes, save for the change in color scheme. I didn't remember picking orange, but also didn't mind as it would make them easy to pick out if I needed to avoid them and would save many of their lives from hunting accidents.

This should have been the greatest day of my life, but it was not. You see, now that everyone was together, all I could think about was how I was responsible for so many people. The king assured me several times that all but a handful of the old religion's local leadership had been present at the battle and were either killed or captured, but I still felt like I had forgotten something. The spoon that contained Axaous was firmly in my hand, so it wasn't that. After Axaous whined in my head about setting him free and then started to dictate his next book on beard styling, I decided to lock the spoon in a chest and have it dropped into the ocean.

I retired early, faking a stomach ache, and lay down immediately. The throbbing of worry in my head kept me awake for hours, so I decided to catch up on writing down notes of the more recent events. I had been extremely relieved earlier when I found out that Didlius saved the writing I had done before we parted. After a while, I dozed off in the middle of recording the fight with Axaous.

∽

I woke up with an intense headache. The coffee-like baeva I had in the dining room helped a little with it; the messenger who arrived in the middle of my second cup did not.

"A second army approaches from the south!" he said.

The collection of followers I was breakfasting with in the great hall stopped eating or even moving. The only sound was the creak of the wooden floor as the messenger got closer. All eyes were on me.

"Is it a good army or a bad army?" I asked.

"Well," the messenger said, "I didn't have time to ask everyone in the army if they're good or bad, but they're being led by some people in red robes, so I'm fairly confident that they mean us no good."

I'm not proud that my first thought was relief. An enemy army was a lot easier to deal with than trying to create an official religious doctrine or deciding what everyone is supposed to wear. Plus, our followers were still a rather disparate group, and another battle would further bond them together. I would have preferred to bond them through team-building exercises and trust circles, since there's usually less death in those, but this would be a lot faster.

"Mount the generals!" I said. "Inform the horses! Men the arms. We ride at dawn."

"Dawn tomorrow?" the guard next to me asked. "Dawn today passed a few hours ago."

"The army that is likely bad should be here by noon today," the messenger said.

"Sorry, I'm not awake yet," I said. "Get everyone ready as soon as possible. Someone inform the king, The Pink Woman, and all the other leaders immediately."

The room cleared in under a minute in a surprisingly organized manner. I was left with a half a cup of baeva and a full cup of problems.

~

I spent the rest of the morning being fitted with armor and then robes to go over the armor. Evidently, Paruxians expected their religious figures to look like Elvis impersonators. I didn't see the point in putting armor on me if anyone who came within one hundred feet would be too blind to target me. At least they gave me new shoes.

"How am I supposed to grab the reins with my arms stuck out to the side like this?" I asked as three servants pushed me on my horse. "There's more starch in this thing than a potato stuffed with bread and pasta."

"Ha," King Fartius said. "It's good to see someone else suffering in these costumes they make us wear."

I managed to turn my neck enough to scowl at the king. He had on a nearly identical robe in purple instead of orange. With reinforcements, the servants managed to push my arms down enough to grab the reins. Another group of servants rushed in and reapplied the starch-like powder to get my arms to stay that way. A squadron of royal guards arrived shortly after to escort us to the battlefield, saving me from the torture of being unable to move with nothing to do.

The Pink Woman and the head of the Paruxian army, General Guxus, agreed that the best place to meet the enemy was to the south a few miles outside of town. The hilly terrain ended abruptly there, making it a perfect place to utilize our abundance of infantry and negate the advantage of their cavalry on the edges of the hills. The muddy terrain to the east—the result of the Paru River's change of course—would also slow any flanking attacks from that direction. They had positioned our meager cavalry to the west.

It sounded like a good plan, much better than my plan of "hold the pointy end out and charge toward the enemy"; not that we couldn't use both plans, but the generals seemed to already have thought of and incorporated mine without even asking.

Now that the dust was beginning to settle in the distance, it was nice to see that our enemy had coordinated their colors. They were the red team and we were the . . . non-red team. First thing after the battle was over, I'd have to work on getting some uniforms. No, second thing. Looking after the wounded would have to come first. Of course, both of those were assuming we won. If they had managed to coordinate their colors, there was no telling what else they had coordinated. A guard handed me King Fartius's spyglass, and I got my first up-close look at their army.

"They don't all seem to be Paruxian," I said.

"Very few of them are," General Guxus said. "Your ragtag group took out most of the priests' local forces. They've coaxed and bought forces from every neighboring kingdom who follow their religion, even some as far away as Zelahadon." He guided the spyglass to the far right to focus on a group of horsemen in silvery ring mail with long bushy mustaches.

"Wow, I didn't know their religion had that much reach. By the way—"

The clomping of hoofbeats cut me off. I looked to my guards, but they seemed unconcerned.

"Heya, Hatatello," Billiam said from behind me. "Don't you dare think you can have a battle without me."

I handed the spyglass back to the guard. "What are you doing here?" I said. "Isn't this the part where you run away or hide behind some shrubbery?"

Billiam snickered. "Your army cut down all the shrubbery and no one would let me leave. I figured near you would be the safest place I could get to. Besides, I want to see this battle. This'll be the pivotal scene in my book, though as soon as your guys start losing, we're making a break for it."

"I never agreed to let you write about this world."

He crossed he arms and pouted. "But you were going to trade me that for letting you know how to get back home."

"And then you changed your mind and told me how in exchange for getting Judas out of the way, which I did."

He screamed something incoherent, so I decided to change the subject. "At least you brought Gu with you. I know I feel safer with a god near me. What are you the god of, by the way?"

Gu ignored Billiam and moved his horse closer to mine. "I am the god of followers and assistants. I mostly picked that to piss my brother off. He kept nagging me about choosing to be god of thunder and wagon crashes." Gu shrugged.

Billiam put his ring on. He eyed mine and his face lit up in a devilish grin.

I looked down at the ring hanging from the cord around my neck. *Harry's ring! I completely forgot about that thing . . . No, I had people to look after now. However, if we lose, it would be a good thing to have a way out as a last resort.* "Could you help me put this thing on, Gu? It took them ten minutes to get my arms like this, and I don't think we have ten minutes before the battle starts to reset them."

"Sure thing." Billiam looked like he wanted to bite Gu's head off, but Gu ignored him. Gu had to snap the cord to get to the ring through my thick costume, but after that he had a much easier time. He put the ring on my finger just in time to see the enemy get in range of our archers.

In the center of our army, the general had arrayed the Paruxian regulars. They looked very professional in their heavy, polished armor and equally polished weaponry. I had to wait for a cloud to partially block out the sun to cut down on the glare before I could get the best look at them. When I did, I could see that quite a few of them appeared to be shaking. At first, I took it to be the wind, but when I caught The Pink Woman out of the corner of my eye, a memory of her conversation with Judas came to mind. She had told him that the Paruxian regulars hadn't fought a major battle in over fifty years.

I grabbed the spyglass from the guard and looked back at the enemy army. None of them appeared to be shaking. As a matter of fact, they looked like they were going to a festival and not a deadly battle. Except for a small minority, my own forces did not present the same impression. I realized I had to do something.

"General Guxus," I said, "I would like to parley with the enemy commanders."

The General nearly fell out of his saddle. The Pink Woman snickered and reached her hand out to catch him before he tumbled over.

"I . . . I don't see the point," the general said. "They're obviously here to kill us all, and no words can possibly change their mind."

I began moving my horse forward. "I'm sure you're right, but I have to at least try. At worst it will buy us some time. Who knows, a plan might come to me." I didn't have my usual gut feeling that I was on the cusp of something, but that didn't mean it wouldn't still come.

"Unless your plan comes with a few extra thousand veterans, we're doomed," he grumbled a bit too loudly.

The Pink Woman slapped him on the back of the head, and the rest of the party followed her through our army toward the center of the battlefield. Surprisingly, even Billiam and Gu were with us. Fred the fake magician hurriedly rushed her horse out of the pack of ghosts to join us. I found her presence strangely comforting.

We stopped halfway between the two armies. One of the general's aides unfurled a great white banner and waved it at the other army. His action was wasted as a group of horsemen had come forward before we even stopped. I assumed them to be our equivalents as their clothing and armor was much nicer and more elaborate than anyone else.

Toward their center rode a person in a nearly identical outfit to my own, save for the color scheme. Two assistants rode to either side of him and had to nudge him occasionally to keep him on his mount. I felt sympathy and kinship to him until I remembered that he was likely the chief obstacle to keeping my followers alive. As that occurred to me, his previously normal-looking eyes began to look extra beady and his face became more wicked and cruel.

I had to get rid of him, but how? I still couldn't feel a plan coming even though I needed it more than ever.

The group stopped when they got about five feet away, their red robes immaculate despite the dust. It appeared they had a representative from every one of their disparate units present. A bald, tattooed woman wearing a green scaly armor sat on the far left. The general informed me she was from Lopanga. Next to her sat a pair of conically helmed horsemen holding long, thin lances to their sides. A Zelahadonian twisted his bushy mustache in impatience on the other side of their leader. Next to him an Ipanian blew a small dust storm to the side of us, more likely out of boredom than as a threat, though she had to stop when the storm caused the heavy knight to her right to almost fall from his saddle. The equally heavily armored man behind the knight almost fell from his saddle as well, though that seemed to be more from his awkward riding skills than from any action of his placid horse. That and his large, square shield indicated he was probably an infantryman.

The entire party stared at us for a great while with cocky, smirking looks. After about three minutes, Beady Eyes finally broke the silence. "What are the terms of your surrender? We'll probably reject them all, but it doesn't hurt to at least listen. By the way, I like my feet massaged three times a day and my baeva chilled, but enough about me. Let the groveling commence."

The Zelahadonian chuckled.

Normally, this would be the part where I'd start talking until a plan came to me, but I was so overcome with worry for my followers that no words would come. The general mercifully spoke instead. "Foot rubs are completely out of the question, but we'll see what we can do about the cold baeva. Ice doesn't come cheap in Paruxia, but I think we can manage it."

The Zelahadonian stopped laughing and raised his eyebrow in surprise.

"You drive a shrewd bargain, general," Beady Eyes said. "We'll also need to sell all the peasants in your army into slavery and for your soldiers to turn over their weapons."

My mind screamed at me to say something, but I couldn't think of a word to say. I glanced back at my army, and I died a little inside. Where was the clever, confident me that emerged on this journey?

"Only three-fourths of the peasants and we get to keep our knives," General Guxus said.

Beady Eyes bit his lip. "Seven-eighths and only whittling knives."

Guxus and King Fartius whispered between themselves for a few minutes. "Agreed."

"Now on the matter of executions. The guy dressed like a poor, orange imitation of me will obviously be executed."

"Of course."

Come on, brain. Where's your sense of self-preservation?

"And one other. I don't want to be accused of racism, so I won't pick the other southwesterner. How about the bald guy next to him?"

Billiam laughed manically. "You have to catch me to execute

me. And how're you going to do that if you don't know where I am?"

"Billy, he said they were going to execute me," Gu deadpanned.

Billiam slipped his ring on his finger and laughed again. "Suckers." He then grabbed a shield from one of our escorts and knocked himself in the side of the head. His unconscious form slid from the saddle and disappeared with a pop just before it would have struck the ground.

The general shrugged and went back to the negotiation. "You can try to execute the bald guy, but he's an Old God."

"Ahh," Beady Eyes said. "So, that's how the loon disappeared. Capturing an Old God would be great PR for us even if we probably can't kill him. We agree."

The Ipanian trotted his horse forward to grab me. "With all the money we're going to get from selling the slaves and equipment, can I have a raise?"

"Raises for everyone!" Beady Eyes said through fist bumps.

I fist bumped the Ipanian as she got closer out of instinct. I don't know where it came from but something came out of my mouth. "Wait a minute. I don't work for you. Who do I have to see for a raise?"

"Well, you're in charge of our new religion," King Fartius said. "So, you have to see you."

"Darn," I said. "I'm not in today. I guess I'll have to see my assistant . . . who is my assistant anyway?" I turned to the Ipanian. "Are you my assistant?"

"No," she said. "I'm here to arrest you." She reached for the reins of my horse.

"If you see my assistant, tell her I need a raise, and then after that, she's fired for not being here to take my note about giving me a raise. No, wait . . . after she gives me a raise, but before she's fired, have her hire a new assistant. But after she hires a replacement, she's definitely fired. That's it! Now read that back to me."

"I'm still not your assistant." She pointed toward the rest of my group, who must have thought I had something contagious since they were moving as far away as possible. "Are one of those people your assistant?"

"No, I think they're here to betray me to save themselves," I said. "When you do find my assistant, see if she can hire some guards to protect me from those guys."

Fred the non-magician raised her hand, and I motioned for her speak. "I'm not here to betray you."

"Ohh, that's very nice of you, Fred. Would you like to be my assistant?"

Her long, fake beard swayed back and forth, annoying her horse. "Not really, since you said you're going to fire her. I'm mostly only good at magic. Would you like to see a trick?"

My gut told me I was finally closing in on a plan, but I couldn't quite put my finger on it. "Whatever, as long as it's a quiet trick."

Fred turned toward the enemy leadership, her floppy hat threatening to leap from her head in the strong breeze. "Behold. Nothing in my hands. Now look over there."

The enemy leadership as well as their army looked behind them. I stared at them in bewilderment. This would have been a good time for the ghosts to pop up. Unfortunately, I couldn't see them. *Hehe. See them . . . Focus, Hat! You can't count on ghosts popping up to save the day. You can't count on anything in this world but you. That's what this journey has taught you.* I gave Fred the "keep going" signal.

"Now keep looking over there." She gave me a questioning look.

I motioned Gu over to me and he quickly responded.

I whispered so the still-near Ipanian couldn't hear. "I know you're a pacifist, but do you think you could do something to subdue these guys?"

He whispered back, "Normally I wouldn't, but seeing as how they plan on killing you and doing worse to me, I suppose I could bend the rules and do something non-lethal like I did earlier to save you. I'm the god of assistants, after all, and it wouldn't be right to let them hurt one of my own." He waved his arms and then a great wind flattened the pack of enemy commanders. Fred nearly fell off her horse, barely managing to catch her pointy hat and yank it back onto her head.

Horses and men screamed, but I blocked out the terrible sound. "Quick, tie them up, assistant," I said.

My terrible assistant didn't respond, but The Pink Woman and three guards charged forward and then leapt from their horses. Soon the entire enemy command was subdued.

"Keep looking over there," Fred said. I shook my head at her. "OK, you can look back now. Behold! I have in my hand a magic ring."

"And behold again," I yelled. "I have your leaders in chains!"

A great clap erupted from most of the enemy army. Some horsemen on the far right began to trickle away and were soon joined by a smattering of others throughout their army.

"Neat trick. Now make the chains disappear," a guy in the middle of their formation said.

"They're not really in chains," I said. "It was more of a way of saying I have them captured."

"Oh, my mistake. Can you let them loose though?"

"Sure. Could you turn back around?" I asked.

The enemy's new spokesman leaned on his sword. "We already saw that one."

I was about to wave Fred off when another idea came to me. "No, this is a different trick. Now, Fred."

Fred raised the pebble she called a ring over her head. "Behold. A magic ring."

A low, rumbling sound started behind me. I glanced back to see our army advancing toward us. I decided to turn back quickly in the hopes that the enemy army hadn't noticed me look back. As I did, I caught the eye of General Guxus, who winked at me. Fortunately, no one in the enemy army seemed to have either caught me looking or noticed our advancing army.

"As you can see, I have in my hands a ring," Fred said.

"We've already seen this one," the spokesman said. "And we're not going to look behind us so you can capture more of us."

Fred cackled manically. It was some exceptionally impressive cackling, but I didn't think it was appropriate to the character she was trying to appropriate. However, it did have the effect of unnerving most of the enemy army, so I decided to give her a pass.

Panicked screams erupted from the enemy army. I looked at Fred to see if this was part of her trick, and her smirk answered my question. As horses and their riders crashed throughout the opposing army, I thought Fred had somehow stumbled onto actual magic, especially when they began attacking each other. As our army finally passed us in their charge into the melee, I was finally able to catch the cause of the confusion as a ghostly head and hand popped through the enemy's newest spokesman and waved at me.

Fred maneuvered her horse to stand next to mine as the last of our troops passed by. "I worked out a plan with Gafenarai. When I started cackling, that was the signal."

I patted her on the back. "How would you like to be my head wizard?"

Fred nodded enthusiastically. "That sounds great. Do you think Paruxians have heard of the 'pull a coin out their ear' gag?"

Before I could answer, my attention was drawn away by the

beating of hooves behind me. At first, I assumed it was our small cavalry force rushing to join in on the slaughter, but their attire told me I was wrong. Bright red really did make it easy to identify friend from foe. I made a note to pick a similarly bright shade of orange for my new force later.

The three guards with us charged forward to meet the five enemy horsemen. These Red Robes were not like the ones I had seen in the earlier battle. Those ones seemed to be more politician, judging by the way they'd flailed about with their weapons. The well-armored and armed cavalry in front of me, however, I could have mistaken for professional soldiers, though with the fight they were giving the royal guards, that probably wouldn't have been a mistake at all. They certainly knew how to hold banners, an important skill for every professional soldier of this era.

Gu grabbed my arm. "We need to get you to safety."

"You mean get *you* to safety." I smirked. "OK. Fine. We'll go find a nice safe bunker away from the bad men. You know, I bet that's where my assistant is. Oh, goodie. I get to fire her myself." I turned my horse and moved after him. The Pink Woman, her two aides, the king, Fred, and the general formed around us as we galloped back to the city. "Now that I think about it, I should probably get my assistant to work on some banner ideas. I was going to use the banners Harry described in the books, but those Red Robes seem to have stolen that. Although . . . it would make sense for the original followers of The One to incorporate their symbols from the ones used by the preceding religion to help ease into the transition. Maybe we can use that as a starting point and change a few things. What's everyone's opinion on glitter?"

"It's kind of messy," Gu said. "The One?"

His statement was interrupted by more Red Robes arriving in front of us. I was fairly confident that he was going to say something similar to "that's an awesome name" or how I should have saved that for my new middle name. Unfortunately, I'll never get to know what he was going to say because he was taken from his saddle by a vicious mace strike to the face.

If that had happened to anyone else, it would have been the end of any hopes for a professional modeling career and also probably their life, but Gu was a god and gods don't take lightly to getting bashed in the head. I almost felt sorry for his attacker, because the only damage he did was to Gu's pants, though that was more than likely from the fall and landing. I mean, the guy had just attacked a genuine god and now he would have to deal with . . . chasing after him. Gu really was serious about that whole pacifist thing, I guess.

My other companions fared better. The general downed his first attacker with a perfectly placed sword strike and knocked the second one off with a well-placed smack to the side of the helmet. The Pink Woman and her men were making mincemeat of their four opponents. Fred tossed smoke pellets in the path of anyone who got near the king. It looked like the two of them would get away as their pursuers were too busy coughing to give chase. That left three more for me and my assistant.

"All right, assistant," I said. "You take the two on the left, and I'll get the ugly one on the right."

"I'm not ugly," the one on my left said.

"He wasn't referring to you," the one in the middle said. "He was referring to Gorgiann, who's on *his* right."

"Hey!" Gorgiann said. "Just for that I'm going to kill you extra hard."

"Fantastic," I said. "How'd you know that was my favorite way to do things?"

"Just for that I'm going to do it extra soft now. What do you think about that?" He put his sword away, took off his gauntlets, and smacked his right fist gently into his palm.

"Not as good, but I can't complain because I have my faithful assistant at my side." I nodded confidently to my left.

The Red Robe in the middle craned his neck. "I don't see anybody. Is she invisible?"

"That's . . . that's really mean." I shook my head. "I know being an assistant isn't the most glamorous job out there, but that's no reason to say she doesn't exist. Assistants are people too, you know. Why, I used to be an assistant. Make a note, fair assistant, for having to put up with such vile vitriol from these awful people, you're getting a raise . . . after I get my raise. If you're good, you'll even get it before I fire you." I scowled at them. "You guys are just terrible. I'm beginning to see why your religion lost."

All three of them pointed their weapons at me: a sword, a lance, and a fist. The one in the middle moved forward. "We haven't lost yet. The One will always come first!"

His sword bounced off my thickly starched costume and slightly less thick armor. I normally would have done something to prevent that—which, given my limited mobility in the stiff costume, would have been moving forward or, even more daringly, moving infinitesimally to the left—but what he said had stunned me into a surprised stupor. His second blow bounced equally ineffectively off my shoulder.

"Do you mind?" I said. "I'm trying to think. Assistant, could you read back what he said about The One?"

He stopped swinging and stared at my left.

"He said, 'The One will always come first,'" the Red Robe on my far left said.

"It's kind of rude to interrupt my assistant like that," I said, "but I'll let it pass this time because your diction is so much better than hers. Assistant, make a note to interview him for your job before I fire you. Now on to that motto of yours. Do you think I could borrow it for my new religion? You see, I'm going to name it 'The One,' and as such, I think it would work better for us . . . Also, don't tell any of my followers our name yet. I want to make it a surprise for the victory speech."

A sword and lance clanged off my outfit. "You can't name it that," the swordsman said. "That's our religion's name."

"And we called dibs," the lancer said.

"Dibs?" I said. "That changes everything. Say, you fellas wouldn't have a calendar handy, would you? My friend told me the year was 467, and I'm beginning to think he lied."

The third one hit me softly on the side of the head. "It *is* 467 on that silly Paruxian calendar but the 2498th year of The One on the calendar we adapted from our Garandian kinsman."

I staggered and barely kept myself on my horse. "That can't be right. Then why do the priests in the books . . . I mean to say, in Garandia, not wear red?"

A lance clanged off my shoulder. "At the legendary Council of Counsel in the tenth century of The One, it was decided that each major geographical area would get to pick their own outfits to mesh with the local cultures. Our region picked red robes as it had long been the sign of religious authority here. In Garandia they went with goofy bowl cuts, Zelahadon has assless chaps, and Lithia has hats shaped like birds."

"Assistant . . . take . . . uh." I didn't get to finish that brilliant line of thought as I was mercifully interrupted by The Pink Woman and her guards cutting down my three opponents. My assistant didn't help at all. I made a vow to fire her, right before I fired myself for not double-checking the date.

My saviors said something, and later the king and a few other people said something too, but I didn't hear any of it. My mind was too busy going in circles to accept any new information. As we entered a lavishly decorated room back at headquarters, someone mentioned Didlius and my mind decided to pause its circle running to gather additional information for more effective circle running later.

"My name is Didlius," one of the royal guards said.

"Mine too," a mercenary said. "Which of us were you referring to, King Fartius?"

The king slapped himself on the forehead. "I was referring to Hat's friend, but I guess I shouldn't be surprised given how really, really common that name is. By the way, you both might want to change that since Didlius was the name of that vile religion's founder we just got rid of."

"Your Majesty is most wise," the mercenary said. "I'm going to change mine to Hat."

The royal guard hit him. "Nuh-uh. I'm going to change mine to Hat."

"You two stop it; you're giving the real Hat a headache." The king put his hand on my shoulder and led me out of the room. "You really, really look like you need to lie down. You'll need your strength for the coming days. We have won a great victory here, but there is still a lot of work to do. I'm sure our victorious troops will want to hear a few words from you. And then you will have to write down the tenets of our new religion of . . . Say, what are we called?" He gently eased me into a bed, likely his own by the size of it.

"We're called . . . we're called 'The . . . The . . . Waaaa.'"

I'm not sure if I was too tired to think up anything, if my brain crashed from trying to figure out where I went wrong, or if I was running away from deciding on a name, but I fell into unconsciousness. I had a lot to figure out when I woke up.

QUINTUPLE MEANS FIVE

I woke with the same dread I had fallen asleep to, my pile of notes from the journey lying on top of me. Nothing better came to my mind than "The Waaaa," and I was tempted to just stick with that. There couldn't possibly be any other religions with that name. There also couldn't possibly be any other religious leaders who were as stupid as me. Stupid. Stupid. Stupid. Was "The Stupid" taken?

No, Hat. You're not going to take the easy way out. You're going to face your followers, explain to them that this was all a big misunderstanding, and tell them you didn't mean to destroy the religion of your favorite book. They should forget everything you said and go back to thinking that the best way to solve any problem is by killing their opponents and that sexually harassing women is OK . . .

Maybe not. The year I'm in is after when the books take place, after all. I would only be changing the future, something Harry had also done in his journey there. It's not like I could cause anything worse than he did. I hadn't killed a single major character in any of the books.

I would make a better future for this world. I would be an influencer. A change agent for the better. Introduce a better moral code. Save lives. Make my favorite place better. I could do it! I could make the religion of The Smile? The Warm and Fuzzy? The Better One? The Two? The name could come later, but the reforms would come now. I opened the door to my destiny and was embraced by the warming light of a dirty lightbulb.

Since when did they have lightbulbs and electricity in Paruxia? The Atlians were thinking of more and more creative uses for their magic, though I doubted even the genius of Hammurabi Joudisz could have come up with the *Thundercats* action figures on top of the bookshelf. I was also fairly confident that they wouldn't have been able to recreate the *Final Fantasy VII* strategy guide that Lion-O was resting on either. (I was sure they were smart enough to figure out all those secrets but doubted they had the right adapters to run a PlayStation.)

I ran down the hallway and came to a stairwell—a stairwell that contained a polished cedar bannister with a familiar notch on it over an even more familiar set of stairs. Stairs that one time held a fantasy author who was knocked out by an assistant who I happened to see in the mirror every morning when I brushed my teeth.

Harry! He's in the hospital, and now that I'm back on Earth, I can finally see him. But Paruxia . . . they need me. Decision time, Hat. Which one's more important? The lives and moral well-being of countless people or the guy whose collective arch-enemy is a kindergarten class?

Harry has guilt on his side. I was the one who put him in that hospital . . . even if he did deserve it. But there are a lot more Paruxians, and they're counting on you.

I took a few sleeping pills, made sure the ring was firmly on my finger, and climbed back into the closet I had left from. It took a few hours to finally go down due to my nerves and doubts. I could feel the same magical pulse overtake me as my last conscious thought faded away. I was going to where I needed to be.

~

I woke up in an area roughly the same size as the one I left in. At first, I thought I hadn't left Harry's cabin at all, but then I remembered waking up in an area roughly the same size when I first arrived in Vyenra. I breathed heavily in anticipation of what I might find when I opened that door. Billiam had said the rings only took you to where "you needed to be," so there was no guarantee I'd be close to where I had left. I could be countries or even a hemisphere away from Paruxia.

I opened the door to my destiny . . . and then the second door. There laid Lion-O in all of his action figurey glory. I hadn't gone anywhere. Either the ring was broken or this was where I needed to be.

I considered punching myself into unconsciousness to see if I ended up in Vyenra, but then decided to trust its decision. Guilt had overtaken me by that point anyway. No, I had to face the music and see if Harry was all right. I had tricked myself into believing my blows would only put him in a temporary coma, but now I had to see if that was only self-delusion or if I really did know how to do that.

If he was awake, I wanted to be able to show him the book I had finished. I decided to quickly check the computer over to make sure nothing had changed with those all-important files. It still shocked me how much dust can collect on a screen in only a few weeks. Fortunately, everything in the files was exactly like I left them, though there were an awful lot of email notifications popping up. I made a note to read them after I got back. I followed that with a note to dust and vacuum the room.

I paused before I turned the computer off, tempted desperately to write my fantastic journey down before I forgot too much, but the guilt of what I did to Harry overpowered me and I finally flipped it off. I turned to leave, but quickly turned back and grabbed a notebook. I would probably be spending a lot of time in the waiting room, after all, and I wanted to get the final battle down while it was still fresh in my memory.

I was about to exit the house when I realized that if I wore the bright orange robes from Paruxia to the hospital, they might not let me in to see him, especially when they were caked in mud and smelled like I had wrestled a hippopotamus. I quickly tossed on my best *Mega-Man* t-shirt, jeans, and winter coat, and then slicked back my hair, exactly the way Harry likes it—not too stylish, so people pay more attention to him, but not so terrible that people think badly of him.

As if the world was telling me everything would be all right, the weather outside was beautiful. I quickly took the coat off and tossed it in the back. I just knew everything would be all right. Harry's favorite song was even on the radio as I pulled in to the hospital parking lot. I was still humming it when I asked the receptionist for his room number. (I was bummed out a little that I couldn't remember it, but I had spent three whole weeks of harrowing adventures in Vyenra.)

As I neared his room, I could hear yelling inside. I couldn't tell who the voice belonged to, but my guess was his agent, Jess. It would be exactly like her to still be arguing with Harry even while he was in a coma, though she may have been on the phone. It was more likely the nurse. Harry had that special ability to make people want to argue with him before he even said a word and that had probably continued even while he was in a coma. I opened the door, fondly remembering the argument where I convinced him that did not qualify as a superpower.

A book hit me in the face before my eyes could adjust to the change in light.

"You! It serves you right to get hit in the head by your own travesty. Hmm . . . that's poetic justice. After you fire yourself, make a note of that brilliance so I can put it in my next book."

"Do you want me to hire my replacement before I fire myself?" I asked. "Wait. You're awake!" I charged forward and embraced him in a big hug. "And it's smarter to have your assistant take notes before you tell them they're fired . . . never mind. You're awake!"

"Ow! Stop it. That hurts. And you better not have hired an assistant while I was asleep."

I let go, having forgotten in my blissful shock how being hugged was his greatest weakness. Remembering my second day of orientation, I patted him on the back instead. "Sorry, Harry. I'm sure you're extra weak having just woken up from your coma."

"Just woken up from my coma? I've been awake for two weeks, and by the way, how dare you not show up for two weeks so I could fire you. For that, you're fired!"

"So, if you're firing me from being fired, does that mean I'm re-hired?"

He scratched his head. "Whatever option results in you not working for me. Now get out and take that stupid book with you."

I picked up the book lying there on the floor. I knew it couldn't be one of his since he would never throw anything he wrote as he had always claimed the strength and power of his words would be too heavy to be aerodynamic. That would explain his mood. He must have been reading one of his competitor's books. He always liked to read anything Billiam or any of his numerous other rivals wrote as soon as it came out so that he could know what not to do as soon as possible, and Billiam's latest had been scheduled to come out a couple of weeks after I left.

"And give me my ring, too."

"Before or after I leave?"

He got up off his bed and held his hand out. "Before, obviously. How could you give it to me after you leave?"

"By mail; I could hand it to one of the nurses so they could give it to you; or I could build an elaborate device using paperclips, rubber bands, and pulleys."

He scratched his chin with his other hand. "This pulley system intrigues me. No, wait. That's my grandpa's ring, and I can't have you sullying it with your very fired touch even a moment longer. Hand it over now."

I put it in his hand. "Oh, by the way, sir. Billiam explained to me how it works to send you to Vyenra. You wear it on your finger while unconscious, and then the ring takes you to where you need to be."

He twirled the ring around his finger. "Billiam . . . how does he know anything about this?"

"He was there in Paruxia. Evidently, he's been there before." I decided not to elaborate further as he already seemed to be in a bad mood and telling him that Billiam had been there first would not help.

He smiled at me, which usually meant he was coming down from his bad mood and that he'd re-hire me. "Paruxia? In Vyenra?"

"Oh, yes. The ring took me there, like it did you."

He crossed his arms and pouted. Usually that meant I needed to hand him some pudding snacks, but I had forgotten to grab some in my haste to check up on him. "So, you knock me into a coma so I won't change the book that details my epic journey in the world I created, and then go off and have a journey of your own?"

I nodded excitedly. "Oh, yes. It was in Paruxia, too. You never did get around to writing about there before."

"Don't you dare tell me your journey was epic too." His

spittle flew everywhere, not a good sign, but I was too happy to notice.

"It was! I thought I was witnessing the formation of The One but it turned out I got the year wrong—and oh, I met the Fanged Trio. Well, there were only two of them and only one was actually a member of the trio, but they were a different Fanged Trio than you met so—"

"I'm not following you," he growled.

The best way to calm him down when he had that face was to not make eye contact, so I turned the book over to see whose it was. It had a pretty blue sky, so it wasn't one of Billiam's. His always had something on fire. By Harry Olson? But I'd never seen this cover before, and I had all his books in every language. Maybe a new edition? But he always loved his books. They'd never put him in this bad of a mood, and he would never throw one of them . . . "and Samuel 'Hat' Feinberg."

"The book about your journey? How is this out already?" I was so shocked I forgot about not making eye contact.

Surprisingly, he looked more bewildered than angry. "It came out over a month ago. How long were you there? When did you leave?"

"I was there about three weeks, and I left on December 12th. What month is it?"

"It's August, you beautiful bastard," a hard feminine voice said behind me.

I almost jumped out of my skin when I saw Jess staring at me with a shark-like grin in the doorway. At least that put a smile on Harry's face.

"Jess," Harry said, "I've been trying to reach you since I woke up. Where have you been for two weeks?"

"The hospital blocked all calls from me. You curse out three administrators and a few dozen doctors and suddenly you're 'too detrimental to the patient's health to take calls from.' I was in the

Dominican for a much-needed three-week vacation. You like?" She held out her deeply tanned arm.

I shuddered and barely managed to hold in the "eww." Not that it mattered anyway because she never heard anything I said.

"You're *my* agent. How could you allow this godawful book to be released?" Harry hit me in the face with another copy of the book. I don't know where he could have possibly gotten that one but developed a theory that they could reproduce.

"Your wonderful assistant had the rights while you were incapacitated." She made sure not to look in my direction, which was fine by me. I'm still not sure how she always managed to make a compliment sound like an insult. "Besides, it's at number nine on *The New York Times* Best Seller list."

Harry stomped forward and pushed me out of the way. He looked like he might get in her face, but one look into her eyes, and he took a step back. "How dare you release something in my world without my permission! How dare you release something that makes me look bad! How dare you take advantage of my comatose state! How dare you . . . *The New York Times* Best Seller list? How dare you not bring party hats and those things you blow into that make noise! What are they called?"

"Noise makers, Harry," I said.

He grabbed my hands, and we jumped up and down in his signature happy dance. He made me learn it on the fourteenth day of orientation.

I suddenly stopped jumping as a dark thought hit me. "Wait. What about the ending? I was so overcome with grief that I admitted what I did to you. Am I wanted?"

Jess looked at me with those lizard eyes of hers and smiled. "The publisher passed it off as a publicity stunt to explain Harry's incapacitation. Besides, it's not like my wonderful boy is going to press charges if someone believes that ending."

Harry's eyes darkened for a split second, but he quickly

relented as his eyes made contact with Jess's. He covered his embarrassment at being so easily cowed by jumping up and down again.

"Does this mean I'm not fired?" I asked.

Jess ignored us and put on a new coat of lipstick. "He better not be. The publisher has offered quintuple your normal advance, but on the condition that . . . the other one—Shoe? Belt? Shirt? Whatever his name is—co-authors the next book."

Harry stopped the happy dance and let go of my hands. "Co-author? But Harry Olson works alone. You tell them no."

She pulled out a tiny mirror to examine her lips. "Quintuple means five."

He grabbed my hand, and we continued the dance for a few minutes until he abruptly stopped. "Wait. I'm in no condition to think of anything new. What could I possibly write about after what happened in the last book?"

"But I just went to Vyenra, Harry," I said. "We could write about that."

"Great. You tell me what happened, and I'll do all the writing."

I let go of his hand and stared at him seriously. "No. We co-write it. I want to write some too."

We locked eyes, and after about a minute, he backed down. He nodded slowly and grinned. "Co-writers! Less work for me!"

He grabbed my hand and we jumped up and down until the nurse made us stop. I was an assistant no longer. I was now so much more.

ᴇ ɴ ᴅ

What will become of Hat's new religion, The Waaaa? Can Harry
work with Hat as an equal? Who became king of Garandia after
Harry accidentally killed Berin in the first book? With Judas and
Beardcules gone, who will be Paruxia's next top beard model?

Find the answers to these questions and more in the continuing
saga of the world of Vyenra.

Want to hear when the next book is released? Sign up for my
exclusive *New Release Mailing List* here:
www.matthewhelbig.com/mailing-list